SLEEPING
TRUTH

Published by Shalom Rav Publications

ISBN 978-1937416027

Library of Congress Control No. 2013920487

SLEEPING TRUTH

Martin Vesole

Shalom Rav Publishing

THIS BOOK IS DEDICATED TO:

My Mother and Father, Esther Vesole and Herman Vesole,
of blessed memory,

and

My Brother, Dr. Bruce A. Vesole,
of blessed memory.

"I will insist the Hebrews have [contributed] more to civilize men than any other nation. If I was an atheist and believed in blind eternal fate, I should still believe that fate had ordained the Jews to be the most essential instrument for civilizing the nations... They are the most glorious nation that ever inhabited this Earth. The Romans and their empire were but a bubble in comparison to the Jews. They have given religion to three-quarters of the globe and have influenced the affairs of mankind more and more happily than any other nation, ancient or modern."

— John Adams, 2nd President of the United States, Feb. 16, 1808

Contents

Foreword

We live in a time when people are searching in new places to find meaning in their lives. Some turn to new or different religions and some turn to various kinds of spiritual self-help books or aids.

It is clear that the traditional religions are not satisfying tens of millions of people the way they once did. The numbers are down across all organized religions as their former adherents lose faith in the "truths" those religions teach and rebel against organized religion in general.

As a Jewish person, I am especially concerned about the future of secular Jews in America. I first became aware of this problem after reading *The Vanishing American Jew* by Alan Dershowitz. And every study I have seen since then confirms the diagnosis that there has been an unrelenting and substantial attrition in the size of the Jewish community in America.

Many reasons have been given for this phenomenon. The most significant among them have been assimilation, intermarriage, disinterest in synagogue life, synagogue membership costs, loss of belief in a seemingly useless God, and the failure of Judaism to speak to people in meaningful ways.

Most current efforts to remedy this problem have to do with "preaching to the choir." Jewish leaders try to make religious services, youth and adult education, and programming more interesting, but those who have already left us go to none of those. Meanwhile, the rate of attrition marches on unabated.

Having somehow survived the Holocaust, the Jewish community cannot afford to continuously lose 50% of our number, which has been the case for the past few decades. In my view, we need to find a way to bring those people back. To do that, I believe Judaism has to change, as it has many times before when faced with an existential crisis.

This book gives some ideas along those lines, and many more ideas can be found at my website www.martinvesole.com. I believe if something isn't selling, you either need to change the customer or the product. In this case, the customer cannot be changed, but the product can. There is a lot more to Judaism than its numerous rules (613 mitzvot) and its perpetuation of the way things have always been done. We need to take Judaism out of the Middle Ages and bring it into the 21st Century. Failure to do this is not a good option.

My non-Jewish readers will find some of the same problems happening to their religions. I am hopeful that this book will show the way to all of us to understand God in a new way, perhaps in a more accurate way, so we understand what to expect and what not to expect from our religion and from life.

I think believing in a just and merciful God is important and good for all of us. I am not one of those who hopes religion will disappear because it has been the cause of so many wars. I hope the wars will disappear, because there is no reason for us to fight with each other. But my idea that God *needs us* to make the world a better place is good for us as individuals and good for the world. I believe all religions can help in this endeavor and if my book can help all ethically-based religions become stronger, I think that will be a good thing.

I'd like to thank a few people without who this book would not exist. They are: Deborah Lanore, my publicist and business consultant, who has helped me immensely every step along the way; Sylvia McConnell, my editor; Diane Yocco, Patty Thompson, Dr. Elizabeth Feldman, Alice Graubart and Jim Shelton, who helped me with the writing or developing concepts; the two focus groups that gave me important advice about changes to the book; and the many friends and acquaintances who helped in various ways through the five years I needed to write this book.

Martin Vesole
www.martinvesole.com

The Condemned

Deliver me from my enemies, O God; protect me from those who rise up against me.
For lo, they lie in wait for me! They conspire against me…
I have done no wrong, yet they prepare themselves to attack me.
[Psalms 59:2-5.]

The jail cell was dank and dark. The rabbi was sitting on the lumpy cot with his head in his hands. He was facing murder charges even though everyone knew he did not do the shooting. A minister had been shot dead and five people had been trampled to death. The rabbi was being indicted for all of them.

He had managed to elude the police for a few days, but with the whole country looking for him, it was only a matter of time until he was caught. Upon his arrest, he was told he would be sent to St. Louis on the morrow for his murder trial. What awaited him after that? That question filled him with tremors every time he thought about it. He feared the worst because the powers-that-be were all aligned against him. He had threatened the religious establishment and the politicians and businessmen associated with it, and they were determined to make an example of him, or worse.

"I was doing what God wanted me to do," he said to himself. He was absolutely convinced of that. But he feared that, like so many others before him, God would not be there to reward him for his loyalty. Rabbi Hertzel knew that when you pray, sometimes God helps you and sometimes He does not. The rabbi had to assume he was on his own this time unless God did something to convince him otherwise. The realist in him knew that he could not count on God's help, and that was why he was so anxious about his future.

Sometimes, like most of us, he wondered if there *really is* a God. Why is God so hidden, why isn't it obvious that He exists? What about all the scientific findings that explain things our ancestors used to attribute to God, but which we now know do not need a god to occur? The attempts by man to prove there is a God by scientific, philosophic and theologic methods have not been totally convincing. It is great to have *faith* — Rabbi Hertzel did have faith — but *knowing* would be so much better.

Meanwhile, despite the overwhelming feelings of foreboding he felt in his bleak jail cell, Rabbi Hertzel knew he was fortunate to have a cell to himself. He was being held overnight in the notorious jail at 26th and California in Chicago, Illinois, his home town. Some of the city's worst criminals were housed there. "Like Daniel in the lion's den," he said to himself when the arresting officers told him where he was going. Fortunately, the lions were not put in the same cell with him.

The officers had arrested him on the first night of Passover, before he had a chance to have dinner. He was hungry and he could not eat most of the food the jailers brought him without violating the Jewish kosher laws or the special laws pertaining to Passover. Although he was not a particularly observant man, despite being a rabbi, he did follow some of the rules. He did not feel that this was a good time to break those rules. "It would be bad karma," he said to himself. So when the guard brought him a pork sandwich with mashed potatoes and corn, the only thing he could eat were the mashed potatoes, and he was not too sure even about that.

He gazed around the nearly empty jail cell. There was the cot he was sitting on, a sink, and a commode that looked like it had not been cleaned in a while. Bars on every side. He was cold and hungry and there was an acrid smell coming from somewhere that made him feel nauseous. He was given nothing to read and his cellular phone had been taken from him. And because he was a high profile case, he was not allowed any visitors.

Feeling totally miserable in every possible way, he was suddenly comforted by a vision of her face, her smile, the loving way her eyes looked at him, and the sound of her voice. Feeling better and with nothing else to do, he decided to lie down on the lumpy cot and try to get some sleep. But his mind would not shut off, and he began to retrace the events that brought him to this place.

It all began two years earlier in Israel, when two Arab boys discovered an ancient scroll hidden in a cave near the town of Nazareth…

The New Scroll

He cuts out rivers among the rocks; His eye sees every precious thing. He stops the rivers so they do not even trickle, and things that are hidden He brings forth to light. [Job 28:10-11.]

The little cave was foreboding but irresistible. Amir and Fareydoun saw the small opening at the bottom of the nearby hillside that had been exposed by yesterday's flash flood. The cave was near the family's olive orchard outside of the sprawling Arab town of Nazareth. Miraculously, the olive orchard had escaped serious harm, and after the boys had helped their father clean up the debris brought by the turbulent waters, they were given permission to play.

The mouth of the cave was just large enough for a small boy to crawl through. Amir, age eight, the smaller and more active boy, urged his older brother by two years to explore the cave with him. Fareydoun, reluctant, yet excited by the possibilities, was easily persuaded by Amir's enthusiastic speculations as to what might await them within.

Amir crawled headfirst into the cave and Fareydoun followed closely after. By wriggling on their bellies and clawing at the yielding pebbly sand beneath them, they were able to navigate themselves forward through the narrow entranceway. It was not difficult, because they were buoyed by centuries of sand that had first filled the mouth of the cave, and then buried it. As the brothers traveled farther along, the cave expanded, but at the same time, it became quickly darker as the light from outside diminished. When conditions told them it was becoming pointless to continue, the boys decided to return later with flashlights.

The next day, after their work in the orchard was done, the boys returned to the cave again, this time armed with flashlights. After crawling through the narrow entranceway, the cave gradually opened up and at the same time, the sandy floor began to give way to stone. Once the sand was gone, the cave was more than large enough for a tall man to stand erect and walk about quite comfortably.

As they began to explore the vast cavernous room they found themselves in, it became obvious to the excited boys that the cave had had its share of human visitors. For scattered about hither and yon, the young brothers found shards of pottery, burnt candles, and assorted other well-used objects, which thrilled them with each discovery.

As they proceeded deeper into the cave, it became harder and harder to breathe, and they decided they would need to widen the cave entrance to let more fresh air in. The next day they brought shovels to the mouth of the cave and dug doggedly at the sand to widen the entrance. The more they dug, the wider the opening became. They were also able to widen the crawlspace beyond the mouth of the cave, and it soon became apparent that the entrance to the cave had once been quite large before the sands of time had filled it up.

After two long hours of shoveling sand in the sweltering summer heat, the brothers felt they had dug enough. But although they were eager to continue their explorations, they were too exhausted to go back into the cave. Their next visit would have to wait for the following day. They decided to leave the shovels up against the mouth of the cave, one on each side of the opening, feeling confident that no one would take the shovels before they returned.

Approaching the mouth of the cave after work the next day, they could not believe what they saw. The shovels were aglow with a soft yellow aura that was still striking despite the intense light of the sun in the cloudless sky above. The brothers were in awe and did not know whether to be frightened or not.

"This is surely the work of Allah," said Fareydoun breathlessly.

Amir, who was usually the braver of the two boys, clung tightly to his older brother. His body was shaking, and he started to cry. "Fareydoun, let's get out of here," Amir finally was able to say.

But Fareydoun did not move. "This is surely the work of Allah," he said again. "I think we better pray," he said nervously.

The brothers got on their knees and put their foreheads down to the ground and began to pray. After a few minutes of heartfelt prayer, the boys looked up apprehensively and were delighted to see that the glow on the shovels was gone.

"What do we do now Fareydoun?" Amir asked, with a little more calmness in his voice.

"I don't know," Fareydoun answered. "We better tell Father."

Up till now, the boys had kept their explorations secret, but now they felt they had to tell their father what they had found and what they had seen. Their father was astonished and did not know what to make of it either, but he decided he should see the cave with his own eyes and asked the boys to take him there after dinner. As they approached, they could see even from a distance that the two shovels were glowing again.

"Yes, yes, this is surely the work of Allah!" Father said, awestruck. "We better go talk to the Imam. He will know what to do."

The next morning, Father and the two boys went to see the Imam together. As usual, the Imam was found in his office in the Grand Mosque of Nazareth. The office was dark and filled with shelves of books. The old man had a long white beard and soft soulful eyes and the boys instinctively felt at ease with him. Taking turns, the boys told the Imam the story about the shovels: about how they glowed the day after they used them to widen the entry to the cave; how they stopped glowing when they prayed; and how they were glowing again when they went back with their father.

The Imam stroked his long white beard as he appeared lost in thought. "Come back tomorrow," the Imam finally said. "I will pray to Allah and have an answer for you."

They returned the next day, full of awe and curiosity about what the Imam would tell them. The boys had hardly slept the night before.

"The shovels glow because Allah is there," the Imam told them. "They stopped glowing when you prayed to show he is listening to you and is inviting you back into the cave. They started glowing again to tell others that Allah is there. You must visit the cave again. Allah wills it." The Imam showed by his body language that he was done talking.

"Salaam, go in peace," said the Imam as the boys and their father rose to leave. "Thank you, Imam," said the father. "Thank you, Imam," said the boys.

Later that day after work, the boys and their father went back to the cave, feeling confident about the Imam's instructions, but also a little fearful. The shovels were glowing, as expected. The boys and their father prostrated themselves on the ground in front of the cave and began to pray. As before, when they were done praying, the shovels were no longer glowing.

A lifetime of hard work and bad-back issues prevented the father from going through the narrow entranceway into the cave, but he was apprehensive about sending the boys in without him.

"Don't worry Father," Amir said bravely. "We'll be okay," Fareydoun agreed. The brothers then resolutely entered the dark and mysterious cave while Father waited outside for them.

They quickly crawled to the area where the cave was large enough for them to stand. They turned their flashlights on and carefully proceeded to explore beyond where they had been before. Soon the boys came to a place where the cave separated into two tunnels.

"Which way should we go?" they asked each other. Amir, the youthful brave one suggested they split up, with one going to the left and the other one to the right. But Fareydoun, the more mature and careful one, said, "No, we better stay together in case one of us needs help."

"Okay then," said Amir, subconsciously relieved. "Which way do you want to go?"

"Let's flip a coin," suggested Fareydoun. "Heads we go to the right, and tails we go to the left." Amir agreed. Fareydoun flipped the coin to the ground and it came up tails. "To the left we go," said Fareydoun.

Suddenly, something happened to change the boys' minds. Before Fareydoun could pick up the tossed coin, it began to glow, and then miraculously flipped over so that heads was showing. The boys were terrified and ran from the cave as fast as they could, leaving the glowing coin behind. When they got out of the cave, the boys told their father what had happened.

"We better go see the Imam again," said their father nervously.

The Imam told them he would pray on it, and they should come back again the next day. Their father winked at the boys knowingly and said they would return; the Imam's pattern of resolving questions was becoming clear.

"The message is quite clear," said the Imam slowly after they returned the next morning. "You need to pray by the coin and then go to the right."

The boys and their father went straight back to the cave. This time there was no question of waiting until after work. Filled with excitement and a feeling of urgency, they arrived at the entrance, where they found the shovels glowing again. Father and the boys prayed before the two shovels and the shovels returned to normal. Encouraged, the boys went back into the cave with their flashlights while their father anxiously took up his post outside the entrance.

The two boys cautiously approached the spot where the cave separated into two tunnels. The coin was still there, and it was still glowing. The brothers prayed by the coin, and when they looked up, they saw that the coin was no longer glowing. Fareydoun carefully picked up the coin and gingerly slipped it into his pocket, not knowing if they would need it again.

As the Imam had instructed, the brothers went down into the tunnel on the right. After several meters, they saw a glimmer ahead of them. It seemed to be coming from around a bend. Cautiously, the boys tiptoed ahead. When they got to the bend in the tunnel and peered around it, they saw a large, highly decorated urn, glowing with the same yellow aura they had seen on the shovels and the coin. Amir ran toward the urn, but he was stopped in his tracks by the glow, which increased in intensity as he drew near.

"I think we better pray again," offered Fareydoun. Amir readily nodded his agreement.

When they looked up from their prayers, the glow was gone. The boys slowly approached the urn, and when nothing unusual happened, they lifted the lid and saw there were many large pieces of parchment inside. Gently, Fareydoun pulled out one of the pieces. It felt fragile, but it did not tear or break. He looked at it in the glow of their flashlights and saw what appeared to be Hebrew lettering on it; however, many of the words did not look like Hebrew words.

"It's probably Aramaic," said Fareydoun. Aramaic was the language that had been commonly spoken in that area in ancient times, replacing Hebrew as the language of the Jews and some of their neighbors. "This could be something important!" Fareydoun fairly screamed, getting very excited.

"Oh boy, we might get rich!" shouted Amir enthusiastically, who was much more the businessman than the scholarly Fareydoun. "Let's take it to Father and the Imam." And so they did.

The Controversy

When word got out about the discovery, experts rushed to Nazareth from all over the world. The Israeli authorities took possession of the urn and the pieces of parchment, which they sewed together and made into a scroll. They stored the artifacts in the Israel Museum in Jerusalem, the same place where the Dead Sea scrolls were displayed. The authorities then allowed the experts to examine the urn and its original contents freely. The Imam negotiated a finder's fee for the discovery and, as Amir predicted, the family became very wealthy.

The experts quickly agreed that the urn was Jewish in origin, and they dated it and the scroll from the first century of the Common Era, probably between 50 and 70 C.E. There were words on the urn that indicated it was probably made by a Jewish Nazarene pottery maker. The urn was of some interest, of course, but the most interesting, and controversial part of the find was the scroll. As Aramaic experts were given the task of reading and translating the scroll into different languages, a startling picture began to emerge.

The scroll was absolutely stunning in its scope. It was nothing less than a new and different account of the life and death of Jesus of Nazareth, the same Jesus that Christians call the Christ (the Latin word for "Messiah"). But, and this was the source of the controversy, this account seemed to have been written by a Jewish friend of Jesus, and it said nothing about Jesus being the Christ or the Son of God. *In fact, Jesus was quoted himself as saying he was not the Messiah.*

The discovery of the scroll set the Christian world on its ear. Even when small things are found that contradict the Bible's account, they immediately become a major topic of international interest and discussion. They are excitedly covered on television news shows, political and religious talk shows, in magazines and newspapers, and on the internet. And this discovery was not a small thing.

Commentators quickly divided into three divergent camps: Most Christians, especially Catholics and fundamentalist Christians, called the scroll a forgery, a hoax, or the work of the devil. Jews crowed that they were right about Jesus not being the Son of God or the Messiah all along. Most religiously neutral historians claimed that the scroll was properly dated, seemed historically accurate, and did not seem to be a forgery or a hoax. Intense passions were aroused on all sides, and it became virtually impossible for those with differing views to talk to each other without acrimony.

They could not even agree on the naming of the new scroll. Some called it the "Gospel of Emet" because it was purportedly written by Jesus' best friend from childhood, whose name was Emet. They called it a gospel because, like the gospels of Mark, Matthew, Luke and John, it told about the life of Jesus. Others called it the "Nazarene Scrolls", comparing it through its location to the Dead Sea Scrolls. The media split the difference and called it the "Book of Emet" and that is the name that came into general usage.

The experts did come to agree on one very important thing, however — the translation and dating of the text. It had taken them nearly nineteen months to reach a consensus about what the text said and how to translate it into contemporary languages. The experts also agreed that the scroll had been written well before the three earliest gospels, Mark, Matthew, and Luke, which were referred to by scholars as the "synoptic" gospels, from the Greek word meaning *to see alike* or *to have the same perspective*. In fact, so much of the wording was the same, it was apparent that the three "synoptic" gospels and the new scroll drew from some of the same sources. According to the experts, the Book of Emet was not only the earliest "gospel," but it was also the only account the world had of Jesus that was written by someone who was his contemporary and who claimed to know him personally.

The Great Debate

And Moses said to God: ... "I pray Thee, if I have found favor in Thy sight, teach me Your ways so I may know You and continue to find favor with You. Remember that this nation is Your people." And God said, "My Presence will go with you..." [Exodus 33:13-14.]

Eventually, representatives of the three divergent camps were brought together in a much-anticipated worldwide televised panel discussion presented by the Public Broadcasting Station (PBS). The "Great Debate," as it was called, would be broadcast worldwide on television, radio and through the internet.

Deciding on who would be the participants in the Great Debate had taken months of discussion and planning among numerous university authorities, religious groups and the producers from PBS. They were eventually able to agree that the highly-respected Unitarian minister and famous television talk-show host George Turner should make the final selections.

Reverend Turner narrowed it down to three panelists. Representing the Christians was the noted televangelist and theologian, Dr. Mary Madelyne Roberts; representing the Jews was Joshua David Hertzel, a Reform Rabbi from Chicago, who was known for his controversial new-age beliefs; and representing the historians was Sir Winston Hamburley from Oxford College in England, the leading expert on the life of Jesus and his times. Reverend Turner, who was also the pastor of the Second Unitarian Church of St. Louis, would lead the panel and be its moderator.

The panel discussion was scheduled for three consecutive nights in the month of April, just a few days before the Jewish holiday of Passover and the Christian holiday of Easter. It was to take place in the renowned

Graham Chapel on the campus of Washington University in St. Louis, Missouri. The chapel was stunningly beautiful, made of pink granite and stone, like all the original buildings on the campus. It was built in Gothic style with high stained glass windows on every side. Inside the building, on the ground level, there were 27 rows of wooden pews with red cushions, seating a maximum of 589 people; and in the balcony, there were 196 fixed seats, also with red cushions and backs. The interior walls were made of gray stone, and above was a series of criss-crossed dark wooden beams, which perfectly matched the wooded ceiling. The members of the by-invitation-only audience consisted of leading political, social, and religious dignitaries from all over the world. Invitations to the event were reportedly the hottest tickets in history, with individual tickets reselling for tens of thousands of dollars in some cases.

There were several large television screens placed at various points outside the chapel, allowing additional hundreds of viewers without invitations to sit on the lawn to see and hear the proceedings. Most of those on the lawn were interested observers, but there were also a group of protestors on the left lawn carrying large signs disparaging the legitimacy of the scroll, and denouncing the whole thing as a hoax, a forgery or the work of the devil. Some of the signs blamed the Jews and others blamed the "liberal" media. It appeared that the protestors on the left lawn were an organized group. The authorities safeguarding the proceedings viewed the group suspiciously and considered them a possible safety concern.

Dr. Mary Madelyne Roberts was the first of the panelists to arrive at Graham Chapel. She was 53 years old, tall and slender, and fair of skin, with a beautiful and charismatic face that showed off her passionate intensity. She had sparkling green eyes and wavy red hair that cascaded energetically to her shoulders. Wearing a white satin blouse with a light gray skirt suit that flattered her curvy figure, she had accessorized her outfit with expensive Manolo Blahnik black and grey suede high heels with a matching purse. She wore conservative jewelry—a set of tasteful pearl earrings and a pearl necklace. Mary was a striking woman who still turned heads when she walked confidently into a room, but she cared little for that, because her life's focus was on her calling to teach the world about her hero Jesus Christ, and the Christian religion he founded.

Reverend Turner was there to greet Dr. Roberts as she walked into the chapel. He was a kindly featured man in his late 40s with a genial and friendly smile, a man who instantly inspired trust and affection. He was tall and slender and Mary liked the way his thinning straight blond hair framed his pale and clean-shaven face. He was wearing his favorite outfit—a light blue suit with a white shirt and a subdued yellow tie.

"Welcome, Dr. Roberts. I'm George Turner," George said warmly. "I am so glad to finally meet you in person. There's a vestibule behind the stage where you can put your things and make yourself comfortable until we begin. Do you have any questions?"

"Thank you, Reverend Turner," Mary smiled. "It's very good to be here. Thank you for inviting me. This is an incredibly important day for all of us."

George led her to the stage and then to the vestibule behind it, where she could wait until the proceedings would begin. Then he left Mary alone there so he would be available to greet the other panelists. She sat down in one of the overstuffed chairs in the vestibule and pulled a small mirror out of her purse to check her makeup and apply a little more red lipstick to her lips. Satisfied, she pulled out her notes and thought about what she wanted to say about the parts of the new scroll that differed from the established gospels. She was passionately determined to defend the *true* gospels against the Emet *heresy* and believed it was her mission to build a convincing case that the new scroll was illegitimate. Over the course of the next three days, she hoped to bury it once and for all in the public mind.

Mary had participated in many discussions about theology and religious beliefs before, of course, usually with other Christians, but sometimes with Jews or Muslims. She always dominated those discussions, which was one of the reasons why George had chosen her to give the Christian perspective. And Mary was no fool — she knew her good looks were one of the reasons the Christian leaders urged George to select her. They believed she would make a better impression on television than any of their other theologians.

Despite her considerable experience in public religious debates, she was feeling quite nervous this time. It would be the first time that she would be addressing a global audience, and she needed to perform convincingly. After all, as an evangelist, it was her mission to bring Christ to as many people as she could. Given the enormity of the effect that the Book of Emet had already had on the Christian community, she was under a lot of pressure to win the debate.

To succeed as a spokesperson for Christianity, which was a field almost totally dominated by men, Mary had to be better, smarter and stronger than the men were. The fact that she was good-looking both helped and hindered her career. It helped in that people wanted to be around her, but it hindered in that men (and even women) did not always want to take her seriously. Now she had to convince the whole world to take her seriously.

Mary looked at her notes again to make sure they were in order. They were. Nervously she pulled out her mirror and checked her makeup and hair again. The face that looked back at her seemed fine, but she was still feeling as if there might be something wrong. Her heart was pounding and her stomach was doing flip-flops.

It was not long before the second panelist arrived. Sir Winston Hamburley was a short pudgy man with a ruddy face and a thick gray drooping mustache that matched his bushy eyebrows. He had wire frame trifocal glasses planted halfway down his nose that give him the look of a university professor, which of course he was. He was wearing a gray tweed three-piece suit with a white shirt and a crimson red bow tie. In his hands were a gray fedora and an umbrella that he carried everywhere he went. His thick white hair always seemed to look as if he had just stepped in out of the wind.

"Good evening, my dear," Sir Winston jovially said to Mary. "This should be jolly good fun." He looked very happy to be there and was quite relaxed.

"Very pleased to meet you too," returned Mary. She took an instant liking to this friendly old Englishman. "I don't know how much fun it will be. We have a huge responsibility to tell the world the truth about this so-called Book of Emet." Winston could see the anxiety on Mary's face.

"Yes, quite so," Sir Winston said sympathetically. "I realize you are under a lot of pressure from your colleagues. I certainly wish you well and I know you will be outstanding."

"Thank you very much," Mary said. She was genuinely touched by Winston's empathy for her circumstances. She was already very glad he was there.

"Ah, I see Rabbi Hertzel has come," Sir Winston announced, nodding in the direction of the chapel's entrance. Rabbi Joshua David Hertzel, 54 years old, walked briskly into the vestibule accompanied by Reverend Turner. The Rabbi was six feet tall, and obviously athletic, which gave him an air of energy and leadership. With his dark brown eyes and his salt-and-peppered brown hair, and similarly colored short beard and mustache, his handsome face radiated warmth and magnetism. His eyes sparkled with interest and curiosity and women found him quite irresistible, despite a certain edge to his personality that accompanied a sharp intelligence. Mary noticed that he was very well put together, wearing an attractive dark blue suit with pin stripes and a blue and red patterned tie over a light blue shirt.

What Mary liked most about him was the intelligence she saw in his eyes, and her womanly antenna started to go up. But she quickly quelled any possible interest she could have in him. She was a married woman who was there on business, and finding this man attractive was irrelevant to her mission. Nevertheless, she noticed an increase in the activity of the butterflies in her already queasy stomach.

Joshua had much the same reaction to Mary. He found her beauty and energy surprisingly compelling but he too had business to attend to. Being a divorced man who dated occasionally, he imagined he might have tried to approach her romantically in other circumstances.

Joshua and Mary had never met, and George did the honors by introducing them to each other. The two would-be combatants eyed each other.

"I'm pleased to meet you," Joshua began. "I've seen you on television a few times, and you make a very nice presentation. I must say you are much better looking in person than on television."

"Thank you Rabbi Hertzel," Mary said graciously, looking Joshua straight in the eye. "I've read your book on Jesus and I think you are almost as good looking in person as you are on the book cover."

Joshua burst into laughter. "Thank you, I think." he said.

Mary laughed too. "You're quite welcome," she said with a friendly smile.

"I believe you are the only woman with a regular TV show like that in my area. Is your show televised nationally?"

"Yes, it is," Mary answered matter-of-factly. "It is one of only five that has that kind of reach. I'm very blessed."

"That's quite impressive!" Joshua exclaimed with admiration. "I didn't realize you were so important. I wish I could figure out a way to get that kind of an audience for myself," he laughed.

Mary smiled back at him. "Maybe someday you will Rabbi Hertzel.

I hear you have some very interesting ideas." Mary had done quite a lot of research on her primary opponent as soon as she knew he would be serving on the panel with her.

"Quite so," agreed Sir Winston. He had become quite interested in some of the rabbi's ideas and was eager to learn more about them.

George was about to share an identical opinion, but there was no time for further conversation. Two theater majors from the university sprang into action, quickly brushing the shine from the participants' faces and equipping them with tiny microphones. George then briefly reviewed the evening's format with the panelists as they awaited the word to move onto the stage.

The stage was equipped with four comfortably cushioned red chairs with mahogany armrests. They were arranged in a semi-circular pattern, with all chairs facing the audience. George Turner and Sir Winston occupied the middle two chairs, while Joshua sat next to George on the left and Mary was placed next to Sir Winston on the right.

At 7:00 p.m. Reverend Turner opened the discussion by thanking the audience for coming and then introduced the panel. Mary was applauded when she was introduced, but Joshua was booed. Reverend Turner put his hands up to quiet the audience. He then provided some background information for the topic of the evening.

"The document that we will be discussing tonight, which is popularly known as the Book of Emet, was discovered two years ago in a cave near Nazareth, the town where Jesus grew up. The document consisted of numerous sheets of parchment, which were later pieced together in the form of a scroll. It has been translated into thirty-two languages so far and has sparked controversy and heated debates all over the world. This is the first time that scholars from the Christian, Jewish, and academic communities have been brought together to discuss this scroll. We are being broadcast all over the world by television, radio, and webcast. I welcome all of you who are joining us tonight. I hope our panel will clear up some misunderstandings and false rumors about the scroll that have been prevalent. I do not expect the panelists to agree on everything, but I do expect them to provide more information.

"Historians are in general agreement that the Book of Emet was written some twenty to thirty years after the death of Jesus. It was purportedly written by a man named Emet, who claimed to be a boyhood friend of Jesus in Nazareth. It was written quite a few years before the

Gospels of Mark, Matthew and Luke, and several decades before the Gospel of John. It is easily the earliest account of the life of Jesus that we now possess. It is also the only account of the life of Jesus we have that was written by a non-Christian.

"For our purposes, the Book of Emet has been divided into eight parts, or chapters. The Public Broadcasting Service has graciously given us two hours for tonight's discussion and another two hours for both Saturday night and Sunday night. We will do the first three chapters tonight, the next three chapters tomorrow night and the last two chapters on Sunday. Each chapter will be presented as a separate segment.

"The panelists have agreed on the following order. First, Dr. Roberts will summarize what the gospels from the Christian Bible teach us; then Rabbi Hertzel will summarize how the Book of Emet differs from the Christian Bible, and give the Jewish point of view; and lastly, Sir Winston will tell us how the various accounts of Jesus' life square with the views of the historians. After their respective presentations, there will be a general discussion among them of the issues presented by that chapter of the book.

"Before each session, the pertinent chapter from the Book of Emet will be narrated to our audience.[1]

"There will not be a question and answer session with the audience. We ask the audience to be respectful of the panel and not applaud or respond in any way that will disrupt the professionalism of these discussions."

Outside The Chapel

Judith and Bryce came early to the chapel and found a good place on the grass to sit and watch the proceedings on one of the big screen televisions posted at various places outside. From where they sat, they had a great view of one of the screens and were well situated to watch the dignitaries parade into the chapel as they arrived. At one point near the beginning of their vigil, Judith pointed to a small group of people entering the chapel.

"There's my father," she exclaimed to no one in particular, although Bryce was the only one near her and listening.

---

1   Excerpts from the Book of Emet are reproduced in the Appendix.

"Which one?" Bryce asked with surprise. "You didn't tell me your father would be here. Is that why you wanted to come so early?"

"No, I wanted to come early to get a good seat and see all the big hoop-de-doo's arrive."

Bryce laughed at her terminology for "big shots." Judith had a spot on the student radio station and wanted to be able to tell her listeners which dignitaries were there and what they were wearing. Despite the grungy way she herself dressed, she was very interested in fashion and the lives of celebrities.

"He's gone now," Judith said after most of the group she pointed at had already disappeared into the chapel. "It's no big deal. I'm just excited he's here."

Judith Isaacson was a free-spirited spunky sophomore at Washington University. She was very loyal to the people she loved, and she would do anything to defend or protect them. As a socially and politically minded liberal, Judith was dedicated to the proposition that all men—and women—are created equal. Like Bryce, Judith believed in the traditional American ideals and was a strong advocate of civic justice and human rights. In addition, helping the underprivileged was very important to her and she especially enjoyed working in soup kitchens and helping to feed the hungry. Her Jewish upbringing was also important to her. She enjoyed Jewish culture and was a volunteer teacher in her synagogue's Sunday School.

Judith was casually dressed. Her long dishwater blonde hair was tied up in a pony tail. Wearing the standard university uniform of faded jeans with holes in the knees, she had thrown on a sweater and a windbreaker to keep the cool spring weather at bay. White socks and well-worn black Converse sneakers completed her comfortable outfit. Blue eyes sparkled in her pale freckled face as she intently watched the crowds entering the chapel.

Judith was majoring in communications and was planning on being in sales or marketing after graduation. She had grown up in St. Louis, yet unlike many "townies," she lived in the dorms.

Although Bryce Patterson was the star football player on Washington U's under-achieving football team, and a quiet leader of the players on that team, he was usually agreeable to being led around and organized by Judith, especially in regard to their social life. He just liked being with her and did not care very much what they did together. In this case, however, Bryce was independently interested in the topic being discussed.

Bryce had been raised a Catholic, but had come to doubt the story of the virgin birth and the resurrection of Jesus. Much to his parents' chagrin, Bryce felt those stories were fairy tales and he had ceased going to church altogether. Not even for Christmas or Easter. He was part of a growing group of independent thinkers who were either apathetic or had antipathy for organized religions of any stripe. Bryce still half-believed in a higher power, but did not have solid views about what or who that higher power was. Someday he would look into that more, he told himself, after finishing football, college and law school.

By now, Bryce had completed his final season as the school's starting fullback, finishing third in school history for most yards gained in a career, and he was soon about to graduate. His father was the first African-American prosecuting attorney for St. Louis County and Bryce wanted to follow in his father's footsteps. He was light-skinned with brown eyes and had what he jokingly called an Anglo nose and African hair. The ladies thought him very handsome. Certainly Judith thought so.

Sitting on the grass, with a blanket under them, holding hands and huddling close to keep warm in the cool air, the young couple waited with great anticipation in the fading evening light for the start of the program.

Dr. Mary Madelyne Roberts

A woman of valor, who can find? For her value is far beyond rubies. "Many daughters have attained valor, but you have surpassed them all." False is grace, and vain is beauty; a God-fearing woman, she should be praised. Give her the fruit of her hands, and she will be praised at the gates by her works. [Proverbs 31:10, 29-31]

The phone rang in Mary Robert's upscale suburban home in Colorado Springs.

"Hello," she answered in her professional voice through force of habit, even though it was mid-evening and after office hours.

"Could I speak to Dr. Mary Roberts please," said a pleasant male voice on the other end that Mary did not recognize.

"Speaking."

"Hello, Dr. Roberts," said the voice even more pleasantly. "My name is Reverend George Turner. You are of course aware that we are convening a panel to discuss that new scroll about Jesus that was found in Nazareth two years ago."

"Yes, of course," she said hesitantly. The Nazarene scroll was considered scandalous by all believing Christians, and they hated it as much as the devil himself. This so-called Book of Emet threatened to do more harm to Christianity than anything in the faith's long and tumultuous history.

"I'm calling to see if you would like to serve on the panel and present the Christian side in the debate."

Mary was flabbergasted. "Me?" she thought, "me????"

"You want me? Why me?"

"I love watching your television show," George said, "and I've seen you in other panel discussions. I can't think of anyone who can present the Christian point of view more forcefully and more cogently — and with more class. And you've been recommended by a number of the people I've talked to."

Mary was stunned, and of course flattered. "Let me think about it," she said. "This is a big responsibility. When do you need an answer by?"

"Do you think you could let me know by this time next week?"

"Yes, I'll know by then."

"I hope you'll say yes," George said warmly. "I think you would do a splendid job."

"Thank you so much," Mary said sincerely. "I'll give it a lot of thought and pray on it."

"Wonderful, I'll call you in a week. Bye for now."

"Goodbye Reverend Turner, and thank you."

"Wow," Mary thought. "I can't believe I'm being given this opportunity to testify for Jesus and bring the good news to the whole world. Show me the way Lord Jesus! You have so many people who love you. How did you come to choose me?"

How, indeed?

Mary Madelyne Roberts was a most unique and gifted woman. She was a popular televangelist and Bible teacher whose weekly television show reached millions of viewers. As her most avid followers knew, she was well-qualified to teach about Jesus Christ, having earned a PhD in Theology from the highly regarded Presbyterian Theological Seminary in Louisville, Kentucky, where she taught for five years during and after receiving her graduate degree. She had begun a "teaching ministry" while at the seminary, leading retreats for women and teenagers, and speaking in churches, primarily to women's groups and mission committees. Mary's interest in preaching began during her sophomore year of college when, for the first time, she heard a female pastor speak about her missionary career.

During that Christmas break, Mary and her best friend Lizzy had driven to a mission conference in Urbana, Illinois. Held on the University of Illinois campus, this conference was that year's version of the every-three-year's convention geared to college students who might be interested in becoming missionaries or evangelists. When Diane Booker addressed the crowd of 17,000 in the Assembly Hall, Mary listened intently to every word, as the former missionary told stories of teaching others about Jesus in far-away nations.

At one point that evening Mary said confidently to her friend, "If that woman can become a pastor, so can I! Can you believe it? This has been a dream of mine since I was a child.... Maybe someday your friend, Mary Madelyne O'Malley, will become a famous preacher!" They both howled at the seeming absurdity of her statement. Neither of them knew of many churches whose pastors were women at that point in time.

"You're talking like a crazy person, you know," Lizzy said.

"I know it sounds like that, but God has a long history of inspiring people to serve Him in new and different ways. Remember the story of Deborah from the Old Testament? She was chosen to be the leader of the Israelites in a very difficult time. If she could do it way back then, why can't women today be leaders? Anyway, if I can't be the pastor of a church, I can teach. I could go to the seminary and study theology, and take every class they have on the Bible. I could really make my mother proud of me!"

Mary's parents were, like the hilarious Irish song, a marriage of "the orange and the green" — except she had a Protestant mother and a Catholic father. They were both from Northern Ireland, which was mostly Protestant and part of the British Empire. The rest of Ireland, which had achieved independence from Britain, was almost totally Catholic. Underground groups in Catholic Ireland were warring with Britain over its occupation of Northern Ireland, while the Protestant majority of Northern Ireland was suppressing the Catholic minority there.

As a rebellious teen, Mary's Protestant mother went to a Catholic school dance, and there met and fell in love with Jack O'Malley, a tall, handsome and exciting man, who was to become Mary's father. Nothing could come of their relationship in that hostile sectarian environment, and as Jack O'Malley was from a poor family, there seemed to be no hope for them to relocate elsewhere. Being a bit of a gay blade and a gambler, Mary's father often bet on the horses and gambled in safe houses. One day he bought a ticket to the Irish Sweepstakes and told Mary's mother that if he won, he would elope with her to America. Amazingly, he was one of ten winners and, after giving his parents half of his winnings, he made good on his promise. He and Mary's mother were soon on a ship to America where they were married *en route* by the ship's captain.

They settled in Chattanooga, Tennessee, and bought a small comfortable house on Lookout Mountain, which was made famous by a battle in the Civil War. From their house, they could overlook most of the city. Mary loved sitting on the front porch in the heat of the summer evening, feeling the cool breeze wafting toward her while gazing at the city lights ablaze below. She liked to look at the houses in the valley beneath her and tell herself romantic stories about what her future life would be like. She knew that the two things that meant the most to her were her love for God and the love of a most wonderful man who would make her feel fulfilled as a woman.

Mary's mother joined a Presbyterian church and was very active there. Her father became loosely affiliated with the nearby Catholic parish but rarely attended Mass. Inasmuch as Catholics were not well-liked in the South in those days, it was not difficult for Mary's mother to get her father to agree to have Mary and her younger sister Margaret raised in the Presbyterian church.

As time went on, Jack O'Malley gambled away much of his fortune and took to drinking heavily. He was a mean drunk and often in his stupor he would beat Mary and Margaret, and often their mother too, for which he predictably was very sorry later. But not sorry enough to change his ways.

Mary often pleaded with her mother to leave her father, but her mother was attached to the church community, and the Christian community in those days did not look kindly on divorce, especially not on divorced women. Thus, this cycle of abuse and meaningless regret on the part of Mary's father, and helpless resignation on the part of her mother, became a central feature of Mary's daily life.

During those years when Mary was constantly afraid of her father, she found comfort and happiness in her faith in Jesus Christ, whose protection she felt even while feeling the fists of her father upon her. She made excellent grades in school and could not wait for the day she could go away to college in order to get as far away as possible from home. She was awarded a full scholarship at the University of Tennessee, where she studied Psychology and Religion. Working part-time there, she was able to save enough money to go to the aforementioned Presbyterian seminary in Louisville.

As a new seminary student in a new city, building relationships with churches and pastors in Louisville was slow going. One day, one of her classmates invited Mary to meet her pastor for coffee. The pastor was so impressed with Mary that he asked her to outline a six-session adult education class on the biblical foundations of Christianity.

The church members who attended Mary's class were impressed at how much they learned in the classes she taught. All agreed that she was smart and well versed in the Bible. But there was more: Mary was an inspired and passionate teacher who obviously loved and believed in what she was teaching — to have total faith in their Lord and Savior, Jesus Christ. When she taught, she gave off a warm loving aura that some students felt was Christ-like. Mary often said she felt like she was imbued with the Holy Spirit when she was teaching. She began to make a reputation for herself as a uniquely gifted and caring teacher who inspired her students to greater Christian faith and action.

Mary expanded her teaching to other churches and venues and she began to build an exceptional résumé for her chosen profession. As Mary often said, "The Lord called me to teach His Word, and He has blessed this ministry to be what it is today."

Mary's ministry was very successful in every sense of the word. She wrote six bestselling books, all of which continued to sell well. CDs and DVDs of her talks and seminars were available from her television ministry and in most Christian bookstores. Her television show was widely watched and she was critically acclaimed as one of the most effective and passionate preachers for Jesus Christ in the country. She organized mission trips to Africa and Asia, which not only converted thousands of souls to Christianity, but provided much needed food, medicine, and education as well.

Mary's life would have been almost perfect, except for the deep disappointment of her marriage to Wayne Roberts. Although she was a beautiful and sexually appealing woman, she had virtually no intimacy with her husband during most of their marriage. They had met at a church in Cincinnati where she was speaking. Like her, Wayne Roberts was a committed Christian, and he was working as a clinical social worker for Christian Charities. He was tall and slender, cute and funny and really liked her, so Mary started seeing him intermittently. When he proposed to her several months later, Mary thought that he must be the one God had chosen for her. She hoped she had found the religious soulmate she had always dreamed of.

She was teaching in Louisville when they married, so Wayne left Cincinnati and with her help, found a job in a counseling center run by Christian Charities in Louisville. His angelic laid-back demeanor provided a comfort zone in her often frenetic life and Mary was happy.

Wayne was a good companion and he provided an atmosphere of peacefulness at home and a soft place for her to land after a hard day.

But they were not without problems in their marriage. Mary and Wayne were both virgins in their early 20's when they married, and even though they had gotten hot and heavy on some dates prior to their marriage, she found that he was only occasionally interested in sex with her after the wedding. She read women's' magazines giving advice on ways to spark the desire for her that Wayne seemed to have before their wedding, but to no avail. He agreed to go to marital counseling sessions with her and the therapist concluded that Wayne had some issues with his mother that inhibited him from being sexual with any woman who had the role of wife in his life. Frustrated, but still content overall with her relationship with Wayne, Mary decided to accept her relatively loveless marriage as one of the challenges God gave her to cope with. "No one gets through life without some challenges," she often used to say. So she decided to face this one with a good-natured cheerfulness and continued to view her glass as half full.

But after the first two years of marriage, even the place of comfortable refuge that Wayne provided for Mary began to deteriorate. Wayne was high maintenance and needed a lot of attention, and with Mary's busy travel schedule, he was not getting what he expected from the marriage. He became easily hurt and angered when Mary was not around, feelings that were heightened by guilt, because he truly did want Mary to be successful in her calling. In addition, Wayne felt diminished as a man because Mary was more successful and prominent than he was and she made a lot more money than he did.

Wayne began to feel embittered and became increasingly passive-aggressive toward her, and the little bits of affection he gave Mary ceased entirely. Their life together became as cold as an Arctic winter in private, while at the same time appearing normal, warm and loving in public. This disconnect was not how Mary had envisioned her life would be, yet this *was* her reality.

The marriage deteriorated further when Mary became pregnant in her late 20's during one of the three times they had sex that year. The pregnancy was troublesome from the beginning. Mary suffered countless infirmities in the early months, and in the middle months had continuous spotting and bleeding problems and was confined to her bed most of the time. Wayne was only grudgingly helpful and Mary's mother came to live with them, over Wayne's objections, to help take care of her. Seven and a half months into her pregnancy, Mary stopped feeling the baby inside of her, and in a panic she went to her gynecologist to see what was happening. To her utter horror, she was told that the baby had died.

The doctor suggested she carry the baby for a while until her body expelled the baby naturally, which her doctor thought would happen within a week. But it did not happen that way. Mary ended up carrying her dead baby for three weeks until they were safely able to induce labor. Those were the longest and most horrific three weeks in Mary's life. The baby was a girl, the daughter who Mary had always wanted, hoping to give her little girl a better childhood than Mary had experienced. She named the baby Rachel, after the Biblical wife of Jacob. Rachel in the Bible had also died too young, something Jacob had never gotten over. Mary had a well-attended memorial service for Rachel, and had her buried next to Mary's father in the cemetery in Chattanooga.

Strangely, Wayne did not share in Mary's grief. Instead, he became even more fervently religious, saying that Rachel's death was God's will, and praising Jesus for giving them their own personal cross to bear. He liked to say that God wanted Rachel more than they did, and he cast himself as some kind of a noble suffering hero.

After the excruciating delivery of the stillborn baby, Mary developed an infection in her uterus, which after several weeks in the hospital and a couple of near-death code-red episodes, was successfully ameliorated. However, she was told that she could never have another child. Mary was heartbroken and sank into a two-year depression. She could not bring herself to work and had no enthusiasm for anything in her life. Sometimes she wished she could join baby Rachel in heaven. Only her faith in Jesus Christ gave her solace and helped pull her through.

During this dreadful time in her life, Mary desperately needed Wayne's support, but none was forthcoming. He was not interested in her sorrow and resented her for moping around the house and not working. Even worse, he let subtle but unmistakable hints drop that he blamed Mary for the baby's death, and increasingly became physically violent toward her, unhappily reminding her of how she had been treated by her father. Whatever sparks of love that had remained for Mary in the marriage up until then were completely extinguished.

Later she learned that Wayne had begun having affairs outside the marriage during the period of her post partum depression. Those affairs have continued to the present time, but Mary has stopped confronting him with them. Each time the subject was brought up, Wayne would immediately confess his sin, apologize to her, ask for forgiveness, and end the affair. Then he would find another woman and do it all over again. If she persisted in pushing the issue, Wayne would become angrily defensive and sometimes physically assaulted her. Since the loss of baby Rachel, there has been no intimacy between Mary and Wayne. It was quite apparent that Wayne had no interest in Mary in that way and she felt the same way toward him.

Like her mother, Mary felt trapped in the marriage because she believed that divorce was wrong. Jesus had spoken against it — "what God has joined together, let not man put asunder." Of course, Mary was aware that the rate of divorce in the Christian community was about the same as the rest of the population. But being a Christian public figure, she believed she had to be a role model for Jesus' teachings and her employers felt the same way.

Only Mary's closest girlfriends knew the truth about her marriage. Except for these wonderful women, Mary felt very much alone in her life. These feelings only increased when Wayne insisted they move to Colorado Springs to be closer to Wayne's family. Living far away from her friends and her roots, Mary's life became even more sad, lonely, and desperate. All that remained was her work, which she happily threw herself into. Now in her late forties, Mary's domestic future did not look bright. But as is so often true of life, things change unexpectedly.

Such a change occurred in Mary's life when her younger sister Margaret was murdered, making Mary the guardian of Margaret's seven-year-old daughter, Christa.

Unlike Mary, who had turned to her faith to protect herself from her unhappy childhood, Margaret had turned to alcohol and drugs. When Margaret was 15, she became pregnant and secretly got an abortion. When her pro-life father learned of this, he threw her out of the house. Distraught and angry, Margaret ran as far away as she could and ended up in New Orleans, in the seediest part of town, where she immersed herself in the local alcohol and drug culture. Margaret went from one man to another, eventually settling in with Jerry, a hard-drinking brutal man who she lived with for ten years until she became pregnant with Christa. This time, Margaret decided to have the child and for seven years raised Christa in a home filled with violence and drugs and alcohol abuse. Then one day, Margaret and Jerry got into a drunken brawl and Jerry shot and killed her, with Christa watching.

Jerry was convicted of murder and sentenced to death, and the court gave custody of Christa to Mary, being that Mary was Christa's only competent relative. Mary was of course delighted at long last to have a daughter in her life. However, there was a problem. Christa had been born with fetal alcohol syndrome, had serious learning disability issues and required lots of attention, more than Mary was able to give with her very busy work commitments.

Mary persuaded her mother to move to Colorado Springs to help her raise Christa. However, Wayne would not allow Mary's mother to move in with them this time, so Mary found a nice condo nearby for her mother to live in. Now Christa is 12 and Mary's mother has shown early signs of dementia. Mary has had her hands full taking care of Christa and her mother, combined with her busy career and taking care of Wayne as well. Still, overall, these have been happy years for Mary compared to what her life had been like before Christa's arrival. She loved Christa as her own daughter and Christa deeply loved Mary, who was more of a mother to her than she had ever known.

None of these changes affected her now non-existent relationship with Wayne, however. They were still sleeping in the same bed, a king bed, but there was no warmth or conversation or touching. They lived like distant roommates in the house, each doing his or her own thing. Mary could not rely on Wayne for very much. On the eve of her departure to St. Louis for the panel discussion, she asked Wayne to take care of Christa and Mary's mother in her absence. But typically, Wayne was not in the least interested in Mary's request and instead decided to go to Denver a few days early to help celebrate his cousin's upcoming wedding.

Rabbi Joshua David Hertzel

And Moses said to God, "May the Lord, the God of the spirits of all mankind, appoint a man over this community to go out and come in before them, one who will lead them out and bring them in, so Your people will not be like sheep without a shepherd." [Numbers 26:15-23.]

Joshua's earliest and fondest memories from childhood involved his immediate family. His father was an outstanding tennis player who tutored him continuously in the sport, starting at the age of 5, and Joshua's play improved every year. His mother was a beautiful, kind and deeply spiritual woman and a caring and dutiful mother. His older sister Esther was born severely handicapped, both physically and mentally, but she was a sweet girl who was always ready to show him her love, and Joshua loved her deeply in return. He felt loved, nurtured and happy. But as is often the case, Joshua's idyllic childhood did not last.

Joshua's father and mother got divorced when he was 11, and he did not see his father again until his Bar Mitzvah two years later. His father did see him occasionally again after that, but only rarely because his father had moved from the Chicago area, where Joshua grew up, to California. There his father remarried and had two more children who he was more devoted to. From that point on Joshua was raised by his mother, who never remarried despite having several romantic relationships. Her dalliances with other men tested Joshua's sense of his own masculinity. Joshua often felt in competition with the other men in his mother's life for her affections, and he felt he needed to contend with the other men to establish who was the real man of the house.

His parents' divorce, his father's virtual disappearance from his life, and his mother's subsequent dating lifestyle took away much of Joshua's childhood optimism and confidence. He learned to give the appearance of being self-assured and competent, although in reality he was filled with deep insecurities and self-doubts. He also felt guilty that his sister Esther was disabled while he was intelligent, athletic and healthy. As a result, Joshua became very goal-oriented, feeling he had to excel at everything he did. A psychologist once told him that he was trying to impress his absent father with his accomplishments in order to earn back the love his father had taken away from him. All Joshua knew was that he felt an emptiness that only success seemed to fill. He eventually learned to suppress his feelings of guilt and inadequacy, but he also began to think a lot about God and God's role in this often unfair and cruel world.

After his parents' divorce, Joshua worked out a lot of his angst on the tennis court, with a great deal of success. In his senior year of high school, Joshua led his school's tennis team to the state finals. He and his partner came in second in doubles competition, and later that afternoon, Joshua Hertzel won first place in boys' singles. He received a four-year scholarship from the University of Illinois to play tennis, was very successful there, and attracted national attention. Joshua was a bit of a celebrity on campus and at one point he was planning to turn pro after graduation.

During his sophomore year of college, Joshua met Patricia, his future wife. Patricia came from a wealthy Chicago suburban Jewish family and was attracted to the excitement that was Joshua's life. Joshua in turn was attracted to Patricia's class and upscale lifestyle.

Joshua's concern about the role of God in the world led him back to studying his Jewish religious heritage. Since he was a little boy, Joshua had been fascinated by Bible stories. He would read them over and over again, sometimes in comic book form and sometimes in the form of children's stories. When he grew older and went to Jewish Sunday School, he loved reading those stories again and again, in a progressively more advanced style. The Bible stories were all the more interesting because there was a family legend that the Hertzels were descendants of the line of King David. However, no one knew if the legend was true or how to check it out.

Joshua's interest in Jewish education stopped after his Bar Mitzvah, and like most boys his age, Joshua became involved in teenage things, particularly sports and girls. He did not become interested in Jewish things again until he started attending Rabbi Kolb's classes at the Hillel Center, the campus Jewish organization, during his junior year in college.

Inspired by the wisdom and kindness of Rabbi Kolb, Joshua attended every Hillel Center class that he could fit into his busy schedule. His relationship with the Rabbi became close, and they typically met one-on-one for an hour two times a week. Joshua looked upon Rabbi Kolb as not only his teacher of the more than 5,000 years of Jewish history and traditions, but also as a mentor, father figure and spiritual guide. Joshua was astonished to discover that the Bible stories were taught on a more advanced level than he had ever imagined. At the university too, there were classes on "The Bible as Literature," "Comparative Religion," and "The Bible as History."

Joshua learned that Jewish thought did not stop at the end of the Bible. He was told that great learned rabbis, called "sages", took biblical analysis to levels that would have dwarfed the Tower of Babel. Most of their efforts were focused on the Torah, the first five books of the Bible (Genesis through Deuteronomy), which they believed were dictated word for word and letter by letter by God directly to Moses, who wrote it down just as God dictated.

During the era of the sages, every word in the Torah was discussed, dissected, analyzed, compared to other words, and then discussed again. The sages wrote down their discussions, and they made decisions on Jewish law that were based on either the prestige of one of the rabbis or by majority vote. Like U.S. Supreme Court decisions, the majority views and the minority views were all written down and saved for posterity. There was something called the "oral law", which was also said to have been passed down orally from God to Moses and to every subsequent generation, but which had not been written down. The oral law amplified the text of the Bible itself, giving color, texture and flesh to the economical biblical verses. Eventually, the oral law was written down too, and it was also discussed, dissected, analyzed and compared by the sages. These various writings were called Talmud, Midrash and Mishneh. One could spend one's entire life studying them, and historically hundreds of thousands of Jews did.

During the centuries following the era of the sages, great commentators arose, with such famous names as Moses Maimonides and Rashi. There were also great local Jewish rabbis, like the Baal Shem Tov, who taught kindness, happiness, and righteousness. Books were written summarizing and compiling Jewish laws and traditions. Standard prayer books were created out of the text of the Bible, the poetry of the Psalms, and the thoughts of the great scholars and poets of the Middle Ages.

There was also a field of study called "Jewish Mysticism" that Joshua had never heard of. The leading school of thought in the Jewish mystical tradition was the Kabbalah (literally "something received"). It was said that one had to be very learned in the subjects discussed above, and be over the age of 40, before Kabbalah study would be permitted. This was a very mysterious field of study indeed and was not considered part of mainstream Judaism. However, Joshua liked the Kabbalah because it talked about more spiritual matters and about non-traditional subjects like reincarnation and the eternity of the soul. It also talked about God needing the help of mankind to help collect shattered shards of light that had been broken at creation and, like Humpty Dumpty, needed to be put back together again. Shards of light are collected when people act righteously and in a God-like manner toward God's creations, especially other human beings. "God needs my help," Joshua learned, and he liked that idea. Helping God make the world better became a significant part of his life.

In short, Joshua found himself completely amazed at how rich Judaism was beyond the Bible stories that were the essence of his initial attraction to Judaism. He wanted to learn more, and the more he learned, the more there was to learn. It seemed endless.

However, the rebel within Joshua found the theology and some of the rulings of the sages and other authorities to be unconvincing. He did not believe that the Torah was written word for word, and letter by letter, by God. Joshua learned in his secular classes that parts of the Bible were written in different eras by different authors, and he became convinced that the historians were right about this. Joshua also came to believe that mainstream Judaism was lacking in some significant ways. He found some of the tenets of other religions more convincing than Judaism, and he came to believe that *every religion has a piece of "the truth" and no religion has "the whole truth."* But Joshua believed there were many more "truths" in Judaism than in the other religions, and he thought that what was good in the other religions should be added to Judaism to make it more complete and more appealing to both modern man's reason and his sense of spirituality. Joshua came to be what some derisively called a "New Age Jew." He wanted to pass his thoughts on to other Jews and pondered how he could do that.

Shortly before he finished his senior year of college, Joshua told his coach that his great passion for tennis would never end; but, from then on, it would have to be second to a greater calling. Joshua David Hertzel decided he wanted to be a rabbi.

Before embarking on this path, which totally surprised his friends and family, Joshua felt he needed to go to his Jewish roots, to the State of Israel. Taking advantage of a program called Birthright Israel, Joshua was able to go to Israel for a nominal sum. Once in Israel, he loved it so much he stayed on for two years. He took classes in English at Hebrew University in Jerusalem during his first year there. The second year Joshua went to kibbutz Naot Mordechai in the upper Galilee, where he worked as a volunteer and was offered additional classes in conversational Hebrew. The two years in Israel was a soul-deepening experience and gave Joshua an even stronger feeling for Jewish history, wisdom and cosmology.

Upon returning to the States, Joshua did two life-altering things; he embarked on Rabbinical School and he married his college sweetheart Patricia. Five years later, Joshua was ordained as a Reform movement Rabbi and had seen two sons come into the world. Even though the Reform movement is considered the most liberal and flexible branch of Judaism, Joshua finished in the middle of his class because his ideas were too outside the mainstream for many of his teachers and his grades suffered accordingly. Nevertheless, most of his fellow students regarded Joshua as the best and the brightest among them.

Joshua has come to believe that the future of the Jewish community in America depends on adopting new ideas with wide appeal to secular Jews, who comprise the vast majority of Jews in both America and Israel. As one of the nation's leading "new age rabbis," Joshua believes that Kabbalistic and Buddhistic notions of reincarnation need to become part of mainstream Judaism's afterlife theology. He also believes that the traditional Jewish prayer service does not speak to the contemporary spiritual concerns and beliefs of most American Jews. And most controversial of all, Joshua teaches that the rules of ancient Jewish law need to be revised and updated for the modern age.

All the Jewish sects are uncomfortable with Joshua's views to varying degrees—the other leading sects being Orthodox, Conservative and Reconstructionist. He would probably have been considered just a flake were it not for the fact that his views have attracted a huge and growing following among American Jews who were voting for him with their feet. His Temple Menorah synagogue in Chicago was growing rapidly and his website was the most frequented one in all of Judaism. Despite his general popularity, Joshua was also the most criticized Jew in America by mainstream Jewish authorities and commentators. He attributed the resistance to his ideas to a fear of change and an unquestioning loyalty to tradition.

In addition to his work with his synagogue in Chicago, Joshua was a frequent invitee to speak and teach in other venues, and was a favorite of the national media when they wanted a controversial Jewish leader to weigh in on the many issues of the day. He has written op-ed pieces for both of the major newspapers in the "Windy City," the Chicago Tribune and the Sun-Times, and for various Jewish newspapers throughout the country and in Israel. He has also published two very controversial books: A new prayer book, which included the wisdom writing from Judaism and other religions, lovely poetry and music, new age self-help ideas, and inspirational writings from various sources. The other book, which was published a few months after the Book of Emet was discovered, was titled *"Embracing Jesus: What Jews Can Learn from this Jewish Prophet."*

While Joshua's professional life reflected his typical ability to excel at things he set his mind to, his personal life became a shambles. His beloved mother passed away suddenly from pancreatic cancer when Joshua was in his early 30's. After that, he became the one who was solely responsible for the care and treatment of his sister. He took care of Esther by himself for as long as he could, but eventually her condition worsened and required the full-time care of a nursing home. Insurance did not cover her care, so Joshua had to pay for it out of his own pocket. He put her in the best quality nursing home he could find, and it was very expensive. No help came from his father, and Joshua's financial situation became precarious.

Joshua's marriage also suffered, for a number of reasons. Patricia was not interested in being a *rebbitzin*, or rabbi's wife, and rarely participated in Joshua's professional rabbinic life. She did not take kindly to having Esther brought into their home and was very upset about the family's financial problems. Her parents had expected Patricia to be married to a celebrity jet-setting tennis pro and frequently expressed their disappointment with Joshua's career choice to Patricia. They were embarrassed at Joshua's failure to be a better provider and did not enjoy hearing back from their friends about his controversial reputation within the Jewish community.

Patricia started having an affair with someone from her parents' social circle who had recently been divorced, and after a few months she took their sons and moved back into her parents' house and filed for divorce. Fortunately, the divorce court judge acceded to Joshua's request for joint custody of the children, so Joshua was able to stay a constant in his sons' lives, thereby avoiding a repeat of what had happened between him and his own father.

Joshua has now been divorced for twelve years. Like many men his age, Joshua has become more distinguished-looking, and women have found him handsome and desirable. They have been especially attracted to his friendly warm smile, and his kind but serious eyes. They also liked his nurturing personality and his respectful and loving attitude toward women. However, very few of the women he met could see themselves married to a rabbi, though that had stopped only a handful from pursuing him. A few non-Jewish women even told him that they would consider converting and a couple of them actually did. Although Joshua discouraged them from converting out of the hope of having a relationship with him, he helped those who were sincere, because he believed that a sincere convert was every bit as good, or even better, than a born Jew. In this, he disagreed with the Orthodox authorities, who believed that would-be converts should be discouraged from converting.

Joshua has not remarried despite having had three serious relationships, all with Jewish women. Those relationships were good for the most part but were not ultimately fulfilling. They left his soul feeling lonely, and he is still looking for the love of his life, his *beshert*, the one who was meant for him.

George Turner's decision to choose Joshua to represent the Jewish point of view was quite controversial in the Jewish community. Besides his contrarian views, the most controversial of Joshua's views involved the nature of God. Joshua had come to believe that God could not be both all-good and all-powerful at the same time, considering all the injustice, pain and cruelty in the world. He had heard the usual explanations: God works in mysterious ways that humans cannot understand; God no longer acts in the world and leaves things for man to work out; and God helps with spiritual issues but does not intervene in the laws of nature. None of these explanations satisfied Joshua and he spent years trying to understand how so much evil could exist in a supposedly *perfect* world created by a *perfect* deity.

Joshua's conclusions were shocking to the religious establishments of all denominations. He taught that God was all-good but *not all-powerful*.

That would explain evil in the world and also support the innate human belief in a moral and just God. Joshua believed that God was opposed by a more powerful force of amoral chaos that Joshua called the "Dark Side," which he compared to another impersonal force like gravity. He believed that God had created mankind to help Him overcome the Dark Side. The essence of Joshua's teaching was both bold and invigorating — that *God needs us as much as we need Him.*

As his beliefs began to attract a following, Joshua became a frequent target of religious writers from the right and center of the Jewish spectrum. In fact, some rabbis refused to share a stage with him because they thought of him as a traitor to Judaism's belief in the One God. Nevertheless, he was quite popular with the more liberal Jews, and more importantly, with the more than fifty percent of Jews who were unaffiliated or disaffected — a rapidly growing group that he was passionately committed to bringing back into the fold.

Joshua's theological diversity was of deep concern to the leaders of the Christian faith community as well. Many Christian leaders saw in Joshua a bigger danger to their faith than might come from any mainstream Jewish authorities. They felt his popularity with liberal and new age Jews would also translate well to Christians who have doubts about Christian theology. Some fundamentalist Christians felt he and the Book of Emet had to be stopped at all costs and they hoped that Dr. Mary Roberts would be the one who could do that. But just in case, they laid contingency plans to make sure Joshua's arguments would not carry the day.

The Book of Emet

Chapter One: In the Beginning

Cast away from you all the transgressions you have committed, and get a new heart and a new spirit. For why will you die, O house of Israel?
"For I take no pleasure in the death of him who dies," says the Lord your God. "Repent and live!" [Ezekiel 18:20-21, 18:30-32.]

Reverend George Turner opened the proceedings. "We turn now to Chapter One of the Book of Emet. Dr. Roberts, would you please start us off by telling us what the New Testament says about the birth of Jesus."

"Thank you Reverend Turner, and thank you to everyone who is watching and listening to this program. I think you will find when we finish this debate that the Word of God in the Gospels is the Truth and the Way, and that this Book of Emet is a fraud.

"The birth of our Lord and Savior Jesus Christ happened like this. His mother, the Blessed Virgin Mary was engaged to Joseph. But before their wedding, she was found to be with child. Her husband Joseph, being a righteous man and unwilling to expose her to public disgrace, planned to dismiss her quietly. But just when he had resolved to do this, an angel of the Lord appeared to him in a dream and said, 'Joseph, son of David, do not be afraid to take Mary as your wife, for the child conceived in her is from the Holy Spirit. She will bear a son, and you are to name him Jesus, for he will save his people from their sins.' All this took place to fulfill what had been spoken by the Lord through the prophet Isaiah:

"The virgin will be with child and will give birth to a son, and will call him Immanuel."

"Immanuel means, 'God is with us.' When Joseph awoke from his sleep, he did as the angel of the Lord commanded him. He took Mary as his wife, but had no marital relations with her until she had borne a son, and he named him Jesus.

"In those days a decree went out from Emperor Augustus that everyone in the Roman Empire should be registered in their ancestral hometowns. Joseph and Mary went from Nazareth to Bethlehem, also called the city of David, because Joseph was descended from the house of King David. While they were there, the time came for her to deliver her child. And she gave birth to her firstborn son, the baby Jesus, and laid him in a manger because there was no place for them at the inn.

"The Bible tells us of two groups of people who were given special notice of the birth of our Savior. In one scripture, there were shepherds in that region living in the fields, keeping watch over their flock by night. An angel of the Lord came to them and said: 'I am bringing you good news of great joy for all the people! To you is born this day in the city of David a Savior, who is the Messiah, the Lord. This will be a sign for you: you will find a child wrapped in bands of cloth and lying in a manger.' The shepherds went to the manger and prayed at the foot of the baby Jesus.

"In another scripture, three wise men from the East saw a star in the sky that led them to the manger in Bethlehem. They could see right away that the baby Jesus was a special child and they prayed to him in awe. They opened their treasures and presented him with gifts of gold, incense and myrrh."

Mary looked over at Joshua to signify that she had finished and that it was his turn now. But seeing Mary's gorgeous green eyes focused on him surprisingly unnerved Joshua for a few moments. George saw Joshua's discomfort and decided to help.

"Thank you Dr. Roberts. Rabbi Hertzel, would you please tell us what the Book of Emet says about this."

"Of course, thank you Reverend Turner," Joshua answered as he regained his composure. "The Book of Emet says Joseph and Miriam, or Mary as we have come to know her, were married and living in the village of Nazareth in the district of Galilee. Mary had no children yet and prayed to God that she might have a child, promising to dedicate him to God's service. God heard Mary's prayers and a few months later Mary and Joseph conceived their first son. Joseph called the child Jesse, named for the father of his ancestor King David. In Hebrew, Jesse means 'God lives', but in ancient Greek it was translated as Jesus. Mary and Joseph raised Jesus to know that he was promised to God's service.

"By the way, Dr. Roberts, the passage in Isaiah that you quoted doesn't say 'virgin'. It says 'young woman'. This passage has been mistranslated by Christians for two thousand years. Isaiah was not predicting a miraculous or 'immaculate' conception."

A nod from George Turner indicated it was now Sir Winston's turn to speak.

"Most historians believe Jesus was born in the town of Nazareth, because that is where Mary and Joseph lived. It doesn't make sense that they would have traveled to Bethlehem for a census just because King David had lived there many generations earlier. That would be like you Yanks traveling to where your great-great-great grandfather lived for you to take the U.S. census. According to the Gospel of Mark, it would have required Joseph to go back fourteen generations to get to King David. If he went back even one more generation, he would have had to go somewhere else. The whole thing is very dubious and few serious historians believe it happened that way.

"Concerning the paternity of Jesus, it was common in those days, particularly with the pagan religions, to believe that the gods impregnated ordinary mortals, and that half-man/half-god offspring were created. Hercules was one example of this. Perhaps that is where the story of Mary being a virgin came from."

Mary Roberts quickly jumped in. "According to scripture, which is the Word of God, Jesus was not half-man and half-God. Jesus was fully human *and* fully divine. The pagans had no legends like *that*."

"That is true," said Sir Winston, "but we think Jesus was not originally portrayed as a god. For Jewish audiences, it was enough to call him the Messiah. But for pagan audiences, which had no concept of a Messiah, to get their attention, Jesus had to be portrayed as a god. We think that is where the virgin birth idea came from."

"That sounds good as a theory," Mary agreed, "but that overlooks the fact that the Scriptures are God's words and what they say is Truth."

Joshua did not agree. "The problem with believing that all the words in Scripture are God's words verbatim is that there are numerous contradictions that can't be reconciled. For example, Dr. Roberts, one of your gospels says Joseph and Mary went from their home in Nazareth to Bethlehem because of the census and then after Jesus was born, they returned home. One of the other gospels says Joseph and Mary first lived in Bethlehem, and then after Jesus was born they fled to Egypt to save Jesus' life, because King Herod ordered that all boy babies be killed. Then it says they went to Nazareth to live after returning from Egypt."

"How can there be contradictions if every word came from God?" Joshua asked. "We have some of the same problems with our Torah, which is the first five books of the Bible — Genesis through Deuteronomy. There are numerous contradictions there also. I personally believe that God was somehow involved in creating these Scriptures, but I don't believe that every word and letter is the word of God as fundamentalists in the Jewish, Christian, and Muslim world believe."

"Rabbi Hertzel is right about the contradictions," Winston said. "Also, we have found no evidence that there was an order for baby boys of Bethlehem to be killed, and there is no evidence that a national census was taken. There are pretty accurate records from those days, so historians believe that none of those things actually happened."

"You should not be so cavalier about dismissing the words of Scripture even if you haven't found the historical evidence for it yet," Mary warned. "It is important to believe. The Bible says that those who do not accept Jesus Christ as our Savior and the Lord's only begotten son are going to hell. Those who accept him and believe in him will be saved. Through Christ, who died for our sins, God made it possible for all of us to have eternal life. I hope you and all our listeners will see God's light by the time these discussions are over and that you all will not be distracted by your so-called 'historical evidence'." Mary's face glowed when she spoke, a glow that came from her absolute and passionate faith in Jesus. It was this conviction that had made believers out of the millions of people who had the chance to see her preach personally or on television.

"Jews don't believe that belief in Jesus determines whether you go to heaven or hell," countered Joshua. "We believe that leading a righteous life is much more important than what one believes."

As none of the panelists had anything more to add, Reverend Turner nodded at Mary to proceed on to the next topic.

The Childhood of Jesus

"Almost nothing is said about the childhood of Jesus in the gospels", Mary said, beginning the next topic. "Although we all wonder about the early years of Jesus, it doesn't really matter much because his ministry did not start until he was a grown man, probably around the age of 30 or so.

"There is, however, one story that tells us something about his childhood. Every year Jesus' parents went to Jerusalem for the festival of the Passover. And when he was twelve years old, they went up as usual for the festival. When the festival was over and it was time for them to go back home, the boy Jesus decided to stay behind in Jerusalem without telling his parents. Assuming that Jesus was among the group of travelers they were with, the parents went a day's journey before they became aware that Jesus was missing. They searched for him among their relatives and friends but did not find him. Now in a state of panic, Mary and Joseph quickly returned to Jerusalem to search for him.

"After three long days they finally found Jesus in the Temple, sitting among the teachers, listening to them and asking them questions. And all who heard him were amazed at his understanding and his answers. When his parents saw him, they were astonished, and his mother said to him, 'Child, why have you treated us like this? Look, your father and I have been searching for you in great anxiety.' Jesus responded, 'Why were you searching for me? Did you not know that I must be in my Father's house?'"

"The Book of Emet has a lot more to say about Jesus as a boy," Joshua said after Mary was finished speaking. "Emet says he knew Jesus when they were both children, while those who purportedly wrote the gospels did not know him at all as they wrote long after his death. I don't have anything to add to what the audience has just had read to them about it. I will point out, though, that what Emet has to say is neither contradicted nor disputed by any other source. Whether it is true or not, I'll let each of you decide."

Mary wanted to help the audience decide in favor of the Gospels' narratives. "The key issue here is that there is no mention of any Emet in the gospels or in any other place. If this Emet was so important in the life of Jesus, certainly one of the gospels would have mentioned him. It seems clear to me that this Emet did not exist, or if he did, he was not anyone important, and he probably made up everything he said that is not in the Bible."

"Dr. Roberts is right about that," Sir Winston agreed. Mary was feeling glad for Winston's support, until he expounded further on what he meant. "There is no evidence that I know of that Emet existed, and there is no outside confirmation of any of the events he wrote about that vary from the Bible. Nevertheless, most historians think Emet's version is more likely to be true than the Biblical version. I share that view as well. I think that by the end of these discussions, most fair-minded viewers will agree with the historians."

Mary was surprised that Winston chose to side with Joshua and Emet on this and she did not intend to let them have the final word. "For true believers," she said, "this is not a matter for the historians. This is the Word of God we're talking about here. What the historians may theorize is not remotely as important as what God tells us in the Bible."

Winston had nothing more to add, not wanting to get into an argument about the value of historical research. He already knew that there is no amount of science or research that can be offered that would change the mind of people who believe the Bible is God's word. He also knew that presenting historical research to those who did not hold that belief about the Bible was sufficient in itself to open their minds and make them think.

John the Baptist

Noticing that neither Winston nor Joshua had anything more to say, Mary introduced the next topic. "John the Baptist prepared the way for the coming of our Lord and Savior Jesus Christ," Mary said in her professorial voice. "The Word of God came to John the Baptist while he was praying and wandering in the desert. After God told him what to do, John went to the areas around the Jordan River, preaching a baptism of repentance for the forgiveness of sins saying, 'Turn your lives around, for the Kingdom of Heaven is near.'

"John was a very holy man. He wore animal skins and had no possessions and ate insects and locusts. He was obviously imbued with the spirit of the Lord. The people came to him from the Jordan River area, Jerusalem and all over Israel. Confessing their sins, they were baptized by him in the Jordan River, as John proclaimed: 'I baptize you with water as a sign that you are changing the direction of your life and beginning to walk with God.'

"Many people believed John the Baptist was the Messiah, but he rejected that notion, saying that 'one who is more powerful than I is coming after me; I am not worthy to carry his sandals. He will baptize you with the Holy Spirit and fire!'"

Mary paused then to give the other panelists a chance to respond.

Joshua spoke up first. "John the Baptist was definitely creating a spiritual and religious rebirth within the Jewish people," he said with admiration, for Joshua was hoping to achieve a similar result with his own work, "and he had a large following. John preached asceticism and said that those who had extra clothes and food should share them with those less fortunate. He told tax collectors and soldiers to treat their fellow Jews honestly.

"The people came in large numbers to receive John's blessing and, as a result, the people felt cleansed of their sins. Being baptized in the Jordan River was like a trip to the ritual cleansing bath called the 'mikvah' where Jews go to cleanse themselves of ritual impurities. But being cleansed in the Jordan must have felt very powerful to them."

Now it was the historian's turn. "The famous first century historian Flavius Josephus wrote that John the Baptist attracted quite a lot of attention, and not only from common people," Winston intoned. "The Jews were very unhappy with Roman rule, and as a result, large and small revolts were constantly breaking out. John was preaching like a fire-brand Hebrew prophet in a highly charged political atmosphere. Some of them thought John the Baptist was the long-awaited Messiah. According to Josephus, that is the real reason Herod Antipas had him put in jail and executed. However, the Gospel of Mark says John the Baptist was imprisoned for criticizing Herod's marriage to his brother's wife.

"I also must point out that there were many others around at the same time as John and Jesus who also performed great healings and miracles, and who were also thought to be the Messiah by their followers. Times were very bad and hopes for rescue by a Messiah were in the air."

"That may well be," challenged Mary, "but all the other pretenders were ordinary people, while Jesus was God's only begotten son, who through his sacrifice and resurrection, brought salvation and eternal life to all those who believe in him. Jesus is the only one who has followers today. That should tell you something."

Seeing that there was no reaction from Joshua or Sir Winston, Mary went on with the narrative.

The Baptism of Jesus

"Jesus came from the Galilee to John the Baptist at the Jordan River to be baptized by him. John would have prevented him, saying, 'I need to be baptized by you, and do you come to me?' But Jesus answered him, 'Let it be so now; for it is proper for us in this way to fulfill all righteousness.' Then John consented. And when Jesus had been baptized, just as he came up from the water, the heavens were opened to him and he saw the Spirit of God descending like a dove and alighting on him. And a voice from heaven said, 'This is my Son, the Beloved, with whom I am well pleased.'"

"That is not exactly what it says in the Book of Emet," said Joshua. "According to Emet, Jesus came from the Galilee to the Jordan River to hear what John had to say and *learn* from him. He was greatly inspired by John's prophetic teachings. When Jesus felt ready, he asked John to baptize him, which he did. The baptism became a profound spiritual experience for Jesus, and from that time on, he felt he was called by God to help continue the work of John the Baptist, preparing the people for the imminent arrival of the Kingdom of Heaven."

"It may have looked that way to others, but we have the benefit of their private conversation," Mary argued back. "And if you think about it, it really makes sense this way. Can God learn about godliness from one of His creations? That's like saying an infant can teach a scholar to read."

Calling the First Disciples

"Jesus called twelve men to be his first disciples," Mary said, beginning the next topic after a nod from George. "Those first twelve men were quite diverse. At least four were fishermen, one was a political revolutionary, and Matthew was one of those hated tax collectors.

"Keeping such a disparate group together while working on the same goals would have been a minor miracle for anyone but Jesus, who was so filled with God's Holy Spirit that virtually no one could resist him.

"Later Jesus sent the twelve disciples out as apostles, telling them what to say to encourage the people to repent. As he traveled around to other towns and villages, Jesus felt compassion for the crowds he preached to, because they were helpless, like sheep without a shepherd. So Jesus appointed seventy-two others to help spread his message, and sent them two-by-two ahead of him to every town and place where he was about to go. He allowed them to perform miracles and healings in his name."

"The Book of Emet agrees with the gospels on these things pretty much word for word," corroborated Joshua. "There is no doubt that Jesus was charismatic and filled with godliness in his soul."

"Yes, word for word," Winston agreed. "Historians marvel how many times these various gospels agree with each other word for word, even though written by different people at different times and in different places. We believe there were many snippets of text floating around that were available to all the gospel writers. There were also oral traditions that were passed on, but those would have been less reliable."

"The reason why the four gospels agree so much is because they were inspired by God," Mary challenged. "And that is why this phony gospel they call the Book of Emet is different—it was not inspired by God. The reason he uses the same words so often is because he copied them from others."

Joshua wanted to change the subject. He knew that Judaism had an even longer and more extensive oral tradition, called the oral law, before it was finally put into writing after the destruction of the Holy Temple because the most educated of Jewish people were thrown out of the Land of Israel.

While he agreed with Winston that oral traditions almost certainly experience changes over time, it was not the kind of topic he wanted to discuss at this type of forum.

"It is interesting to me," Joshua said, "that Jesus told the apostles to go out only to the Jews. Jesus was not interested in bringing the Kingdom of God to the gentiles. Yet, in an irony of history, it was primarily the gentiles who came to be the ones who made Christianity so successful. In his day, Jesus was preaching *to Jews for Jews* and that is who his teachings were meant for. If Jesus did think of himself as the Messiah, which Emet says he didn't, he would have thought of himself as the Messiah only for the Jews. That is totally in line with what the prophets who preceded him also thought and taught."

Winston agreed. "Yes, yes, it seems quite clear that Jesus was interested only in preaching to the Jews. It would have amazed the earlier prophets that the Messiah could be for the gentiles and not for the Jews. The Messiah was prophesied to be a Jewish military superhero who would save the Jews from their oppressors and lead them to freedom and begin a golden age. That is why it was important to them that he be descended from King David, the greatest warrior in their history."

"You both have it wrong," corrected Mary. "The Messiah was supposed to bring love, peace and justice on earth to all peoples. And if we would all believe in him, we would have that now."

Further Discussion

"Do any of you have anything more you would like to discuss concerning this chapter of the Book of Emet?" George asked.

"I do," said Mary promptly. "This Emet tale leaves out the account of the temptation of Jesus by the devil in the desert. After his baptism, Jesus was led by the Holy Spirit into the desert to pray and purify himself for his coming mission. He fasted forty days and nights and—afterwards—he was very hungry! So, the tempter, the devil, came to him and offered him three temptations.

"First the devil said, 'If you are the Son of God, tell these stones to become bread that you may eat.' But Jesus answered that man does not live by bread alone.

"Then the devil took him to the holy city of Jerusalem to the highest point of the holy Temple. 'If you are the Son of God,' he said, 'prove it by throwing yourself down and see if God's angels will save you.' But Jesus answered that one should not put the Lord to the test.

"Again, the devil took Jesus to a very high mountain and showed him all the kingdoms of the world and their splendor. 'All this I will give to you,' he said, 'if you will bow down and worship me.' But Jesus said, 'Away from me, Satan! For it is written: Worship the Lord your God, and serve Him only.'

"Then the devil left him, and angels came and attended him. And Jesus went to Galilee, proclaiming the love and grace of God, saying, 'The time is fulfilled, and the Kingdom of Heaven has come near; repent, and believe in the good news.' And he spoke with such authority that those who heard him believed he had brought the Kingdom with him!"

"Rabbi Hertzel..." George called out after waiting a few seconds for Joshua to take his turn to speak next.

Joshua had been watching Mary, transfixed by her beauty and her poise. Every gesture made her more alluring.

"Nothing in that story requires superhuman or mystical powers," Joshua replied refocusing on the task at hand. "Jesus never allowed himself to fall—or jump—for the three temptations. He seemed to do just fine by reciting and applying the Scriptures and Talmudic sayings he learned as a child. Now, there's a good reason for going to Sunday school, so you know what to say to 'beat the devil!'" There were chuckles in the audience.

Joshua smiled, enjoying that his little joke met a friendly reception.

"But getting serious now," Joshua said, getting serious now, "Jews don't believe in Satan or the devil. We believe the evil in the world comes from the world being inherently imperfect. We don't believe it comes from a conscious outside force. I have a little bit different view about this, which I'm sure we will get to later."

"What is our historian's view?" asked Reverend Turner with a soft smile, cocking his head in Sir Winston's direction.

"It is a nice embellishment to have the devil go up against his primary adversary," said Winston jovially. "It is jolly good story telling. However, it is highly doubtful that this episode ever took place. The supernaturalism of it boggles the mind. It might make some sense were it a dream or a hallucination, but it is not portrayed that way."

Mary was unhappy at the easy dismissal of what she felt was an important Biblical narrative, but seeing she was not going to get anywhere against those two, she decided to change the subject. "I want to go back to the beginning, Sir Winston, when you mentioned pagan myths about half-man/half-god creatures. Christianity is nothing like a pagan religion, with many gods fighting each other for power and domination. Christianity grew out of Judaism and developed just as God intended it to, fulfilling His plan of eternal salvation through His son, Jesus Christ."

"I don't agree," Joshua interrupted. "Christianity started as a minor sect within Judaism, but strayed way off course when they chose to characterize Jesus as God...."

"We did not *choose* to characterize Jesus as God, Jesus *was* God, and his resurrection proves it!" Mary interrupted. "God loves us so much he sacrificed His only son Jesus to atone for our sins and allow us to be saved and have life eternal."

"But in that sense, Christianity did *not* grow out of Judaism," Joshua insisted. "There are no stories in the Old Testament about God assuming human form and we cannot even imagine Him doing something like that. The only thing close to that is that sometimes God sent angels as messengers. The idea of God coming to earth in human form comes from pagan myths, not from Judaism."

"That is quite right," seconded Winston. "When Christianity was not being successful converting Jews to this new religion, it turned to the many non-Jews around them. These people believed in the Greek and Roman gods and in their experience the only way to have a mortal child of a god was to have the god impregnate a mortal woman. I believe that is why the story of the virgin birth was created, because it was not initially a part of Christian beliefs."

"Jesus was not a pagan god and did not act like a pagan god. He acted like he was God's son, as God incarnate." Mary was speaking passionately. "And he was also the Messiah forecast by Isaiah and the other Jewish prophets — who was sent by God to save the world and grant eternal salvation for those who will believe in him."

"But Jesus did not do any of the things the Messiah was supposed to do," Joshua objected. "Our prophets taught us that the Messiah, which means *the anointed one*, would restore Israel to its previous prominence as an independent nation. Isaiah and others had been promising this for four hundred years before Jesus of Nazareth was even born. But Jesus didn't restore Israel to independence and, as near as I can tell, he never even tried.

"He was a peaceful man who said turn the other cheek, *not* the great warrior that the Messiah from the line of David was supposed to be. Jesus was not the Messiah, first and foremost, because he did not bring about the things the Messiah was prophesied to bring — peace on earth, where the lion lies down with the lamb, and men beat their swords into pruning hooks, and make war no more. Wouldn't you agree, Sir Winston?"

"As a physical, historical and spatial reality, I would agree that peace on earth as the Jewish prophets thought about it has not yet arrived," Winston responded. "So Jesus definitely did not achieve what the prophets predicted the Messiah would do."

"The things Jesus left undone will be done with the Second Coming," Mary affirmed. "In the meantime, he brought love and salvation and God's grace to all who believe in him. He makes it possible for us to overcome our original sin and go to heaven when we die. That is no small accomplishment."

"For the things that are supposed to be done with the Second Coming, I say let him come again and do those things, and then I'll believe in him." Joshua said smiling, using his favorite comeback line to that argument.

Someone from the audience shouted "You Jews are Christ-killers and you will all be going to hell, especially you Hertzel!"

"All right, everyone, let's stick to the point," George interrupted.

"Let's not get into anything personal here." He paused to let his words settle in, and then continued, "Do any of the panelists have any more comments or questions about the first chapter?"

No one spoke, so George thanked the panel and adjourned the discussion, ushering the panelists backstage for their first break between the chapters.

As Joshua stood up, he noticed, in the far right corner of the balcony, a man dressed entirely in white. "Oh my God!" he thought to himself. "What is *he* doing here?"

Backstage

Joshua was still feeling stunned as he joined the others backstage. "This is going to be a tough three days," he muttered.

"Don't worry, we'll protect you," Mary said kiddingly.

Joshua looked at her with a funny expression on his face. "I hope we won't need protecting."

"I hope we won't have any more outbursts like that," George said apologetically. "Obviously there are strong feelings out there about this. Let's try not to take any of it personally."

"That's not just strong feelings," Joshua said with a hint of anger in his voice. "That's anti-Semitism. And we do take it personally because anti-Semitism has led to the death of millions of Jews, and not just in the Holocaust."

His historical Jewish memory of Christians who used to make Jews convert or face death began to surface. Visions of Roman cruelties, European pogroms, the Spanish Inquisition, and of course the Holocaust flashed before his eyes. Almost 2,000 years of anti-Semitism has left its mark on the Jewish consciousness.

"Well some would say it's your own fault," Mary said cautiously. "Jesus was the Messiah, the Christ! The one prophesied by your own prophets. The Messiah your people had been waiting for. If the Jews had just followed him, you'd all be…"

"We'd all be what?" Joshua fired back angrily. "Christians?"

"No, we would all be Jews, faithfully following our common Messiah, Jesus."

Joshua was surprised by her answer. Did this great spokeswoman for the cause of Christianity really say that she thought Jesus' goal was not to make people Christians, but to make them even better Jews? Of course, that is exactly what he believed about Jesus, but he did not expect that from her. He stared in Mary's direction without really looking at her.... Suddenly a feeling of warmth coursed through his body. "She isn't anti-Jewish, she is pro-Jesus," he said to himself happily. He was not sure what to say, so for a few moments he was not able to say anything.

Mary noticed the confusion in Joshua's eyes and felt a surprising maternal twinge. Part of her wanted to help him, but she caught herself, realizing that her mission was to spread belief in Jesus Christ. "Get a grip Mare," she said to herself. "Stick with the program."

Joshua was finally able to speak. "Well, first of all, we Jews can't agree that Jesus was the Messiah, and even more importantly, we can't agree that Jesus was God incarnate. So we can't be Christians, and you can't be Jews." He paused for a few moments to see if Mary would object to what he just said. And when she did not, he continued thoughtfully. "If we all agreed that Jesus was a great prophet and teacher, and not more than that, I suppose we could all be Jews."

"If we all thought that about Jesus, many of us would still be pagans or something else," Mary said sweetly. "Judaism was not capable of spreading beyond the little country of Judea. It took the gospels to spread the word to the rest of the world. You might say Jesus did your work for you in spreading the word of the One God. Just look at the results, and you'll see which of us has been doing God's work."

"Great point," Joshua said, thrown off balance by Mary's remarks. "I hadn't really thought of it that way. But the Christians don't follow the Torah — they have their own very different rules. So at best they could be thought of as only doing part of God's will."

"We believe the Torah was updated by Jesus and the gospels," Mary said, feeling very confident now. "God certainly has the right to change His message if He wants to."

"I agree with you about that," Joshua said warmly. His personal mission in life was to convince his fellow Jews that Judaism needed to be updated with the times. That what does not grow, dies. "But we can't agree that Jesus was God incarnate. That is an 'update' we can't believe in. Besides, Jesus himself said that not an iota of the Torah should be changed. What do you say to that?"

Mary was about to say something when Joshua's cell phone buzzed, and he jumped at the sound. He grabbed it from the table beside his chair and fumbled it open. As Mary watched him intently, Joshua appeared to be totally absorbed in reading something on his cell phone. Though Mary could not tell from her vantage point, it turned out to be a text message. It read: "Watch yourself tonight. Remember our deal. You are not doing what you promised. WE ARE NOT HAPPY! You know what that means."

"O dear God," thought Joshua. He did not know for sure what that meant, but he knew who it came from and it sounded ominous. Feelings of dread swept through him. That text sounded very much like a threat and he hoped they were not threatening anything really serious. But he had a bad feeling that they were *very* serious. A lot of very important people felt there was a lot at stake in these debates.

Watching him, Mary wondered what was going on. Joshua's cheeks were flushed, and she could almost hear the blood pounding in his head. She became afraid he might be having a seizure or a stroke. Finally, with some difficulty, Joshua laid his phone on the table. His hands were visibly shaking.

The call came to return to the stage, but Joshua did not move. "Rabbi Hertzel," Winston said with concern, "we must go back on stage now." Joshua took a drink of water and poured some on his handkerchief, wiping his face quickly before joining the others.

The Book of Emet

Chapter Two: The Ministry Begins

The men of the city said to Elisha, "We pray to you, this town is pleasantly located, as you can see, but the water is bad and the ground is barren."
And he said, "Bring me a new bowl and put salt in it." And they brought it to him.
Then he went forth to the spring and cast the salt into the waters, saying, "Thus says the Lord: 'I have healed these waters. Never again will they cause death or make the land barren.'" And the waters have remained healed to this day, according to the words Elisha had spoken. [II Kings 2:19-22.]

When everyone on the panel was seated, George welcomed the audience back. "We now resume our story at the point after Jesus' baptism by John the Baptist and the calling of the first disciples. Dr. Roberts, would you please begin the discussion of Chapter Two of the Book of Emet."

"Thank you Reverend Turner," Mary said. "Jesus initially attracted a following by going around the countryside healing the sick, expelling demons, raising the dead and relieving suffering. In doing so, Jesus showed to everyone — past, present, and future — that he *was* God, because no mortal could work such wonders. Then, once he had a large following, he taught them about God's great love for them and told them they would inherit the Kingdom of Heaven if they came to accept Jesus as their Savior. The crowds that came to hear him grew larger and larger and began to scare the Jewish authorities of that time."

Joshua was only half listening while Mary spoke. He was distracted by his undeniable attraction to Mary and his disaffection for her views. "She is very literal in her thinking, almost like a fundamentalist," he said to himself. He did not like fundamentalists of any stripe, not Christian, not Muslim, and not Jewish. In his experience, most fundamentalists believed everything was totally black and white — things were either right or wrong — with no shades of gray allowed. He knew Mary was not a fundamentalist, but sometimes she reminded him of one. "How could that soft and gorgeous face hide such a doctrinaire and narrow mind?" he thought. The protective part of his male psyche wanted to reach out and help her, to show her that the world is much more subtle and colorful than she realized.

"Rabbi Hertzel," he vaguely heard George say, "is there anything you would like to say now about the Book of Emet?"

George's voice reverberated like a gunshot through Joshua's ruminations. "Oh… I'm sorry….I was thinking about something that… um…Dr. Roberts said." He quickly refocused his mind, a bit embarrassed that he was thinking of Mary in such a non-professional way.

"The Book of Emet affirms that Jesus initially became known as a healer and exorcist, and it was in that capacity that he began to achieve a following. Whether his success came from faith healing or a special talent is not clear. In any case, Jesus was very good at those things and people flocked to him wherever he went. But while God may have given him a special talent, or even worked through him, that does not make Jesus a god himself."

"Well just listen to some of the healings Jesus performed before you say he was not God. He healed Peter's mother who had a high fever just by touching her hand; he healed several demon-possessed people, including one who was so possessed he broke whatever chains they put on him; he healed a blind beggar and a man who was mute and deaf; and he healed a woman who just touched his cloak without him even seeing her.

"Jesus was not the only healer of his day," Winston chimed in. "There were many others and Jesus' healings were no more remarkable than theirs. What made him remarkable was they charged for their healings and Jesus did them for free.

"As a historian, I doubt that these narratives of Jesus healing people can be called miracles, as so many people believe. I think those stories were passed down in oral form and were in circulation when the first gospels came to be written. It may well be that Jesus engaged in paranormal activities, which could account for his prominence as a healer."

"You are both missing the point," Mary insisted. "These healings performed by Jesus were signs of the power of God working through His son. The gospels quote Jesus as saying that his miracles of healing are part of the Kingdom of God coming into its own on earth. It's like Jesus taught his disciples to pray in the Lord's Prayer: '…Thy Kingdom come, Thy will be done, on earth as it is in heaven'. The realm of God in heaven is completely supernatural. Thus, God coming to earth in human form is also supernatural. Christ's power came entirely from his being God in human form. The Heavenly Father was right there with Jesus, working through him each and every day."

Jesus Goes to the Feast of Tabernacles

Observing that no one else had anything to add, Mary went on to the next topic.

"For the most part Jesus' ministry took place in the Galilee region of Israel. If Jerusalem was like today's New York, Galilee was like the American South, mostly farming country and resentful of central control. Like tens of thousands of Jews all over the country, Jesus made an occasional pilgrimage to Jerusalem for the three major agricultural holidays: the Feast of Tabernacles in the autumn, which is the Jewish holiday of Sukkot; the Feast of Passover in the spring; and the Feast of Pentecost in the summer, which is the Jewish holiday of Shavuot and which commemorates the day when the Ten Commandments were given. Going to Jerusalem for the Feast of Tabernacles was a sort of coming out event for Jesus, because for the first time he began to teach to a wider audience.

"At first Jesus didn't want to go to Jerusalem, but his brothers urged him to go so that the people there could see his miracles. He ultimately decided to go, and while he was there, he taught in the Temple courts. The crowds that heard him were amazed at the authority with which he taught.

"Besides his teachings, Jesus singled out the Pharisees for criticism, calling them hypocrites and chastising them for being insincere and untrustworthy. It was the beginning of the hatred that the Pharisees came to have for Jesus and eventually led them to seek his death. Instead of catering to the Pharisee authorities, Jesus praised the poor, like for example, the widow who gave only a couple of coins to the Temple. He said her gift was greater than any the others because she gave all she had."

Mary nodded to Joshua that it was now his turn. Joshua smiled back.

"This thing about the animosity between the Pharisees and Jesus is quite overdone," Joshua began. "It is certainly true, *according to the New Testament*, that Jesus criticized the Pharisees as hypocrites and challenged their sense of priorities, but he never disagreed with them about the importance of the law. I don't believe the Pharisees ever looked at Jesus as a heretic — he was just one among many who were critical of them and their interpretations. I seriously doubt they sought his death because he called them hypocrites, if that was in fact what he really said. They may have been a pompous group, but there is no evidence they were vicious.

"Jews have always disagreed with each other over the years. There is a joke about two shipwrecked Jews who were finally found after many years on an uncharted island. The captain of the ship that rescued them noticed that there were three synagogues there. 'Why three synagogues for two Jews?' he asked. They answered that one synagogue was for one, and the other synagogue was for the other. 'What about the third synagogue then?' asked the captain, puzzled. 'That is the one neither of us would set foot in,' the two Jews answered scornfully."

The audience laughed appreciatively.

"The point is that Jews have always disagreed with each other about all sorts of things, but rarely do they kill each other over their disagreements. As an example, I am highly unpopular with large segments of the Jewish community because of my views. But though they castigate me in their writings and speeches, no one has suggested I should be killed and no one has threatened my life.

"The other point to be made here is that Jesus almost never refers to the Pharisees in the Book of Emet, which is because, I think, Jesus was a Pharisee himself. The Pharisees were the teachers and the sages of that time, which is exactly what Jesus was."

"I am afraid I will have to generally agree with Rabbi Hertzel on this," Winston chimed in. "Whether Jesus was himself a Pharisee, I don't know. But Jesus and the Pharisees certainly did not disagree about anything important. While the Pharisees may not have liked what Jesus said about them, nothing he said was so dangerous or threatening to them to merit seeking his death."

"I totally disagree with you," Mary said emphatically. "Jesus had a mass movement going that threatened the power of the Pharisees. They had him put to death because they were afraid of a mass revolt and losing their cherished positions in the pecking order of Jewish society at that time. Jesus was not a Pharisee or a member of any of the other groups that existed at that time. He was God's messenger on earth and everything he said was the truth."

Winston felt a need to respond further. "Historians are in general agreement that Jesus' following was not as large as you seem to think, my dear. Most of his following came from the Galilee and similar areas. He did not have much of a following in Jerusalem or other parts of the country at all. The Pharisees had no reason to fear that Jesus was a threat to them. Furthermore, it was the priestly class—the Sadducees—not the Pharisees, who were in power in those days.

"The priests were the only ones who were allowed to minister at the Holy Temple in Jerusalem. And they were the only ones who didn't have to work and were supported by the sacrificial offerings made at the Temple. In the days when the Holy Temple in Jerusalem was still operational, it was the priests who were considered to be pompous and arrogant. They were the descendants of Moses' brother Aaron and their positions were inherited, so they were the true privileged class of Jewish society at the time Jesus lived. Jesus was nothing more than a flyspeck to them. Rather, they had more to worry about from the Romans who had the real power in Judea and who could have given them the boot from their places of importance at any time.

"By the time the New Testament gospels were written, many years after the death of Jesus, the Temple in Jerusalem had already been destroyed by the Romans and the priestly class had functionally disappeared. So the Pharisees were the only group left to take the lead in carrying on the Jewish tradition. And of course, we know that most of them helped lead the Jews in opposing conversion to Christianity. So the Pharisees were the ones the early Christians saw as their opponents and it is likely they changed what Jesus said to reflect that."

Observation of the Sabbath

"The gospels tell us that several times the Pharisees confronted Jesus about things he said or did," Mary countered, "and these were not conversations that occurred at the Temple in Jerusalem, so it would not have been the priests who were involved. For example, the Pharisees challenged Jesus for letting his disciples pick grain to eat on the Sabbath and for healing people on the Sabbath. Jesus answered with these familiar words: 'The Sabbath was made for man, not man for the Sabbath. For the Son of Man is lord of the Sabbath.' After that, the Pharisees began conspiring to kill Jesus."

"Frankly, we don't know why God created the Sabbath," said Joshua. "It might have been for man or it might have been for its own sake. We don't know why God did what He did or why He directed us to do the 613 commandments in the Torah. As they say, God acts in mysterious ways and we are not given to know His ways or His why's. Jesus obviously had his own point of view, which I agree with by the way. But the ancient rabbis ruled that the Sabbath laws must be followed precisely because the Sabbath was created by God on the Seventh Day and then given to man to observe. Jews are told to rest on the Seventh Day, because God rested on the Seventh Day.

"What Jesus and the disciples did was a kind of work, or so the legalists of the time believed, but Jesus had an answer for them," Joshua continued. "Jesus said that it is permitted to violate the Sabbath to maintain health or to save a life. This was not a heresy. It was a minor dispute over theology and practice, about how to observe the Sabbath, and what is permitted and what is prohibited. In fact, Jesus was proven right, because his view is now what Jews everywhere believe."

"So you agree that it would have been the Pharisees who criticized Jesus for violating the Sabbath," Mary asked Joshua.

"Yes, that is true. But it was also the Pharisees who later changed the rules to agree with what Jesus taught about the Sabbath. So I seriously doubt that they wanted to kill him over this."

Discussion

"It's time now for us to discuss any issues that may have been raised by Chapter Two of the Book of Emet," George said. "Dr. Roberts, would you care to begin?"

"I'd be glad to," said Mary. "To summarize what the Bible says in relation to this chapter, Jesus began his ministry with words and actions that healed people physically and spiritually. They had a strong sense that he was no ordinary man. They knew with absolute certainty that he was sent by God. The buzz heard among the people was, 'A great prophet has appeared among us,' and 'God has come to help His people.' Soon they came to know Jesus was the Messiah who would give them everlasting salvation."

"Jesus most certainly was not the Jewish idea of the Messiah, who we believe was supposed to bring peace and justice on earth to all peoples," disagreed Joshua. "Jesus preached that the Kingdom of Heaven—peace on earth—was at hand, which he said would occur in his own lifetime. This was something he fervently believed and was the essence of what he taught. But he clearly got it wrong because peace on earth did not happen then, and he came to know that as he was dying. And after 2,500 years of continuous hope and expectation, by both Jews and Christians, the Messiah still has not come to bring us peace on earth."

"He is coming again, and soon!" Mary stated confidently. "The Bible says that Jesus will come again when the Jews go back to the Promised Land. They are there now."

"Yes, we are there now," Joshua agreed. "But our existence there is constantly threatened and who knows how long we will last. So if he is coming again, he better hurry and bring peace on earth before it is too late." Like most Jews, Joshua was worried about another Jewish holocaust, this time coming at the hands of the Arabs of the Middle East, who had never given up their hope of throwing the Jews into the sea and remaking the Land of Israel into an Arab state of Palestine.

"From my research, I am not convinced that Jesus thought of himself as the Messiah," Winston said. "Those thoughts may have been attributed to him many years after his death by the second or third generation of his followers, but he never claimed that title for himself. And as Rabbi Hertzel said, Jesus definitely believed he would see the Kingdom of Heaven arrive in his own lifetime. He said so several times."

"I can't agree with that," Mary responded. "The gospels *clearly* state and show that Jesus knew he was the Son of God and the Messiah, whether or not he ever made such an announcement. That is the evidence you are looking for, Sir Winston. There is no need to look further than that. The Kingdom of Heaven that Jesus taught us about was both spiritual and sociological. He was supposed to bring peace on earth, that is true Rabbi Hertzel, and for that he will come again. But Jesus did bring us the kind of Kingdom of Heaven that he talked about, which he said is *within us*. That part he brought with him during his lifetime on this earth. He brought us God's grace and love and forgiveness and eternal salvation for those who believe in him. That is what we needed the most. Jesus did not 'get it wrong'."

"In my view," countered Winston, "Jesus may have thought of himself as an important instrument in God's plan to usher in the Kingdom of Heaven on earth, but I don't believe he thought of himself as the Messiah. In those days there were many other people performing healings and miracles. And unlike Jesus, some of them *did* proclaim themselves as the Messiah. So in retrospect, Jesus' followers obviously needed to portray Jesus as the Messiah too, to compete with those others. And then by claiming that Jesus was the only begotten Son of God, and that he was also resurrected, Jesus' followers effectively put him above all the other claimants."

"Actually, he did call himself the Messiah at the end of Mark," corrected Mary. "But, did he even have to? He announced the Kingdom's arrival but taught that it would take time for the Kingdom to come into its fullness. He told the people they needed to make drastic changes and turn their lives toward God. His miracles were signs of God's power. Why would Jesus need to introduce himself further?"

"Suppose you call your doctor's office to set an appointment for as soon as possible. Your physician is booked for three weeks, but his colleague, Dr. Susan Jones, can see you tomorrow. The next day, a nurse checks your vital signs and takes your information, telling you that Dr. Jones will be in momentarily. A few minutes later, a nicely dressed woman wearing a white lab coat enters the exam room. She is holding a medical chart with your name on it. She apologizes for how busy they are that day, examines you, says it's just a bad cold, and recommends two over-the-counter medications. As you leave, do you question if she really was Dr. Susan Jones? No. Why would you? After all, you just witnessed her act out who she is. By the same token, Jesus did not need to hand out Messiah business cards to show who he was."

Many of the people in the audience clapped. George smiled and gave them an indulgent look, but motioned with his hands that they should be quiet.

"I'd like us to return to the use of disciples, if we might," said Mary changing the subject after her "victory" with the audience. "Emet agrees with the gospels that Jesus called the twelve disciples to be his followers. John the Baptist obviously preferred to work on his own, and none of the other prophets in Jewish history had disciples either. That shows that Jesus knew he had a huge mission to fulfill that was greater than any of the prophets who preceded him. Jesus' mission was to spread the good news that the Messiah had arrived and that all who believed in him would be saved and granted eternal life."

"That's a good point," Joshua admitted. "But here is my take on it. The message Jesus was trying to spread was that the Kingdom of Heaven was about to arrive in their own day and that the people needed to make ready for it. There wasn't much time and that is why he needed the disciples to spread the word. He didn't have time to reach everyone himself.

"The disciples were extremely loyal to Jesus, but not particularly bright or sophisticated," Joshua continued, "and they quite often did not get what Jesus was trying to teach them. I think they were so over-impressed by what Jesus said and did, that they later came to make up stories about him. I think Jesus seemed magical to them and that is why they started telling everyone he was a god, especially after they thought he was resurrected."

"The disciples were not dull or stupid, as you so nonchalantly suggest!" Mary retorted. "The reason they did not seem to understand many of the things our Lord taught was that they did not yet have ears to hear. What I mean is they were not very spiritually attuned to Jesus' message. They heard the words just fine, but were still learning how to see the world as Christ saw it."

Mary paused briefly, and then continued. "Rabbi Hertzel, do you practice your religion today just as you did when you were 12 and preparing for your Bar Mitzvah? I imagine you could only absorb a limited amount at that time and came to learn much more later."

"Of course, you're absolutely right," agreed Joshua. "I memorized the assigned Torah verses in Hebrew, and learned everything else I needed to know. I was quite serious about it, but appreciated very little of what I had learned…until much later in life when I came to appreciate the incredible sophistication of Judaism. It began when I was at the university and started taking classes at the Hillel on an adult level.

"I was amazed at how little I had known and understood previously, and that amazement only increased as I continued to study and learn. That is true even now. On the other hand, studying Judaism as an adult and a scholar, I learned that there are problems with some of what I call the 'simplistic views' of mainstream Judaism, which is why I am not in sync with most of the authorities today."

Joshua paused out of habit after using the term "simplistic views." Most Jews were offended at that characterization and he had to explain what he meant. The most controversial part of Joshua's philosophy was that he did not agree with Orthodox Judaism that the Torah was written by God. And almost as bad, Joshua believed that the way the Old Testament characterized God as a punishing God was flat out wrong.

A lot of Jewish belief was tied up in the view that God punished the Jews for not following His laws. That was how Judaism could maintain that the Jews were God's "chosen people," and reconcile that belief with all the horrible things that happened to the Jews throughout their history. Jews had been taught for centuries to believe that the bad things that happened to them were brought on by themselves for not doing what they were supposed to do. Those teachings, Joshua believed, were simplistic and wrong. He did not believe that everything bad that happened to the Jews was intended by God as a punishment.

"In getting a more adult understanding of Judaism," Joshua mused, "I was also able to develop a better personal relationship with God, and a much more humble one too, I might add. So I get your point about the disciples not having the ears to hear what Jesus was saying. It took decades for me to hear what I believe God was saying. Point well taken."

Mary was quite surprised at Joshua's words. His genuine and self-effacing answer to her question had thoroughly disarmed her. One might say she began to look at him with "new ears."

George got a signal from the producers that it was time for a break. As was becoming his custom, George stayed with the audience to chat while the other panelists went backstage.

Backstage

Mary was glad for a break in the action because she had other things to worry about that evening. Her mother had not been feeling well the past couple of days and Mary wanted to make sure she was okay.

Mary went to the chair she had been sitting in, took her purse from the circular wooden table beside it, and pulled out her cell phone. She then sought a quiet corner of the backstage area so she could talk privately. Her niece Christa answered the phone.

"Hi sweetheart. How is Grandma?"

"Oh, she's feeling much better, Aunt Mary," Christa responded. "She's been watching you on television and hasn't stopped smiling."

Mary sighed with relief.

"I'm not sure she understands what you all are talking about," Christa continued, "but she is definitely feeling better and having a great time." Christa laughed, and Mary joined in.

"And how are you doing?" asked Mary with concern. Her mother was actually babysitting Christa while Mary was out of town. Her mother had a touch of dementia and Christa had learning disability problems. She would have liked to be able to trust her husband Wayne to look after them both, but he was out of town at pre-wedding events for a cousin and could not be persuaded to wait until Mary returned.

"I'm doing fine," Christa answered. "How do you feel it's going there?"

"It's been fun so far, but the rabbi is very tough and he is being backed up by the British guy at almost every turn. But I'm doing as well as I can."

"It's so much fun to see you on television," Christa said excitedly. "The phone has been ringing off the hook all night. Everyone is so proud of you, especially Grandma!" Christa and Mary laughed again.

"Are you recording it?" Mary asked.

"Oh yes, and almost everyone else we know," Christa laughed.

"This is exciting for me too," Mary added. "I'm trying really hard to convince everyone to let Jesus into their lives, but it's not as easy as preaching at a church or on my show."

"I'm praying for you Aunt Mary," said Christa. "It will go the way it's supposed to go." Christa believed that everything happens for a reason.

Mary was not so sure. "A lot of people are depending on me and I don't want to disappoint them."

"You're the best," Christa said. "I love you Aunt Mary."

"I love you too," Mary said. "Keep an eye on Grandma."

"I will. Talk later."

"Bye bye sweetheart. I love you."

Meanwhile, Joshua and Winston were using the intermission to review their notes and take a breather from the tension of the discussion. They both knew, as did Mary, that hundreds of millions of people were watching or listening, and that every word they said could have significant consequences in the thoughts and lives of their audiences.

George, meanwhile, was still out on the stage schmoozing with members of the live audience. He was a very social person, a people person, and he enjoyed talking to people about whatever was on their minds. The time had just flown by for him, and he was surprised to see the signal from the networks that it was almost time to resume the discussion. He went backstage to see how the panel was doing and give them a pep talk. The first day's debate was almost over and George was relieved that the emotions generated by the Book of Emet were not interfering with the professionalism of the discussion.

"I'm very pleased at how this first half of the evening is going," George said with a warm smile. "I believe that we are accomplishing our stated purpose — to give the Book of Emet a good and reasoned introduction to our audience and show how it differs from the New Testament. I have been out there talking to them, and they have been responding positively to your contributions and to the lively discussions. However, we all have strong beliefs on this subject and we have to be careful not to get personal about the things we are discussing. That would be the last thing we want to happen." He was looking directly at Joshua and Mary, and they nodded their agreement.

Reverend George Turner was a noted peacemaker in clerical circles. Whenever arguments broke out at ecumenical events, he was always the one who introduced calm and reason into the discussions. He had what they call a "presence" and people just naturally looked up to him and respected him. The fact that he was tall and gregarious, immaculately dressed and well-groomed, with a broad smile and a firm, but friendly handshake, all undoubtedly had something to do with it.

"How about if you two shake hands and play nice," George said with a smile and a wink.

Mary and Joshua both laughed and moved toward each other. Mary put her hand out first and Joshua took it. The electricity they felt in their handshake shocked them both. Mary looked Joshua in the face with surprise. His expression mirrored her reaction. For a few embarrassing nanoseconds their eyes fastened on each other as their hands were locked together. Quickly, they both released their handshake and actually jumped back from each other. Joshua cleared his throat and Mary pulled her suit jacket over her breasts, which were tingling. Joshua adjusted his pants a little higher on his waist.

Just then, Joshua's phone signaled the arrival of yet another text message. Mary's antenna went up and she studied him closely as he read it.

"THINK ABOUT YOUR SISTER," the text said. "What will happen to her without the money? We can't guarantee her safety. Or yours." He closed his phone, only to hear George say that it was time to go back on stage. He quickly composed himself, but his escalating anxiety did not escape Mary's notice.

Outside the Chapel

Bryce was getting restless. "Let's go for a little walk," he said to Judith after the break was announced. They had both read the Book of Emet before the Great Debate, so they did not need to stay by the outdoor TV to hear the next chapter's narration.

"Isn't this so interesting!" she gushed as she got up to join him. "So this historian says the Pharisees didn't want to kill Jesus at all. So how is it we got blamed for killing him all these years?" Judith's mother and stepfather were Jewish, and she had been raised in the faith.

"The Bible says the Pharisees wanted to kill him, so they probably did," Bryce answered. "Why would it lie about that?"

"I don't know, but it was the Romans who actually killed him. Maybe we'll learn more later."

"I don't know that I would believe any of them. I don't trust the Bible or this Emet thing, or even the historians. Who knows what really happened way back then. And does it even matter that much?"

"I don't know if it matters that much to you and me personally, but it certainly has mattered to the Christians and Jews over the years. More wars have been fought in the name of religion than for any other reason.

And certainly millions of Jews have been killed because of Christian animosity. Thank God it isn't so bad anymore, at least not in this country."

"Amen to that," Bryce said with a grin. "Here is one Christian that wants to make love, not war, with a certain Jew."

Judith blushed happily. "I love your attitude!"

Then Bryce grew serious. "I hope none of that stuff ever happens again. Right now, I am more worried about these radical Muslims than anything Christians and Jews might do."

"That is something we can both agree on," Judith said squeezing Bryce's arm affectionately. "I really love this man," she was thinking. She leaned her head on Bryce's muscular arm feeling very content. She saw another student looking at her watch, which broke her reverie. "We'd better get back to our spot before they start again," she purred.

Bryce put his arm affectionately around her and they walked back to their spot awkwardly as they held each other tightly, laughing as they went. They sat down again on the blanket, warmed by each other's presence in the cool night, with anticipation shining on their moonlit faces, and wondering what would happen next.

The Book of Emet

Chapter Three: Parables and Miracles

When Elisha came into the house, the boy was dead and was laid upon his bed.
Then he got on the bed and lay upon the boy, and put his mouth on the boy's mouth, and his eyes on the boy's eyes, and his hands on the boy's hands; and as he stretched himself on the boy, the boy's body grew warm; and the boy sneezed seven times and opened his eyes. [II Kings 4:32-35.]

"Welcome back," George greeted the audience. "The third chapter of the Book of Emet contains an interesting mix of parables and miracles. Jesus' favorite way to teach was through parables, in which he told a story that had a specific spiritual—though sometimes a very hidden—meaning to it. It appears that the crowds he preached to were able to understand some of the parables, but at other times they had no clue what he was talking about. Come to think of it, that sounds like my congregation every Sunday!"

He paused while the audience laughed.

"Dr. Roberts, would you please begin our look at Chapter Three."

"Thank you, Reverend Turner; and, thank you to everyone in our audience for your obvious interest in learning more about our Savior Jesus Christ. Oh, and for laughing at Reverend Turner's jokes!" Mary wanted to start out this chapter with a light touch because she had some scathing criticism of the Book of Emet planned.

Legitimacy of the Text

"Tomorrow," she began, "we will look at some more parables, but there are four in this chapter of the so-called Book of Emet.

"Jesus traveled about from one town and village to another, proclaiming the imminence of the Kingdom of God. The twelve disciples were with him, and also some women who had been cured of evil spirits and diseases, including Mary Magdalene, from who seven demons had been exorcized. These women traveled with Jesus and the disciples and helped support them financially.

"Wherever they went, large crowds gathered to hear the words of Jesus. When he began teaching by parables, his disciples asked him why he spoke in parables and he said: 'The knowledge of the secrets of the Kingdom of God has been given to you, but to others I speak in parables, because though seeing, they may not see; though hearing, they may not understand.'

"Jesus told them the Parable of the Sower, in which he said that the seeds of his teaching, which are the words of God, grow best in good soil, and that the good soil stands for those who listen with a noble and receptive heart. They hear the words and they remember them.

"In another parable, he said that finding the treasure of the Kingdom of Heaven is worth more than all of one's earthly riches.

"I need to point out that these and the other parables are exactly the same, word for word, in the Book of Emet as they are in the Bible, although there are many more parables in the Bible than in Emet. To me, it is obvious that this 'gospel of Emet' is a fake and totally plagiarized the Bible. I think it is ridiculous that anyone takes this forgery seriously. I think it's only being taken seriously because of the publicity it's been given by the secular media."

Mary felt she had the momentum going for her and thought she might have Emet on the ropes. She wanted to push for the complete defeat of Emet right here. She was afraid that the longer the debate continued unresolved, the more likely the viewers and listeners would become confused and possibly take Emet more seriously than it deserved.

However, Joshua had other ideas. "Maybe the New Testament gospels copied the parables from Emet. Emet was written earlier than the other gospels so maybe they copied the parables from Emet. Did you ever consider that?"

"We don't need to consider that," Mary fought back. "There is no mention in Christian literature or any other forms of ancient literature of any Emet, whereas there are lots of references and copies of Matthew, Mark, Luke and John. There probably never was an Emet in Jesus' life, and this whole thing is just a hoax. And we only have some historians' word for it that Emet was written before the gospels. They are almost certainly wrong about that. We all know that sometimes scientists vastly overstate their own capabilities."

Some in the audience cheered at the last thing Mary said. George smiled briefly and then motioned for them to quiet down.

Seeing that neither Mary nor Joshua had any more to say, Winston decided it was a good time to reiterate something he had said earlier. "Many historians believe there were chunks of text floating about and that the biblical gospel writers used them. That would explain how the four gospel writers and Emet said exactly the same thing in so many places even though they were written by different people in different times and different places. It is true that there is no evidence that there ever was an Emet except for this scroll. However, this scroll is quite old, and if it is a forgery or a hoax, it is a very old one. I am inclined to think of it as real and legitimate. It is possible Rabbi Hertzel is right that those common passages could have been written by Emet first."

Mary knew that she had better say something after Sir Winston essentially endorsed Joshua's position. "The reason the same words are used in different gospels is because the writers were all inspired by God. God spoke to them using the same words and so the gospel writers used the same words too. This Emet character never even claimed to be inspired by God."

That was a good argument Joshua thought, but he had a better one. "Assuming Dr. Roberts is right about God inspiring the gospel writers, isn't it possible that God inspired Emet too, even if Emet didn't know it? Sometimes when I write a sermon or a speech, the words seem to come from somewhere other than me. Some writers call this feeling their Muse. Some writers say their Muse is God.

"Maybe Emet had it right, and where the gospels differ, they were changed by later copyists to reflect the Christian ideology of their day. Historians all say that the original New Testament gospels do not exist, and that all we have today are copies upon copies of them. And the copies don't agree with each other."

"That is correct, Rabbi," Winston agreed. "The earliest gospels we have date from 300 years after the death of Jesus.

"Getting back to Jesus' use of parables, if I may," Winston continued after hearing no further objection from Mary. "It is well for us to note that parables were quite common in Jesus' day. Many other first century rabbis used them, much like the ones Jesus used. Jesus taught in parables because they were easy to remember, like Aesop's Fables. Parables invited those listening to reflect on his words and see the lessons in them. They were also like a secret code. If some people in the crowds were seeking to get Jesus in trouble, they might not understand what he really was saying."

"I want to call special attention to the parable about the yeast," Mary interrupted. "This goes to the point you keep making about the Kingdom of Heaven not being here yet," she said, looking squarely at Joshua. "It is just as Jesus said in Matthew 13:33 — 'The Kingdom of Heaven is like yeast that a woman took and hid in it three measures of flour until all of it was leavened.' Can you, or anyone else, tell me, from God's point of view, how long the yeast — in other words how long the Kingdom of Heaven — will take to arrive? Maybe it's still rising and not done yet."

"Well, my dear," Winston chuckled, "when my wife is preparing her delicious homemade bread for baking, she maintains that the dough has risen when she says it has, so you'll have to ask her!" The audience, particularly the women, broke into laughter. "Of course, you were speaking in metaphors or, should I say, in parables. As I've studied Jesus' use of teaching in parables, he confounds his audience by never precisely defining the Kingdom of Heaven. The gospels never quote him as saying what it is. He only reveals what the Kingdom of Heaven or Kingdom of God *is like*. In this case, it may very well be a continuous process that remains hidden until it is revealed."

"Exactly, Sir Winston!" Mary exclaimed, glad that at least one person understood the point she was making. "It is a continuous process that is still unfolding and much of it is still hidden from us. Meanwhile, those who believe in Jesus will receive God's grace in their lifetimes and will be saved."

"I believe the world *is* improving over time," said Joshua. "But that is because I believe in reincarnation. As we become more enlightened as individuals, the world becomes more enlightened as a whole. So I see small incremental improvements in the world over time, but I don't see where the world has gotten *suddenly better* since the time of Jesus."

"Well," Mary said proudly, "the world is immeasurably better since the time of Jesus because it has gained many millions of Christians who try their best to emulate our Savior by being like him in their daily lives. Look at all the soup kitchens and other charitable activities that Christians engage in that are not done by anybody else."

"Yes, yes," agreed Winston jovially. "You are absolutely right about that!" Mary noticed that George and even Joshua nodded their assent.

A Prophet Without Honor

"The next topic shows some of the difficulties of being the kind of teacher Jesus was and also the difficulties of being one of his followers," George said. "Dr. Roberts, would you please continue."

"Yes, of course," Mary smiled. "After Jesus had been preaching for a while and had accumulated a large following, he went back home to Nazareth and astonished the worshipers at the synagogue with his teaching. But no one there believed a local boy could become so wise, so they dismissed him as offensive and audacious. Because of their attitude, he did not perform many miracles there.

"Apparently he felt his family sided with the townfolk. He said that those who do God's will—for example, his followers—were more his family than his actual family."

"I imagine most of us have had the feeling from time to time that our friends are more on the same page with us than our family is," Joshua concurred. "I know I've certainly felt that way at times. Jesus comes across as both ungrateful and disloyal on the one hand, and sad and hurt on the other hand."

Mary was reminded of her own family, and how she would rather be with almost anyone than her own father. She identified with the imaginary Jesus who might have been hurt by his family in some way, although of course that would not have happened to the real Jesus. After all, his parents had worshipped him as God from the time of the Immaculate Conception. But she could not let Joshua get away with that negative characterization of Jesus.

"I assure you that our Lord Jesus Christ never had an unkind bone in his body or thought in his head, Rabbi Hertzel. And he was most certainly not ungrateful or disloyal. He was perfect in every way. He said those things about his family to teach a lesson to the others that they should be focused more on God than on their own families."

"Not an unkind thought in his head?" Joshua thought. He remembered the story of Jesus getting angry at a fig tree and causing it to whither. But he decided not to say anything about it, hoping to avoid further antagonizing the people who had been texting him.

Mary waited a few seconds to see if Joshua would have a rejoinder. When none was forthcoming, she went on to her next point.

"Jesus went on to note that his life was not easy. He said that foxes have holes and birds have nests, but the Son of Man had no place to lay his head. His followers too had to leave their families to help bring the Good News to others. And sometimes they had no help—he said each one has to carry his own cross."

"And like his followers, I had to leave my family to do God's work," Mary thought to herself. She missed her family when she was away, and even missed her father when as a young woman she used to daydream that he would change someday, but she knew her calling required her to leave them anyway. She also wondered if her marriage would have turned out differently if she could have stayed at home more.

"In the Book of Emet, Jesus does not call himself the Son of Man," Joshua reported. "And it also says nothing about each man carrying his own cross. That sounds like something Christian writers added later. How could Jesus know about carrying his own cross at that stage of his life?"

"I don't know why Jesus called himself the Son of Man so often instead of the Son of God," Mary admitted. "That has always puzzled me. I think he was trying to be circumspect so as not to scare people too early with who he really was. As for talking about carrying a cross, he already knew what his mission on earth was and how it would end. He did not need later Christian writers to alter his words."

"If Jesus had called himself the Son of God, he would indeed have scared people," Joshua replied. "Jews don't believe in a God that comes to earth in human form. We believe that no one person is God's 'son'. We believe we are all children of God. We are all made in God's image and we are all equal in His eyes."

"Historians have also puzzled about the phrase 'Son of Man'," Winston confirmed. "Jesus never called himself the 'Son of God'. Some historians think 'Son of Man' was an expression used in Jesus' time that meant 'a person' in general and was not referring to Jesus in particular at all."

"That could be, Sir Winston," Joshua chimed back in. "In Hebrew, the expression for 'a person' is *ben adam*, which technically means *son of Adam*, or *son of man*, but is used in every day conversation to mean 'a human being' or just 'a person'."

George could not resist abandoning his master of ceremonies role to join the discussion. "When I see soldiers from my congregation return on leave, their conversation is heavily peppered with obscenities. They call everyone a 'son of a...,' um, let's just say they call everyone a 'son of a gun'." George smiled broadly as the audience roared with laughter, but he was also a little embarrassed by his unexpected success as a comedian. "Uh, let's continue with the next section," he said, his face slightly flushed.

Woe on Unrepentant Cities

"After leaving Nazareth," Mary said, following George's lead, "Jesus had similar experiences in other cities nearby. Finally, he had enough and expressed his frustration that his miracles were not causing them to repent. He said that non-Jewish cities like Tyre and Sidon in what is now Lebanon would have already repented if they had seen what he had done. This was the beginning of Jesus' frustration with the Jewish response to his ministry."

Joshua felt an unwelcome pang in his stomach at Mary's words. Whenever Christians said anything negative about Jews in connection with Jesus, his historical Jewish memory of Christians who used to make Jews convert or face death began to surface. For two thousand years, Christians blamed the Jews for killing Jesus and felt entitled to persecute them for that alleged crime. They called Jews "Christ killers" and accused them of deicide. They said the Jews were forever cursed by God, so anything negative they did to the Jews was acceptable.

"Well, the Torah often calls us a stiff-necked people and it's true that we can be stubborn sometimes," Joshua admitted. "I've had the same experience with some of the out-of-the-box changes I've tried to make, so I can appreciate Jesus' frustration. On the other hand, during his lifetime Jesus' followers were all Jewish as well. So it's not about all Jews being this way or all Jews being that way." Like most Jews, Joshua was concerned about Jewish stereotypes—any Jewish stereotypes—knowing that they were often used negatively by anti-Semites to justify all kinds of heinous acts against the Jews.

"Even in the United States," Joshua continued, "a heavily Christian country, we have liberals and conservatives, and all kinds of views in between and on both fringes. We are split fifty-fifty on many important issues. So I don't think it's fair to knock just the Jews for not becoming one hundred percent followers of Jesus."

Winston chuckled. "I would have to agree with that, Rabbi. It is the same in my country as well. There are many things we can't agree on and probably never will."

"Yes, and even Christians can't agree on many things," added George. "We have multiple Christian sects and they do not agree or even get along with each other. A lot of people become Unitarians because of the infighting among the various Christian groups. And although we believe we exemplify the best that Christianity has to offer, because we are not dogmatic we are labeled non-Christian by many."

Mary Magdalene

Mary did not want to get in a squabble involving liberals and conservatives or the various kinds of Christianity, which she considered beyond the purpose of this gathering, so she decided to go on to the next topic—Mary Magdalene.

"I found the section on Mary Magdalene really interesting." It is one of the passages from this so-called gospel of Emet that I personally like, and there is nothing comparable to it in the New Testament. But since this whole Emet thing is obviously illegitimate, we cannot trust any of it, even the parts we like.

"The Bible tells us this about Mary of Magdala: She had seven demons exorcised from her, probably by Jesus, and she provided for him and his disciples from her own financial resources. She was at the cross when Jesus died and at his tomb when his body was placed in it. She was among the first disciples to see the empty tomb and to see the resurrected Jesus. And she became the apostle to the Apostles, being the first one to tell the others that Jesus was alive.

"The Catholic Church used to say Mary Magdalene was a prostitute who was saved by Jesus," Mary added with a tinge of displeasure, "but there is nothing in the Bible that says that. There are others who think that Mary Magdalene was Jesus' lover, but there is nothing in the Bible that says that either and I think it is sacrilegious to say that about him."

It was now Joshua's turn to tell what Emet said about Mary Magdalene. "According to the Book of Emet, Jesus found maybe his best friend in the friendship of Mary Magdalene, but it appears that Jesus' relationship with her was very respectful and purely platonic. She became someone he could confide in when he needed to talk. She understood him better than any of the other disciples and he learned he could respect her judgment and advice. When he was absent, Mary's was the voice the disciples listened to about what Jesus would or would not do in particular situations."

"I agree with Dr. Roberts that there is no evidence that Mary Magdalene was either a prostitute or Jesus' lover," said Winston. "There is also no evidence that the Book of Emet is correct either. However, if Emet is legitimate, as I think it is, we learn more about Mary Magdalene from him than from any of the other gospels."

John the Baptist Beheaded

"The next part of our story, the beheading of John the Baptist, seems to have been a seminal event in the life of Jesus," George said in introducing the next topic, and then nodded at Mary to continue.

"I'm not so sure about that," Mary answered. "John was a precursor to Jesus, but not essential to his mission. But yes, when Jesus heard about John's death he was deeply moved. He also saw close at hand what happens to those who preach about the coming of the Kingdom of God, and was reminded of his own imminent fate.

"John the Baptist got in trouble by criticizing Herod for illegally marrying his brother's wife Herodias, and thereby he earned her undying hatred. One day, Herodias' daughter Salomé danced for Herod and pleased him so much he said he would grant her any wish. After consulting with her mother, Salomé demanded the head of John the Baptist on a platter, which Herod reluctantly granted."

Joshua agreed with George. "The reason the death of John the Baptist was important in the life of Jesus was because John the Baptist was a hero in the eyes of Jesus and many of Jesus' followers. Many Jews in those days thought John the Baptist was the Messiah. When he was killed, his mantle fell to Jesus."

Winston agreed with George as well. "The Flavius Josephus version, and the one narrated in the Book of Emet, said Herod had John arrested and executed because he feared John's teachings were leading to unrest among John's followers. Many historians say that Jesus was arrested and executed by the Romans for the same reason. We will be getting to that later.

"Some historians doubt that the followers of Jesus were ever as numerous as the followers of John the Baptist. There were two other significant differences between them. Jesus took his message on the road and also to Jerusalem, the capital and the largest city in Judea, while John stayed by the Jordan River and waited for the people to come to him. The second difference, and the most significant one, is Jesus was said to have been resurrected, while John the Baptist was never heard from again."

Jesus Feeds 5,000 and Walks on Water

"Two amazing stories about Jesus that every child knows," Mary narrated with a soft smile on her face, "are where he feeds 5,000 people with almost no food and then later that day walks on water. There were 5,000 people gathered in a remote place to receive healings from Jesus and after they had been with him three days, he became concerned about them because there was no place to get food nearby and he didn't want them to go away hungry. There were only seven loaves of bread and just a few small fish. He told the disciples to divide them among the 5,000 people there, and not only did they all get fed, but there was enough to satisfy them, *and* there were still seven basketfuls of bread and fish left over.

"Then Jesus sent the disciples away in a boat to go to the other side of the Sea of Galilee. Jesus stayed behind, probably to mourn the death of John the Baptist. When evening came, the boat was only halfway across the Sea because of buffeting winds. In the middle of the night, they saw Jesus walking to them on the water lost in prayer. At first they thought he was a ghost, but then he spoke to them, and they worshipped him and said 'Truly you are the Son of God'. Jesus did not deny it or correct them, so contrary to what Sir Winston says, Jesus did indirectly call himself the Son of God."

"Emet does not say that they worshipped Jesus or that they called him the Son of God," countered Joshua. "But Emet does tell the story of walking on water the same way as the gospels do. That makes even me doubt Emet to some extent," he added graciously. Joshua looked up at the balcony to see if the man in white would give him an approving look. But he did not see him there at all.

"While these are smashing stories that I also learned as a child," Winston said with a fond look on his face, "they are very hard to believe as an adult. With just seven loaves of bread and a few fish, Jesus and the disciples fed 5,000 people and still had pieces of bread and fish left over? I have to assume these stories are entirely made up, or possibly they were based on some actual events that were still surprising but much smaller in scope."

"Well, that is the rationalist in you," Mary said kindly, because she was growing quite fond of Winston even when he disagreed with her. "The whole point is that it was not possible to feed that many with such a small amount of food unless it was a miracle. I noticed a lot of the miracles that Jesus did are missing from Emet, but it's good that he included some of them. That tells you that contrary to what Emet wants you to believe, Jesus was God and whoever forged this Emet hoax knew it."

Leprosy and Lazarus

"Let's go on to the next section," George said with a smile, nodding at Mary.

"Yes, of course, I'd be glad to," Mary said still pumped up. "First, Jesus heals a man with leprosy, which in those days was incurable. And then even more amazingly, Jesus raises a man named Lazarus from the dead, even though he had been dead and entombed for four days.

"This is a significant event in Christ's ministry. The sisters of Lazarus, Mary and Martha, are predictably in deep mourning. The people in the town are weeping openly, moving Jesus' soul. Jesus assures Martha with the words, 'Your brother will rise again.' Martha says she believes he will rise again at the resurrection at the end of time. But Jesus gives her even more assurance when he says:

I am the resurrection and the life.
He who believes in me will live, even though he dies; and whoever
lives and believes in me will never die.

This is how we know that eternal life is granted to those who believe in Jesus."

"When I was growing up in the Church of England," Winston said with a twinkle in his eye, "I recall being quite fond of this story. It was mysterious and sad, but with a happy ending. However, this story is only from the Gospel of John. The other three gospels make no mention of it and many historians believe the author of John made it up to back up a changed theology about Jesus.

"In those days, the early Christians gave up on the belief that eternal life would come to them by the Kingdom of God coming in their own day. Instead, they decided that eternal life would come through being resurrected, as they believed Jesus was. I am very surprised this story is contained in Emet, and that gives me some reason to doubt Emet's authenticity."

"There are two major differences between John and Emet," Joshua piped up. "In Emet, no mention is made of how long Lazarus had been dead, which gives the impression he had not been dead long. Also, the passage Dr. Roberts just quoted does not appear in the Book of Emet."

Discussion

"It is now time to go to the discussion phase of this chapter," George said after getting a cue from the show's producer. "Who would like to begin?"

"I will," Mary said, jumping in quickly. "When Emet tells us about Jesus teaching in the synagogue in his home town of Nazareth, he says that the people in the synagogue were *un*impressed. If you ask me, I'd say Jesus made quite an impression on them. They got angry and, in Luke's telling, some of them tried to push Jesus off of a cliff!"

"I assume Emet meant that Jesus did not make a favorable impression on them," said Joshua.

"Yes, that is probably true," Mary agreed. "The point I want to make here is that Jesus really tried to stir people up, so they'd have to take him seriously and decide whether to change their ways so they would be ready to accept God in their hearts and souls. Apparently, those who knew him from childhood, *including Emet,* if he existed at all, were not ready or able to listen to his message with ears that could hear, which is a shame. Perhaps that is an analogy to the Jewish people in general, who were not able to listen to the revolutionary things he was saying to them because he was 'one of them'."

A bolt of anxiety ripped through Joshua's body after Mary's critical words about the Jewish people. "I agree that Jesus probably wanted to stir people up," Joshua replied coldly, "and that the people in his home town probably didn't take him seriously, but I don't agree he was all that revolutionary and I definitely don't agree that there was something wrong with the Jewish people for not accepting him."

Joshua believed that the Christians changed Jesus' message to ideas that Jews could not accept. The Jews of that time could have accepted Jesus as a healer and a teacher, and maybe even a prophet or the Messiah in some cases, but they could not accept that he was God incarnate or that he could change the laws God gave them in the Torah. Like most Jews, Joshua did not believe that the Jews had been in some way sinister and blameworthy for "rejecting God." They believed with all their hearts and souls that they were absolutely loyal to God and felt, because of God's covenant with Abraham, and the Ten Commandments and the Torah, that they were given a special mission to represent God on earth. Millions of Jews throughout history had affirmed God to their dying breath while they were being tortured and murdered by Christians for "rejecting God" (in other words, not accepting Jesus as God). In the minds of the Jews, "rejecting God" would have meant converting to Christianity in order to save their lives.

But Joshua had enough presence of mind to discuss Mary's more general point. "Many of the Jewish prophets in history were not well received in their own day. Jeremiah, for example, had his life threatened numerous times and spent many years in prison. You could say the same thing about some artists too, like Van Gogh, who were not popular in their own day. Being a prophet who tells people things they don't want to hear is often a thankless task. Jesus found that to be the case in his hometown, but he was well received everywhere else he went, so the Jewish people did like him *then*. What they didn't like was that the early Christians said Jesus was resurrected and then decided to call him God."

Mary, of course, did not believe it was a *decision* of the early Christians to call Jesus God. She believed Jesus openly presented himself as the Son of God and as the Messiah forecast by the Hebrews' own prophets.

"I want to return to this issue of Jesus calling himself the Son of Man," she said. "In Matthew 8:20 Jesus says: 'Foxes have holes and birds of the air have nests, but the Son of Man has no place to lay his head.' Jesus used the term Son of Man to refer to *himself*. In Mark, Jesus answers

'I am' when the Jewish High Priest Caiaphas asks if he is the Messiah. Then Jesus goes on to say, 'and you will see the Son of Man seated at the right hand of the Power,' and 'coming with the clouds of heaven.' In this case the Son of Man refers to the Messiah, by which of course he meant himself."

Winston jumped in again on this subject, for it was a topic that many historians had written about. "I do not believe Jesus generally used the words Son of Man to refer to only himself. It is likely that later Christian writers changed or added words to make it sound as if he did."

"In Emet, Jesus *never* refers to himself as the Son of Man," Joshua pointed out happily.

Winston would have none of it from that quarter either. "Well, that is a good reason to question the legitimacy of Emet then because 'Son of Man' was an expression that was in general use at that time. In fact, one of my colleagues texted me that she did a word search for 'Son of Man' in the *Old Testament*, and it came up one hundred times. So it obviously had a history of being used frequently long before Jesus was even born."

"Or," Joshua said with a red face born of being too presumptuous, "it may be that Emet already knew how the Christians were using that phrase, so he changed it to make it clear that Jesus did not use it to describe himself."

"The gospels were inspired by God and Christians believe that every word is true," Mary insisted firmly. "No one rewrote anything or changed anything, except this Emet character. Jesus said what they say he said and Jesus meant what they say he meant. This other stuff is pure academic puffery and presupposition." Several people in the audience clapped.

Joshua saw an opening to redeem himself. "Oh Mary, please, we know that the gospel writers changed things. There are no two handwritten versions of the gospels that are identical with each other from the early days. Some variations were due to copying mistakes and some were due to deliberate changes to reflect the thinking at the time."

"That is correct," confirmed Winston.

Mary felt hurt by Joshua's patronizing manner and by his use of her first name. "More academic puffery," she blurted out. "The Gospels turned out as God meant for them to be. All you need to be saved is to believe."

A few seconds of embarrassed silence ensued, finally saved by George coming to the rescue.

"Does anyone have anything else to add?" George asked firmly.

They all shook their heads no.

"Well then, that is the end of tonight's debate. We look forward to seeing you all tomorrow night when we'll do Chapters Four through Six. Please drive carefully," he urged the audience as they headed for the doors. "And God bless!"

Outside the Chapel

Toward the end of the evening, Judith noticed that Bryce was getting restless and looking bored.

"What's the matter, Bryce? Don't you find this interesting at all?" asked Judith.

"I did for a while, but then this supposedly new gospel is just more of the same. It isn't that different at all."

"What do you mean? There seem to be a huge number of differences."

"Once I heard about Jesus feeding 5,000 people with a few loaves of bread and some fish, and then he walked on water—this Emet thing is just so much BS, just like the other ones. If this Emet thing is supposed to be the true story of Jesus, then it wouldn't have that ridiculous stuff in it."

"Oh, I see what you mean," said Judith thoughtfully. "But there are miracles throughout both Bibles, so do we disbelieve all of them?"

"I don't know," said Bryce in a discouraged voice. "I wish I could believe some of them, but they are probably all made up. You don't see any miracles today do you?"

"I see a lot of miraculous things happening all the time. Just watch the news. The only difference is that nobody says God did it. I think it's possible they were right in those days and we are the ones who are wrong."

"That is really something to think about," Bryce admitted with a smile. "You are sooooo smart," he said feigning sarcasm. Then he gave Judith a big hug and a kiss.

Judith hugged him back with delight, and then noticed everyone was leaving. "Let's go get something to eat. I'm hungry."

"Where do you want to go?" Bryce asked, almost always ready to do whatever Judith wanted.

"How about a steakburger," Judith suggested referring to one of their favorite hangouts, Steak 'n Shake.

"Sounds good to me. I like their chili too. Hey, it's Friday night. Let's go to a late movie after."

And holding hands, they walked to Bryce's car, looking forward to a lovely late evening.

Friday Night

How good and pleasant it is when brothers live together in unity!
[Psalms 133.1.]

After the conclusion of the first night's discussions, the panel participants returned backstage to collect their belongings. George told them that a limousine was waiting for them outside to take them back to their hotel. Winston, who liked a good nightcap, suggested they stop in the hotel's first floor restaurant to relax, have something to drink and get better acquainted. "It will do us good to let our hair down a bit," he said.

George and Joshua readily agreed, and Mary wanted to go to, but she demurred because she was worried about leaving her rental car at the campus parking lot overnight. George told her he would take care of it, for which Mary was very grateful.

Sir Winston, being the heaviest of the four, sat in the front seat with the chauffeur, while the other three sat in the back seat, with Mary in the middle. Sir Winston carried on a chit-chat with the driver on the way to the hotel, but those in the back seat were lost in thought and did not speak.

Mary and Joshua were uncomfortable sitting next to each other, with their hips and thighs touching. The sexual tension between them was inescapable, but neither could be sure if the other one felt it. They both pretended to ignore those feelings, while secretly wondering if the other one felt the attraction too. Both Mary and Joshua knew it was an impossible situation. They were as different as chalk and cheese. How could anything come of this? It was obviously just a passing fancy that would go away as soon as they could get out of the car.

After arriving at the hotel, George led the four of them to a U-shaped booth in the hotel's cocktail lounge. The lounge was dimly lit and few people were there. Mary sat on the outside next to Winston and Joshua sat at the other end of the U next to George.

George had been given an expense account for the group by the radio stations broadcasting the debate. He ordered a basket of chicken wings for the panel, as well as their choice of drinks. Mary ordered a glass of pinot grigio, George asked for an ice tea, Joshua ordered the house merlot and Winston requested a pint of Guinness.

For the next hour, they engaged in light-hearted banter while sharing food and drinks. There was a lot of laughter and they found that they actually enjoyed each other's company. It became apparent that they were beginning to really like each other.

After they finished the wings and the second round of drinks, Winston went upstairs to his room and George drove home, leaving Mary and Joshua alone. Mary started to leave with them when Joshua spoke up.

"How about if I buy us another round of drinks and talk awhile." Joshua was a night owl and was not ready to call it a day. Also, he was totally fascinated by Mary and wanted to get to know her better. He was hoping she would accept his invitation, but was afraid she would not.

Mary was not ready to retire for the night either. She was still wound up and was curious what Joshua wanted to talk about. After doing the Lord's work so wonderfully that evening, she felt she could tease the devil a little. She was absolutely certain she had the will power to resist whatever temptations Joshua might put in her way.

"Well," Mary joked, both to herself and to Joshua, "I can resist anything but temptation."

Joshua laughed heartily. Mary liked his laugh and immediately felt more relaxed. She joined his laugh, and added coquettishly, "Of course, there are some temptations I have no trouble resisting."

"Touché!" Joshua answered, and they both laughed again.

"I'll have to see if I can make myself more irresistible," Joshua said with a wink. Mary just smiled.

Joshua waved at the young dark-haired waitress and made a circular motion toward the table, indicating he wanted another round of drinks. The waitress was right on top of it, bringing their respective drinks within less than a minute.

"You are a captivating speaker and powerful debater," Joshua said after taking a sip from his wine glass. "Where does your passion come from?"

"My beliefs are very dear to me and they have gotten me through a lot of troubles in my life," Mary said softly. She paused before continuing, as some of the highlights of her life popped into her consciousness. "My father taught me how to argue. He was a proud hard-drinking and hard-fighting Irishman. He always said I should stand up for myself and never back down from a fight. If something is important to me, I let others know. People rarely mistake where I am coming from."

"From all I've witnessed tonight, I'd have to agree," Joshua laughed. "What about your mother, if I may ask? How did she get along with your father? She must have had her hands full."

"Oh yes, she did," Mary laughed. "My mother learned early in their marriage how unrelenting my father could be. She rarely engaged him, unless it had to do with the children or safety issues. She had more of a 'keep the peace at all costs' personality. My mother liked being active in the church and took to heart Christ's words about loving our enemies and praying for them."

"So here you are…the product of a fighting Irishman and a peace-making Christian! I see a lot of both sides in you and from my standpoint they blend in very well."

Mary's eyes warmed at the compliment. "Thank you Joshua," she cooed in a voice that Joshua was beginning to love. He could not stop looking at Mary's green eyes.

Joshua forced himself to look down at his wine glass and took another sip of wine, which helped break the spell. He cleared his throat, adjusted the napkin on his lap and had another sip.

"Which parent do you think you're most like?" Joshua asked lamely, trying to continue his side of the conversation so Mary would not notice the effect she had on him.

Mary did notice, but being a lady, she chose not to let on. "I'm afraid this apple did not fall far from her father's tree. I'm a lot like my father, which meant that each of them had their hands full at one time or another with me." Mary laughed and Joshua laughed with her.

"My mother was very passionate about those less fortunate than ourselves, especially children. Though she never went to college, she was well read, and educated herself about social issues. My mother raised us with a strong social conscience based on Jesus' admonitions to care for the poor and helpless."

"Jews are also taught to care for the poor and the helpless, and the widow and the orphan," Joshua said, impressed and delighted he had found something in common with Mary.

"My mother was someone special when it came to that," Mary continued lovingly. "She was always baking pies for others and giving them food, and helping them when they were in trouble. She thought we should combine a social conscience with Christian religious values. I found that I also wanted to help people, and believed the best way I could do that was to bring them peace and joy and salvation by leading them to Christ. At some point when I was in college, I heard the call from God to go into the ministry."

"That is quite wonderful," Joshua said, glowing inside with admiration. "You are one of the good ones."

"Thank you Joshua," Mary said again, "I try to be." She was also feeling a connection with Joshua and it felt good to be appreciated by a man just for being herself. She noticed that she was feeling warmly toward him, and quickly decided to cut those feelings off at the pass.

"I'm very tired and my brain is fried and I don't want to discuss anything serious anymore Joshua," Mary said gently. "I am going upstairs to my room. Are you going to stay here a while?"

"No. I'm ready too. We can ride up in the elevator together."

Joshua, ever the gentleman, walked Mary to her room and, after they wished each other a good night, not daring to try shaking hands again, he walked a few yards down the hall to his own room.

In Paul Lindenbaugh's Room

The phone rang in Paul Lindenbaugh's suite in the luxurious Chase Park Plaza Hotel.

"Hello…okay come on up."

Reverend Paul put his white suit coat back on, rebuttoned the top button of his white shirt, and pulled his white tie up against the front of his neck. He checked his hair and mustache to make sure they were in place and turned the television off.

Reverend Paul Lindenbaugh was of medium height and a bit chunky. He had hypnotic blue eyes, thinning black oily straight hair combed prominently to the left side of his head, and a pencil thin black mustache. He always dressed in all white and his associates did the same. Reverend

Paul, as he liked to be called, was a dapper man and his numerous followers thought he could do no wrong. His ministry was the largest and richest ministry in the country. He filled football stadiums when he preached in person and healed countless crippled and sick believers. If he took a political stand on an issue, dozens of politicians immediately echoed his views. Many people believed Reverend Paul was the most influential man in the country, even bigger than the President.

There was a knock at the door and Reverend Paul let in three expensively dressed gentlemen. Sometimes he derisively called them the three wise men; more often he called them the three godfathers.

The three godfathers were very important and influential leaders from Wall Street financial institutions. They were in the habit of making things happen financially, politically and legally according to their will. Although nominally they were in competition with each other, in actuality the three of them almost always agreed on what results they wanted to achieve. When they got what they wanted, the consequence was always more power and more profits. What was good for one was good for all. Those in the know said the three godfathers ruled not only the United States, but also most of the capitalist world.

They had many strings they could pull to make things happen, and Paul Lindenbaugh was one of their favorites. Reverend Paul brought in millions of dollars per year from his megachurch, his preaching tours, and his television network. He invested those millions with the godfathers, who in turn funded politicians who fought on behalf of the wealthy, the corporations, and the special interests. Over time, they had succeeded in making the rich richer and more powerful, while the rest of the country became poorer and more inconsequential. In return, Reverend Paul was able to increase his influence on social, political and religious issues. Through their religious preaching and political speaking, Reverend Paul and the politicians allied with him and Wall Street were able to persuade their followers to support the issues that helped the rich and the powerful, while at the same time convincing their followers that in doing so they were becoming better Christians and truer Americans. In reality, their followers were usually helping the powerful and hurting themselves.

"This guy Hertzel could hurt us," said Godfather A, a short squat balding man who was the oldest in the group. He spoke with a thick New York accent. He lit up a cigar, an accoutrement he was rarely seen without.

"They don't allow smoking here," Reverend Paul admonished.

"Screw them!" Godfather A bellowed impatiently as he sat down in a maroon overstuffed chair and puffed away.

"Let's get down to business," said Godfather B, a tall, silver-haired, elegant man. He had Hollywood good looks, exuded class, and had a voice like sugar. He was the darling of the media and was often interviewed about issues of the day. He was also the most coldly heartless of the three.

He joined Godfather C on the matching maroon sofa while Reverend Paul made himself comfortable in the other overstuffed chair. A cherry wood coffee table separated the sofa from the two overstuffed chairs.

"We're going to have to do something about this Hertzel guy," Godfather A continued. "He's going to dry up some of your contributions Paul."

"I've done all I can," said Reverend Paul, nodding his head in agreement. "I've threatened him and I've also threatened his sister. It doesn't seem to be having much of an effect."

"We're going to have to stop him once and for all by the time this damn debate is over," Godfather B said coldly. "Are you on top of this Paul?"

"I've got it covered," Reverend Paul said with a sinister smirk. He loved being part of the Godfather conspiracies. "We have a plan and a backup plan. We're not going to let this Jewish sonofabitch slow us down."

"Good," said Godfather C, "I've got the police and the D.A. on board, and our boys will be there too. And if we need the courts to get involved, we know of a judge who believes like we do and who could use some extra cash." Godfather C was a gaunt-looking man with a pinched face. He looked like an accountant, but he commanded the largest and most prestigious financial institution in the country. His company had a pattern of making risky and often disastrous investments, and it really needed the contributions Paul Lindenbaugh brought in. "I'm afraid if he keeps talking the way he is now, this Book of Emet thing might catch on. That would be very bad for all of us."

"Yes, all of us," Godfather B said malevolently. "Our friends will be *very* disappointed. We cannot allow that to happen."

"That is *not* going to happen," Reverend Paul assured him as he stroked his mustache and his blue eyes turned to steel. "I'll make sure of that personally if need be." His face smiled, but his eyes took on a murderous hue.

"Good," said Godfather B. "We have backup plans too. And I have a plan of my own that could explode this whole thing wide open. One way or another this guy is going to stop hurting us and that scroll of his will be buried too. I expect we'll meet here again Sunday night and toast to our victory," he smiled. They all laughed. These men were unaccustomed to tasting defeat, and they never did for long. In the end, they always got their way.

"How are we doing with the schools Paul?" Godfather B asked. Reverend Paul and the political arm of his fundamentalist Christian movement were trying to get the Book of Emet banned from as many school systems as they could. In many cases, they were able to get entire state legislatures and governors to ban the book statewide. In other places, they had to go district by district. "We're up to over 40%," Reverend Paul stated proudly, "and we have a good shot at another 15%."

"That's terrific!" Godfather B replied enthusiastically. "Let's see if we can put pressure on all the others. We can ask our other friends to help. I'd like to see us get up to seventy percent if we can. We won't get the liberals or the Jews, but we should be able to get most everyone else."

"Screw the liberals!" Godfather A declared, mashing his cigar into a saucer on the coffee table. Godfather A hated the liberals and any mention of them elicited a reflexive profane response. "Let's get out of here. I've got some family business to attend to."

The three Godfathers rose and headed for the door. Reverend Paul ushered them out, shaking hands with each of them individually as they exited. He closed the door behind them; his blue eyes glowing darkly in his head. He stroked his mustache again and smiled a sinister smile. "We're going to get thee Rabbi Joshua my friend," he said. And then he cackled gleefully at the thought of it as he rubbed his hands together.

Saturday

And God said: "Let the earth put forth grass, herb yielding seed, and fruit-tree bearing fruit after its kind, wherein is the seed thereof, upon the earth." And it was so. And the earth brought forth grass, herb yielding seed after its kind, and tree bearing fruit, wherein is the seed thereof, after its kind; and God saw that it was good. [Genesis 1:11-12.]

At 8:45 that morning, Joshua was awakened by the hotel phone ringing.

"Hello," he said, struggling to know what was happening.

"Top of the morning to you, Joshua! This is Winston. George and I are going to meet for a spot of tea in a bit and then go to the Botanical Garden. Perhaps you would like to join us."

Joshua could hardly muster the energy to answer. "Thank you for thinking of me Winston, but no, I don't think so. I have other things to do today."

"Alright, we shall see you later." Joshua started to hang up, when he heard Winston say, "By any chance have you seen Mary this morning?"

"No, I haven't seen her yet," he mumbled. "I'm still in bed."

"Oh, so sorry if I woke you old chap. Well then, Mary must be up and out early. She did not answer her phone."

"She said she is going out with her girlfriend today. Maybe that's where she is."

"Quite right," said Winston. "Then George and I will go it alone to 'stop and smell the roses' as they say. Good day, Joshua. We shall meet up with you later."

"Good night," Joshua said without thinking, and finally managed to hang up the receiver on the third attempt.

Meanwhile, in Mary's room, she slept soundly as the ringing of Winston's call fell on deaf ears.

"This is pure delight," Winston commented as he and George ate lunch in the Ridgeway Visitor Center of the Missouri Botanical Garden. "It is a microcosm of Earth's vegetation. Mollie would love this if she were with us. She would be giving us a guided tour…lasting weeks, I fear!" he chuckled lovingly. Truth be told, Winston had learned so much about plants from his botanist wife, he could have given a half-way decent tour himself.

"This is one of my favorite places in St. Louis," George said. "Coming here soothes my soul. When I'm walking a path or sitting on a bench, I feel surrounded by God's Creation—its purity, its holiness. I feel a strong sense of the Spirit here. It's as if the Spirit itself lives in every plant, giving off the oxygen that sustains us—the very breath of life."

"That is a rather heart-felt statement for a Unitarian. You sound more like a…a Celtic Quaker, if there are such people."

George laughed as he said, "During my years at the university I often attended Quaker Meetings. The time of worship at the Friends Meeting House was disorienting at first. Over time it became a place for re-orienting my soul, my whole self. All day long I would be in a continuous dialogue with my books, with my teachers, with other students. When I tried to pray, all I could hear was endless chatter. I craved the silence I found as I sat with the others gathered in the Meeting House."

"You were learning how to meditate?" asked Winston.

"I was learning—and it took a long time. I was learning that real prayer is as much listening to God as it is speaking to God. Coming here, to this arboretum, is for me like attending to the Spirit with the Quakers. I pray differently when I'm here; or, shall I say, here there is less to listen to, so I end up hearing more."

"I can see why. I am happy for you that you can experience your beliefs like that. I never could, especially since…." Winston's gaze drifted off as he was reminded of his son.

"I know," responded George, as he reached across the table and squeezed Winston's hand for a moment. "I can't imagine what that must be like." The two men sat in silence for about thirty seconds until George said, "If you have finished your lunch, I have something to show you. It's a magical place!" They walked outside and rode the tram down to the southwest corner of the Botanical Garden. As they stepped off, George announced, "Welcome to the Japanese Garden."

"Goodness me," Winston exclaimed, "breath-taking!"

"They named this garden '*Seiwa-en*, which means the garden of pure, clear harmony and peace. Designed with great care by the late Professor Koichi Kawana to ensure authenticity, this fourteen-acre garden is the largest Japanese strolling garden in the Western hemisphere. A four-acre lake is complemented with waterfalls, streams, water-filled basins, and stone lanterns. Dry gravel gardens are raked into beautiful, rippling patterns.'"

"You sound like a tour guide. Did you memorize all that?"

"No, I'm reading the sign over here," laughed George, pointing to it.

Winston scanned the sign and replied, "Clever boy. My wife often tells me I should spend more time reading the signs…but I dare say this is *not* what she was referring to!"

"There is more. Would you like me to keep reading?"

"Thank you, no. I read to the bottom," Winston said. "Where shall we begin? Why not show me your favorite parts of the garden."

George thought for a moment. "I think we'll go this way; there's a traditional Japanese bridge on this side that you must see first." George led the way down the path to the right. "At a leisurely pace we can circumnavigate the pond in an hour. You will notice…"

"Look at all the tulips!" gushed Winston breathlessly, as he stopped in his tracks. "They are quite beautiful!" For the next two hours, it was one exclamation after another as Winston stopped frequently. "Ah, the magnificence of nature…. I have not seen cherry blossoms like these in several years' time."

"The azaleas will bud soon and the rhododendrons too," said George, "and the whole place will explode as if a rainbow had landed. I've been coming here since my mother had to push me in a stroller, and I never cease being awed by it all.

"Have you ever noticed that nothing clashes in nature? Put all of the flowers' colors together in one spot—pink, orange, red, lilac, white, green, yellow, blue, or the leaves as they turn in autumn—and they form a harmonious song. No wonder I enjoy wildflowers growing by the side of a roadway. If a decorator tried putting all of those colors in one room, the occupants would go mad! In nature, though, it's calming. I find it clears my brain."

"Yes, yes," Winston enthusiastically agreed. "My Mollie arranges the plants at our house, and no matter how she does it, the arrangement always looks proper and gorgeous."

The two men decided to sit on a bench in the middle of the arboretum and take in the sights and smells all around them. After a while, George broke the silence.

"So my dear Winston, what do you personally think about the Book of Emet?"

"You probably know what I think, George," Winston answered. "You went to the seminary and took Bible classes and learned what historians believe."

"Yes, of course," said George. "Still I'd like to hear your take on it."

"Almost all historians agree that the gospels were written in the name of Jesus' disciples many years after those disciples were dead and gone. None of those writers knew Jesus and none of them were present to hear what Jesus said or see what Jesus did. Those initial writings were also lost. The earliest writings we have actually come from centuries later—copies upon copies upon copies—and we know they were changed many times. So they are not very reliable at all."

"Yes, I know that," said George. "We all know that," he added, referring to all the others who had studied at Protestant seminaries.

Winston continued. "So earlier gospels do not agree with later gospels, even those attributed to the same author. For example, earlier gospels of Matthew do not agree with later gospels of Matthew, and so on. Then there is the problem that the gospels do not agree with each other on many points."

"Yes, that is true," agreed George. "We don't know if anything said in any of the gospels is really true and we don't know whether Jesus really said or did any of the things attributed to him."

"Righto," answered Winston enthusiastically, realizing he did not have to convince George of things most historians had been agreeing on for the past two hundred years or so. "So this Book of Emet is at least three hundred years older than the oldest gospel we currently have. To me, that makes Emet the most trustworthy information there is about the life and words of Jesus."

"But, wouldn't Emet, if he even existed, have an axe to grind portraying Jesus the way he did. Certainly, he would not have wanted to say things that would have helped the early Christians."

"Yes, that is possible," said Winston, "but the Christian writers did not want to say things that would offend their contemporaries either. So I consider it a wash at best, and I definitely lean toward Emet as the real truth."

"I agree with you," said George. "I just wanted to hear what you thought. Come, let's get you back to the hotel and we will have time for a little nap before we hit the stage again."

They rose from the bench they were sitting on, and eventually wound their way back to the entrance, stopping occasionally to admire or discuss something that particularly caught their eye in the arboretum. George drove them back to the hotel and let Winston out at the front entrance. "I'll return by 6:00 to pick you up along with the other two."

"I shall be ready, my head filled with flowers and ancient texts," Winston remarked as he closed the car door and walked to a door held open for him by a young man in a fancy uniform. "Thank you, young man," said Winston, with a smile.

"Have a good afternoon, sir," the doorman replied.

"I have had a most wonderful afternoon in your fair city."

As Winston made his way to the elevator, he yawned and decided that George's advice about taking a little nap in his room was quite the thing.

Observing the Sabbath

Joshua's alarm went off at 9:15, just a half hour after Winston's phone call. Joshua was still tired, having been up rather late the night before watching an old movie on the hotel television. Having been showered before going to bed, he did not have much to do to get ready to go to Saturday morning services at a Conservative synagogue near the Washington University campus.

Joshua, a Reform movement rabbi, had three reasons for choosing this Conservative movement synagogue — he was acquainted with Rabbi Levy, the rabbi who presided there; he wanted to see if there were many students or other young people attending; and there were not any nearby Reform synagogues having Saturday morning services (they usually hold their services on Friday nights).

He knew he would be arriving late for services, but he was okay with that. Conservative services typically begin at 9:00 a.m. and run until around noon, or even later. But unlike Reform services, which usually run for only an hour and a half to two hours, the Conservative service essentially does most of the prayers twice, which Joshua believes are unnecessary. So, according to plan, he arrived at the synagogue at 10:00.

No sooner did he walk into the synagogue than a buzz began to circulate around the room. Most of the congregants had watched Joshua on television the night before and those who recognized him spread the word. Rabbi Levy, of course, recognized Joshua too, and taking note of the buzz, stopped the prayers at the first appropriate moment, which was within three minutes after Joshua arrived.

"We wish to welcome Rabbi Joshua Hertzel," Rabbi Levy announced with a broad smile from the *bima* (dais). Some of the congregants began clapping and some gave Joshua a standing ovation, thoroughly embarrassing him. Rabbi Levy's smile grew even broader. "Perhaps we can persuade Rabbi Hertzel to say a few words and answer some questions we might have. I'd be happy to postpone my 'most wonderful' sermon until another time."

The congregation laughed appreciatively at Rabbi Levy's little joke. Although Rabbi Levy's sermons were better than most, rabbis in general were notorious for giving bad sermons, and some of the men liked to joke about what a great time it was for taking a nap or going to the bathroom.

All eyes turned expectantly on Joshua, who had taken an inconspicuous seat about halfway into the pews. Joshua looked undecided, and several members in the congregation shouted words of encouragement. What could Joshua do? So he graciously nodded his head yes, and the congregation applauded again. "Let's turn to page 133," Rabbi Levy announced happily, and continued the prayer service.

The time for the rabbi's sermon came toward the end of the service, just before the *Aleinu* (the traditional prayer praising God), the Mourner's *Kaddish* and the concluding hymn. "Rabbi Hertzel will now say a few words and answer any questions you may have," Rabbi Levy announced. Joshua strode to the front of the sanctuary, climbed the four stairs to the *bima*, and joined Rabbi Levy at the pulpit. After shaking hands enthusiastically and giving Joshua a warm hug, Rabbi Levy sat down in the rabbi's chair behind the pulpit, and Joshua became the center of attention.

Joshua looked around the room. He estimated there were about 70 people there. About one-third were elderly and most of the rest were between 35 and 55. He was disappointed to see only 8 young people there.

"Good morning and Shabbat Shalom," Joshua began. "How many of you watched the debate last night?" Joshua guessed 55 out of the 70 raised their hands. "The Book of Emet is an important find for the Jewish people. It shows that Jesus was a Jew through and through and that when he died, the Jews had nothing to do with killing him. It was the Romans who did that and they didn't need our help. The Christians and Jews will always disagree whether Jesus was the Messiah and the Son of God, but I have hopes that we will come to agree that the Jews were not responsible in any way for his death.

"If such an agreement were achieved, that would add immensely to the security of the Jewish people, because nothing has caused us more grief than being labeled Christ-killers. However, in today's world, where we have seemingly found a safe home in the United States, and the primary antagonist of our people comes from Arab countries in the Middle East, I think the greatest threat we face as a people comes not from the Christians, not from the Arabs, but rather the greatest threat we face comes from our shrinking numbers.

"Look around you. I count only 8 young people here this morning, and this from a synagogue close to a major university. And I must tell you, I have been to many synagogues in many places, and most of them look just like this. How many of you have children or grandchildren who, for whatever reason, are not very interested in Judaism and who will probably not raise their kids Jewish?" Everyone looked around the room to see how many hands were raised. Joshua counted about 50 hands. "It looks to be about two-thirds of you, and that is what it usually is when I ask this question. Between that and the low birth-rate of the non-Orthodox, we are in big trouble if these trends continue.

"We need to make a lot of changes to Judaism, I believe. If something isn't selling, you need to either change the product or the customers. I don't believe we can change the customers, so we have to change Judaism to make it more attractive to our own people. I hope you all will join me in trying to make the changes we need to save the Jewish people in this country. Please check out my website to see what I think needs to be done. I will now open the floor to questions about this or the debate over the Book of Emet."

A young woman in her early 20's, sitting in the back corner, raised her hand. Joshua nodded in her direction.

"Rabbi, you have advocated including Jesus in the pantheon of Jewish sages and the Book of Emet supports that position. How do you think doing this would affect the direction of Jewish education?"

"Great question," Joshua answered. "I think including Jesus' teachings into our curriculum will lead us to a softer and less legalistic Judaism. I think studying Jesus' teachings will expand the scope of Jewish learning and bring Christians and Jews closer to each other without us having to give up any of our core beliefs."

A middle aged man sitting behind Joshua on the bima asked "Rabbi, what kind of changes do you want us to make that would help bring our lost people back?" Joshua later learned that the man who asked this question was the President of the synagogue.

"An excellent question! If you ask unaffiliated Jews why they aren't members, most of them will say it's because of the high dues synagogues charge. Another reason is that synagogues rarely have programs that appeal to them. In particular, they say that Sabbath services are boring and don't speak to their lives.

"That is unfortunate, because in today's world, synagogues are the only communal organizations Jews have. We have to find ways to make them relevant to our people. I think some synagogues need to be free, like churches are. I think the prayer books and the organization of services need to be redesigned with out of the box thinking. Our prayer books follow a routine that was established hundreds of years ago. We read the Torah every week, week after week, year after year, even when it is boring. Meanwhile, we ignore every other form of Jewish literature, including the rest of the Bible, the Talmud, and the great writings from the Middle Ages and modern times."

An elderly lady in the front row, a long-time member of the synagogue, asked "If we don't charge dues, how will we be able to support our building and our rabbi?"

Rabbi Levy jumped in and jokingly said "Yes, I want to know about that too!" Everyone laughed.

"The Christians support their churches by passing the plate and in some churches, members are expected to tithe. *Tithe* is an ancient word that means 'tenth', which means each member is expected to give a tenth of their income to the church every year. Most people don't know this, but the idea of tithing comes from the Torah, so while Christians follow this mitzvah, Jews do not. Some synagogues will be self-sufficient with tithing or charging dues. But others will need outside help, which I think can come from philanthropists and community Jewish organizations. I think it is important to have some free synagogues so Jews do not grow up feeling alienated from what they call 'institutional Judaism'."

Rabbi Levy spoke up and said "We have time for one more question."

An elderly man sitting six rows back raised his hand and Joshua pointed at him.

"Rabbi, there have been a lot of threats made by the Christian right and right-wing politicians that the Book of Emet is not valid and must be destroyed and not taught in the schools. What do you think will be the outcome after your debate is over?"

"I doubt very much if those people will ever accept the validity of the Book of Emet, no matter how the debate turns out. They have their beliefs and nothing will change them. For example, they still don't accept the existence of evolution and won't allow it to be taught in some of their schools. You can be sure that the Book of Emet will meet the same fate. In other places, I think the Book of Emet will be studied alongside the New Testament, like perhaps in seminaries and comparative religion classes."

"Thank you very much Rabbi Hertzel," Rabbi Levy said. "We now turn to page161 in our prayer books."

Rabbi Levy concluded the service in another 20 minutes and the congregation adjourned to the Dining Hall for a Sabbath lunch prepared by the Sisterhood. The lunch was served buffet-style, with bagels and lox and cream cheese, as well as egg salad, tuna salad, tomatoes and other accessories, and of course a wide selection of desserts. Joshua sat with Rabbi Levy, the President of the synagogue, and other synagogue dignitaries. Synagogue issues were discussed at the table, with some mention of whether Joshua's suggestions could be implemented there. Occasionally, congregants from other tables came by to shake hands with Joshua and give their opinions on some of the subjects touched on during his speech.

After about an hour, Joshua excused himself and went back to his hotel room, where he celebrated the rest of the Sabbath afternoon quietly, reading a little, napping a little, and watching some pro basketball on the television in his room.

Shopping with Lizzy

Mary woke with a start. She stretched and yawned and immediately started smiling. Today was the day that Lizzy Anderson, her long-time friend from high school was coming to meet her and spend the day.

She was excited to see her as it had been several months since they had been able to spend quality time together. Mary swung her feet over the edge of the hotel king bed and got up. She checked her cell phone for any messages and then headed into the bathroom.

After a quick shower, she brushed her teeth, combed her hair and started to apply her makeup. She never wore too much like some of the ladies in her field. She had very beautiful alabaster skin that set off her deep green eyes. She did not need much makeup to look very well put together.

She walked to the closet where she had hung her clothes and carefully looked for something stylish but comfortable to wear. She knew they would be doing a lot of walking and shopping and so she reached for her flats. As soon as she was dressed in her dark navy slacks and white sailor top she gave herself a quick onceover glance in the mirror. "Good, this should be comfortable all day long," she said to herself.

Lizzy would be arriving around lunchtime, after driving the 260 miles from Louisville, where she now lived, to St. Louis. Mary wanted something light, healthy and non-fattening for breakfast, so she walked down the street to the nearest Starbucks coffee shop. She liked their coffee and especially their yogurt and granola cup. She had already bought all the newspapers she could find in the hotel lobby giftshop, so she settled in for some reading and a leisurely breakfast. She was especially interested in reading all the articles and editorials she could find on last night's Debate.

As she expected, the more liberal newspapers favored Joshua and the Book of Emet, while the more conservative newspapers favored her and the New Testament. Both she and Joshua got good reviews for their parts, but Sir Winston seemed to be the star "performer". She knew this was a big problem for her, because neutral historians rarely believed the miracle that was Jesus. They always looked for a scientific, rational explanation for everything. "You're not going to get science to prove what is a matter of faith," she always said to her viewers. "If God wanted there to be proof, then there would be no role for faith. It is faith that God wants we humans to have."

At about 12:30, Lizzy called on her cell phone and said she was about a half hour away. Mary finished her coffee and returned to her hotel room. Just as she finished redoing her hair there was a knock at her door. She opened it. "Lizzy," she almost shouted as she grabbed the woman standing in the doorway around the waist and hugged her tightly. "It's so great to see you again," she gushed. "Oh Mary, I have missed you so much," Lizzy hugged her back, while jumping up and down. They kissed each other's cheeks and hugged again, laughing the entire time.

"So, how is the world treating my very best friend?" Lizzy asked while watching Mary's expression with concerned interest.

"Oh Lizzy, this conference is so important. I was really afraid to tackle it for fear of doing something wrong." Mary was shaking her head as if to throw the idea of fear out of her mind.

"Oh pooh, you never do anything wrong. That good looking rabbi fella probably has you distracted." Both women laughed but Lizzy noticed a strange expression on Mary's face. "Come on, let's have lunch and do a little shopping therapy and you'll be rarin' to go."

"Yes, let's get going. I'm starving all of a sudden." Mary threw back her head and laughed. They headed out the door and down the hallway to the posh hotel restaurant off the main lobby.

Lizzy was famished after her long drive and ordered a full slab of St. Louis ribs. Mary ordered a Julienne salad with oil and vinegar dressing. Both were content with ice water with lemon for their drinks.

"So what's this gorgeous rabbi like in person?" Lizzy asked with a twinkle in her eye after the waters came.

"The rabbi?" Mary was surprised by the question but again had that strange expression on her face. "He is really rather nice. Seems like a real person." Lizzy was disappointed with the answer, even moreso when Mary changed the topic.

"Wayne left my mother and Christa alone this weekend so he could party with his cousin up in Denver. I'm so worried about them, but they seem to be taking care of each other so far."

"That Wayne is disgusting," Lizzy snorted. "I used to like him way back when, but he's a different man now." Lizzy watched as Mary's face darkened.

"You're right. He's such a jerk any more, Lizzy. He hates me I'm pretty sure and I am starting to feel the same way about him, God forgive me. He is arrogant and pushy and does nothing around the house to help with Christa or anything else for that matter." Mary's voice went to a whisper. "He also has his women on the side." Lizzy's mouth fell open and she stared at Mary.

"Oh, for God's sake, you mean he is still cheating on you too?" she asked incredulously. Mary just nodded her head, tears rolling down her cheeks. She had not talked about Wayne's infidelity since Christa came into the house and Lizzy assumed it was not happening anymore.

Lizzy got up from her side of the booth, went over to Mary's side, sat next to her and gave her a hug. "Mary, I'm so sorry you're in this mess of a relationship. Why don't you just leave his sorry ass?" Lizzy had no problems with divorce. She had gone through one herself. A very nasty one. He husband had been physically abusive to her on a number of occasions. She had nursed more than a few split lips and black eyes. If someone was miserable in a relationship, as far as she was concerned they needed to get out of it.

That was one thing that she and Mary had never agreed on. "You know I don't believe in divorce Liz. But, I'm also getting very tired of never knowing where he is or who he's with. Then there's the problem of having Christa know about this. She is getting older every day and it won't be long before she is painfully aware of what's going on in my marriage." Lizzy nodded sympathetically.

Their lunches arrived and Lizzy dug into hers enthusiastically while Mary, who was less hungry, barely picked at her salad, lost in thought. It was not long before Lizzy was ready to talk again.

"So Mare, do you think this scroll is for real?" Lizzy asked between bites. "Everyone in Louisville is upset over this. No one wants to believe it's true."

"I know Liz. Everyone I know is upset too. I know what I believe. Jesus was the son of God. He was sent to us by the Father to save us from our sins and give us eternal life in heaven. I don't think this Emet ever really knew Jesus, and if he did, he didn't understand what he was seeing no matter how well he thought he knew him." Lizzy saw the passionate conviction in Mary's eyes. She had always admired Mary for the strength of her beliefs.

"Well, I'm sure you will do your best to convince everyone of the truth Mare. You have always been a soldier for Christ and I am sure you will win out in this debate too. People will believe you, especially the Christians. The Jews are another story. They have never believed that Christ was the son of God. You probably won't be able to convince them to change their minds. But you will make your points for our side." Mary knew she was right. But by the same token, she was worried about Joshua and Winston continuing to gang up on her. She had the feeling they were winning with the doubters and the newspapers she read that morning tended to confirm that.

"You know this has been a real learning experience for me Liz. This Rabbi Hertzel is simply amazing. He is very smart and well spoken and very open-minded toward other ideas. He doesn't say the things Jewish people usually say. I have to really stay on my toes with him," Mary smiled.

Lizzy sat back and studied her face for a second. "You really like this Rabbi don't you?"

"Yes, I do." Mary admitted reluctantly.

"He is very handsome isn't he?" Lizzy asked the question already knowing the answer.

"Yes, he is handsome. But he doesn't act like it. He is very passionate about his religion and why he is here. I don't think there is a conceited bone in his body. He is very mild mannered and polite also."

Lizzy was getting the impression that Mary's attraction to Joshua went beyond respect and admiration. But she sensed Mary was not ready to talk about it on that level so she changed the subject to goings ons in Louisville since Mary had moved away.

They finished their lunch and Mary wanted to pay for both of them. Then they headed for the upscale stores in downtown suburban Clayton. They used Lizzy's car because Mary's rental car was still at the campus parking lot. Like many women, shopping was one of the most fun things they liked to do together. It seemed like old times, and they laughed a lot and had a ball. In one dress shop both women liked, they each bought a new dress and shoes to match. They giggled like school girls at the thought of dressing alike again after all these years.

Lizzy had auburn hair, was a little taller than Mary and had a lean and muscular body. She had been on the school track team and still tried to run at least 3 miles every other day. Lizzy liked staying in shape and was proud how attractive she still looked at her age in her early 50's. She also felt really good and did not understand why other people would not take care of their bodies and health.

After they finished shopping, multiple bags in their hands, they stopped in one of the bistros on the main strip in town. Mary was feeling very good after a couple of glasses of wine. She started to snicker and Lizzy caught it.

"What's going on in that over active mind of yours now?" she asked with a huge grin.

"Oh, I was just wondering what Wayne would do if I brought Joshua home with me." Mary giggled again very naughtily. "I'm sure he wouldn't know what to do."

Lizzy grinned at the thought. She was very angry that Wayne had made her best friend so unhappy. "When did all the cheating start?" she asked when Mary first told her about how unhappy their marriage had become.

"After I lost the baby. He became very aloof and didn't want anything to do with me after that. I don't know if he was afraid I would get pregnant again or what, but he stopped touching me or even coming home some nights. It was very painful and hard on me. I even started to question my faith at one point, but I managed to work through it. I knew my faith was all I had at that point. I knew Jesus would watch over me and help me get through it. And he did."

They finished their wine and the cheese and cracker tray and headed back to the hotel. Mary was so happy she had gotten to spend almost the entire day with her dear friend. They were like sisters and had been since the first day they met all those years ago. Mary had not been so relaxed in ages. Lizzy always had that effect on her.

"So Miss Mary, am I going to get to meet the handsome rabbi or not?" Lizzy interrupted Mary's reverie after they arrived back in Mary's room. Lizzy really wanted to meet Joshua and size him up for herself.

Mary smiled and nodded. "I'll call his room and see if he has time to meet you before we go back for the Debate." Mary dialed Joshua's room number but he did not answer. He was taking a shower and was all soapy and could not make it to the phone in time. "Oh well, I *guess* he's not in," Mary said. "I *guess* you're out of luck."

"I *guess* I am," Lizzy said laughing, joining in the word play. "I *guess* I won't get to see him tonight except on television." Lizzy had a cousin in the St. Louis area that she would be spending the night with. They would of course be watching the second night of the Debate on television. PBS had announced that viewership was higher for the first night of the Debate than ever in its history.

"I *guess* I better start getting ready for tonight," Mary chimed in laughing.

"Enough with the *guesswork*," Lizzy was almost hysterical by now. "I *guess* I better leave and let you get ready."

"I *guess* so," Mary almost could not get the words out she was laughing so hard. She escorted Lizzy to the door and the two friends gave each other a long lingering hug.

"Good luck tonight," Lizzy said with emotion. "I love you Mare."

"I love you Liz. Let's talk later tonight or tomorrow."

Lizzy nodded her head, gave Mary a big hug and a kiss and left. Mary was still laughing and needed to calm down before she could jump in the shower and begin organizing herself for tonight's Debate.

Sir Winston Hamburley

And the Lord appeared to Solomon in a dream during the night,
and God said, "Ask what shall I give you."
"Give your servant an understanding heart to judge your people,
that I may discern between good and evil. And these words pleased
the Lord, that Solomon had asked for this thing.
"Behold, I have done according to your words. I have given you a
wise and an understanding heart, so that there have has been none
like you before you, neither after you shall any arise like you." [I
Kings 3:5, 9-12.]

Sir Winston Hamburley was a well-established and venerated religious historian, specializing in the ancient Near East, and particularly in Judaism and Christianity at the time of Jesus and the five centuries thereafter. He had written dozens of articles for scholarly journals and some for popular magazines, as well as several books, including a well-regarded book on the real historical Jesus. Sir Winston was often interviewed on these subjects for television news and special programs and both the BBC and The History Channel often used his expertise as a consultant or as a host. In fact, this erudite scholar with the cheery voice was probably more often heard and seen than read. His burly figure, along with his full white droopy mustache and wind-tossed hair, made him a recognized figure wherever he went.

Sir Winston was raised in the Anglican Church and sang in the cathedral's boys' choir for six years. As a boy, he was fascinated by the architecture of church buildings. Every week, it seemed, he noticed something new on the exterior or on the interior of the church. He would find the nearest adult—preferably the vicar—to answer his questions about the many spires all pointing up to the sky, or the meaning of an ancient symbol he had discovered carved into the stone some twenty feet above the pulpit.

By his eleventh birthday, young Winston could have given the churchwarden—or the entire vestry, for that matter—an extensive tour of the cathedral, with all of its religious symbolism explained. He even requested permission to do just that, but was told by one curmudgeonly gentleman that he was too young. Winston thought about telling the man that he looked old enough to have watched the construction of the six-hundred-year-old building personally, but he bit his tongue just in time.

Winston's love of church life and buildings continued upon his matriculation at Queens College, Oxford. He read history and theology, taking first class honours in all subjects. Rumor had it that Winston, the up-and-coming scholar, received firsts in some courses that had not been taught at Oxford in over 300 years. When asked, he would typically remark that such legends were best kept in the towers—with the ghosts.

For several years, Winston prepared himself to become a priest in the Church of England, and was continuing toward that goal when he came to a fork in the road. Later, he would joke to his friends that he would have taken that fork, but saw nothing good to eat in either direction. By the twentieth telling, they asked him to find a new joke.

The summer before he was to begin a Master's degree in theology, young Winston joined a group of twenty-three students and professors on an eight-week trip to the Holy Land. While they did as much sight-seeing to the known biblical sites as time allowed, their primary mission was to join an archeological dig at a village that was estimated to be 1,700 years old. Several more layers of construction were being discovered, and the dating of the village went further back in history. Artifacts had already been unearthed that included Christian symbols—apparently English in origin—from the Middle Ages, alongside fragments from the Koran in Arabic. That summer, team members painstakingly uncovered pieces of Jewish pottery dating to the first and second centuries of the Common Era, and nearby, a French priest called Roland de Vaux brushed dirt off of a small coin. It appeared to contain the image of Trajan, Roman Emperor from 98-117 A.D.

One Saturday, a dozen members of the team drove to the Mediterranean coast to hike up Mt. Carmel, just above the modern

Israeli town of Haifa. This was the site of the contest between the ancient Israelite prophet Elijah and the four hundred prophets of the Phoenician god, Baal, as described in the Old Testament in 1 Kings 18:1-46. That afternoon after they had returned to Haifa, Winston went for a walk alone and found a bench on the beach to sit on and reflect. As he gazed into the amazing blue waters of the Mediterranean Sea, he did not think of the tale of Jonah and the Whale (big fish, actually) or of St. Paul's voyages to far-off ports in Asia Minor (modern Turkey) and Italy. No, he pondered whether he would be happier as a priest, tending to the needs of a church in "who-knows-where" England, or in an academic life of research and teaching about the Ancient Near East.

Each day as Winston worked in the hot Israeli sun, one simple question haunted him. It started in some nether region of his brain and slowly migrated to the front. With every discovery, with the incredible histories of the several civilizations that had occupied that tiny one-half-square-kilometer space of arid and rocky land, Winston asked himself, "What is behind this?" It became his daily mantra: "What came before this? Who—or what—destroyed the walls that this newer building replaced? How did each generation live, cook, or teach their children? What animals did they tend? Was the land more fertile in those days and did anything of value grow here? Had they heard there was a great sea just twenty kilometers to the west or that a small lake called the Sea of Galilee (or Lake of Gennesaret) lay the same distance to the east?"

Then, one evening after dinner, the question of the summer presented itself again, but Winston was not sitting by an ancient wall in the 100-degree heat holding a small, soft-bristled brush in his hand. This time he was lying on his cot in the shade of the tent looking at a leather-bound copy of the Jewish and Christian Scriptures and saying to himself, "What is behind this?" He had already studied what is called Historical Criticism in some classes at Oxford. He had read Albert Schweitzer's ground-breaking book, The Quest of the Historical Jesus, which traced the late 19th and early 20th century attempts to ascertain what is behind the pages of the gospels. He had been curious about what might be learned about Jesus Christ from non-biblical sources, but was even more focused on the content and meaning of Jesus' message.

Winston could barely sleep that night as light bulbs turned on in his head, like the stars that become visible as dusk turns to darkness. The following morning at breakfast, Winston asked one of his teachers from

Oxford if he knew how many days a letter would take to travel between there and England. He explained that he wanted to enroll in a different graduate course of study. Knowing Winston's scholastic achievements, the teacher was hoping Winston would want to study biblical archaeology with him. But no, Winston asked his dean at Oxford if he might pursue graduate study in New Testament and Christian Origins. In large script on that thin airmail paper, he told the story of his aha moment and his favorite new question. Just a few years later, Winston Hamburley was granted the Oxford D.Phil., his thesis having been supervised by the highly respected New Testament scholar, Samuel L. Cairo.

In the meantime, Winston calmed the fears of his fiancée, Mollie Hannigan Wright, by assuring her she would never have to bear the cross of being "the Vicar's wife." They wed, and soon he was happily lecturing, telling bright-eyed students about the world into which Jesus was born and the cultural and religious milieu that influenced the shaping of the Christian writings of that era.

In due time, Mollie and Winston (she called him Winnie, a term of endearment he hated at first; but later he gave in because she always said it with that twinkle in her Irish eyes) had a baby boy. They began attending a nearby Anglican church as a family, but the rising New Testament scholar received many invitations to teach—and preach—in churches across England. Winston was delighted with the chance to see so many churches of varying size, décor and design. He thanked God for showing him his calling and giving him such a rich and rewarding life. His contented life continued for nearly a decade, but ceased abruptly when his only child was killed in a freak accident and he lost his faith in God.

Tragically, Winston knew that by rejecting all things mystical and supernatural he had painted himself into an intellectual corner. After the accident that killed his son, he was never again able to reconcile the biblical picture of God as loving, just, and merciful with such a seemingly random act of violence. He would either have to change his picture of God or get rid of God altogether. Where he once viewed prayer as a doorway one walks through to be a bit closer to heaven, its current futility was akin to opening those same doors and falling into a bottomless pit. He saw other parents of tragedy relying on their faith; they seemed to have more hope and assurance as they tried to make sense of their losses. Even his next door neighbor, Mrs. Blackwell, had shared with Winston and Mollie how her relationship with Christ had brought her a peace that made no rational sense. It had been ten years since her daughter had taken her own life, yet the comfort of her faith elicited joy.

Mollie tried going to church after the loss of their child, but sitting there alone, where once there had been three, was too much to bear. She and Winston had now been married for 50 years and Mollie was retired from her career as a botanist. Since then, Mollie mostly spent her days happily stewarding their greenhouse and garden. As for Winston, he became an even more rationalistic historian, and his carefully researched works had recently earned him a knighthood. Sir Winston was no longer bitter, and had mellowed considerably, but he has never recovered his personal faith in God.

Reverend George Turner

*A kind man does good to his own soul, but a cruel man brings
trouble on himself.
Those that are perverse of heart are an abomination to the Lord,
but those who are upright are His delight.
Be sure of this: The evil man will not go unpunished, but those who
are righteous will go free. [Proverbs 11:17, 20-21.]*

George Turner majored in Psychology, with a Religious Studies minor,
at Washington University in St. Louis. His interest in studying religion
was first sparked after he took an Introduction to Religion class in his
freshman year.

He had started out intending to do a double major with Psychology
and Social Work, with the thought of staying at WashU for his Master
of Social Work degree. It was—and still is—one of the most highly-rated
social work programs in the nation. George did a lot of soul searching the
summer after his freshman year. He even prayed about his future, asking
God to give him a sign. His parents suggested that he not be expecting a
dove with an olive branch to fly through his window, or the stars to spell
it out for him in the sky on a hot, muggy St. Louis summer night.

The pastor of the United Church of Christ (UCC) congregation,
where most of George's family were members, offered a slightly different
approach to reading "signs from God." He reminded George of the
hurdles he had to jump over to get his Eagle Scout project approved
by the church's governing board — how relentless he was in convincing
the leaders he really could complete the project. Once George had
commitments from the Building and Grounds Committee and the
Pre-School Board, plus eight church members willing to give an entire

Saturday to construction, he returned to the leaders. They unanimously approved George's request to build additional playground equipment for the pre-school.

"George," the pastor continued, "I haven't seen you as excited about anything as you were about that project—until now. In every conversation we've had since this spring, your whole face lights up when you tell me about your religion class. You are asking some thought-provoking questions, much the same as I did when I was in college evaluating a call to the ministry. I'm not saying that's what you will end up doing, but if you are serious about studying religion for the next three years, I would say your enthusiasm for it is the sign from God you are looking for."

"No lightning bolts or engraved stone tablets coming down from the clouds?" George asked, with a smile.

"Those are rarer than you might think… even in the Bible! There are times when people believe that God has spoken to them with a message of some sort—and I'm not talking about hallucinations. Typically it's a message just for them, like an answer to prayer, or when they 'just know' what they're supposed to do. George, it sounds like you 'just know' that you are supposed to study Religion this fall."

"There's just one problem here; well, two really," George confided. "I've been feeling sad about giving up Social Work. I'll definitely take Psych, still. The other one is that WashU doesn't have a major in Religion, only a minor. And I really do not want to transfer. Besides, WashU gave me a lot of scholarships and grants, and I might not get those if I go somewhere else."

After looking at a few different colleges, George decided to stay at Washington University, major in Psychology, and take every Religion course they offered. One of his professors was a Unitarian, a group George knew little about. George met him in his Introduction to Christianity course, part of which was an introduction to many denominations within the Christian faith. He learned that the Unitarian Universalist movement had its origins in European Christian traditions. To George it sounded more like Humanist philosophy than Christianity, believing that religion must be supported by reason.

These Enlightenment teachings from Europe were first taught in America at its oldest colleges. Schools such as Harvard and Yale, originally founded to train young men for Christian ministry, started teaching their students to question generally accepted dogmas of faith. They were taught that anything having to do with the supernatural world, like miracles or exorcisms that could not be explained by reason, did not belong in a thinking religion. God in human form? No. Resurrection from the dead? Not likely. A woman impregnated by the Spirit of God? Impossible!

By the turn of the 19th century, a number of Congregationalist churches in New England—churches founded by Pilgrims and Puritans—moved from being Trinitarian to Unitarian. In some circles, belief that Jesus Christ was God was dwindling, so the idea of "God in three persons" (trinity) was replaced by the notion of God as one spiritual, mystical entity (unity).

In fact, the Congregationalist church in Massachusetts that Abigail Adams regularly attended was "[s]o influenced by the Enlightenment that it later joined the American Unitarian Association." Like her, her husband, second President of the United States John Adams, was no orthodox Christian. More accurately, they would have been described as Christian Deists.

Over the coming years, George thought a lot about the places of faith, reason, heart, and mind in religion generally and for his beliefs in particular. To supplement his studies in religion, George attended worship services and other events in a variety of St. Louis churches, including his home church. He was fascinated by the diversity in the worship and theology and preaching he experienced.

It was in one of the smaller advanced Religion classes that George met Raymond. They developed a good friendship and soon discovered that the other was gay. Raymond had "come out" to his family and friends during his junior year in college, but George had not…yet. George knew that the upcoming Christmas break would be like none before. He was excited to tell those he loved most in the world that he was in love, yet afraid they might not be accepting of his orientation.

One evening George and his mother were sitting in the kitchen eating warm Christmas cookies with hot spiced apple cider, while his dad was engrossed in a University of Missouri basketball game on television. George segued the conversation from his seminary studies to "something personal," as he called it. He told her why he had never been attracted to girls growing up, and then all about Raymond. His Mother's first response was, "Well, Dad and I had wondered about this since you were in high school."

George's eyes widened. "Really? Was it that obvious?"

"You never dated, and you went to your Prom with a mixed group of friends—there weren't the same number of girls as boys, as I recall."

"That's right. I was trying to figure out if I was straight or gay. The problem was I really liked everybody in that group of friends, male and female."

"And then there was Marcie."

"Yes," he said, a warm smile crossing his face.

"I still remember the way Marcie would look at you when she'd come over to work on a science project. You seemed completely oblivious; and she's so attractive. I think she went into social work because of you."

"Mom!" he said with a hint of exasperation. "She wasn't Homecoming Queen runner-up for no reason. I just never thought of her in those ways. Marcie was one of my best friends in high school and still is."

"How do you think she'll react to your news? You haven't told her about this, have you?"

"About Raymond?" he replied, looking down at his mug of cider. "Yes.... I'm sorry, Mom. I wanted to tell you and Dad first, but...."

"You weren't sure how we'd react."

"Right. Actually, I came out to Marcie a couple of months ago. She was disappointed but it didn't last long, because shortly afterwards she got serious with someone and she's pregnant now and engaged. And then, when Raymond and I started dating, she was the first person I called.

"She was really happy for me and asked when I was going to introduce her to Raymond, so she could see if he was good enough for me." The look on George's face was one of pure delight, and his mother intuitively saw a contentment she had not seen in some time.

"Guess we should go tell Dad," George offered.

"*We?*"

"Alright, alright; I should be the one to tell Dad, but I want you there, too."

"For moral support?"

"Intervention, more likely!" They both laughed.

"It'll be fine," his mother said. "Remember, I told you he and I were already wondering, and he was not upset at the possibility. Wait! You'd better be sure the game is over. You know how Dad gets when Missouri is playing."

"Oh, yeah. He might not be so accepting if we interrupt his *spiritual time.*"

The evening ended on the most positive note possible in the Turner home. Mr. Turner said exactly what his wife had said earlier, "Your mother and I had wondered about this since you were high school." He went on to tell George how proud he was of him — that if George was happy with what he was going to do with his life, he was happy also.

"Are there any more cookies in the kitchen," Mr. Turner asked, "or did you two eat them all?"

"I baked twenty dozen today for friends and neighbors, like I always do. There might be a broken one you can have," Mrs. Turner replied with a wink.

"Nothing you say could ruin this evening, my dear; not even a cookie that wasn't good enough for a gift basket. My Missouri Tigers won and all's right with the world!"

"It's good to know some things never change, Dad. I will leave you two to your cookie banter. I'm going upstairs to call Raymond."

"Honey," Mrs. Turner called as George reached the top of the stairs. "Tell Raymond…we're looking forward to meeting him."

"Thanks, Mom. I love you."

After his senior year of college, George decided to spend a year in Europe, studying the various Christian churches, theologies and historical sites in that fountain of culture and history. He also went to Israel for a year to study early Christianity and Judaism at Hebrew University in Jerusalem. Upon returning to St. Louis, he worked in underprivileged areas as a social worker for two years. He found that he enjoyed the camaraderie of his co-workers and the closeness they achieved both during and after working hours. After four years of touring, studying and working, George was ready to pursue his calling, which still pulled at him as strongly as ever.

The following autumn, George drove to New Haven, Connecticut, to attend Yale Divinity School. He was truly in his element. Every course was exciting — he could not learn enough or discuss enough to satisfy himself. Like a sponge, he soaked it all up. He took a Psychology of Religion class his first year which helped him make important connections between his two major academic interests.

Every semester after that, George took a class in Pastoral Care and Counseling, including two from the late renowned pastoral theologian, Henri J. M. Nouwen. Father Nouwen had a unique way of wedding the hurts and longings of the human heart with divine love and forgiveness.

The students packed his classes, and not just to feed their minds. Father Nouwen was able to feed their spirits with grace and holy embrace, fueling their spiritual quests to love and be loved.

As graduation neared, it was time to choose a denomination where he would feel most at home. He had become increasingly uncomfortable with the more conservative Christian denominations, and found himself gravitating to the more liberal ones. After he received his Master of Divinity at Yale Divinity School, George chose to be ordained by the Unitarian Universalist Association. He served churches in Connecticut and Massachusetts before receiving the call to be minister of the Unitarian Church in St. Louis. This was a dream come true. His parents were still healthy and active in their "golden years," and the congregation and their new minister seemed to be a good fit for each other.

He and Raymond had been together for eight years at that point. During the interview process, he had told the congregation's search committee about his relationship with Raymond. The committee chairwoman said that should not be a problem. Their previous minister had come out six months after she and her friend arrived. She felt the church had done a fine job of welcoming the new pastor's partner and adjusting to the changes. Her assurance proved to be true. George and Raymond were immediately embraced by the church.

George always had a well-balanced personal life. He and Raymond neither hid nor flaunted their sexual orientation. He exercised regularly and ate healthily. He was popular with the members of his congregation, had written many books on spirituality and achieving happiness, and was a frequent guest on television and the lecture circuit.

After a number of years, he was invited to host a new liberal Christian talk show program on Sunday morning television. The show became very popular and was widely acclaimed by the critics. He was able to get almost any guest he wanted because he treated everyone with love and respect. Even when he disagreed with someone, he allowed the guest to have his or her views presented in the most favorable light. George truly loved all people and all religions. "They all point toward God," he always said.

The Book of Emet

Chapter Four: The Sermon on the Mount

In the third month after the Israelites had gone forth out of the land
of Egypt, they came into the wilderness of Sinai.
Then Moses went up unto God, and God called to him from the
mountain and said, "You have seen what I did to the Egyptians,
and how I carried you on eagles' wings and brought you to Myself.
Now therefore if you will hearken unto My voice and keep
My covenant, then out of all nations you will be My treasured
possession. And you will be for Me a kingdom of priests and a holy
nation." [Exodus 19:1-6.]

The three panelists staying at the hotel assembled in the lobby at 6:00
p.m. and George arrived with the limousine a few minutes later. They
arrived at Graham Chapel at 6:20 and immediately noticed that the
protesting group outside had gotten much larger and were much more
boisterous. They gave every appearance of being a well-organized mob.
All four panelists looked at them nervously, Joshua moreso than the
others because he was the target of most of their signs.

The Debate was scheduled to resume at 7:00. As in the previous
evening, students from the drama club came to apply some makeup and
give the panelists some finishing touches. When everyone was ready,
George led the panel back on stage.

"Welcome back everyone, to the second of three nights in which we
will be comparing the Book of Emet to the Bible," George said opening

the proceedings. "Tonight we will be discussing three more chapters of the Book of Emet, Chapters 4-6. Chapter 4 is about the famous Sermon on the Mount. It encompasses a lot of topics, and some would say they are Jesus' most important teachings. For those who are looking for places where Emet is very different from the Bible, pay particular attention to what Jesus says about women and homosexuals. Dr. Roberts, would you please begin."

"Thank you again Reverend Turner for bringing us together for this discussion," Mary said warmly. "You have been a wonderful host. The Sermon on the Mount is found in Matthew, with parallel readings in Luke. There are quite a few topics here and we will go through them one by one."

On Prayer

"The disciples asked Jesus if prayers are answered. Jesus responded that our Lord in heaven is like a father and will surely give an answer to his children who ask. He said: 'Ask and it will be given to you; seek and you will find; knock and the door will be opened to you'."

Winston's emotions went raw. "The analogy of God being a father and all of us being his children does not ring true because we all know that many, or even most, of our prayers are not answered the way we want them to be." He dabbed his tearing eyes, as he remembered the son who had been taken away from him at such a young age. Everyone on the panel waited patiently to let him gather himself.

"I beg your pardon," he said to the audience. "Just a personal matter." Almost no one in the audience knew what he was talking about, but they were respectful just the same.

He quickly gathered himself and concluded his comments on a more professorial note. "I would like to add that many historians believe that the words of the Sermon on the Mount are more likely authentically Jesus than any of the other words attributed to him in the New Testament."

The Beatitudes

"The verses that we call the Beatitudes are very special," said Mary. "I would like to read them if I may."

Mary glanced over at George, who gave her a broad smile and a nod. They were special verses to him too.

Blessed are the meek, for they will inherit the earth.
Blessed are those who mourn, for they will be comforted.
Blessed are those who hunger and thirst for righteousness, for they will be filled.
Blessed are the merciful, for they will be shown mercy.
Blessed are the pure in heart, for they will see God.
Blessed are the rich in spirit, for they will sit with God.
Blessed are the peacemakers, for they will be called sons of God.
Blessed are those who are persecuted because they prophesy for God, for theirs is the Kingdom of Heaven.

"These blessings are amazing to me," Joshua said admiringly. "They are not the kind of blessings we find in the Jewish Bible or in Jewish prayer services. I like them very much and feel sad they have not been part of Judaism for all these centuries."

Salt and Light

"Jesus called his followers 'the salt of the earth and the light of the world'," Mary continued, and quoted Jesus as saying: "'A city on a hill cannot be hidden. Let your light shine before men, that they may see your good deeds and praise the Lord, our Father in heaven.'"

"This passage sounds very Jewish to me," said Joshua. "We like to call ourselves 'a light unto the nations' and believe that we have been chosen to spread the truth of the One God. When Jesus said this, he was talking not just to his followers, but to all Jews."

The Fulfillment of the Law

"Jesus spoke many times about the Law of Moses and how to honor it and keep it," said Mary going on to the next topic. "He said that not even the tiniest stroke of any of the words—such as dotting an 'i' or crossing a 't'—would disappear from the Law 'until everything is accomplished'."

"This is a teaching most Jews would be surprised at," Joshua interjected. "Paul claimed that the advent of Jesus made the law irrelevant. He quoted Jesus as saying he came to replace the law. That is one of the reasons Jews have rejected Jesus as even being a prophet, because no Jewish prophet would have said that.

"It seems clear from what Dr. Roberts just said that Jesus would have been appalled at the notion he came to replace the law," Joshua continued. "He believed just the opposite, and that is what he preached. Jesus was an Orthodox Jew for his entire life and never wavered from that. When he said 'not an iota, not a dot' will be changed, he was referring to the Torah, which has always been written by hand, in ink, and on parchment by the best and most learned scribes in the Jewish world

"There was no concept in Judaism that the Law would ever be replaced. The rabbis taught that the Torah existed before the universe was created and would be in effect forever in heaven as on earth. Jesus obviously believed that too, despite the words that Paul incorrectly put in Jesus' mouth."

"Paul discarded many Jewish practices and beliefs," agreed Winston. "My research suggests that Jesus would not have concurred with most of those changes. Essentially, Paul replaced Judaism with Christianity, somewhat as we know it today. Most historians believe that Jesus had no desire to replace Judaism, only to broaden it and in some cases to reaffirm the strictness of it. Like other prophets of the past, he encouraged the people to repent of their erroneous ways and to renew their connections with God and God's laws."

"Jesus was exceedingly revolutionary in one way," Joshua added. "Although in Emet, Jesus gave total respect to the words of the Torah, he did not feel the same way about the rules made by the sages and rabbis of his time, such as those in the Talmud. To make an American comparison, if you think of the Torah as the Constitution, the Talmud would be Supreme Court decisions.

"I believe the sages and rabbis went too far in some of their 'Supreme Court decisions'. But those decisions are the rules the Orthodox Jews of today follow, and of course, they believe all other Jews should follow them too. I agree with Jesus, that those decisions are 'advisory' and not mandatory upon us. All the non-Orthodox movements in Judaism believe that way too to varying degrees."

"That is a very interesting way of looking at it," mused George out loud. "So you would say that a lot of what the Orthodox Jews call Jewish Law is only 'advisory'?"

"That's right," said Joshua. "That is what I and most Jews today believe. But the Orthodox are not tolerant of our views. They think of us the same way traditional Catholics regard the various Protestant movements. The Protestants do not agree with the Catholics that the Vatican is the final arbiter of God's Word. Similarly, we do not regard the rules laid down by the Orthodox rabbinic authorities as God's Word."

"Like most Europeans today, I think it is dangerous for people of any religion to be sure they have all the answers," said Winston. "That is the attitude that is most responsible for all the religious wars and strife we have had throughout our human history."

"I entirely agree with you Winston," said George.

"I do too," said Joshua.

"Well, I for one don't agree," Mary said firmly. "When we know what God says and what God wants, to be anything but strictly obedient is just plain wrong. God's rules are not subject to human dilution. The Bible gives us God's Word and we don't get to decide what parts we like and what parts we don't have to follow."

Mary paused to let the other panelists respond. No one had anything else to add, so she went on to make her final point.

"If God came down to you and personally told you what He wanted you to do, you would do it, right? This is what we have in the Bible. The problem of those who don't follow the Bible is that they either don't really believe in God, or they don't believe the Bible is His word."

Joshua and Winston nodded their assent to what Mary just said, but for different reasons. Joshua was one who did not believe the Bible is literally God's word. Winston was agreeing because he was one who did not believe in God anymore.

Mary continued, "Jesus went on to talk about six specific laws and told how they should be understood and observed."

"In Emet, there were eight topics Jesus talked about," Joshua added. "The two extra topics—on women and on homosexuality—may have been eliminated from the gospels by later writers because what Jesus said about them didn't agree with church doctrine."

Murder, Anger and the Judicial System

"Jesus compared anger to murder and urged people to be reconciled with each other," said Mary. "He also recommended that it is better to settle your legal differences with each other than to go to court, because you are just as likely to be thrown into jail as to win. That is why there is a rule that Christians should not sue other Christians."

"In Emet, Jesus added that the laws always favor the rich and powerful," said Joshua, "which certainly seems to have been true throughout history. I would like to think that is not true in this country, but everyone knows the special interests have a much bigger voice than ordinary citizens have." Little did Joshua know how much the truth of this observation would come back to bite him later.

Adultery

The subject of adultery was in the forefront of Mary's mind because of her own husband's infidelity. Although in theory she might have been tempted to do the same, Mary never let herself contemplate committing adultery and told herself she never would.

"This passage on adultery is extremely timely today," she said with an irony only she understood, "when cheating on one's spouse is more rampant than ever in our country. Some people act like it's a normal activity, like taking out the garbage or walking the dog! I see couples out together and so often the husband or boyfriend is ogling the waitress or a woman at the next table. Men should be looking at their wives like that!" Mary's eyes teared up and she did not feel able to continue.

Joshua did not know anything about Mary's private life, but he saw she was upset, so he picked up where Mary left off. "Here Jesus was drawing from the 7th Commandment, 'Thou shalt not commit adultery'. He said that 'anyone who looks at a woman lustfully has already committed adultery with her in his heart'. He said if your eye or hand causes you to sin, it is better to cut it off and throw it away, because it is better to lose one part of your body than to have your whole body thrown into hell.

"I want to make two points here. Judaism believes that you don't get punished for your thoughts — only for your actions. So Jesus was apparently stricter than even Jewish law was. However, I don't believe he intended to change Jewish law that way — I believe he was only trying to make a point. I think he was trying to steer people toward a more pure *inner* life so as to prepare them for the coming of the Kingdom of God.

"The other point is the use of the word 'hell'. 'Hell' is the English translation of the Hebrew word 'Gehenna'. Gehenna was one of the two principal valleys surrounding Jerusalem. It was a place where the idol-worshippers of that time sacrificed their children by fire to their pagan gods. So Gehenna became synonymous with the place the wicked went to die. The fire sacrifices became associated in Christianity with burning in hell. That is how Jesus could say that it is better to lose your hand to 'hell' than your whole body.

"Judaism does not believe in hell and mainstream Judaism doesn't really say what happens to the wicked. However, according to the mystical beliefs in the Kabbalah, those who are wicked must spend more time in a purgatory-like state to purify their souls, before they can be given another chance and are reincarnated. I personally believe that really evil souls, like for example Hitler and Stalin, do not go to purgatory to be given another chance. I believe their souls are either permanently consigned to purgatory or are completely extinguished."

"Are you saying Judaism believes in reincarnation?" Mary asked with surprise. "I've never heard that."

"Most Jews have never heard of it either," Joshua answered her. "Mainstream Judaism does not believe in reincarnation, so it is something most of us are not taught. But the mystical tradition of the Kabbalah does talk about reincarnation. Mainstream Judaism has not adopted very much from the Kabbalistic teachings — the most important exception being what we call *tikkun olam*, repair of the world. But I personally believe the Kabbalah is right about the existence of reincarnation and I have incorporated a form of reincarnation into my theology of Judaism. That is one of the reasons they say I teach new age Judaism."

On Women

Joshua introduced the next topic, because there was no comparable passage in the gospels. "On the subject of women, Emet quoted Jesus as saying:

"Eve was given to Adam to keep him company for he was lonely without her.
Do not think of women as secondary, for they support you and all that is best in you.
God gave them smaller bodies but greater love. Hearken unto them and do what they say, for the word of God is within them."

"Well, obviously Jesus never said those things about women," Mary objected. "If he had, at least one of the New Testament evangelists would have quoted him. He definitely would not have said that men should do what women say."

Then she said in a whisper, "If I didn't tell my husband what to do, nothing would get done around our house." The microphone picked it up and the audience roared with laughter. Mary got red with embarrassment at first, and then she too broke into a good-natured laugh. Her professional face relaxed, and her natural beauty radiated throughout the chapel.

Joshua looked at her transfixed. Mary noticed him looking at her and her face glowed even more. She looked at him coquettishly and Joshua had to look away because now it was his turn to feel embarrassed. George saw what was going on with them and broke into a wide smile.

"Joshua, do you have anything to add?" George could hardly restrain himself from laughing out loud, knowing he was catching Joshua at a weak moment and was good-naturedly enjoying his befuddlement.

Joshua became red-faced and needed a few moments to gather himself. An unconscious part of him was wishing he was close enough to Mary to have her tell *him* what to do around the house.

"Um...this passage from Emet shows that Jesus understood women a lot better than most of the men of his time and that he was not a male chauvinist, which I find very appealing in him. I'll bet he really said these things about women and that later writers took it out of the New Testament because it didn't support the male-centered doctrine of the

Catholic Church. You can see by his relationship with Mary Magdalene that he respected women more than most men did."

"Such a statement in his time and place would have made Jesus most extraordinary," Winston added, also enjoying Joshua's momentary embarrassment. "But we already knew that about him!"

Homosexuality

Joshua also introduced the next topic, because again there was no comparable passage in the gospels. "On the subject of homosexuality, Emet quoted Jesus as saying:

"You have heard that it was said, 'Do not lie with a man as one lies with a woman; for that is an abomination to the Lord.'
But I tell you this law was meant to apply only to those who are given to procreate.
For the Lord made men who lie with men as well as men who lie with women and He loves them both."

Mary became very serious. "For Emet to claim that our Lord would excuse homosexuality is blasphemous! The Old and New Testaments are both very clear on the matter of same-sex relationships! God condemns both the sin and the sinner! Jesus would never change God's eternal word; it is Truth then and now and forever… 'until heaven and earth pass away!'"

George did his best to maintain his composure while Mary spoke. She had not been looking at him, but he felt her piercing words personally nonetheless.

"Well, I think what Jesus said in Emet makes sense," Joshua said with equal seriousness. "After all, gay and lesbian people do exist and were created by God, so why would God make them that way and then send them to hell as sinners. I think Jesus was much more loving and accepting than he has been given credit for."

Winston disagreed with Joshua. "It is highly doubtful Jesus would have said this in the pre-scientific age in which he lived. This passage is something that gives some credence to Mary's contention that all or part of Emet is untrue."

George could not let this discussion pass without adding his views. "I have to agree with Joshua. We need to be tolerant and accepting of all of God's creatures, without regard to their sexual orientation, color of their skin, ethnicity, or religion. Jesus, the great man and prophet that he was, felt and believed this. He was ahead of his time in so many other ways, it makes sense that he was ahead of his time in this way also."

Mary had more to say, but decided to wait until it was time for the Discussion segment

The Golden Rule

"The next three sections of Emet are almost verbatim from Matthew and Luke," Mary observed. "They say:

Keep your word; you don't have to take an oath to convince others how sincere you are.
Turn the other cheek; remember that everything we have and all that we are is a gift from God, who expects us to be giving and loving.
Love your enemies and pray for those that persecute you; and remember the Golden Rule — do unto others as you would have them do unto you."

"You summarized it very well, Mary," Joshua concurred. "I like many of the softer things Jesus taught. Judaism is often very legalistic — you can't do this and you must do that. Jesus focused a lot on thoughts and attitudes toward others, which, while not absent from Judaism, does not get the emphasis Jesus gave to it. Jesus' teachings about loving your enemies remind me of when God said not to rejoice at the deaths of the Egyptians in the Red Sea. He said the Egyptians are 'My children too'. Of course, what you call the Golden Rule was essentially said by the great Jewish teacher Hillel years before Jesus was even born and is as old as Leviticus — 'Love your neighbor as yourself.'"

"One cannot understand these texts without understanding the culture Jesus dwelled in," Winston pointed out. "The Law of Moses already contained a provision to limit revenge — it said the punishment must not be greater than the crime. But here Jesus took up the idea that there must be *no* revenge exacted. Jesus also used some irony in his preaching and the section on turning the other cheek is full of irony.

"There is so much more that a reader of the gospels needs to know to really get a clearer perspective on the world of Jesus. He did not preach like a preacher in our day, either from a pulpit so high it is just a bit removed from heaven or in front of a gigantic television screen projecting his image to the masses. He did not use 21st century images or patterns of thought. He walked, he stopped, and he talked.

"He talked in Aramaic, but all the gospels except Emet were written in Greek. Who knows what was lost or changed in the translation. There are concepts in every language that cannot be exactly translated into any other language. We do not know which things Jesus said that could not be correctly translated. Historians such as myself try to help the reader understand what Jesus meant—and what his listeners understood—by the phrases and metaphors he used.

"When Jesus said turn the other cheek to an evil one who hits you, he was not just teaching morality; he was being ironic and the people he taught knew that. Today, we might call that being passive-aggressive. Turning the other cheek after getting hit invites the aggressor to hit you again, but enables the victim to keep his dignity. Giving away your coat when you are only asked for your shirt? Now there are half-naked people all over the place! Quite jolly, that! Go two miles when only one is demanded of you? Jesus was telling us to show the other person he was being unfair by giving more than he asked.

"People living under brutal Roman occupation were being told not to resist but also to show the Romans *they* were acting immorally. The people who were listening to Jesus understood the double purpose of his teaching."

Heavenly Values

"Jesus gave very explicit instructions on exercising three well-known religious requirements," Mary began, introducing the next topic. "They are usually called 'Practicing our Piety' and have these components: giving alms to the poor, praying, and fasting for spiritual reasons. His basic message was: do these things that God requires, but don't do them as show-offs. The treasures that matter are those we accumulate in heaven, and the one who is pious gives light to those around him. The only praise that really matters is in knowing we have pleased God."

"These are beautiful passages that have been echoed by some of the great rabbis in the Middle Ages," Joshua said. "But if Jesus said them, Jews would ignore them because they came from Jesus. That is because the Christians have used him as an excuse for killing us over the years. I don't think that it is necessary any more for us to ignore the good teachings of Jesus, and I hope the discovery of this Book of Emet will help us recognize what wonderful things Jesus has contributed to Jewish thought. Our own texts teach us: 'Who is wise? He who learns from every man.' How much more so should we be willing to learn from one of our own!"

"Very well said Rabbi," said Winston.

"I want to make a comment about The Lord's Prayer," Mary continued. "The familiar version, of course, comes from Matthew 6:5-15. And in Luke11:2-4 we find it in shorter form. Jesus taught us this prayer so we wouldn't get long-winded and kid ourselves into thinking that God honors only long prayers. It has everything the Heavenly Father knows we need when we pray to Him. We are to begin with praising God for His glory, then end with bringing our needs to Him. Praise first, petition last. It always works.

"Jesus also taught us not to worry about tomorrow for the Lord will provide," Mary added.

"By the bye," Winston chimed in, "the saying in America that 'God helps those that help themselves' does not come from the Bible, but rather from Benjamin Franklin's *Poor Richard's Almanac*. In point of fact, Proverbs says that he who relies on himself and not on God is doomed to failure."

Who Is Righteous

"'Judge not lest ye be judged'," quoted Mary. "In saying this, Jesus taught that we should not judge others unless we apply the same rules first to ourselves, and then judge them in like manner. The apostle Paul in Galatians 6 wrote that when a brother or sister sins, they are to be restored gently to the fellowship of believers. The point here is that we should not think of ourselves as being better than we are.

"Jesus also taught us to stay on the straight and narrow path, and not listen to false teachers who could lead us astray. You will have a strong foundation if you build your life on the teachings of Jesus, but if you do not follow his teachings, you will have a shaky foundation that won't stand up to life's storms. Only Jesus can help us through those rough times."

"The key thing to understand about Jesus from a Jewish point of view," said Joshua, "is that when he said follow these words of mine, he meant follow the words of God, because like the other prophets who preceded him, when he said 'me' or 'mine' or 'I', he was quoting God, not himself. Most Christian leaders say the way to heaven is through Jesus. A Jew would say, and Jesus would say, the way to heaven is through God and God's Torah."

"That is absolutely not true," said Mary quickly. "Jesus said: 'I am the way and the truth and the life. No one comes to the Father except through me.' There is no way you can interpret the 'I' in that statement as coming from the Father."

"I agree with you Mary," Winston concurred at first, "that would have been what Jesus meant when he said 'I' in that statement. But that statement comes from John 14:6. John was written much later than the other gospels and most historians don't believe the narrations in John are very accurate. While no one can disprove that Jesus made that statement, none of the more respected earlier gospels contain it. Therefore, I would doubt that Jesus said it at all."

Mary was taken aback at Winston's words, but she could not let them pass without objection. "Sir Winston, you can't just dismiss things Jesus said just because they came from John. That we have to go through Jesus is the essence of Christianity. I assure you that whether the earlier gospels said it or not, it was always known to be true."

Now it was Joshua's turn to object. "We Jews don't believe you need an intercessor to get to God. We pray to Him directly. We find it strange that you believe you need to go through Jesus to get to God, especially since you believe that Jesus *is* God. That you have to believe in Jesus to be saved also seems strange to us. We think believing in God is enough, and even that isn't required if you lead a righteous life. We believe God loves all His children of whatever faith, even the ones who don't believe in Him. If they are good people, He is as happy with them as He is with us. In Judaism, what you do is much more important than what you believe."

We Are All Children of God

"Certainly the next section of the Book of Emet supports your view, Joshua," said Winston. "It says we are all children of God and that we each have a God-given soul and we all have been given our own special mission from God. I know I've always felt that way—that something inside me told me what direction to take in my life."

"That sense of mission you feel, Winston, comes from Jesus, who speaks to you on behalf of the Father," Mary explained. "This section of Emet is not in any of the gospels and implies that Jesus is not any more special than anybody else. Those of us who have invited Jesus into our lives and felt the happiness that brings know that is not true."

"I don't doubt for a minute the truth of what you say, Mary, insofar as it concerns true believers," George said in a rare contribution to the discussions. "But you must understand that those of us who are not true believers also receive messages from God about what to do with our lives. I know I did."

Joshua nodded his head in agreement.

The Little Children

Mary went on to the next topic. "After Jesus was done with his sermon, little children were brought to him to receive his blessing. The disciples tried to stop them, but Jesus said 'Let the little children come to me for the Kingdom of Heaven belongs to them'. And he added 'Anyone who does not receive the Kingdom of Heaven like a little child will never enter it'.

"His point was that to receive the Kingdom of Heaven like a child is to totally depend on God. We are to trust Him in everything. Jesus was so in tune with his Father in heaven that he just broke into prayer as if he had been talking to the Father the entire time. We who have the Holy Spirit in our hearts can connect with Jesus any time we want. Isn't that wonderful!" Mary's face was glowing.

Joshua was enchanted by Mary's luminous beauty, but he had to tear his eyes away so he could object to what Mary had just said. "I don't think you have to have the Holy Spirit in your heart to be able to pray sincerely to God. The Holy Spirit is a Christian concept. Observant Jews pray to God several times a day and some synagogues have prayer services twice a day, every day. Jesus said a simple prayer over the children, which is very sweet. Rabbis say a benediction for the congregation after every synagogue service. Muslims pray five times a day. I don't see anything specifically Christian about this."

"Jesus told the little children that the way to the Kingdom of Heaven is through him, through Jesus," Mary reiterated. "He said 'Come to me, all you who are weary and burdened, and I will give you rest…for I am gentle and humble in heart'. Jesus was talking about himself, not about the Father. He wouldn't be saying the Father is gentle and humble in heart."

"I disagree," said Joshua.

"What else is new?" Mary thought ruefully to herself.

"For the sake of the children," Joshua continued, "Jesus was trying to humanize God so none of the children would be afraid. We do that at our synagogue too, because we don't want to scare the children. Those preachers who preach fire and brimstone scare children half to death. Adults too for that matter. That is not the Jewish way.

"So I think he was telling the children about God when he said 'I am gentle and humble of heart', but he was also talking about himself, because children need a trusted human to relate to. Adults do too sometimes. I think that is why Christianity became so popular — because by making Jesus divine, God became more human and accessible."

Mary was finally able to agree with something Joshua said. "That's exactly right, Joshua. When it comes to God, we are all children. Jesus made it easier for all of us to come to the Father. God, in his great love for us, gave us his son so we can feel the love and give it back."

Discussion

"Reverend Turner, I'd like to start the discussion, if we're ready," Mary said when it did not appear anyone had anything else to add.

"Please do Mary," said George happily. He was enjoying the back and forth interplay of the two theologies.

"I've noticed that in Emet the disciples addressed Jesus with lesser names. In the first section of this chapter of Emet, On Prayer, a disciple of Jesus referred to the Heavenly Father as Lord and Jesus as only 'Master', as in 'Master, does the Lord answer our prayers?' But in Luke 11:1 and throughout the real gospels, the disciples called Jesus 'Lord' as in 'Lord, teach us to pray'. That shows that Jesus and the disciples shared the understanding that Jesus was the Son of God. Sir Winston claimed Jesus never referred to himself in this way."

"Excellent point, Mary," answered Winston. "Let us remember that the canonical gospels we have today — Matthew, Mark, Luke and John — were written long after the death of Jesus, by people who never knew him. They saw Jesus as the Messiah, the Christ, the Son of God, and wrote about him that way. Many historians believe that Jesus did not see himself that way."

"So you're saying the gospels deliberately misquoted Jesus and the disciples? That sounds like more conjecture by historians."

"It is most certainly not conjecture," Winston objected. "We have many copies of the gospels from the First Century through the Third Century. We can see that the words attributed to Jesus changed over time. Christians did not always believe that Jesus was God. That came many decades later. The various copies we have of the gospels reflect those changing views."

Mary was unconvinced, but what the disciples really called Jesus was a minor point and she had bigger fish to fry. She decided to change the subject.

"We need to talk some more about homosexuality. The Bible says God forbids it—that it's an abomination to the Lord! One of the best proofs that the Book of Emet is illegitimate is that it sanctions homosexuality, contrary to God's Holy Word. God made us male and female in order to procreate. 'Be fruitful and multiply' He commanded us in Genesis.

"Everyone who is physically normal has the ability to procreate. The Creator does not do anything that is against His holy and perfect will. That's why I believe homosexuality is a choice, not a condition as some say."

"Mary, I want to ask you a question, to help me clarify something," Joshua asked.

"Okay," she said suspiciously.

"How many gay and lesbian Christians do you know personally?"

"I've met a few former homosexuals that were healed through reparative therapy ministries."

"Okay. How many do you know that believe God created them gay, that it wasn't a choice?"

"None that I know of. Those people don't come to us for help. What are you getting at?"

"That when our worldview paints everyone the same, we don't make room for anyone to be different. Unless we sit down one-on-one with a person whose experiences differ from ours, and we really listen to that person share from the heart, we assume there is no more for us to learn on that topic.

"Young people in my synagogue have gay and lesbian Christian friends who sincerely believe God made them that way. A couple of years ago we offered an eight-week course on human sexuality and some of these young Christians attended. I was privileged to hear some of their stories. To a person, none of them could recall a time that they consciously chose to be gay. I remember one young man said, 'With all the hassle and prejudice and hatred against us, why in the world would I *choose* to be something I'm not?'" Some grumbles of affirmation could be heard in the audience.

"I really liked those kids," Joshua continued. "They were honest and clear thinking. They didn't know what to do with those negative verses in Genesis or Leviticus, and in Paul's Epistle to the Romans, but they were asking hard questions about them as they were moving from adolescence into adulthood. And, many of them loved Jesus more than our Jewish young people love Torah. I was really hoping some of their religious devotion would rub off! Bottom line, we are talking about real people, not some group that can be written off as immoral just because they are different."

George nodded his head approvingly as Joshua spoke.

"I can appreciate that these people have feelings and that many of them want to follow Christ," Mary argued, "but their choices get in the way, just as the sins any of us commit get in the way of maintaining a good relationship with the Lord. The Scriptures were written for all time by God Himself. We don't get to change them or make them say something they don't say. And the personal feelings or 'experiences' of the homosexuals you talked about don't change the Word of God. Scripture is the final authority on all matters under heaven! I'm sorry that those young people have been led astray, but there is hope and healing for them in Jesus."

"You can say that so positively because you believe Emet is fiction. What if Jesus really did say what Emet says he said? What if Jesus really did speak for God, as God's chosen prophet, to tell us that God loves gays and lesbians too?"

Mary was thoroughly touched by Joshua's words and his humanity. "What if Jesus really did say that?" she thought. "That would change everything. What if God's Word could be updated by later spokesmen, prophets, God's son? What might Jesus say when he returns? I'm really going to have to give this some thought. Wouldn't it be nice not to assume all those people are going to hell?"

Mary took a deep breath as the enormity of that possible revelation sank in. "Oh my, that would be sooooo confusing! But I like the way this Joshua thinks. He really has a big heart. No wonder he has such a large following."

Before anyone else could speak, George noticed that there were only 30 seconds remaining. "Time for a word from our sponsors," he joked. We will be back in a few minutes.

Backstage

Joshua excused himself and went to the Men's Room down the hall. Just as he was coming back, he felt his cell phone vibrate in his pocket. Nervously, he retrieved it and found another text message on it, again from Reverend Paul Lindenbaugh. "Now you're saying Jesus defended homosexuality? You are full of the words of Satan. We cannot let this go on!!! Stop and think! Think of your sister…"

A worried look crossed his face, and Mary, ever the observant one, noticed.

"I can't help noticing that you are getting messages that you find upsetting," she said softly. "Every time your phone beeps you jump."

"I'm sorry, I really can't tell you. It's…uh…personal. You wouldn't understand, anyway."

"Try me. I went to divinity school, remember?"

"No. I have to deal with this by myself. I cannot involve anybody else."

The phone signaled a new message. Joshua quickly looked down at it but he was so nervous he dropped the phone. "Oy!" he instinctively uttered under his breath as he stooped down and fumbled for it. When he opened it and saw who the message was from, he sighed with relief. "Ahhhh, thank God."

"Well?" Mary began, "Good news I hope?"

"Yes," Joshua smiled. "It's one of my friends from Chicago. He says I'm doing a kick-ass job and he's cheering me on."

"Tell him all the Gentiles are rooting for me," Mary quipped back.

Joshua laughed. "Okay, but he's not Jewish. He's a not-so-good Italian Catholic boy who now practices Buddhism and teaches yoga at the meditation center near my synagogue. We met at an interfaith dialogue and became good friends. I give him tennis lessons and he gives me meditation lessons."

"I see," said Mary laughing. "But what about the other messages? Right now you look like you just dodged a bullet. May as well tell me. I'm very persistent."

Joshua glanced around the room to make sure no one else was listening. He exhaled loudly before continuing. "I have a sister, Esther, my only sibling. She is severely mentally and physically disabled. I had to put her in a specialized nursing home after my mother passed away, because she needs more help than I can give her. I tried home health aides and nurses, but she needs more than that. It is very expensive, more than $10,000 a month. I do fairly well as a rabbi and writer and guest speaker, but not *that* well."

"I'm so sorry to hear that," Mary said sympathetically. "Are you being threatened by bill collectors? They hounded my sister unmercifully."

"I wish it were that simple." Joshua was speaking very softly. "I was so desperate I made what I thought was an innocent deal to make some quick money."

"What did you do? Sell your soul to the devil?" Mary asked jokingly with a smile.

"It seems to have turned out that way and…Oh, my God! I can't tell you this! You'd want to hang me from the nearest tree."

"Whatever are you talking about, Joshua? You are starting to scare me."

"Oh God…. Here goes, and you cannot tell anyone what I am about to tell you."

"Okay, I promise."

"Do you know the name Paul Lindenbaugh?"

"Of course, Reverend Paul! He is well known among Evangelicals. He has a mega-church and a terrifically successful TV show and he is a huge contributor to many ministries around the world. He takes in more money in a day than I do in a year. Why?"

"Somebody called me...someone who said he worked for Paul Lindenbaugh. He told me he had heard about my sister and that I could use some help with her care. He said Reverend Paul would pay me a million dollars if I would 'let some things go' during the debates. He told me that this would be better 'for all concerned.' It turned out he was talking about me and my sister. The implication is that if I don't do as he says, Paul Lindenbaugh will not 'guarantee' our safety."

"This is incredible! Reverend Paul *Lindenbaugh*? Really? It can't be! Why would he do such a horrible thing? And besides, surely he knows I can handle myself quite well. I've been called a spitfire more than once or twice before!" Mary smiled with pride at the understatement.

"I don't know why, but I can guess some reasons. All I know for sure is he wants me to 'let you win,' so to speak. The texts I'm getting keep alluding to the health and safety of my sister. I am worried sick."

"So are you trying to 'throw' the debate to save your sister? I sure don't get that impression."

"Not really throw the debate, no, but I told him I would go easy on you. There have been times I think I've done that a little. You know, letting some things pass more than I usually would. I'm not so worried about myself, but I am terrified they will do something to Esther. She is so helpless. And she is in Chicago and I am here. Apparently, they think I am doing too well anyway because the threats are increasing.

"And then last night I saw Lindenbaugh himself in the balcony wearing his usual white suit, which really scared me. But I can't and won't give in to him because these issues are too important to me and the Jewish people. It's not really about Jesus or even Emet. It's more about how we Jews see ourselves and how others see us. It's very complicated. Maybe someday I'll explain it to you. I didn't realize when I made this deal that there would be threats. If I disappointed him, I just figured he wouldn't pay me the money. Now it almost feels like I am dealing with the Mafia and that someone is going to get hurt if I don't do exactly what he says. I hate to admit it, but I am scared they have something really bad planned."

Mary was deeply touched by Joshua's concern for his sister and his people, and the threats against him "got her Irish up". She always had a special feeling for the Jewish people, and she did not like seeing *anyone* threatened. And she felt insulted on some level that Reverend Paul did not think she could "win" the debate on her own. She suddenly felt aligned with Joshua and wanted to help him see this through. Suddenly, "winning" the debate was no longer her only motivation.

"Don't worry Joshua, we will get you through this," Mary said defiantly as she squeezed his hand reassuringly. Joshua wanted to take her in his arms and kiss her to show his appreciation of her new-found support. But at that moment, George entered the room and motioned for everyone to return to the stage.

Outside the Chapel

Judith and Bryce had come early again to see the second night of the Great Debate and were able to get the same place on the lawn they had the night before.

"What an amazing segment that was," whistled Judith with awe. "I really like the way Emet talks about gays and lesbians and women."

"I do too," Bryce agreed.

"You know my real father is gay," Judith confided.

"No fooling!" Bryce exclaimed. "Before he came out of the closet, eh?"

"It's a long story. I'll tell you some other time. Let's go for a little walk and unwind a little. This debate may not mean much to you, but for me it is almost earthshaking."

"Why is that?" Bryce asked as they began walking.

"To think of Jesus as being Jewish, saying Jewish things, trying to make Judaism better, I never imagined such a possibility. We all grew up either thinking Jesus was irrelevant to us or that he was our enemy. The Christians did so much harm to us in his name. It never occurred to me to think of Jesus as a *Jewish* prophet, a Jewish patriot."

"The same for us," Bryce concurred. "We never thought of Jesus as Jewish. He was the first Christian, our leader, our inspiration, our friend. 'Oh what a friend we have in Jesus,'" he sang and then laughed. "It's been a long time since I've sung that. If we thought of Jews at all, it was in a negative way because they fought Jesus every step of the way and they ended up killing him."

"That's the other earthshaking thing," said Judith. "Rabbi Hertzel is saying the Jews really didn't fight Jesus and that they had no reason to, because he was saying Jewish stuff to them. He's saying the later Christians changed what Jesus really said."

"That wouldn't surprise me at all," Bryce affirmed. "I mean, I wasn't there and who knows what really happened. You have the Bible and you have this Book of Emet. I don't really believe either one of them but the people at my parents' church are going crazy over this. They feel like everything they believe in is under attack and they don't like it one bit."

"A lot of the Jewish leaders are the same way," Judith said with annoyance. "They are so committed to their usual way of thinking, they can't deal with anything involving Jesus in a positive way. But some of the others — the ones who are involved in ecumenical groups, are really happy, because they think it will bring Jews and Christians even closer together. It is really very confusing.

"Looking at this crowd over there tonight, I don't get the feeling that anything will change for some of these Christians." The organized mob on the left lawn had Judith feeling nervous and apprehensive.

Bryce nodded and put his arm around Judith's shoulders. Judith immediately felt better.

"We better go back to our spot," he said. "The next segment will be starting soon."

The Book of Emet

Chapter Five: Teachings

You have broken faith with the wife of your youth, though she is
your partner, the wife of your marriage covenant.
Has not God made them one? In flesh and spirit they are his. And
why one? Because he was seeking godly offspring. So guard yourself
in your spirit, and do not break faith with the wife of your youth.
"I hate divorce," says the Lord God of Israel. [Malachi 2:13-16.]

Divorce and Adultery

As usual, Mary opened the first topic. "Jesus said whoever divorces his
or her wife or husband, except for marital infidelity, and then remarries,
commits adultery. In those days, anyone who committed adultery could
be punished by being stoned to death. On this issue, he was stricter than
Jewish law because he wouldn't permit divorce at all, except in cases of
marital infidelity."

"Yes, he was very strict about marriage and divorce," Joshua added,
"but then there is the story that tells of Jesus coming to an adulteress's
defense. He said 'let the one without sin cast the first stone.' So it's like
Jesus said there should be no divorce, but if you did divorce or commit
adultery by having sex with another person, no one should be allowed to
punish the adulterer because no one else is without sin either."

"Yes," said Winston, "that is an interesting juxtaposition, where Emet
had the divorce prohibition and the 'cast no stone' story in successive

passages. They are not united in this way in the Bible. Most historians believe the story about casting the first stone was made up and added much later, because that story is only told in the Gospel of John and the oldest versions of John do not include this episode. So it is very doubtful Jesus ever said this."

"I have heard that also," Mary said, "but I still believe it came from our Lord. Maybe it was just found later."

Joshua cautiously ventured out to say something. "Emet shows us a Jesus whose prophetic gifts included…"

"There's only one Jesus, Hertzel!" cried a voice from the balcony, "and the one you talk about is not him! You speak for Satan! Only Roberts speaks for God!" The panel was stunned by this brief tirade, and watched in silence as security officers grabbed the man, who was standing in the balcony, and removed him from the building. Everyone could hear his voice as it trailed off in the distance, "They are blaspheming the Bible, God's Holy Word! Jesus was and *is* the Son of God! You don't know what you're talking about! Go ahead, arrest me! *There are a lot more of us.…*"

The entire chapel was buzzing with shocked and fearful conversation. As the man was yelling, George noticed for the first time the security officers surrounding the panelists on stage. In the balcony, he saw two officers escorting out several people from the area where the man had been sitting. An officer told George that the other people taken out were just being questioned to find out what they knew about the man. The other panelists sat in stunned silence, observing everything and wondering what might happen next.

Soon, the officer came back and whispered something in George's ear and gave him the thumbs up sign. The host quieted the room and explained the situation: "Campus security tells me the building is secure, and as far as they know this was an isolated incident. Let's see…where were we? Oh, it was Rabbi Hertzel, I think. Rabbi?"

Joshua heard nothing. All his brain could focus on was this — the man who yelled was sitting in the exact same far right corner of the balcony where, the previous evening, the man dressed all in white had been.

"Joshhhh…shua," Mary cooed softly, "I said something about the story of the adulteress being legitimate, and you were starting to say that the Book of Emet.…"

"Uh, uh…I'm sorry, yes, I remember what I wanted to say. Emet shows us a Jesus whose prophetic gifts included a more complex understanding of human nature than we see in the New Testament. Thank you," he mouthed silently, smiling at Mary, but still visibly shaken.

"Also, I wanted to add that Jewish law today is not as strict as Jesus was, and is much less strict than some branches of Christianity. The Orthodox Jews believe that God does put you together with who you marry, but that sometimes, human frailty being what it is, if the marriage becomes untenable, then divorce is permitted."

The Rich Young Man

"In this next story," Mary began, "a wealthy man came to Jesus telling him that he had obeyed all the commandments of the law and wanted to know what more he must do to have eternal life. Jesus praised the man for his religiosity, but then told him that he should give up all his wealth to the poor and become one of Jesus' followers. Jesus told him his earthly wealth would be replaced by the treasure he would have in heaven. The rich young man could not bring himself to give away his wealth, because he had many things he could not let go of. Jesus famously said: 'It is easier for a camel to go through the eye of a needle than for a rich man to enter the Kingdom of God.'"

"By his emphasis on giving to the poor, Jesus spoke like the wise Jewish sage he was," said Joshua. "He knew that we study Torah, not only for its own sake, but also to live it. What you do is more important than what you believe. This is and was the Jewish view.

"However, Paul said that what you do in life doesn't matter — all that is needed for eternal life is for you to believe in Jesus as the Son of God and your savior. I think that this is a contradiction in the theology of Christianity that cannot be reconciled. Obviously Jesus took the Jewish view, that *what you do in life is what matters, not what you believe.*"

"I agree with Joshua about this being a contradiction," Winston said, "and so do most historians. My reading of the source material tells me that this encounter probably occurred and Jesus may well have said this to an inquirer. Jesus often used aphorisms to make a point. This one about the camel is an example of his use of humor. The crowds might have forgotten the rest of what he taught, but no one can forget the impossible picture the teacher painted for them of a camel trying to go through the eye of a needle."

"I don't see any contradiction here," Mary said firmly. "Jesus also said the way to salvation is through him. So belief and good works are important. We believe that good works naturally follow your commitment to Christ, so while belief is the most important thing, it is also expected that if you are a true believer, you will also do good things."

No one offered any further comments on this point, so Mary went on to the next part of the story.

"The disciples then asked Jesus, if the rich man could not get into the Kingdom of Heaven, what will happen to them, who had left everything to follow Jesus. He answered that the Son of Man—that would be Jesus—will sit on his heavenly throne and give thrones to the twelve disciples. From those thrones, the twelve disciples will then rule the twelve tribes of Israel. Jesus also said that anyone who left their families, their land, and their houses to follow him would receive eternal life."

"In Emet, Jesus said it will be God's messenger, the Messiah, who will sit on the heavenly throne, and Jesus did not say he was this messenger," Joshua reported. "Also, there were not thrones for the disciples, but Jesus said those who follow him would be rewarded for doing God's work. Then Mary Magdalene asked Jesus what will become of him when the Kingdom of Heaven comes. Jesus said he had a special relationship with God that would continue in death as in life."

"This is where, as you Yanks like to say, the rubber hits the road," Winston said to a light chuckle from the audience. "The New Testament says that Jesus will be on a throne, like God Himself, and the twelve disciples will be ruling the twelve tribes of Israel. The Book of Emet says Jesus has a special relationship with God, but otherwise he is almost as uncertain of what comes next for him as the rest of us are. Which version is the correct one depends on what you think of the Book of Emet."

The Parable of the Good Samaritan

"Probably the most famous story in the New Testament is the Parable of the Good Samaritan," Mary said with a big smile on her face. This was one of her favorite stories. "Samaritans lived in a separate region between Galilee, to the north, where Jesus was from, and Judea, to the south, where we find Jerusalem and Bethlehem. Jews looked down on Samaritans because they were the products of intermarriage with

Assyrians, dating back to the 8th century B.C. when Assyrian armies invaded Israel, settling there and taking Hebrew wives. Intermarriage was banned under the Law of Moses."

"Perhaps the greatest offender of the law against intermarriage," Joshua interjected, "was none other than the 'wisest' king in Israel's history, King Solomon, who reportedly had ten thousand wives and concubines from all over the world. Those numbers boggle the mind. To pay for his extravagant lifestyle, he raised taxes so high that the people groaned under them. When his son Jeroboam became king, Jeroboam was asked to lower the taxes but refused to do so. The result was a revolt against him from the tribes to the north, the ones who later became the ten lost tribes. The ten tribes made a separate country that they called Israel, and the other two tribes called what was left of their country Judea."

Mary jumped back in, feeling that Joshua was off subject. "The point is that Jews and Samaritans didn't like each other and didn't get along with each other.

"In this parable, two Jewish priests came upon a fellow Jew who had been beaten and robbed and left beside the road, and they did nothing to help him. However, he was saved and helped by a Samaritan. This parable shows that kindness can come from any person attuned to God, even from those who you don't like and who don't like you. This parable also shows that Jesus was thinking beyond just serving the Jewish people, for he found value in all peoples."

"Personally, I like that Jesus saw value in other peoples," said Joshua admiringly. "Although Jesus said he was sent to help only the flock of Israel, he had a world-wide perspective too. Most of the great Jewish leaders of the past also had a broad world view. In fact, the idea of the Messiah was not only to bring safety and justice for the Jewish people, but also to bring peace on earth for all peoples."

Three Parables

"The next three parables related in Emet continue the theme of mercy—God's mercy on us, and our responses of showing mercy to others, or not. The theme of self-centeredness is here, as well." Mary went on then to summarize those parables:

"In 'A Brother Who Sins Against You', Jesus says that the appropriate response to being wronged is to go to the other person and try to work out your differences. You try to raise your brother's consciousness so that your relationship can be reconciled.

"'The Parable of the Unmerciful Servant' shows, with very extreme consequences, what happens when we refuse to be merciful to others. A servant whose debts to his master were forgiven did not forgive the debts that other servants owed him. Therefore, the master said he would not forgive the debts owed the first servant either and had him thrown in jail.

"Finally, 'The Parable of the Rich Miser' takes a hard look at selfishness which shows its ugly head as greed. A rich man decided to build a new building to hold all his possessions. No sooner was he done, than he passed away. The lesson being: be greedy with your possessions and God will take them *all* back, since He gave them to you in the first place."

"The first parable reminds me of Yom Kippur, the Jewish Day of Atonement and the holiest day of the year," said Joshua. "It is a day when God renders judgment on us: who is to live and who is to die, who is to be happy and who is to be struck low. It is also a day when we repent and ask God for forgiveness of our sins. However, the rabbis say that God will only forgive and atone sins against God. God does not atone or forgive sins against other people. To get forgiveness from them, you have to ask each person you sinned against to forgive you. And you have to offer to forgive them for any sins they committed against you. So, if you are a religious Jew, it is the custom on Yom Kippur to go to everyone in your life and ask them to forgive you for anything you have done to them in the past year, and to offer to forgive them for anything they did to you."

"I have always liked that custom, Joshua," Winston said.

"Yes, and it shows why we don't need someone to die for our sins," Joshua added. "We are not perfect and God does not expect for us to be perfect. By atoning for our own sins every year and having the slate wiped clean if we are sincere, we have the responsibility of trying to live up to the ideal. We do not give that responsibility to someone else and have a free ride through life. I am quite sure that Jesus would not have approved of that and I know God wouldn't."

There was a smattering of clapping from the audience, which George quickly quelled with a gesture. Mary, being a responsible person in her own life, saw some virtue in what Joshua was saying. But it did not have the feeling of total relief Christians have knowing that their sins are forgiven in advance if they believe in Jesus.

Seeing that Mary wasn't forthcoming with a rebuttal, Joshua went on to the third parable, which embodied what he believed in concerning social justice. "I wish 'The Parable of the Rich Miser' would have more influence than it does on the wealthy in our society. They seem to want more and more, and let those less fortunate than themselves have less and less. At some point, if they don't change their ways, somebody will take it away from them."

"That is certainly one of the lessons of history," Winston agreed. "The French Revolution is an excellent example of that."

Jesus Anointed by a Sinful Woman

"This next story is a profound statement about faith and God's forgiveness," Mary began. "The woman in the story had a bad reputation. She was a sinner who was moved by faith, and she hoped to be forgiven for her lifestyle. She went to the home where Jesus was staying, and without a word, began to wash his feet and anoint his hair. Due to her faith, she came to minister to Jesus without any strings attached and without asking for anything. And because of her faith, he forgave her sins."

Joshua said nothing. He was wondering if he would be forgiven by God for compromising himself with Paul Lindenbaugh. He knew he had a mission to fulfill and he silently reaffirmed his intention to do it the way it needed to be done. He did not care so much what would happen to him, but he prayed that his sister would not be made to pay a price.

"Mary, is not this episode more about love and forgiveness, rather than faith and forgiveness?" Winston suggested. "Jesus said that whoever loves little will be forgiven little."

"No Winston, I don't believe so. That interpretation would contradict two thousand years of Christian understanding. Jesus did not teach that the more loving a person is the more God will forgive him. God's grace and forgiveness cannot be earned by loving. What this woman did was show her faith, and her faith made her capable of turning her life around. She acted out her confession and her repentance, which made room in her soul to receive forgiveness from God."

Mary was feeling inspired, and looking at the audience said in her best preaching voice, "If you open your heart to Jesus and let him come in and give you his love, he will do so and change your life. You will be given a new soul and a new body. That is what trust in Jesus brings you."

George was signaled by the program's producer that time was up for this segment, which George dutifully passed on to the audience.

Backstage

"Are you alright Joshua?" Mary asked after taking a drink from her water bottle. "You looked pretty shaken during that man's outburst. I was wishing I could help you somehow." Her face showed the deep concern she felt.

"You did help!" he replied warmly. "I felt your good wishes coming my way, and they helped me bounce back to say what I wanted to say."

Mary felt happy that she was able to help him. "I was proud of you for standing in there — it was so scary! I kept scanning the auditorium for the next crazy person to start shouting. Even though that man agreed with my positions, I truly do not want support like *that!*" Mary's eyes flashed proudly.

"Yes yes," Winston joined in. "We need to keep everything civilized and on the up and up. We are just exchanging views here, not trying to change anyone's beliefs."

"We need to keep things professional," George added.

"Quite so, quite so," Winston agreed. "The constables are doing a jolly good job here. They will keep things orderly I presume."

"People are entitled to their beliefs," Joshua said. "It's when they try to force them on others... That is wrong!"

George and Winston nodded their heads in agreement, but Mary did not join in.

"You know, we used to force Christianity on others because we believed they would go to hell if they didn't believe in Jesus. Our missionaries felt that we were doing them a favor, even if they didn't like it. I used to feel that way too, but as I've gotten older and met proponents of other religions, especially those who believe in the same God we do, I have trouble believing they are all going to hell. I just don't believe it works that way."

"Unitarians don't believe it works that way either," George concurred. "It makes no sense that good people go to hell because there is something they don't believe, while bad people go to heaven just because they believe in Jesus. I agree with Joshua that neither God nor Jesus would be happy with that result."

"It made more sense when Christians thought they could convert the whole world to Christianity," Winston said in his professorial voice. "In those days, the Christians thought all the good people of the world would come to believe in Jesus because he was the son of the one and only God. All that was necessary was for the 'good news' to be brought to the ignorant. If that was insufficient, the Christians forced them to convert on pain of death, believing they were only doing what was good for them. Christian missionaries thought they were the ultimate idealists. Nowadays, no one believes the entire world will be converted to Christianity, so now even many Christians wonder what will happen to the good people of the world who are not and never will be Christians."

"That's an interesting way of looking at it Winston," Mary said thoughtfully. "When you get down to it, that probably explains why I don't believe all non-Christians are going to hell. However, I believe letting Jesus into your life brings you peace and happiness and God's grace and I have met many converts who have experienced that in their lives."

Joshua felt his cell phone vibrate in his pocket and apprehensively pulled it out to see if there was a message on it. The text said "You are treading on dangerous ground. You are not keeping your agreement." A wave of anger rose up within him and he wanted to throw the offending cell phone out the window.

He sat in the overstuffed chair he had been using and took a few gulps out of his water bottle. Soon he calmed down and felt better. He noticed Mary looking at him and he just shrugged his shoulders, which she correctly read as a sign he had received another message from

Reverend Paul. He laid his head back into the chair and closed his eyes, trying to take a break from the tension he was feeling. He was able to doze off for a few seconds before one of the students stepped into the room to announce, "It's time to return to the stage, everyone."

The Book of Emet

Chapter Six: Toward the Kingdom of God

And it shall come to pass in the end of days, they will beat their swords into plowshares and their spears into pruning hooks. Nation will not lift up sword against nation, nor will they learn war anymore.
The wolf will dwell with the lamb, the leopard will lie down with the goat, the calf and the young lion and the yearling together; and a little child shall lead them. . [Isaiah 2:4, 11:6.]

As usual, Mary started the discussion. "In this section, the disciples asked Jesus what signs will appear to tell them that the Kingdom of God is coming. Jesus told them to watch out that no one will deceive them, for many will come in God's name, claiming to be the Christ. And there will be wars and famines and earthquakes and those things will be the beginning of the birth pains of the coming of the new age. And Jesus told of many other disastrous things that will happen, but assured them that he who stands firm will be saved. Then Jesus said that when the new age comes, he will appear in the sky with power and great glory and the angels will gather the elect from one end of the heavens to the other.

"He told them that the day and hour are unknown, even by the angels. So be prepared, for it will be like Noah and the ark. One day, without warning, the flood will come, and they need to be ready."

"Jesus also said those things would happen in his own lifetime," Joshua responded. "But as I said before, those things did not happen in

Jesus' lifetime or in the lifetime of that generation, or any generation till now. So obviously Jesus was not that Messiah."

"Kill the Jew! Kill the Christ-killer!" someone shouted from the audience. Joshua's face became flush with anger and he was about to say something when Mary beat him to the punch.

"There is no place for that kind of talk here!" Mary admonished in her teacher's voice. "This is a civilized exchange of views. We are just having a discussion. There is no reason to want to kill anybody!"

George seconded her. "Please people, let's keep decorum here. If you can't listen like adults, you will be removed."

Meanwhile, the man who did the shouting managed to escape from the inside security guards by ducking out the side door of the chapel. However, the outside security guards were able to capture him. He was promptly arrested and taken away in handcuffs.

Judith and Bryce witnessed the whole scene inside the chapel on the big screen television, and then saw the capture of the shouting offender on the outside with their own eyes. Meanwhile, the mob outside became even more unruly and had Judith shaking with fright.

"Do you want to leave?" asked Bryce, feeling her shaking body next to his and seeing the look of a frightened animal in her eyes.

"No," she said bravely. "My father is in there and the security forces seem to have everything under control. We have to stand up and be counted against the haters."

Bryce was not so convinced. As the son of a prosecuting attorney, he had seen unruly crowds intimidate police forces before. But he did not want to say anything to scare Judith even more.

Repent or Perish

With the situation quieted, Mary bravely resumed the discussion. "Jesus used two recent tragic events—where some people were executed and others had a tower fall on them—as examples of people who perished before they repented. He said that everyone is given ample opportunity to turn their lives around. But if you do not confess and repent your sins, there is a good chance you will die before you repent, and thereby lose your chance for eternal life."

Joshua mostly agreed. "Judaism teaches that God is ever merciful and gives the sinner many chances to repent. *For it is our repentance, not our destruction that He seeks.* But we don't feel there is any deadline on this or that we should be in a panic to repent 'in time'. We don't believe in hell or eternal punishment. We believe that God looks at the totality of our lives in judging us, not whether we are fortunate enough repent our sins before we chance to die."

Winston was thinking of his deceased son. "In my view, Jesus was telling us that the people who died in these instances were not killed because they were judged adversely by God. As Jesus said, they were no more blameworthy than others who did not die. Rather, they were victims of political violence or natural disaster—two tragedies God does not cause. From this we learn that bad things can happen to good people and that the bad things that come to us do not mean we have been judged harshly by God."

"My view is that the bad things that happen in this world do not come from God," Joshua said softly, instinctively feeling Winston's anguish. "I believe God is all good, but I don't believe God is all powerful. I believe there is an evil side to this world. I like the Star Wars term for it — I call it the Dark Side. I believe that the Dark Side, not God, is responsible for the bad things that happen."

"I am somewhat aware of your views Joshua," said Winston, "but it does not give me any more comfort that my son may have been killed by the Dark Side instead of God. He is still gone."

Winston pulled out his kerchief and dabbed his eyes. George put his arm around him to comfort him. Winston looked up at George with gratitude and patted his knee. "Thank you George," he said warmly. George smiled back at him with that benevolent smile that made him such a beloved figure by all who knew him.

The Tax Collector of Jericho

Mary waited a few moments while Winston composed himself, and then went on to the next topic.

"This is a beautiful story, in which our Savior called upon a tax collector, who was hated in his community, to join the rest of the community in welcoming Jesus to town. The tax collector was so moved by the invitation that he gladly welcomed Jesus into his home *and* into his heart. He also promised to return all the overcharges he collected from the townspeople. The fruit of saying 'yes' to the Lord is a changed life. That's what having a personal relationship with Christ is all about."

"It would be nice if Judaism talked more about turning our lives around for the better," Joshua said appreciatively. "The tax collector in this story was a man who made a fortune by gouging his neighbors for much more than they really owed. It was legal for tax collectors to do that, but it was morally wrong. I think the tax collector knew that at some level. But it was not until Jesus welcomed him without judging him that the tax collector turned his life around and decided to treat his fellow Jews fairly."

"I believe it was because it was the first time he had experienced the loving-kindness that Jesus offered," Mary said added. "We let the loving-kindness of Jesus into our lives and the feeling makes us rejoice and we become a new person."

"This story is one of many showing that Jesus had a strong social conscience," Winston added. "Part of Jesus' agenda was to lift up the poor and oppressed, and bring healing and hope."

"Yes," Mary agreed, "Jesus sought to bring God's love and justice and salvation to all people, regardless of social status. Even the hated tax collectors were offered salvation if they accepted Jesus and changed their ways."

Joshua could not resist adding his liberal political views. "Those who profess Christianity, but don't believe that the government should help people who cannot help themselves, run counter to the teachings of Jesus. They may not like 'big government', but that is a legitimate way for our society to help the less fortunate among us."

"Yes, I agree with that," seconded George. "But let's get back to discussing the Book of Emet."

The Treatment of Workers

"Yes, of course," Joshua said, but he was on a roll and started the next topic out of turn.

"The next three parables show the confusing nature of Jesus' social conscience. They involve the treatment of workers. In the Parable of the Workers in the Vineyard, the landowner appeared to treat his workers unevenly, maybe even unfairly, because some agreed to work for less than others. In the Parable of the Talents, Jesus suggested that the workers act like capitalists and invest what they were given to provide a greater profit for their bosses. In Doing Your Duty, Jesus said that servants were due no special thanks because they were only doing what they were told. Frankly, I don't understand how they go together."

"I never have either Joshua," Winston agreed. "There is another parable in the gospels that is not in the Book of Emet where Jesus said the workers have the right to all the profits from the land even though they were renting it from the owner. When the owner sent people to collect the rent, the workers rightfully killed them. It is quite peculiar that Jesus would have been so inconsistent in his teaching."

"Mary, don't you have anything to say about this?" George inquired with surprise at her silence.

But Mary was busy watching someone moving around in the balcony and did not want to lose track of him. She only partially answered George's question. "The parable about Doing Your Duty is about our relationship with God. When we are in a personal relationship with God, it is our duty to obey God and we should never expect a reward for it."

A Seat at the Table

"The next parable has to do with humility," Mary said, getting back to the business at hand. "Jesus said a person who is invited to a banquet should not sit at the most prestigious place at the table. The reason was that if someone more prestigious than you arrived, you would be humiliated by being asked to move down. And if someone less prestigious than you arrived, you would be flattered by being asked to move up. The lesson is that he who exalts himself will be humbled, and he who humbles himself will be exalted. He also said it is more worthy to invite the poor who cannot repay the invitation than to invite the wealthy, who can be expected to return the favor.

"Then he told about those who were invited to the banquet but found excuses not to come. He said those who were poor and hungry should be invited and that those who rejected the invitation should be given nothing to eat."

"This last part has been read by some as being anti-Semitic," said

Joshua. "They say it teaches that the Jews rejected Jesus' invitation to the heavenly banquet, so he was telling the church to exclude them and instead bring others to the dinner, such as sinners or even Gentiles."

"If I may ask Joshua, what do you think?" asked George. "Is this parable anti-Semitic?"

"Not as I read it," answered Joshua. "I would label it as anti-Jewish perhaps, but not anti-Semitic."

"What's the difference between them, in your mind?" asked Mary with great interest.

"The way I think about it is that anti-Semitic is an attitude of hate toward all Jews," Joshua explained. "Anti-Semitism implies that Jews are different from others, and always in negative ways. For example, anti-Semites say we are greedy and care more about money than anything else; that we never want to associate with non-Jews; and that we all look the same with big ugly crooked noses. On the other hand, being anti-Jewish means rejecting Judaism as a means of salvation or as a way of life."

"Can you give us an example?" Mary asked.

"Sure. The Christians say we have to believe in Jesus as God or we are all condemned to hell. In other words, Jewish life and practice have no value.

"But we see ourselves as God's 'chosen people'—chosen by God to obey the laws in His Torah, and be messengers to the world to testify that He is the 'one true God'. When Christians say Jews are going to hell because we rejected Jesus, and give us no credit for doing what God told us to do, that is anti-Jewish!"

"I don't think that is anti-Jewish at all Joshua," protested Mary. "It's true that we believe the Jews tragically rejected Jesus as their Messiah and Lord, but we believe all peoples should come to Jesus to be saved, not just the Jews. That is why we go to non-Christians and try to convert them, so they will be saved too."

Winston joined in the discussion. "As you know Joshua, a lot of people have trouble with the Jews calling themselves the 'chosen people'."

"Yes I know Winston," Joshua answered. "But they misunderstand what that means. It means we were chosen to follow God's commandments and to testify that He is the one and only God. It does *not mean* we are better than others. We believe we were chosen in the sense that God gave us a special mission. In other words, He 'chose' us to be the group that is required to follow His laws and bear special responsibilities. If you look at our history, there is no sign that He treated us better than others. Just the opposite, in fact.

"There is a joke about how we came to be chosen. God originally offered a tablet of only five commandments, and He looked around for a people who would take them and obey them. He asked the Egyptians and the Assyrians and the Babylonians and every other group if they would take them on, and all the groups said, 'No'. Then he asked the Jews. The Jews asked Him if the laws on that tablet were really good and God of course answered that they were really, really good. So the Jews said, 'Well, if they're really that good, we'll take two!'" The audience broke into laughter, as did the panel.

"But in reality," Joshua continued after the laughter subsided, "God charged the Jewish people to 'obey Me fully and keep My covenant,' and the people all responded together and said, 'We will do everything the Lord has said.'"

"As I recall Scripture," George remembered, "God told the Israelites that if they obey His laws and keep His covenant, they will be a kingdom of priests and a holy nation, and they will be given the land of Canaan to live in. But let's steer the discussion back to the banquets."

"Right," said Mary. "The lesson of the wedding banquet is to be humble, or someone else may humble, if not humiliate, us. Instead of hoping for an earthly reward, we should do good things for those who cannot repay us in kind, and God will bless us for it. Also, Jesus scolded those who said they wanted to follow him into the Kingdom of God and then offered excuses when he asked something specific of them."

"These parables again show Jesus' concern for the humble and underprivileged," seconded Winston. "He really cared about who we sometimes call 'the little people', which is partly why his popularity has been so widespread and so enduring."

"I totally agree," said George.

Preparing for the Kingdom of God

"When Jesus was asked when the Kingdom of God will come," Mary continued, "he said the Kingdom of God is not coming with things that can be observed. This has a deeper meaning than many think, especially when paired with his statement, '…the Kingdom of God is among you.' It means that the reality of God's Kingdom is present and available, because the Kingdom is among us in the person of Jesus. But what God has begun, almost no one can observe.

"Jesus compares it to the yeast in flour that makes bread rise; or a small seed that, when planted, grows a bush big enough to nest the birds of the air; and so on. The Kingdom of God is like that, he said. It moves slowly, it gains ground in people's hearts and minds, it infiltrates systems and bureaucracies, and it brings the good news of God's love and saving grace wherever it goes. Jesus brought it, he announced it, and he *was* and *is* it. His said we should rejoice in the new life Jesus gave us, always having a sense of expectation and joy, and with an excitement that draws others to it!"

"That is very sweet," said Joshua admiringly. "I have never heard it put quite that way before, and I personally think that is how the world becomes better. But I disagree that this happens because Jesus was the Messiah. According to Isaiah, the Messiah will bring peace on earth, where the lion lies down with the lamb, and people will beat their swords into plowshares and learn war no more. Those things obviously have not happened, nor are they in the process of happening."

"The statements Mary described have led some scholars to the conclusion that Jesus did *not* believe the world would end soon," added Winston. "That is why Christians believe that the peace on earth will come with Jesus' second coming."

"As many Jews say, let him come again and do the things the Messiah is supposed to do, and then we will believe," said Joshua. "Until then, he is not the Messiah foretold by Isaiah."

"Sometimes I am surprised Missourians don't agree with you Joshua," George said with a wide smile. "We are called the 'show-me state' you know." The home state audience roared with pride and approval at George's joke.

Suddenly, there was a loud banging somewhere at the side of the building, and it continued for several moments. The panelists looked at each other with fear in their eyes. What could possibly be going on? Were they in real danger?

There was more banging, and even louder this time. Then, in a flash, an explosion came from the side door on the left. People were shouting and screaming at each other. An officer's radio crackled, "Breach of security at the side door. Security stat to the Graham Chapel side door!"

Immediately the panelists were surrounded by security officers and rushed to the secure room offstage. Out of the corner of her eye as she was hurrying out, Mary noticed the suspicious man, whose movements she had been following on the balcony, pulling a gun out of his black jacket and pointing it in their direction. She heard a gunshot but did not see where it went before she was hustled off the stage.

Then she saw Joshua stumble.

"Oh my God!" she screamed.

Backstage

The panelists huddled together in the back corner of the room. George was pacing back and forth. He was nervous and anxious. Even Sir Winston remained standing, staring at a framed print of some pastoral scene, thinking the original could have been painted in an English countryside.

"Are you okay Josh," Mary asked frantically.

"I'm scared out of my wits," Joshua whispered.

"I mean are you hurt?"

"No, I don't think so. Are you?"

"I'm fine. I thought you were shot. I saw you stumble."

"Oh that," Joshua almost smiled. "One of the security guards stepped on my heel." They found out later that the gunshot had hit the wall behind the dais in exactly the spot where Joshua's head had been before he stumbled.

Mary felt relieved and gave him a big hug. Joshua was pleasantly surprised by Mary's spontaneous gesture of concern and he hugged her back gratefully. He wanted to kiss the top of her head but thought better of it.

Sounds of struggle were coming from the auditorium. Several voices competed with each other to be the loudest: "That woman is a poor excuse for a Christian! She gives in to him every time he talks now. The bitch needs to put that Jew in his place!"

Joshua felt Mary's hand and instinctively took it in his hand. Mary was startled but liked the feeling. Each of them felt like they were prepared to protect the other from any danger that might come their way.

More voices drifted their way. "That beady-eyed son of a bitch says he admires Jesus. That'll do him a lot of good in hell!" Sinister laughter was heard.

George looked at Joshua and Mary, as if to say, "I'm so sorry!" Joshua met his eyes and nodded understandingly.

"Where's that fag minister?" someone shouted, followed by more sinister laughter. More scuffling ensued, with cries of, "Don't touch me! You can't arrest us—we have a right to speak!" They could hear an officer shout back, "You lost your freedom of speech the second you broke into this building! You are under arrest! Come quietly, or we'll drag you out of here!" Which is exactly what they had to do in some cases.

The officer in the back room received a radio report that the building was being swept for intruders and firearms, and that the panelists should be kept inside the backstage room until the "all clear" signal was given. After a few more minutes, a captain of the campus security entered the room to debrief everyone, while one of her colleagues tried to calm the audience so they would file out of the building at a measured pace and allow themselves to be searched for the offending weapon.

The nine men who had broken in and were doing all the shouting had come from the mob on the left lawn. They were now in the custody of the St. Louis County Police, on their way to be booked for criminal trespass, creating a public disorder, criminal damage to property, resisting arrest, and cursing inside a chapel or other house of worship. (This antiquated ordinance was still on the books, so why not?)

Then came the report that the man suspected of being the shooter had been arrested. He was dressed all in black, which is partly what had drawn Mary's attention to him as he moved around in the balcony. Of great concern was that no gun was found on him. Of even greater concern was that he was a known hit man, hired by who he would not say.

The three guest panelists wondered silently if the Debate would resume the next night, but no one said anything. Winston mentioned something about wanting to use the men's room, but he felt somewhat wary about going down the hall. The captain of campus security said she would escort him and even check the restroom before he went in. "Thank you so much," he replied. "I'm at sixes and sevens over this."

In a few moments, Winston returned, looking a bit more refreshed. The police security officer told George that it was up to him if he wanted to return for the third night of the Debate.

"I wonder if it's wise for us to continue…," George said to no one in particular.

"Yes, yes, we can't give in to terrorists," Sir Winston said. "If we do that, they will always control what gets said and what doesn't. A form of censorship I dare say."

"There are only two chapters of Emet to go," agreed Joshua nervously. "I think we have to go for it, or this whole Debate will have been in vain. And the whole world is watching and depending on us." Mary nodded reluctantly in agreement, but she was worried about the safety of Joshua and the others.

"Okay," said George. "This isn't a decision I would want to make by myself. You are brave and dedicated people. I definitely invited the right people for this." But George was still worried that the shooter's gun had not been found.

Outside the Chapel

Bryce had fallen asleep, bored to some extent with the debate going on inside. He was moderately interested in the subject matter, but to be honest, he was mainly there to be with Judith. Judith cuddled his head lovingly in her lap, stroking his face when he stirred and soothing him back to peacefulness. She was amazed at how he could sleep through all of the hubbub going on with the mob outside.

At one point, Judith saw a group of young men who had been drinking and making fools of themselves get encouragement from some in the mob. "Great," she thought, "bubba meets hubbub!" She laughed out loud at her own cleverness. "Wait till I tell Sarah about that one! She will be absolutely hysterical!" Sarah, of course, was her best friend.

As the sixth chapter of the Book of Emet was winding down, Judith noticed that the "bubbas" were getting increasingly animated and loud. They were working themselves up into a frenzy and the mob was egging them on. Suddenly she heard one of them say, "Let's git that sonofabitch and teach them Jews to keep their Satan worship to themselves!"

The nine "bubbas" ran to the side door of the chapel and tried to push their way in. Like flies to honey, security guards ran to the side door from their posts to help thwart the intrusion. There was a lot of pushing and shoving and shouting. At the height of the melee, there was an explosion at the other side of the chapel.

Judith found out later that a Molotov cocktail had been thrown at the stained glass windows on the other side of the chapel, shattering one of the windows in the balcony. Some of the mob was nearby, waiting to rush in the front door if the police left their posts to check out the explosion. However, the four security guards stationed at the front door did not leave their posts so the mob held back.

What Judith did not know was that when the Molotov cocktail went off, the man in the black suit was waiting to take a shot at Joshua.

The sound of the Molotov cocktail explosion woke Bryce up with a start. He jumped to his feet before he was even fully awake, and then looked around dumbly for trouble. He instinctively put himself between the possible unseen threat and Judith.

"What's going on?" he asked Judith breathlessly.

Judith was shaking visibly and could not answer immediately.

"Are you okay?" asked Bryce with concern.

Judith nodded her head affirmatively, but her body was still shaking and tears were pouring down her face.

"Let's get out of here! This isn't that important."

Judith was about to agree when she saw people exiting from the chapel in droves. Most of the viewers on the grass left too, but not the people from the mob.

"Wait! Maybe the program is over. Look at all those people leaving."

"Is your father with them?"

"Not yet. I don't think he would leave until everyone else got out safely."

"He must be a brave man."

Judith nodded, a fresh set of tears streaming down her face.

Suddenly, Bryce noticed something coming out of the shattered second floor window of the chapel. It was a brown paper bag folded over some object. He could not make out what it was. A man dressed all in white was waiting below to catch it and quickly returned to join the mob, apparently not being noticed by anyone other than Bryce. "That's odd," he thought, but then returned to the crisis at hand.

Judith moved closer to Bryce and asked him to hold her, which of course he did. She felt safe now in his big strong arms.

A few minutes later, Paul Lindenbaugh came out of the chapel to talk to the mob. Bryce saw the man who had caught the package hand him something, which Paul Lindenbaugh put inside his white jacket. He then returned to the chapel, nodding at the security guards as he passed by them, unobstructed.

After the Debate

A few minutes later Judith and Bryce saw the panelists leave the chapel and head for the parking lot. Still feeling wound up, Judith and Bryce decided to go their favorite pizza place, Talayna's in the western suburbs, where they could also get themselves a stiff drink. They got in Bryce's convertible and, with most of the traffic gone, had no trouble getting on the westward-bound highway. Bryce loved the unique taste of the St. Louis style pizza and laughed when the grease rolled down his arm when he picked up a slice with his hand. Judith loved the cheese noodles on their signature dinner salad. Both loved that it was open late into the night. College students always depend on a late night pizza place for special occasions.

As they were enjoying their pizzas, Bryce started to talk about the evening's activities.

"You know what amazes me the most about this Book of Emet is that he portrays Jesus as a man who could walk on water and heal people and all those things, but without the virgin birth and that kind of thing. I don't believe in this Son of God stuff, so I thought all the miracle stuff was made up too. I thought maybe he was a great man who got really exaggerated."

"I never thought much about him at all," Judith admitted, "until I met a born again Christian last year. She really wanted to convert me, and I listened to her and thought about it, but in the end I was too involved with Judaism to change. But she did get me interested in the New Testament. That is why I wanted to go there in person. It's all so fascinating!"

"What do you Jews think about it?" Bryce asked.

"Most Jews are not very interested in Jesus or the New Testament," Judith answered. "They mostly think of it as a Christian thing that has nothing to do with them."

"But Jesus was Jewish!"

"Well we don't think of him that way. We think of him as Christian."

"Do you think this new gospel will change that?"

"I have no idea," said Judith. "We're pretty set in our ways about this. You know, we've been blamed for killing Jesus for centuries, and the Christians have used that as a reason for killing us. The Holocaust was the last straw. They almost wiped us out that time."

"Yeah, we've been pretty horrible. But now most people I know find Jews rather interesting. I don't see the hate there used to be."

"Not in this country, no, but in Europe the hate is still there. Do you notice how they always side against Israel whenever anything happens in the Middle East? It is so unfair!"

Bryce put his arm around her and gave her a hug and a kiss. Judith kissed him back gratefully and put her head on his shoulder. She could not wait to get him back to her room so she could show him how much she loved him.

Saturday Night

Let him kiss me with the kisses of his mouth; for your love is better than wine. [Song of Songs 1:2.]

Like the night before, George offered to take the panelists to the hotel to have some drinks and eats. Everyone gladly accepted. They were able to get the same U-shaped booth they had before. They also decided to have the same food and drinks they had before. As Joshua said, "When you're on a winning streak, you need to do the same thing you did before so you don't jinx the streak." That of course was a baseball superstition, but Joshua said he used it in tennis as well.

Naturally, the main topic of conversation this night was the gunman. The group guessed he was aiming for Joshua, but could not figure out why. "What good does that do them to kill any of us?" George asked diplomatically. "It has nothing to do with the Book of Emet."

"Maybe they think by getting rid of the Book of Emet spokesman, that will somehow discredit Emet in the eyes of their public," Joshua ventured. "If you can't kill the message, kill the messenger instead."

"Quite right!" said Winston. "Sometimes it works. All of us better be careful tomorrow."

"Well Mary should be safe," said George. "She isn't a messenger of Emet."

"I don't *feel* safe though," Mary responded. "If I say something someone doesn't like, I could become a target too."

"Well well my dear," said Winston in his fatherly voice, "we shall certainly not let that happen." Mary gave him a loving look.

"The idea," George added, "is not to let that happen to anyone."

"I for one totally agree with that," Joshua joked, and everyone laughed.

"Hopefully that was the beginning and end all of this nonsense," said Winston.

"Amen to that!" said George.

The group changed the subject to the problem of religious fanatics generally, and when that topic was exhausted, the chicken wings were gone and the drinks were emptied and they decided to adjourn early. Before they split up, George invited everyone to attend his church service the following morning, and they all readily agreed.

Winston wanted to spend a little time in the hotel lobby as he saw a newspaper that he wanted to read lying on a coffee table there. Like the night before, Joshua and Mary went up in the elevator together.

In Mary's Room

On the elevator ride up, Mary looked at Joshua and said, "You know Josh we were all laughing about it down there, but I was really worried when I thought you'd been shot."

"That was very sweet of you to worry about me like that," Joshua said with a grateful smile on his face. He was feeling close to Mary since then and he instinctively reached out and took her hand.

Mary was initially startled at this unexpected physical gesture, but she found that she liked it and took his hand in hers and unconsciously leaned into him. Joshua was delighted at this unexpected closeness while Mary found she was attracted to the smell of Joshua's body. They were both disappointed when the short elevator ride came to an end and the elevator doors opened on their floor. Like the previous night, Joshua walked Mary to her room, but this time they were holding hands.

When they got to Mary's door they turned to face one other. Mary found herself looking at Joshua's lips as he was saying goodnight. They were so soft and inviting. And his eyes—they were so gentle and bright—and they danced when he laughed. And the way he was looking at her made her...

Before she could finish her thought, Joshua's mouth swooped down from above and, catching her by surprise, he pressed his lips firmly to hers. He was unable to resist her any longer. His lips had to have hers. He had to have her body close to his, and feel her warmth.

Instantly, Joshua found himself transported back to a similar moment when he was in junior high school. He was in the 8th grade and had just walked his girlfriend to her locker following final period. All day long Joshua had planned his strategy. He had memorized the words he would say to her. He would be confidant and cool.

Debby opened her locker and turned toward him with a smile. Joshua became so flustered that he forgot his lines, grabbed her head with his awkward hands, and smothered her mouth with his. It was the best kiss he'd ever had—or imagined—until he stuck his tongue through her lips, and she abruptly pulled away. "Josh," she cried, "I don't French!"

"Is Mary going to pull away, too?" he asked himself wordlessly. And to Joshua's utter dismay, Mary did pull away! He felt like the limb he had climbed out on — by venturing to kiss Mary without knowing how his kiss would be received — had been totally sawed off.

Mary's eyes were as big as dinner plates. He saw her look up and down the hall, and then in a soft voice he heard her say, "We can't do this here. Somebody might see."

Joshua's heart fell through the drain of déjà vu, but stopped just as suddenly when she opened the door with her key card, grabbed his necktie, and with an unbridled passion born out of years of frustration and neglect, pulled him into her room. In a single movement, Mary shut the door, pressed Joshua against it, and zeroed in on his mouth hungrily. She was unable to deny herself this time—she had to have this man. Mary pressed her body against his and Joshua could feel her breasts and hips against him. She felt something press against her abdomen that had not been there previously, and that made her even more excited.

After a good (really good!) few seconds—neither had any sense of time—she broke their kiss and breathlessly said to Joshua, "Why don't you have a seat on the sofa. I'll be right back."

Mary disappeared into the bedroom. Joshua's heart was pounding. He paced around the sofa and over-stuffed chairs in the living room portion of Mary's suite. "What's she doing in there? Is she in the bathroom or getting into 'something more comfortable'? What should I do? Slip off my suit coat, this necktie… my shoes?" Joshua heard a voice within him asking, "Josh, what do you want to do with her when she comes out? Talk? Kiss? Touch? What if she expects more?"

It felt to Joshua as though there was an angel on one shoulder and a devil on the other, each whispering into opposing ears. "It's in your hands, Josh," the devil was saying. "You will never be in this place with this woman again. What happens in St. Louis stays in St. Louis. Go for it!" That voice had his libido racing wildly.

"You like her, don't you?" the angel was asking. "You don't want to ruin it by going too far too fast do you? You're a rabbi—she might lose all respect for you if you come on too hard."

"You two are not a match," the devil countered. "She is a Christian who believes in Jesus and you are a Jew who is dedicated to trying to change Judaism. You have very different goals and personalities. There will never be anything between you. You probably will never see her again after tomorrow night. If she wants you, and you want her, go for it!"

"But you really like her," the angel affirmed. "If you treat her with dignity and respect, no matter what she wants or expects, you will be laying the groundwork for a good relationship that just might happen despite your differences."

A noise came from the bedroom. Mary was coming back. Joshua was crazed with anticipation. He slipped off his suit coat and threw it over the back of one of the chairs. He loosened his tie and unbuttoned the top button of his dress shirt. He sat down quickly, only to rise again when Mary entered the room, still wearing everything but her jacket. Her breasts looked full in her pink satin blouse and they beckoned to him. Her lipstick was refreshed and her glowing face touched his soul. In his stomach, hundreds of butterflies were jumping everywhere.

Mary had gone to the bathroom to calm herself down. She found Joshua incredibly exciting, and knew if she spent another minute kissing him, she would totally lose herself in his embrace. That, she knew somewhere deep inside herself, she was not prepared to do.

Once in the bathroom, Mary splashed some cold water on her face and played with her hair, anything to distract herself from her powerful feelings for Joshua. "Oh Lord Jesus, what am I going to do with him in my living room?" she wondered. "I should send him home right now!" But she knew she wouldn't. He filled the void of her loneliness like no one had in years. She knew she could not let him go just yet — she needed him. She had not been touched or held by a man in years and her craving for a man's warmth was unbearable. Mary dared to look at herself in the mirror. Her face was flushed and passionate, her eyes were filled with excitement, and her insides were wanting.

"What is Joshua thinking?" she wondered. "Does he like me or is he just hoping to get laid?" Mary's upbringing had taught her never to give too much to a man on the first date. "He won't respect you in the morning," she laughed to herself at the old saw. Of course she knew that no such thing was going to happen. She was a married woman and she did *not* play around, even if Wayne did. But, oh, she really wanted to! She *really* wanted to.

"Okay Mare, time to go back out there," she said to herself encouragingly. She was feeling very warm. "Is it the heat, is it him, or is it a hot flash?" Mary wondered laughing nervously at herself. She decided to take her suit jacket off and hoped that would be enough. She fanned herself and eventually began to feel cooler and more in control. Taking a deep breath, she said to herself out loud, "Time to go out there again!"

Mary reappeared into the living room, but as soon as she saw Joshua rise up for her, all her strict admonitions to herself turned to mush. She noticed the excitement in his eyes and she desperately wanted to jump into his arms and unleash her passion upon him again. "I better do something to 'change the subject' or I'm a goner," she said to herself.

"Sorry to keep you," she said huskily, as she walked to the little refrigerator in the kitchen section of the hotel suite. "Are you thirsty? I have some bottled water," she opened the door and looked in, "and some fruit juice."

"I'll have whatever the lady's having," he said gallantly. Mary nervously dropped one of the water bottles on the floor. "That was good Mare," she said to herself,

"Good one," Joshua teased. "I was afraid I was the only nervous person in the room!" They both broke into laughter, relieving some of the tension.

Mary brought each of them a water bottle and then profusely apologized for her behavior. "I'm really sorry Josh and I'm so embarrassed. I've never done anything like that before. I'm a married woman and a professional. I should never have kissed you like that. It's just that it's been a long time and I guess I got a little carried away."

Joshua was disappointed she regretted kissing him, but he kind of understood. He decided that a little humor was in order to put things back in balance. "It's okay. I just hope you don't do it again. You almost strangled me and my insurance isn't paid up." Then he winked at her and she laughed heartily.

"Good, now we've got that settled," Mary said lightheartedly. They clinked their water bottles together. "To Jesus the Christ," Mary said with a grin. "L'chaim," Joshua responded with a chuckle.

The cold water was refreshing after the wine they had been drinking downstairs. Mary slipped off her shoes, set the bottle down, and propped her stocking feet on the edge of the coffee table next to the water. "It's late," she thought, "and I would rather be more informal with him. He'll either like me or he won't, but I'm too tired to worry about how I look to him with my feet on the table."

"Is it okay if I put my feet up too?" Joshua asked.

"Please do," Mary smiled happily.

"Oh good! The first thing I do when I get home is take my shoes off," Joshua said. He removed his shoes and put his feet on the table near Mary's.

"Me too," said Mary, who was beginning to feel more comfortable now. "It seems like we have informality in common if nothing else." They both laughed.

Turning toward Joshua she asked, "I told you a bit about my family. What about yours? Have you always lived in Chicago?"

"My whole life. I'm Windy City born and bred."

"A good name for it. Every time I've been to Chicago it's been windy, especially by the lake."

"It is that," he replied, "but that's not the origin of the nickname. It originally referred to the abundance of air coming from long-winded politicians. The political cartoonists must have had a *field day* drawing people and buildings blown over by gale-inducing orations!"

"A *Marshall Field* day?" she winked, referring to the well-known downtown department store, now owned by Macy's.

Joshua laughed. "Very good! Did you ever go to Field's?"

"About three years ago. I was in Chicago on a book tour the week before Christmas and took an extra day to sight-see and shop. I even got to eat under that giant Christmas tree in the… what's the dining room called?"

"The Walnut Room. Isn't it amazing? I don't celebrate Christmas, of course, but I try to eat there every year at Christmastime. The whole experience is so magical, even when one of the teenage girls comes to the table and sprinkles fairy dust on you."

"Yes, it's beautiful! Don't you get sprinkled with fairy dust at your favorite kosher deli?" she teased.

"My friend Sy, who owns the deli I like to go to, squirted me with a water bottle there once when I didn't laugh at one of his jokes. Does that count?"

"Poor baby! So, what did you do then?"

"I took it out of his tip," Joshua laughed. Mary laughed too. They enjoyed seeing each other laugh and liked that they could laugh together.

"You are so cute when you laugh," Joshua said admiringly.

"I love your laugh too."

Joshua had an almost irresistible impulse to lean over and give Mary another kiss, but stopped himself because he knew it would not be welcome. Mary felt it too, but did not want to encourage and then disappoint Joshua again, so she pretended not to notice. They both took a gulp of water and managed to calm themselves down.

"What were your parents like?" she asked, continuing the conversation from before. Joshua leaned back in thought.

"My mother was the kindest person I have ever known: warm, considerate, and very patient. She learned to be patient—she told me—from spending so much of her time taking care of my sister. Mom had been an elementary school teacher, but quit teaching when Esther came along. I know she missed it, the kids especially, but taking care of us was more important to her. My grandparents—my mother's parents—were wonderful, too. I loved visiting them every summer in upstate New York. My mother was an excellent student who moved to Chicago at 18 to attend Northwestern University. That's where she met my father.

"My father was a successful businessman who never achieved his dream of being an attorney. He would have been a good one, too. But his father wanted my dad to apprentice at the family bakery, while my grandmother wanted him to become a rabbi. As a compromise—sort of—my father agreed to learn the bakery business if he could get his degree in business. You see, my grandfather's dream was that both his sons would carry on the family name and the family business. My uncle was a natural in his white apron and baker's hat. Give him some flour and water and he could bake a masterpiece. It's like he was raised in the bakery."

"How much yeast did that take?" Mary said with a straight face.

"What?"

"How much yeast did he need to be *raised* in the bakery?"

"Haha…think you're funny, don't you?" Joshua's eyes were dancing.

"Yes…I think I'm funny and so do all my friends. I'm glad you think so too. I love to laugh. "

"I do too," Joshua smiled back. He really liked getting to see this side of Mary. He realized he truly was enjoying her company.

"I love it when you're not so serious *Mister Rabbi*," Mary teased. Joshua laughed the hearty laugh that Mary was beginning to fall in love with. She really liked it that Joshua could laugh at himself and yet was not too full of himself to let her be the funny one sometimes.

"Hey, *Ms Preacher Lady*, I'm not serious all the time. Even rabbis have a lighter side once in a while," Joshua winked. "Especially when in the presence of a woman who is prettier and smarter than I am." Joshua smiled at Mary mischievously and Mary felt her heart melt. She looked at him longingly, wanting the feel of his lips on hers.

Joshua, in turn, could hardly sit still he wanted her so badly. He took another gulp of water and decided he better go back to their conversation. "Let's see, where was I before you so *rudely* interrupted me?"

Mary gathered herself together and gratefully followed Joshua's lead.

"Something to do with *raising* your uncle," she said with a gaiety she did not entirely feel.

"Right," Joshua laughed as Mary smiled.

"Soooo, my father was mostly interested in the business aspects of the bakery. He was always coming up with ideas for expanding profits, but his ideas were seldom accepted. Grandpa often said, 'We've never done it that way before,' and that was it. Bottom line, there was not enough profit to support my grandparents and their two sons unless they expanded the business.

For thirty years, the bakery was in the same location on the west side of Chicago. My father's idea was to open a second bakery on the north side, where more and more Jews were relocating. It took awhile to convince my grandfather that this would work, but he finally saw the writing on the wall. Eventually, almost all the Jews on the west side moved to the north side. There were already two successful Jewish-owned and operated bakeries on the north side by the time my grandfather decided to move, so on my father's advice he went to the northern suburb of Skokie, which also came to have a large Jewish population. My folks moved even farther north, to Highland Park, and that is where I was born and grew up."

"Did they want you to take over the business, too, like your father and uncle had?"

"Well, my father never took over the business. When my parents got divorced, he moved to Los Angeles and got a job in business development. I never saw him much after that."

"I'm so sorry," Mary said softly. "Do you speak to each other much?"

"No, not really. My father wanted me to be a professional tennis player. He spent an incredible amount of time teaching me to play when I was a kid. But he probably wouldn't be talking to me that much more even if I had turned pro. He got remarried out there and had a couple more kids and to him, that's his real family."

"I'm so sorry," Mary said again, this time with tears in her eyes. She reached out and touched his hand. Having her own father issues, she was especially sensitive to that problem in others, particularly those she felt close to.

Joshua was deeply touched. "This woman has a good soul and a big heart," he thought to himself with the alacrity of a lightning bolt. Those were the two qualities he valued most in others. He found himself reaching out to her and the two of them hugged silently for a few moments. Joshua felt surprisingly comfortable with Mary. He was able to let down his emotional guard and his eyes began to tear up. He gave a deep sigh, which made Mary hold him even tighter.

They both knew that something special was happening. Joshua thought he felt Mary's soul touch his, something he had always wanted to feel with a woman but never had. He hugged her with all his being. He hugged her like she had never been hugged before. Mary was overcome by her emotions. She felt like maybe she had fallen in love.

The moments of togetherness ended suddenly when Mary's cell phone rang. It was Christa, calling in before going to bed, as Mary had asked. Joshua used this interlude to walk unsteadily toward the big picture window that looked out over the city. Looking out at the night lights of the city, he became lost in a reverie. How much time passed this way, he did not know, but something jarred him back into consciousness. He turned around and saw that Mary was putting her phone down and smiling at him.

"Could we please continue what we were talking about," Mary asked, wanting more than ever to learn more about the man she had developed such feelings for.

"Yes, of course," Joshua answered. He sat back down on the sofa, leaned back and tried to remember where they had left off.

"Getting back to the bakery then, the whole family assumed I would play tennis professionally, so I never got involved with it. Thankfully, my two cousins, my uncle's son and daughter, took over the business. I just enjoy the family discount and the delivery of fresh challah every Friday.

Theirs is sooooo good, especially right out of the oven. It almost melts in your mouth."

"What is challah? Is it a bread or a pastry of some sort?"

"It is bread made with eggs and usually made for Shabbat—the Sabbath—and other holidays. Before it is baked, it is braided."

"Oh yes, I've seen pictures of it, but never tasted it."

"You haven't lived till you've tasted a good challah."

"Next time I'm in Chicago, I will expect some family discounted challah," Mary laughed. Joshua's face lit up. The thought that he might see her again in the future made his heart skip a beat.

"My turn to ask some questions about you," Joshua said gaily. He really wanted to ask Mary about her marriage, but decided to ask her about something else that also interested him.

"You told me you had been called by God to your ministry, but how does a young woman keep following that inspiration when all the voices around you are telling you, 'You're a woman; women don't do that.' I mean, were there other voices that encouraged you?"

"Of course. A few of my friends backed me all the way, even if they didn't totally understand what I wanted to do. Two of my college professors—who taught Bible and Theology classes—encouraged me to go to seminary and become a teacher or a Director of Christian Education for a church. Then, there was the librarian at the college, who suggested I read Dorothy Sayers...."

"Who is that? I've heard that name before but I don't remember who she is."

"Dorothy Sayers was a British mystery writer. When I had studied all day, I often relaxed with one of her books; they were a great escape. Over time, I learned that she had written some non-fiction also. In fact, my favorite Sayers quote, is from the non-fiction book *Are Women Human?* I'll get it for you."

Mary disappeared back into her bedroom and came back smiling with a paperback book that looked quite the worse for wear. "I take this with me wherever I go. I have a nice hardback at home, but this is my travel version. Let me read to you my favorite passage:

'Perhaps it is no wonder that the women were first at the Cradle [of Jesus] and last [to remain] at the Cross. They had never known a man like this Man ... A prophet and teacher who never nagged at them, never flattered or coaxed or patronized ... who rebuked without querulousness and praised without condescension; who took their questions and arguments seriously; who never mapped out their sphere for them, never urged them to be feminine or jeered at them for being female ... Nobody could possibly guess from the words and deeds of Jesus that there was anything [inferior] about woman's nature.'"

"I can see how that would inspire you to keep at it," Joshua said. "It sounds a lot like what Jesus said about women in the Sermon on the Mount in the Book of Emet."

"Wouldn't it be wonderful if that was true," Mary said, glowing at the thought of it. "Maybe you're right and the other gospel writers left that part out or it was suppressed by later authorities. That by itself wouldn't make Emet legitimate," she quickly added.

Joshua laughed. "I don't want to get into that stuff again right now," but silently he thought "Hey, maybe I'm making some progress here, with her anyway. I hope so." Then he stood up and stretched. "May I use your bathroom?" he asked. Mary nodded and yawned simultaneously.

As Joshua walked away, Mary glanced at her watch. "Oh my goodness!" she said out loud. The time was almost 2:00 a.m. She had not seen time move so quickly in ages. Or, was it that time had stood still? She smiled at the latter thought. "How romantic!"

Joshua returned and Mary asked if he knew how late it was. "Didn't notice. Wow! Almost 2:00? I don't believe it. I better get to bed or they'll never 'get me to the church on time'," Joshua sung the last words, which were from a song in *My Fair Lady*.

Mary loved it and laughed heartily. She loved musicals and knew the words to most of the famous songs from them. "Yes, you better leave. I have a lot more to do to get ready tomorrow morning than you do. I need my beauty sleep."

"Then you must have gotten a lot of sleep lately," Joshua teased while Mary smiled and blushed. Then Joshua was inspired to sing another song — "You must have been a beautiful baby, cuz baby look at you now."

"The you-know-what is getting piled pretty high in here," Mary joked. "But you're not going to get me in the sack tonight *Mister Rabbi*."

"Oh yeah? Well who asked?"

The Phone Call

Before Mary could answer, her cell phone rang again. "Who could be calling at this hour?" she said, thinking that maybe something happened to Christa or her mother. To her surprise, it was her husband Wayne. She did not like the sound of his voice. She could tell he had been drinking.

Joshua started to leave and waved goodbye, but she motioned for Joshua to stay.

"We were watching you tonight Princess. You let those guys walk all over you."

Wayne often called her "Princess" sarcastically. Ever since she had lost their baby and went into depression, he had chided her for laziness and started calling her a princess. Mary, of course, hated when he did that.

"Where are you?" she asked suspiciously.

"You know where I am," he answered defensively. "I'm at my cousin's in Denver."

Mary knew that was not true. No one in Wayne's family touched alcoholic beverages. If he was drinking, he was with one of his "honeys."

"I really wish you'd go back home to watch my mother and Christa."

"Watch them and miss all the fun we're having watching you get trampled in this 'Great Debate'? I wouldn't miss this for the world. After this, your name will be 'Mudd' with them." He cackled and Mary's eyes teared up out of a combination of hurt and anger. Wayne sure knew how to push her buttons after all these years. She noticed Joshua was watching her and her eyes teared up some more out of embarrassment at having this conversation overheard by a man she really liked but hardly knew.

"I can't talk now," she said. "Do you know what time it is? I have to get some sleep for tomorrow."

"What difference will it make," he slurred. "Maybe you'll do better without your wits around you." He cackled again. She hated that sarcastic laugh of his. She had heard it far too often over the years and made her almost hate him every time he did it.

"Wayne, this really is not a good time…"

"It's a good time when I say it is," Wayne interrupted belligerently. "Maybe you'd be doing a lot better if your senile old lady and that retarded brat weren't around." Then his voice got menacing. "When I get back, we're going to have a little talk about that." He was not cackling this time.

Mary involuntarily shuddered. She knew what that tone of voice meant. He would get his way or she would pay the price physically. She certainly did not intend to give Christa away, so she knew she was letting herself in for more bruising that "wouldn't show."

"If anyone has to go, it should be you," she said bravely, knowing it would anger him more. She was not going to let fear of a beating change her path. She often dreamed that somehow she would be free of him, but she believed it would never happen.

"I really have to go," she said firmly and hung up on the call.

Joshua had seen her shudder and her face darken with fear and anger. "Are you alright?" he asked with concern. Mary turned away from him without answering and put her hands over her face. She was sobbing and her body was shaking. Sometimes she got this way after a confrontation with Wayne, but she never let him see it. She did not want to let Joshua see it either, which added to her angst.

Joshua went over to her but she shook her head no and he stepped back. Then the phone rang again. Mary looked at the incoming phone number and rejected the phone call. A few moments later it rang again. This time Mary put the phone on mute and turned it off.

"I'm really sorry," Mary told Joshua after she had gathered herself. "He was drinking and with another woman, and he gets real mean."

"It sounded brutal," Joshua commiserated.

Mary turned solemn and motioned for him to go with her to sit on the sofa. She needed a male friend just now, and for whatever reason she trusted Joshua.

"My marriage has not been good for a very long time. I can't remember the last time we…I mean, the last time he looked at me with any sort of interest. I'm quite sure he doesn't love me anymore and hasn't for years. So, I stay busy. I channel my feelings into my work. It's almost like my work, my ministry, is my partner. I give it my all, and I receive gratitude in return…. And the satisfaction of knowing I am doing what God wants me to do with my life."

"But that's not enough—for any of us I mean—is it?"

"No, not if I'm honest with myself. The problem is that I almost have myself convinced it *is* enough, so I repress my desires and pride myself in remaining virtuous and obedient to the Lord. Then you come along, kiss me like I can't remember when, and don't try to take advantage of me. You feel like a shelter in a storm, and I have so been missing love in my life."

"The Good Book says, 'It is not good for the woman to be alone',"
Joshua said smiling, giving his best Tevye imitation from Fiddler on the
Roof. Then he began singing, 'It started long ago in the Garden of Eden,
/ When Adam said to Eve, / Baby, you're for me...'

"What *are* you singing? Did you just make that up?" Mary asked
with a smile.

"No. It's a 60's pop song called 'The Game of Love.' Shall I sing
more?"

"No thanks. That's not my music. I was raised on gospel and classical
music. My oldies are Bach, Mozart, and 'The Old, Rugged Cross.'"

"Is that a hymn? The only Christian hymn I know is 'Amazing
Grace.'"

"That's a good one. You should sing it every day."

"I'll keep that in mind," Joshua said with a wink.

"Josh, do you think love is just a game?" Mary asked guardedly,
referring back to the song Joshua had been singing. She was wary of
letting her heart go out to a man who would not feel the same way about
her.

"Not at all!" Joshua said with a bit of hurt in his voice. "I take love
and relationships *very* seriously. I have been looking for real love all my
life. Along with my mission to change Judaism, finding my life partner
has always been the most important goal in my life."

"I feel the same way," Mary said. "But I'm married and have had to
give up on that dream. I miss that piece of my life horribly every day."
She had tears in her eyes.

Joshua gave Mary a look of longing and wished he could help her in
some way. But he knew there was nothing he could do. In his frustration
and his desire to escape the quandary they were in, he walked over to the
picture window and looked out. "Hmmm," was the only sound he made.

"What do you see out there?" Mary inquired.

"Just looking at the lights over St. Louis," he replied, startled that she
changed the subject.

"Anything of interest?"

"You can see the top of the arch from here."

The St. Louis arch is the landmark icon of the city, like the Eiffel
Tower is for Paris. Mary joined him at the window. The glare from the
room was bright on the window, so she went to the front door and
turned off the lights. She opened the floor to ceiling drapes and standing

next to Joshua, she joined him taking in the view to the east, facing the Mississippi River. Joshua put his arm around her again and pulled her close. Her body yielded to his embrace and he felt her melt into him. It was a very exciting feeling. He leaned over and kissed the top of her head.

"What's the stadium on the right?" Mary asked.

"It's Busch Stadium, where the Cardinals play baseball. This is the third incarnation of it I think."

"You mean they've had three different stadiums with the same name?" Joshua nodded affirmatively.

"How old is this one? It looks pretty nice from this distance…to a girl who's never been to a professional baseball game, and is looking at it in the dark, I mean."

"Oh it's been several years now, as I recall. It's nice enough, for a newer one. The best baseball park in the country, in my humble opinion, is Wrigley Field in Chicago, which is about 100 years old. My father took me to see the Cubs play at home several times each summer. There's nothing like 'The Friendly Confines' for watching a game…and my favorite team."

"I didn't know you had any humble opinions," Mary said teasingly.

"I rarely do," Joshua said with pretended boastfulness. "You've never been to a baseball game? The national pastime? You've been spending too much time in church young lady."

Mary just moaned. "It's must be about 3:00 in the morning. Why are you so wide awake? I could fall asleep just leaning on you."

"That's the best idea you've had all night."

"You are incorrigible, you know?"

"Oh, come on; I'm corrigible at least some of the time."

"Is that even a word?" she laughed.

"I don't know," he joked. "Look it up online. That will be your homework assignment for tomorrow."

"I don't need any homework assignments," Mary laughed. "*You* can look it up — you are the one who used it. Anyway," Mary said sleepily. "I need for you to take your fancy words and go back to your room. I need to sleep so I can poke more holes in that crazy Emet thing tomorrow."

"Okay," Joshua said, as put his shoes back on and grabbed his suit coat. "I'll see you in church," he said pretending to sound like a lawyer.

"That's right," Mary said playing along, "and your God better be a good one because mine is the best in this here county." They both laughed heartily.

"Say, why don't we have lunch together after church," Joshua said, and then joked "Whoever's God loses has to buy."

Mary's eyes lit up and she gave him a warm smile and a nod. She walked him to the door and gave him a gentle goodbye kiss. Almost overcome, Joshua wrapped his arms around her and gave her a firm and lingering hug, which she returned. Joshua stepped out into the hall, but Mary grabbed his arm.

"Thank you for making me laugh," she said gratefully. "I really needed that."

Joshua smiled, and then put his fingers on his puckered lips and then placed them on Mary's cheek. She blew him a kiss in return and went back in her room, shutting the door behind her. Joshua turned and walked down the hall to his room, "The Game of Love" playing in his head as his body swayed to the music.

Mary quickly disrobed, washed the makeup off her face and fell into bed, not even bothering to put her nightgown on. Her heart sang as her eyelids drooped. She was asleep within seconds, her head full of happy dreams.

The Bomb

Now the Philistines had captured the Ark of God and took it from Ebenezer to Ashdod.
And the hand of God was heavy on the people of Ashdod and He brought devastation upon them and smote them with tumors. [I Samuel 5:1-6.]

A few days before the Great Debate started, Christopher Moskowitz found himself sitting in the waiting room of Godfather B's office. He had been summoned there by a phone call from Mrs. Thompson, Godfather B's secretary and receptionist. She had called Christopher's boss at the stock exchange and asked to have Christopher sent over immediately to the company's ultra-modern signature office building. He had no idea what Godfather B wanted to see him about and he was quite nervous.

Mrs. Thompson's phone rang. "You may go in now," she told Christopher.

Nervously, Chris rose from his seat and following Mrs. Thompson to the door of Godfather B's office. Mrs. Thompson showed him in and announced him to her boss.

The office was stunning. It was on the 28th floor of the reflective blue glass-plated high-rise in the Wall Street area of downtown Manhattan. There were windows all around with magnificent views of the Statue of Liberty and the downtown Manhattan skyline. The office was plushly carpeted and the furniture was made of cherry wood. There were bookcases on one wall and pictures and plaques on another wall.

Godfather B rose to meet Chris and came out from behind his desk to shake his hand and usher him into one of the four cushioned chairs sitting opposite the 12 foot wide desk. After exchanging some pleasantries, Godfather B got down to business.

"I need you to go on a top secret and dangerous mission for me," he said. "You don't have to do it, and there will be no repercussions if you don't, but it is an important Christian mission.

Godfather B was aware of Chris' background and beliefs. Everyone was, as Chris was not shy about telling anyone who would listen. He was president of the largest Jews for Jesus organization in the State of New York. Jews for Jesus was an organization of Jewish people who accepted Jesus Christ as their Lord and Savior.

Daniel Moskowitz—which had been Chris' name before he converted to Christianity and changed his name—had come from an ultra-Orthodox Jewish family, where he was very devout. He probably would have remained that way forever, but his faith was completely altered when he miraculously survived a bloody eight-car accident while commuting from Brooklyn to the Diamond District in Manhattan. He was pinned inside his crumpled car and he believed he saw Jesus come to him and pull him free, which allowed him to escape the car just before it burst into flames.

His family, friends and the Orthodox Jewish community told Chris that it must have been God or an angel sent by God who saved him, but Chris was convinced it had been Jesus. He began studying the New Testament, which he had never read, and going to various Christian churches to learn more about Jesus. He prayed, and Jesus answered him. He believed he had a new body and a new soul and became a born-again Christian. After affiliating himself with Jews for Jesus, Chris' energy and total belief soon catapulted him to the top of the organization. He preached the Gospel to Jews and Christians alike, hoping to bring them to his faith in Jesus Christ as their Savior.

The discovery of the Book of Emet infuriated and consumed Chris like nothing he had ever experienced before. He joined every protest march he could find, and participated in talk shows blasting Emet as one of the many fake documents Christianity had to overcome in its history. He believed the Book of Emet was the work of the devil and had to be destroyed to save the world.

It was this last belief that had come to the attention of Godfather B, who on his own volition and without consulting with the other Godfathers, decided that he would make sure the Book of Emet would be destroyed. He saw in Christopher Moskowitz the perfect tool for his plan. After discussing the matter with Chris and obtaining his eager consent to do what was asked of him, Godfather B dispatched Chris to the Holy Land to carry out this mission. The timing of the destruction of the Book of Emet was to be between the second and third nights of the Great Debate in St. Louis.

In Bethlehem

To avoid suspicion, Chris flew to Israel on El Al, the Israeli national airline, dressed in the Orthodox garb he used to wear before he found Christ. He remembered getting dressed like a soldier getting ready for battle. First the prayer shawl with the fringes all Orthodox Jews wore. Then the long-sleeve white shirt and the black pants. And finally the black coat and black hat. After adding a very real-looking black beard and a pair of black eyeglasses, he was ready. He was very comfortable in that disguise, for he knew how to look and he knew how to act and he knew how to talk. No one would suspect he was anything other than what he appeared to be.

Godfather B's special missions group had arranged for Chris to be further outfitted in the Christian district of Bethlehem. A middle-aged Christian Arab medical supply store owner, known to Chris only as Ibrihim, gave Chris a specially designed walker to use on his mission. Inside the legs of the walker were substantial quantities of C4 plastic explosives that would escape detection by Israeli security and enable Chris to blow up the Book of Emet where it was housed for public viewing at the Israel Museum in Jerusalem.

Godfather B wanted the blast to take place in the late afternoon St. Louis time, approximately three hours before the start of the third and last night of the Great Debate. Israel was seven hours ahead of the time in St. Louis, so the bombing needed to occur at about 11:00 p.m. Sunday night. He guessed it would take about an hour for the news to become known internationally. With the scroll destroyed, little attention would be paid to the debate as most people would be focusing on the bombing and who could be behind it. Also, with the scroll gone up in smoke, people would be much less interested in the debate and the crisis in Christianity would largely be over. Or so it was hoped.

The Israel Museum

The Book of Emet was on display at a special Annex attached to the Israel Museum in Jerusalem. Located very close to Israel's Knesset (Parliament), the Israel Museum was the largest cultural institution in the State of Israel, and as the home of the Dead Sea Scrolls, was the natural resting place for the Book of Emet. Thousands of visitors per day paid the extra admission charge to see a few of the original pages of the Book of Emet and learn about its discovery.

It was early evening Jerusalem time when Ibrihim drove Christopher Moskowitz to the front of the Israel Museum. During the short 8 km drive from Bethlehem, Ibrihim went over the plan again and again to implant it firmly in Chris' mind. Chris was to enter the front of the Israel Museum and pay the admission fee there. If questioned, he would say that he is an Orthodox Jew from Brooklyn who wanted to see the museum, and particularly the Book of Emet. Using his walker, he would pretend to be seriously disabled and huff and puff as he seemingly walked with great effort.

Once inside the museum, he would pretend to look at the various exhibits in the Museum until closing time, at which point he was to hide in the men's room until the lights were turned out and it was safe to go out into the Book of Emet annex. A revolver with a silencer was previously secreted away under one of the sinks in the men's room in case Chris needed it. Fortunately, the day of Chris' mission was one of the days the museum was open until 9:00 p.m., so Chris would only have to hide for two hours after closing before he could set the explosives that would destroy the Book of Emet.

Everything went according to plan initially. When the time came for the museum to close, Chris went into one of the stalls in the men's room. After a few minutes, a guard came in and told him he had to leave, and Chris said he was having a problem and would leave when he could. The guard accepted Chris' story and left. Chris hoped the guard would forget about him and not come back. But this was not to be.

"Sir, you have to leave now," the guard said to the closed door of the stall Chris was in.

"I'm still having trouble," said Chris in a breathless whisper, with a couple of moans worked in. "Give me a little more time. I will definitely leave when I can."

"I can't leave you here," said the guard decisively. "It is not permitted for you to stay. Do you want me to call an ambulance?"

"No," said Chris, realizing that this tactic was not going to work anymore. "I'll try to come out."

Chris made a lot of noises, moaning and huffing and puffing and dropping things and saying "oy" repeatedly, hoping the guard would leave. But the guard did not leave.

Finally, Chris came out of the stall. The guard looked more miffed than sympathetic. Chris knew what he had to do.

"I just have to wash my hands," Chris said in a pained voice.

As he walked excruciatingly slowly toward the sink with the revolver under it, the guard impatiently turned his back on Chris and looked at his watch. With the guard not watching him, Chris was able to easily procure the revolver from under the sink. The guard heard something that alerted him to danger, but it was too late. As the guard turned around to face Chris, several shots burst out of the revolver, hitting the guard several times in the chest and killing him instantly.

Chris hid the guard's body in one of the stalls and then turned the bathroom lights off. He hoped no one would come looking for the guard before he had a chance to apply the explosives. It was now 9:30 p.m. and Chris had to remain hidden until about 10:30. It was a long wait, but no one new entered the bathroom during that time.

The Bombing

At 10:30 p.m., Chris cautiously opened the bathroom door and looked around. No one was to be seen and only a few lights were on, giving the Museum a half-lighted appearance. Slowly, Chris worked his way toward the annex where the Book of Emet was housed. There was no one to be seen and Chris started to feel very confident.

Inside the annex, portions of the Book of Emet were on display under a thick protective glass casing. Chris unscrewed the legs of his walker and carefully removed the C4 plastic explosives. Slowly and carefully, he placed some of the explosives in little white upside-down mounds under the ledge of the case holding the Book of Emet. Then he placed more of them around the room so the whole annex would be destroyed.

Then, not seeing guards anywhere inside the building, Chris had some extra C4 material to put in the main part of the Israel Museum. He chose to put the remainder of the explosives in areas that were the most flammable, hoping to destroy the entire museum, because he did not know where the undisplayed portions of the Book of Emet were stored.

At exactly 11:00 p.m., Chris pulled the trigger mechanism, disguised as a cell phone, out of his coat pocket. He stood near an emergency exit door, hoping to escape the exploding building unharmed. Just as he was about to push the red button that would set off all the explosives, the ground beneath him began to shake. He was knocked off his feet and dropped the trigger mechanism. The disturbance to the building, which turned out to be a mild earthquake, set off the sprinkler system, turning on the fire alarms in the building.

Chris recaptured possession of the trigger mechanism and was about to push the red button again, when he saw the pages from the Book of Emet glowing. Astonished, he was distracted from his task, and then he heard the feet of several people coming his way. The glow of the Book of Emet grew stronger, and suddenly a bolt of electricity shot toward him from the pages behind the heavy glass and knocked Chris down to the ground. A second bolt of electricity shot out at the trigger mechanism and melted its circuits. Realizing there was nothing he could do to fulfill his mission, Chris decided to flee the scene, to fight another day. But before he could get up and escape via the emergency exit, two burly guards were upon him.

The guards took the trigger mechanism away from him and placed him in handcuffs. Exploring the building, they found the C4 explosives Chris had planted. The Israeli police came and took Chris away, intending to interrogate him to see who was behind this bombing attempt.

Ibrihim and his 25 year old son Mustafa were waiting for Chris in a stolen getaway car. When they saw Chris coming out into the well-lighted plaza in handcuffs, accompanied on both sides by Israeli police, they knew what they had to do. Godfather B had told Ibrihim that if the mission failed and Chris was captured, Chris had to be kept from talking at all costs.

"Aim true for Jesus our Lord," Ibrihim said to his son. Mustafa was an experienced marksman, having fought for the Christian side in Lebanon during some street skirmishes there against the dominant Islamic group known as Hezbollah. Mustafa gave his father a knowing look and motioned for him to get the car moving.

Ibrihim stepped on the gas, and as the car squealed forward, Mustafa took aim with his AK-47 machine gun, and with Chris only a few yards away, sprayed him and the two policemen with bullets, killing Chris and seriously wounding the two policemen in a murderous hail of gunfire. Then they sped off quickly away from the museum, with the other policemen in the area too stunned to give chase fast enough to catch up with the fast-disappearing Ibrihim. Once back in Bethlehem, the two conspirators ditched the stolen car, blew it up, and were given a ride to a safe house that had been set up for them. The police never found any clues to tie them to the day's events.

Soon the story of the attempted bombing and the assassinations were emblazoned all over the international media. On cable news in the United States, nothing else was talked about that evening. It was in that context that the last night of the Great Debate was scheduled to resume.

Sunday

Hide me from the conspiracy of the evildoers, from the actions of the wicked. They sharpen their tongues like swords and aim their words like poison arrows. They encourage each other in their evil plans; they talk in secret about laying their traps; and they ask, who would see them? [Psalms 64:2-5.]

George sent the limousine to pick up his three colleagues at 10:00 a.m. Winston and Joshua were already in the lobby waiting, and Mary came down shortly after the limousine arrived. The Unitarian Church service was scheduled to begin at 10:30 and it was a 15 minute ride from the hotel. George was presiding over the service as usual, and he needed to be there early, so he was already there when Mary, Joshua and Winston arrived. George was standing outside the door of the church, greeting everyone who entered. He gave his three colleagues a warm greeting.

"So glad you could all make it," George said happily, his face glowing. "You can sit anywhere you want inside. I'm sure you will enjoy the service." The three colleagues chose to sit near the front, directly across from the pulpit, so they would have a good view of George.

The Unitarian Church got its name because it did not believe in the trinity: the Father, the Son, and the Holy Ghost. It believed in one God and that Jesus was a prophet, not God incarnate. It evolved to include compatible portions of other religions and therefore, had a distinctly non-sectarian feel to it. The service in Reverend George Turner's Unitarian Church was designed by George and a committee of the church's most interested members. While there was some general structure to the service, no two Sundays were ever alike.

On this Sunday, there were hymns and prayers and poetry from all over, primarily from Christian, Jewish and Buddhist sources. All three of George's colleagues were fascinated by the service, though none of them would have been happy being a Unitarian: Winston because he did not go to church anymore and did not believe in God; Joshua because he was committed to Judaism and its enhancement; and Mary because she had an unshakeable belief in Jesus Christ as her personal friend and savior. However, George was a very popular pastor and his church had a lot of members and often an overflowing crowd of attendees.

At 11:30, it was time for George's sermon. Naturally, he wrote it to coincide with the topic that was on everyone's mind—the Great Debate. He entitled the sermon "What if?"

"What if the Book of Emet is the one and only legitimate account of the life of Jesus?" George began. "What if some parts of the gospels are incorrect? What if the mainstream tenets of Christianity are unsupportable? What if most of the ideas we have about Jesus today are wrong? What if, what if, what if?

"For Unitarians, it is not much of a problem, because we don't believe in Jesus as God incarnate anyway. And for Jews and Muslims and every other religion in the world, it is not a problem at all because they never had any belief in the Christian version of the life of Jesus. But for Christians, it is a problem.

"Or is it? According to Emet, I don't want to give away the ending for those who don't know it, Jesus was clearly a special man in the eyes of God. He was a great thinker and a great leader and a great teacher and a great healer. He loved the downtrodden and taught us the Golden Rule. In many ways, he was the greatest of all of God's prophets, with the possible exception of Moses. We could do worse than to build a religion around him and learn from his teachings.

"The Jews built a religion around Moses, the Buddhists built a religion around the Buddha, and the Muslims built a religion around Mohammed. Those very successful religions didn't need their prophets to be a god. I believe Christians can do the same thing, and they probably will at some future time. They haven't really lost very much if the Book of Emet is the true account of Jesus."

A few people walked out in unison, as if on key. But they were respectful and quiet as they left. George guessed they were committed Christians who wanted to hear what he would say that morning, and obviously did not agree with him. He understood their unhappiness and had a lot of empathy for them. He remembered how disappointed he was at various stages of his life when he found out his heroes were either childhood fantasies or were real-life tarnished imperfect humans.

His own personal last refuge was a belief in God, and atheists and scientists and others wanted to take that away from him. "No one knows what the truth is," he often said privately. "It's all a matter of faith. No one can tell you what to believe and what not to believe. I choose to believe in God because that makes sense to me. Others believe in something they call a 'higher power' or 'the creator' and of course some believe in Jesus. And there is a growing group of people who identify themselves as agnostic or atheist. No one knows where we will end up, if there ever is an 'end up'."

A few concluding prayers followed the sermon and then there were some coffee and tea and light snacks for the congregants to socialize around. Winston stayed for the snacks, while Mary and Joshua headed back to the hotel for their lunch date.

In the Coffee Shop

Joshua and Mary arrived back at the hotel at 12:30. Mary wanted to go to her room to freshen up, while Joshua was content to stay in the lobby and read one of the newspapers he found there. Mary came down 20 minutes later and they went to the hotel coffee shop and were seated at a booth next to a large window.

Mary spoke first about the subject that was on both of their minds. "I don't know what we were doing last night. I never should have let you in my room. It was a mistake and if anyone finds out, I'll lose everything! Everything I've worked so hard for...all of it would be gone in the blink of an eye if I was accused of having an affair!"

"But you didn't—we didn't—have an affair! We were two friends that stayed up and talked for a few hours. There's nothing wrong with that!"

"Have you forgotten that I am married?" Her whisper had increased in volume, turning a few heads in her direction. Mary noticed and whispered more softly. "The way we kissed last night was not just two friends talking. What I did last night with you bordered on adultery!"

"I guess it was," Joshua said dejectedly. "I'm really sorry."

The waitress came with two glasses of water and asked if they were ready to place their order. They had not looked at the menus yet, so they asked for a few minutes. Neither one said anything as they looked at the menus and decided what to order.

"I'm just going to have a salad and an ice-tea," Mary quickly decided.

"That sounds good, I'll do the same, except I'll have coffee," said Joshua in a low voice.

They closed their menus, which signaled the waitress to come back and take their order.

Mary looked at Joshua's sad eyes and said softly, "Don't be sorry, dear Joshua. Your kisses went straight to my heart." Mary unconsciously put both hands over her heart as she said that. "Every time you touched me, my body felt alive and I had goosebumps all over. It's been more than twenty years since a man touched me like that. But it wasn't just that. I don't want to admit it, but I have feelings for you Josh. My first waking thought an hour ago was how much I wanted you to be there with me. But I can't," she concluded unhappily.

Joshua began slowly, searching his own heart as he spoke. "I don't know about the married thing, but I know I have strong feelings for you. I may be falling in love with you, Mary."

"Oh Josh, that's how I feel about you too! But I don't feel like I can divorce Wayne. Jesus said divorce is a sin, and I've believed that my whole life."

"But you told me about Wayne's affairs. Jesus said it's not a sin to divorce if your spouse commits adultery."

"Yes, well, that's true…but it's just not that simple. I would be humiliated in my community and I would probably lose my television show…" She reached across the table, where Joshua took her hands and held them tightly as they silently looked at each other.

"We will work this out, however long it takes," Joshua said reassuringly. "I'm going to go out on a limb here—I believe God brought us together this week for a reason."

"Don't blame Him for this," she said with a smile. "We are mature adults who deal with the consequences of our own choices. And, yes," she teased preemptively, "you are a mature adult…most of the time!" Mary paused and squeezed Joshua's hand. "We *will* work this out, one way or another. I think God brought us together for a reason too."

The waitress came with their salads and beverages. Mary squeezed a lemon into her ice tea, while Joshua added milk and sweetener to his coffee. Hardly had they begun to eat when Joshua's cell phone rang. Joshua pulled it out of his pocket casually, and then his body tightened and his face darkened. It was a call from Paul Lindenbaugh's office.

"Rabbi Hertzel, our people are not happy at all with your performance. You need to change your attitude *and* your words tonight! We want your sister to get all the care she needs, Hertzel, but we made a deal and you signed on! What are you going to do when that nice nursing home accidentally gives her the wrong medicine?"

"Stop it!" Joshua said with desperation in his voice. "I will do what I said I would do! Please don't hurt my sister!"

"Then stop disagreeing with Mary Roberts. She's a scholar who knows what she's talking about."

"I know she's a scholar and a fine one at that. But you can't expect me to lie down and just agree with her about everything. Even *she* would not want me to do that! People would smell a rat."

"Let me talk to him," seethed Mary, as she signaled to Joshua that she wanted to take the phone. "I'll give him a piece of my mind...!"

Joshua held up his left hand in front of Mary's face, as if he were a traffic cop. Covering the mouthpiece of the phone, he whispered, "You want him to know we're together? Stay here; I'm going to finish the call out on the sidewalk." He touched Mary on her shoulder as he walked toward the door. She poked at her salad mindlessly, impatiently and nervously waiting for Joshua to return. Five minutes elapsed before Joshua rejoined her, looking like something had just squeezed all the air from his lungs.

"What on earth happened? Are you okay?" Mary asked as she reached over to him.

Joshua sat stunned and glassy-eyed, looking at her but not really seeing. He took a long drink from the glass of water and that seemed to calm him down and bring him back to consciousness. It was time to tell Mary everything he knew.

"That was Paul Lindenbaugh himself on the phone. This is very big. It is political as well as religious. He said conservative politicians and Evangelical leaders want you to 'win'. They don't want to have significant doubts raised by Emet. They want the scroll to be totally discredited. He said I need to make sure that the views expressed in Emet do not catch on, or else there will be severe consequences for me and my sister."

"I cannot believe this! This is outrageous!"

"Wait, it gets worse," Joshua continued. "Lindenbaugh also said that some of their people would be there tonight, *just in case....*"

"Just in case of what?"

"In case I don't do what they want."

"That sounds like a threat! What are we going to do, Josh?"

"I think I have to get ahold of George...."

"And tell him about the bribe? You can't...."

"I have to, Mary. Before...before the threats, I thought it was just about getting some money for my sister. Now, they are making real threats and there are other powerful people behind this too. Maybe that shooter last night wasn't acting alone."

Joshua paled as the full import of what he had just said hit home. Mary started shaking. "Oh Josh," she finally was able to say, "I'm really frightened now. I don't think we should go back there tonight."

That idea sounded wonderful to Joshua at first. It would save him and his sister. But then on reflection he realized that people would think he knew he couldn't defend the Book of Emet on the final night.

"I can't back out Mary. I would lose all my credibility and so would Emet. I'll call my friend Barry. He'll know what to do to protect Esther. And I really think I need to tell all to George and see what he wants to do."

"Good. Can we change the subject until then?"

"Sure. I'm feeling better now." He smiled at her warmly, grateful for her support. "Hopefully this will turn out to be no big deal." They finished their meal quickly and left the restaurant, neither having much of an appetite anymore. Joshua suggested going for a short stroll. The exercise would help with the stress, and he needed time to decide just what he would say to their host.

Sitting in Joshua's hotel room, Mary listened as Joshua called George on the speaker phone setting. He managed to tell George about the threatening phone call and the texts he had received. Like Mary, George had noticed how strange Joshua had been acting when getting messages on his cell phone, so now it all made sense. He reassured Joshua that he too believed the "show must go on" and that he would make sure there would be a heightened police presence around and in the chapel. He added that they should all meet in the hotel lobby at 6:00 where they would meet the limousine that would drive them to the campus.

Breaking News

At about 5:00 p.m. St. Louis time, all the news stations were reporting about the attempted bombing of the Israel Museum in Jerusalem and the shooting of the alleged bomber. As usual when a dramatic story is new, there were conflicting reports and a lot of misinformation. However, it became clear early on that the bomber was an American citizen with an Orthodox Jewish affiliation. None of the commentators could understand why such a person would want to blow up the Israel Museum.

Some time later, it was learned that the man was named Christopher Moskowitz and that he was not an Orthodox Jew at all, but rather the President of the Judeo-Christian group known as Jews for Jesus. His fanatical view about the Book of Emet was also uncovered, and it became clearer what his goal had been in setting off the explosives in the Israel Museum. Because he had been assassinated before he could be questioned, it was assumed that he was not acting alone. However, there were no leads yet as to who else might be involved.

As planned, George was outside the hotel lobby at 6:00 p.m. to pick up the other panelists. Because of the attempted bombing and the information George had supplied to the police about the threats to Joshua, the limousine was given a police motorcycle escort to the chapel. All four of the panelists were shocked by the bombing attempt and they sat mostly in silence, listening to the news on the radio during the drive to the Washington University campus.

The traffic around the University campus was a nightmare, but the police escort managed to navigate through it with minimal difficulty. Following the police motorcycles, the limousine was allowed to drive on the pedestrian parts of the campus and let the panelists out right in front of the chapel.

The four could not believe what they saw when they looked around. They were told that the latest crowd estimate was around 7,500 people, up from a few hundred the day before. Most of them were part of the mob on the left side of the chapel, but there were other groups there as well. Although there were some signs in support of the Book of Emet, most of them denounced it. Somewhere off in the distance, Mary thought she saw an effigy of Joshua hanging from a tree, but thankfully, Joshua was looking somewhere else and did not see it.

Within the mob on the left, all of the signs were pro-Jesus or anti-Joshua. Many warned that one or more of the panelists, and non-believers in general, would be going to hell. Some threatened natural disaster, such as lightning striking the chapel, or an earthquake swallowing it up. Several signs called Joshua the Anti-Christ. Others called Emet a tool of the devil. One of the policemen whispered to George that some people had firearms. The crowd was boisterous and loud and frightening, and many of them were drinking beer. Between fifteen to twenty police and campus security personnel surrounded the building, hoping to keep the crowds at bay, but Winston noticed the unmistakable look of fear in their eyes.

"Aye," said Sir Winston with a shudder, "this reminds me of Yeats' 'The Second Coming,' —

The best lack all conviction, while the worst
Are full of passionate intensity.

As the panelists got themselves settled in the backstage area of the chapel, a liaison from the campus police came to brief George and the others about security. The county police had placed a walk-through metal detector at the front door, with all the other entrances blocked by security officers. The extra security measures delayed the start of the discussion for nearly forty minutes. The television and radio hosts filled the delay in with discussions and interviews, including interviews with some of the most outspoken group members outside. Some of them made a variety of threats if the panel did not reaffirm Jesus as the Savior. One person waved his revolver in the air, yelling it was loaded and ready to go.

A few minutes after 7:00, George walked onto the stage to greet the first audience members to pass through security. The audience this night was much smaller than it had been. Many who had tickets to the Chapel decided not to go, scared off by the shooting the night before, the bombing attempt in Jerusalem and the mob outside. There were enough seats on the main floor, so no one had to sit in the balcony.

After everyone was seated, and the security guards gave the go-ahead, the other three joined George on stage, ready for…they knew not what.

Outside the Chapel

Bryce and Judith were again able to sit in their favorite spot by the trees in front of the chapel. But this time, they saw that the environment around them was much different. The mob on the left lawn was many times larger than before and it appeared to be shepherded by five men dressed all in white. While many of the people in the crowd had brought their own signs, others were provided signs by the five shepherds. The crowd was angry and animated, and their anger was stirred up, and sometimes even directed, by the five shepherds. Plenty of free beers were available. and they were being passed around liberally.

"That group looks pretty organized," observed Bryce.

"They scare me," shivered Judith.

"Me too," agreed Bryce. "Hey, look over there!"

The two students saw a man in a white coat, white pants, and white shirt with a white tie meet with the five shepherds. He was quite animated and clearly directing them what to do.

"That looks like Paul Lindenbaugh," Bryce said with surprise.

"Who is he?"

"He is one of those TV preachers, who's also very active politically. He has his own TV talk show and is a real big shot in Christian evangelical circles. He's like their leader."

After Paul Lindenbaugh concluded his conversation with the five shepherds, he pulled out his pass and joined the crowd entering Graham Chapel. Without being seen by anyone, Reverend Paul went up into the empty balcony where he unwrapped a package he was carrying. Inside the package were a black coat and fake beard, which he put under one of the seats. Then he found a seat near the back of the Chapel on the main floor.

Soon the show was ready to begin. Outside of the Chapel, Bryce and Judith cuddled together again to watch the big screen TV televising the Debate. At the same time, they cast a wary eye at the mob to their left, with an uneasy feeling of muted terror settling in the pits of their stomachs.

The Book of Emet

Chapter Seven: To Jerusalem for Passover

After the suffering of his soul, My servant will see the full of life;
and who by his knowledge did justify him to the many, and he did
bear their iniquities.
Therefore I will give him a portion among the great, and he will
divide the spoils with the mighty, because he bared his soul unto
death, and was numbered with the transgressors; yet he bore the sin of
many, and made intercession for the transgressors. [Isaiah 53.11-12.]

At 7:40 p.m., George received word that it was time to begin. The
audience had been seated and the media were ready.

"Good evening, everyone," George said warmly. "Welcome to the
third and final evening of our discussion on the scroll that has been called
the Book of Emet. I am Reverend George Turner, pastor of the Second
Unitarian Church of St. Louis, and your host for this event. I want to
thank all of you for your patience tonight. As you may have heard, the
discussions here have generated much interest and enthusiasm."

The audience tittered nervously at George's euphemism for the angry
crowds they saw outside and the attempted bombing of the Israel Museum.

"The Public Broadcasting System has given us another two hours
for our discussion of the last two chapters of the Book of Emet. Again,
we ask you to be silent during the discussion and refrain from clapping
or making any disturbance. I also welcome again our national and
international viewers and listeners.

"Joining us again are our other three panel members:

"Dr. Mary Madelyne Roberts is a nationally televised Christian minister, who describes herself as a conservative theologian and teacher of the Bible. She is representing those who dispute the authenticity of the Book of Emet.

"Joshua David Hertzel is a Rabbi from the Jewish Reform movement. He is known to synthesize aspects from a variety of different religions into the practices and worship of Judaism. He is representing the Jewish point of view about the Book of Emet.

"Sir Winston Hamburley is a Doctor of Philosophy at Oxford University in England. He is a noted scholar of Christianity and Judaism, with a specialty in the life of Jesus and his times. He is representing the point of view of the secular historians.

"Just as we did the last two nights, Dr. Roberts will summarize what the gospels from the Christian Bible teach us; then Rabbi Hertzel will summarize how the Book of Emet differs from the Christian Bible; and lastly Sir Winston Hamburley will give us the views of the historians. After their respective presentations, there will be an in-depth discussion of each chapter and the issues presented by it.

"As in the past, the pertinent chapter from the Book of Emet will be narrated before each session.

"I have been pleased that this very important conversation is happening in a dignified manner despite the passions that have been generated by the discovery of the Book of Emet. On a personal note, I have been fascinated by the study of religion since my first year of college and have really enjoyed the various views presented here."

The Arrival

Shaken as they were by the mob outside, the panelists were still able to project a calm and focused demeanor as the next session began. George was the first to speak as he introduced the next chapter.

"In the spring, Jesus pilgrimaged again to Jerusalem, this time for the freedom-celebrating holiday of Passover. When he entered the city, a large crowd of people who had heard of him gathered together and cheered him. Some historians think he was virtually unknown outside of his native Galilee, but there were obviously many people in Jerusalem, possibly there for the pilgrimage just like Jesus, who had heard of him and thought well of him. It was in Jerusalem that the tragic events that led to Jesus' death occurred. Mary, would you please continue."

"Jesus Christ's triumphal entry into Jerusalem demonstrated that God would rule through the power of love," Mary said with gladness in her heart. "During his last week before the crucifixion, Jesus showed that the Messiah was truly the *suffering servant* mentioned by the prophet Isaiah. Also, where Emet says Jesus came to the Holy City to '…restore [the] nation and drive out the pagans,' the gospels say he came to save all people from the powers of evil and sin."

"The gospels and Emet made consistent use of the Old Testament in this section," observed Joshua. "Emet directly quoted Psalm 118:25 and 26, as did the gospels. And the verse from Emet you just questioned, Mary, was a definite allusion to the prophet Zechariah.

"Certainly the Jewish people of that time believed the Messiah would restore the nation as it was in the time of King David. That is why they believed the Messiah would come from the line of David, because King David was the one who first created a nation for the Jewish people and made them feel safe. They did not have a belief that someone needed to suffer or die for their sins. That is not the Jewish way of thinking.

"We do not believe in Original Sin. We know we are not perfect and we know that God does not expect us to be perfect. And God does not punish us because we are not perfect. What God wants is for us to recognize our sins, repent them, and improve ourselves and grow as individuals. Putting our sins on a Jesus-like person would be considered a cop out by most Jews."

Though unseen by the panelists, Joshua's words riled the mob outside and it was all the five shepherds could do to keep them from charging the Chapel. "Now is not the time," the five shepherds told the mob.

Back in the Chapel, Winston wanted to make another point about Jesus' arrival in Jerusalem. "I have always thought the narratives of Jesus' entry into the city would have been improved if they also described the other parade that occurred that day.

"It was the custom of the Roman governor, Pontius Pilate, to ride a stallion into Jerusalem during every major Jewish Festival. It was like any military parade of the time: scores of soldiers marching with spears, swords and shields; banners proclaiming Caesar as Lord; the stallions dressed for battle.

"It was a reminder to Jews from near and far that they held their public religious feasts only through Rome's beneficence. And it was also a reminder to them not to get stirred up politically, because Rome was too strong to defy. It was during these religious pilgrimages that Jewish unrest was most likely to occur, and Rome wanted to head that off proactively."

"Think about the contrasts between the two parades," said Mary. "One was pompous, the other humble; one was militaristic, while the other was peaceful; one displayed the power of might, the other the power of faith; one was declared triumphant, though they would lose in the end, the other was initially seen as a failure until later, when it became clear it was the ultimate triumph of God!"

No one disagreed.

Jesus at the Temple

"When Jesus arrived at the Temple for the last time, he was not playing around!" Mary began. "He saw the moneychangers on Temple grounds and threw them out.

This was not 'street theater' as I heard it described once. He was angry that those doing business in the outer court had so little regard for his Father's home, and for keeping the spirit of the Temple holy. They had desecrated the Temple and he wasn't going to stand for it."

"This was far more political than most of us realize," said Joshua, "and the Book of Emet tells us why. The moneychangers represented Romans, not Jews. Jesus went to the Temple to preach and teach as he had done before, but this time he noticed that the vendors near the Temple, who were making change and selling animals for sacrifice, were cheating the people. He lost his temper and disrupted their businesses.

"According to Emet, the moneychangers were working for the wealthy Romans who had come to settle in Jerusalem. Like most occupiers, the wealthy Romans skimmed off the cream from the top and took the best of the best. Cheating the poor ignorant masses was something they felt entitled to do. When Jesus disrupted their commerce, and they saw that Jesus had the support of the people, they were worried he would cut into their profits and decided to have him eliminated."

Mary, of course, disagreed. "There may have been some political involvement between Pilate and the high priest, Caiaphas, but the bottom line was that Jesus was certainly a threat to the cold-hearted religious elite who knew he was more than just another itinerant rabbi. They were the ones desecrating the Temple. There is no mention in the gospels of Roman merchants or that the moneychangers worked for the Romans."

"I have to agree with Joshua on the political thrust," Winston said thoughtfully. "I do not believe that the Jewish elite would have felt threatened enough to have wanted Jesus dead. On the other hand, the Romans had plenty of reason to fear him. Jesus was rabble-rousing at a time when Jews from all over the country were in Jerusalem for the festival and were capable of being stirred up to violence against the hated Romans. It was already a tinderbox. And the fact that some of the people called Jesus King had to be considered a threat the Romans would not ignore. The fact that the Romans put 'King of the Jews' on Jesus' cross showed that was what they were concerned about."

Paying Taxes to Caesar

Mary went on to the next subject. "I know there are well-meaning Christians who question paying taxes in this country, but Jesus was clear on this, that we 'give unto Caesar what is Caesar's'. As the apostle Paul wrote in Romans 13, we need to obey the governing authorities because God gave them their authority to begin with. As an aside, I've always liked something Supreme Court Justice Oliver Wendell Holmes once said, 'Taxes are the price we pay for living in a civilized society'."

"Citing Romans 13 reminds me of the provocative American writer, William Stringfellow, no longer with us, I'm afraid," said Winston. "He wrote that if one wanted to read what the New Testament says about a Christian's relationship with the state, one must also read Revelations 13, in which the government is pictured as a beast rising from the sea, in league with a second beast that enforces worship of the first beast."

"What Paul was sanctioning later became known as the 'divine right of kings'," Joshua pointed out. "In other words, if they were kings, it must have been because God wanted them to be kings. That was what the kings used to say to explain why they were kings and other people weren't. And for hundreds of years, the people believed it. The kings are mostly gone now because the people quit believing in their divine right to rule. I don't think many of us miss them. In this country, we don't believe in kings at all and we prohibited them in the Constitution.

"Jesus, on the other hand, said to pay your taxes, but he did not say they had a divine right to rule. He didn't trust the government and he knew that it didn't care about the people he cared about. I doubt if he would have agreed with Paul, that whoever rules is ruling because God chose them to rule. Rather, he was hoping God would help the Jews overthrow them."

Marriage at the Resurrection

Mary looked at the other panelists to see if anyone had anything else to add, and since no one did, she went on to the next topic. "Someone asked Jesus which woman a man would be with at the resurrection if he had more than one wife in life. Jesus taught that when the resurrection comes, being in a relationship with God is more important than any temporal relationship, such as marriage. Faith in God leads from death to life."

"There is clear evidence in the Torah that there is existence after death," Joshua said. "The Torah indicates that the righteous will be reunited with their loved ones after death, while the wicked will be excluded from this reunion. The Torah also names several noteworthy people as being 'gathered unto their ancestors' when they died: specifically Abraham, Ishmael, Isaac, and Moses and Aaron.

"The Kabbalah teaches that soulmates were together before birth, and that the search for one's love partner in life is an attempt to find one's other half. So the right marriage partners would be together after death, as they were before birth, and during life."

"I find it interesting," Winston observed, "that Jesus in the gospels said there should be no divorce because God put the married couple together, yet in the afterlife earthly marriages are irrelevant. Those two ideas don't go together."

The Greatest Commandment

"In the next topic," said Mary, "a man asked Jesus to tell him what the greatest commandment is. Jesus answered by quoting Scripture from the Old Testament — that the greatest commandment is to believe in the One God, and to love Him with all your heart and soul. And the second greatest commandment is to love your neighbor as yourself."

"The first part of Jesus' answer is what Jews call the *Shema*," Joshua said. "It reaffirms the belief in the One God. This is the prayer traditionally said by Jewish martyrs as they are dying due to persecution. It is also said at all Jewish prayer services and is the last prayer we say before we go to sleep at night. It is usually the first prayer a young Jewish student learns to say. It reads 'Hear, O Israel, the Lord is our God, the Lord is One'."

Signs of the End of the Age

"Jesus said that in times of great tribulation people naturally listen to almost any authority figure, real or fake," said Mary. "So he warned them about the dangers of false Messiahs, because he was the true Christ."

"Some New Testament scholars believe that Jesus' prediction of the end of the age actually referred to the destruction of Jerusalem by the Roman armies in 70 C.E. rather than end of the world," Winston offered. "Jesus was quoted as telling the people to get out of Jerusalem, which is exactly what happened. Jews—and Jewish followers of Jesus—were evicted by the Romans and dispersed to all points around the Mediterranean Sea."

"It is possible that is what Jesus meant," said Joshua, "an amazing prediction! But from the sound of his prediction, a lot more was supposed to happen than just the destruction of Jerusalem and the exile of the Jews. He said they would see the end of the world in their own lifetimes, and as I said before, that certainly did not happen."

The Authority of Jesus Questioned

"Then, as now, people question whether Jesus was truly sent by God for us," Mary said, giving Joshua and Winston a knowing look. "But only those who have let Jesus enter their lives can see the real truth."

"I truly believe that Jesus was sent by God," agreed Joshua, "but not as His *divine* Son or Messiah. I think Jesus is right up there with the greatest Jewish thinkers of all time; certainly a prophet of God echoing Moses, Isaiah, Jeremiah and the others."

"That he spoke authoritatively no one really disputes," Winston added. "But on whose authority — that is the question. When he was asked who gave him the authority to say and do what he did, he dodged the question."

"Yes, he did in that particular conversation," said Mary, "but we all know where he got the authority. He often said that he was representing his Heavenly Father on earth. He was the Christ—that was all the authority he needed!"

Helping the Poor and Needy

"I really like this next subject, about where Jesus advocated for the poor and needy," said George.

"I do too," agreed Mary warmly. "Jesus beautifully proclaimed that those who help the poor and needy will have a place in the Kingdom of Heaven, while those who do not help the poor and needy will not have a place there. This is one of the gifts people get when they accept Jesus as their Savior. They naturally want to help others who are in need. People who don't have Jesus in their heart, and don't know the love of God, don't have the love to help others."

"How can you say that, Mary?" Joshua asked a bit offended. "Millions of non-Christians, even atheists, give billions of dollars and countless hours of their time to fight homelessness, poverty, disease, and starvation. Surely they have a place in heaven for their good deeds."

"I have to agree with Joshua on this one," Winston chimed in. "Jesus said that all the nations will be gathered and judged. And those that were righteous will go to heaven, and those who were not righteous will not.

It does not only refer to Christians, or even Jews for that matter. So Jesus clearly said that there will be non-believers in the heavenly Kingdom. It was Paul, not Jesus, who said that only belief in Jesus will get you to heaven."

"The Old Testament and Rabbinic literature require us to care for the poor and needy among us," agreed Joshua. "Jesus is totally in line with those teachings."

Mary was feeling outnumbered again, but was not giving up. "I've noticed that Emet omitted all references to punishment and hell, whereas Jesus talked about them frequently in the gospels."

"Mainstream Judaism doesn't really talk much about heaven and doesn't believe in hell, so I'll bet Jesus didn't either," Joshua countered. "I think that when Jesus talked about heaven, he meant the Kingdom of Heaven—in other words, the Messianic period. And when he talked about hell, he meant the valley of Gehenna, as I said earlier, not the Christian version of hell.

"However, in the Jewish book of mysticism, the Kabbalah, there is a heaven and a purgatory and an afterlife and reincarnation. I think the Kabbalah is more likely to be right about those things than mainstream Judaism *or* Christianity."

The Parable of the Prodigal Son

Mary noticed George glancing at his watch and quickly went on to the next subject before their time for this segment was up. "The next two parables — about the Prodigal Son and the Lost Coin — are about finding what has been lost, and rejoicing in what has been found. God rejoices when any person turns from their sins toward their Savior. These parables are repeated in the Book of Emet with no changes."

"The Prodigal Son parable is very Jewish," added Joshua. "God seeks the repentance of sinners, not their punishment. At the Jewish High Holy Days, we are told repeatedly to examine ourselves and confess and repent our sins. So like the father in the parable, God is delighted to welcome us back if we repent and change our ways."

George then asked if anyone had anything they wanted to discuss before he closed the current session. Winston nodded that he did.

"I just want to add something about why the older brother in the

Prodigal Son story was not so happy that the younger brother returned and got such a grand reception. According to Mosaic law, the younger brother would be entitled to only one-third of the total inheritance. I suspect the older brother was concerned that his father would re-slice the pie, so to speak, and give the repentant prodigal son a larger share."

Outside

Bryce and Judith were thankful when the discussion of Chapter Seven ended.

"Only one more to go, honey," Judith said. "I'll be so happy for this night to end."

"Yeah, everybody came through this session unscathed. With all the rumbling in that crowd, I think we dodged a bullet."

"Couldn't you have picked a better word? Bullets and guns are the last things I want to hear about!"

"Sorry. I should have phrased it differently," Bryce said with embarrassment. "It's hard to think of our campus being a dangerous place."

"I know," Judith said softly, "but that crowd looks dangerous to me and the way they have been drinking and getting riled up, I am scared they might do something awful before they leave."

"Me too," said Bryce with deep concern in his voice.

Judith suddenly had a flash of insight. "Say, remember the package that was thrown from the upstairs window that you told me about?"

"Of course. What about it?"

"Didn't that seem really strange to you?" Judith asked.

"Absolutely! I mean, throwing something out of a window after a shooting is very suspicious if you ask me."

"Even stranger than that was the guy from the mob who walked up to the chapel right under the window as the package came down. It's like they both knew the window would be broken and it was all prearranged. And why didn't the police who were there watching say anything to him? He simply caught the package and nonchalantly walked back to that mob."

"I wonder why the police left him alone. It's almost like...wait! That's too crazy; it's preposterous to think..."

"To think what? What's preposterous, Bryce?"

"To think they knew what was going to happen before it happened; the police and the person inside and the one who caught the package. It might be some kind of conspiracy or something."

"Oh, my God!" Judith fairly shouted with tears filling her eyes. "I'm really scared now. Something's happening, my father is back in there, and I don't know what to do!"

At this, Judith began sobbing and gasping for air. As Bryce held her, she started to cough, and in between coughs she sputtered, "I hope I didn't leave my inhaler in my room! It's not in my pocket..."

"Here it is honey," responded Bryce, handing it to her. "You gave it to me because my jeans have more pockets than yours." In a moment, Judith was breathing normally. Her tears subsided and she used her fingers to wipe them from her cheeks. She leaned in to Bryce and he put his arm around her. "I'm glad you're okay. You really frightened me."

She nodded. "I frightened myself, too!"

"It's probably really nothing," Bryce said trying to console Judith. "The police arrested the shooter. Whatever that package was, it's probably nothing serious. And even if it is, there are so many cops here, there's nothing that can really happen."

Judith nodded her head, feeling a little better. "I hope you're right honey."

"I hope I'm right too," Bryce said to himself.

Backstage

"Just one more session to go," Mary exhaled as she addressed the other panelists. "I can't wait till it's over. I am so scared and worried. That crowd outside seems to be getting louder and louder."

"Quite so. Thankfully we are almost done," Winston agreed. "Just one more session to go. Then I venture to say that we shall all enjoy a few drinks at the hotel."

"I'll be ready for that," Mary smiled broadly. "God has blessed us so far by keeping us safe. I just pray He and the police will keep things quiet so everyone gets out of here without any trouble."

"This old skeptic will gladly join you in that prayer, my dear," said Winston humbly.

Suddenly, Joshua's cell phone dinged; he had a new text message. He read the short message and his face suddenly reddened in anger. "What?" Mary asked quickly. "What does it say?" He showed her the tiny screen: "YOU FAILED JUDAS. WE'LL TAKE OUR POUND OF FLESH NOW!"

"I'm getting really tired of their threats," he said firmly. "Bring it on!" he said, recalling his days as a championship tennis player. He drew himself up straight, head up, chest out, a determined look on his face. Mary fairly gasped in admiration.

Joshua placed a call to his best friend Barry back home to make sure his sister was okay and being well-guarded. Barry assured him that she was. Without his sister to worry about, Joshua felt he could take on whatever came his way. "I'm not going to duck any more questions," he said defiantly to Barry. "I'm ready for them."

"We'll all be ready for them," George seconded. "We are not going to be bullied by that mob outside. There are plenty of police here and they wouldn't dare do anything on international television."

One of the officers in the room said to the panelists, "We just got the signal, folks. Time to go back on stage."

"I have to go now," Joshua told Barry through the phone, "we're due on stage. If anything happens, please let me know right away. Yes, I'll take your call on stage. I don't care how it looks."

Joshua's jaw was clenched and he had a determined look on his face as he put the phone back in his pocket. He started walking toward the stage, but then the conflicting emotions of determination, anger, and fear for his sister temporarily overcame him. Suddenly Joshua became light-headed, he began to stagger, and he felt like he was going to faint. Mary was watching him closely and quickly rushed over to help hold him up.

"Are you going to be alright?" Mary asked with deep concern. "We don't have to rush out there right now. They can wait. Do you want some water?"

Joshua nodded. Mary asked the officer who had come backstage to bring some water so she would not have to leave Joshua's side. Joshua slowly drank the water and soon the color returned to his face and he got his strength back.

"I'm ready, thank you," he said gratefully to Mary. "Let's go and finish this thing up right. We owe it to our public." He said the last remark with a touch of ironic humor, knowing that he and Mary had different publics in mind. Mary recognized the humor and smiled at him, her eyes dancing. "Our public will certainly find it *very* interesting," she said with a wink. "I certainly did."

The two friendly combatants walked side by side toward the stage. They would be discussing the most important and the most controversial part in the story of Jesus — his death and resurrection. It would be the final chapter....

The Book of Emet

Chapter Eight: The Final Events

And the angel of the Lord said: "Lay not your hand upon the lad, neither do anything unto him; for now I know that you are a God-fearing man, seeing that you have not withheld your son, your only son, from Me."
And Abraham lifted up his eyes, and looked, and behold behind him was a ram caught in the thicket by his horns. And Abraham went and took the ram, and offered him up for a burnt-offering in the stead of his son.
Then the angel of the Lord called to Abraham and said: "Because you have done this thing, and have not withheld your son, your only son ,I will bless you, and I will multiply your seed as the stars of the heaven, and as the sand which is upon the seashore; and your seed shall possess the gates of their enemies; and in your seed shall all the nations of the earth be blessed; because you have hearkened unto My voice." [Genesis 22:12-18.]

"We have now reached the final chapter of the Book of Emet, the part we have all been waiting for," George said in his best portentous voice. "Mary, would you please start us off."

"Judas was the greatest villain in the history of the world," Mary said with anger and sadness in her voice. "He betrayed our Lord and Savior for a few coins of silver. It was a conspiracy between Judas and the Jewish priests. As I said before, there is no mention in the gospels of any Roman merchants being involved."

"The Book of Emet says that Judas was forced to betray Jesus," Joshua countered. "If he was so sinister, why would he hang himself afterwards?"

"We don't know why he decided to hang himself," said Mary. "Luke tells us, 'Satan entered into Judas,' and that was the motivation for the betrayal. We assume the magnitude of his villainy hit him and Judas became riddled with guilt and he didn't want to live anymore, or maybe Satan made him do that too."

"The explanation given by Emet makes more sense than the one in the gospels," Winston joined in. "If Judas was so money hungry, why would he be running around the country helping Jesus spread the word for no money? There must have been some pressure on Judas to make him change his values so dramatically."

"Maybe he was behind on his mortgage payments," Mary joked. "But you both miss the point. It doesn't matter what sounds logical to our ears. The gospels we have are the word of God. What they say is what happened. This so-called Book of Emet is a fake. God wouldn't play tricks on us and keep His word buried for two thousand years. *That* is what doesn't make sense."

"I agree with that," Winston said to Mary's surprise. "But, what if God didn't write any of the gospels, and they were all written by men, using the best information they had available to them. It is possible that Emet knew more of the behind-the-scenes story than the gospel writers did. Certainly, from a historian's point of view, this sleeping Emet rings more true than the gospels.

"By way of example, Emet says the High Priest Caiaphas was a Sadducee appointed by Pontius Pilate, while the gospels suggest he was a Pharisee. The gospels had to be wrong about that. The Sadducees, not the Pharisees, were the high born and the priestly class. But even the priests served at the pleasure of the Romans because the Romans controlled everything important in the lands they occupied."

Joshua was quick to agree. "Yes, and from a Jewish point of view, Rome had a more compelling reason to get rid of Jesus than the Jewish religious establishment did. As I mentioned earlier, Jews rarely seek the death of other Jews for theological disagreements. Jesus posed no real threat to the religious establishment at the time, and in fact, he was less of an opponent than other groups that were in existence then. And as Winston pointed out, there were other claimants to Messiah status in those days."

Someone in the crowd yelled, "Kill the Jew! He is the Antichrist!" Other voices echoed the same thing. Joshua rolled his eyes at yet another interruption. Mary just felt angry.

George tried to maintain order. "Let's move on. No one can settle the differences between faith and logic. I again ask the audience to show respect to all the participants here. What we are discussing here has nothing to do with your faith. You already know that there are those who do not believe as you do. Your faith is not being disparaged here. We're just discussing different points of view by well-meaning people."

"We'll get you too," someone in the crowd answered from the back of the Chapel. "We'll get all of you!"

Guards quickly removed the offending cat-caller. Some in the crowd cheered him as he was being escorted out of the Chapel.

The Last Supper

George was getting a bit annoyed with the ill-mannered members of the audience and apologetically nodded at Mary to continue. She saw his nod, gave him a sympathetic understanding smile, and went on to the next topic.

"The Last Supper was the origin of the celebration that we call The Lord's Supper," she said. "We meet together to pray and sing. We break bread, share it and eat it as a way of remembering the body of Jesus, broken on the cross in his death. Then we share the cup of wine—though some of our churches use grape juice—as a symbol of his blood, shed as a sacrifice for the sins of the whole world. Next to a public confession of faith in Jesus Christ and being baptized, receiving communion at the Lord's Table is the most important religious observance in a Christian's life.

"Catholics believe that the bread or wafer has become the body of Christ and the wine has been transformed into the blood of Christ. Although most Protestant churches don't see it that way, the Catholic Christians I know say their belief is quite spiritually transforming for them."

"To the Jews, what Christians call the Lord's Supper or the Last Supper, is in reality the Passover Seder," said Joshua. "'Seder' means 'order' in Hebrew, which comes from the orderly way in which the Seder is organized. We have the unleavened bread and the wine too, but it is not anything like taking communion. To us, communion seems rather pagan, or even cannibalistic. What I have always wondered about, Mary, is why your gospels have Jesus and his disciples planning a Passover meal, but then not having one. Jesus doesn't lead the traditional Seder service: there are no bitter herbs; no parsley dipped in salt water; only one cup of wine when there should be four; and most importantly, he never mentions the Israelites' exodus from slavery in Egypt! It's no wonder most Jews don't think of Jesus as Jewish."

"Neither do most Christians," Mary added. "In Jesus, the Passover was reinterpreted, not only by his followers later, but by him that very evening. Jesus taught us that God was offering freedom from more than slavery and political oppression. He was granting freedom from sin and death. It was almost as if Jesus broke the unleavened bread and said, 'By means of my death, there will be a new exodus'. Jesus himself was to be the sacrificial lamb."

"This is where I quarrel with Christianity the most," Joshua objected passionately, "this view of Jesus as the sacrificial lamb. God showed us once and for all, by stopping Abraham from sacrificing his son Isaac, that He doesn't want human sacrifice. I don't for the life of me understand why Christians think that Jesus had to die because Isaac was allowed to live hundreds of years earlier. Furthermore, if a sacrifice was needed in the Isaac story, it was fulfilled by the ram that God provided. Now, today, we don't even believe in *animal sacrifice*. So I just don't get why Jesus had to die so that God would give us freedom from sin and death. If that is what God wanted to do, He didn't need Jesus' death to do it.

"In Judaism, God teaches us that all He wants is for us to repent from our sins. He does not expect us to be perfect. No one had to die to free us from our sins. Just the opposite, God wants us to work at making ourselves better. He doesn't seek the death or punishment of sinners; He seeks the repentance and betterment of sinners. "

"Jesus had to die because he was the sacrifice that enabled us to be forgiven for our Original Sin, which is in all of us, and thereby allow us to escape going to Hell and let us have eternal life," Mary patiently explained.

"Judaism doesn't believe in Original Sin," Joshua countered. "It's a myth that we were perfect until Adam and Eve sinned in the Garden of Eden. They were imperfect already, and of course they sinned, just like any of us would. That is who we are and how we were made. There is not and never was an Original Sin that needed to be erased. And even if there was an Original Sin, God didn't need the death of Jesus to erase it. He could have eradicated it whenever and however He wanted.

"And we don't believe in Hell, so there was nothing we needed to be saved from. This view of why Jesus died is not at all Jewish and I doubt the early followers of Jesus, who were all Jews, looked at it that way. I think those views came later to appeal to the pagans the early Christians were trying to convert. To the pagans, human sacrifice to please 'the gods' and a virgin impregnated by a god made perfect sense. And they believed in Hades or some kind of horrible underworld."

Joshua's cell phone signaled a new message. He was hoping it was from Barry giving him good news about his sister, but it was from Paul Lindenbaugh. It said: "YOU ARE A DEAD MAN."

Mary noticed Joshua looking at his cell phone, but he did not betray any emotion. She was worried about what kind of message he was getting. Was it about his sister or another message about his performance? She knew he probably crossed over Reverend Paul's line and did not want him to dig an even deeper hole for himself, so she decided to go on to the next topic.

Jesus Arrested

"Well Joshua, those sound like good arguments, but we have the truth from the gospels to tell us why Jesus had to die for our sins. Jesus himself had a lot of anguish over this at the end. After the Last Supper, Jesus led his disciples to the Garden of Gethsemane because he wanted to pray. His divine appointment was to go to the cross. He understood this and was fully committed to giving his life as a sacrifice for all our sins. But, the human Jesus, with a physical body capable of feeling pain, as we do, wished to avoid the suffering waiting for him — the torture of the beatings and the slow death on a Roman cross. Who could blame him? He knew where he was going and humbly went."

"Yes, he did, but not without inner struggle," added Joshua, who was having his own inner struggle. He could identify with Jesus needing to see his mission through to the end, come what may. Joshua felt he had his own mission — to set the historical record straight and tell the world what really happened to Jesus, as described accurately, he felt, in the Book of Emet. If death was to be the consequence of his telling "the truth," then he wanted to get the most out of whatever time remained for him.

"Emet never indicated that Jesus thought he was being sacrificed for the sins of others or that he had any hope of being brought back from death," Joshua continued bravely. "But God was obviously at the center of Jesus' life and he prayed hard to ask God to protect him from the evil he knew was about to come upon him. Even though Jesus must have been terrified about his future when the arresting officers came to take him away, he opposed the use of violence against those who came to arrest him. That is the mark of a very great man."

"That is the mark of a very great God!" Mary declared firmly.

Before the Council of Priests

Mary resumed telling the story. "The gospels tell us that after Judas gave Jesus 'the kiss of death,' the guards took Jesus to the High Priest and the Jewish high court, the Sanhedrin. Jesus was asked if he was the Christ and the Son of God. And Jesus answered that he was, and for that, he was unanimously condemned to death for blasphemy."

"Emet says the so-called trial of Jesus took place before a Council of Priests, not the Sanhedrin," Joshua responded. "That makes sense because the Sanhedrin was the Jewish equivalent to our Supreme Court, and probably could not be convened so quickly to hear this case. They also would not have met during the Passover holiday and the day before the Sabbath. Not only that, but Jewish law in those days was extremely opposed to the death penalty, and many years went by at a time with no executions under Jewish law.

"Emet goes on to say that the Roman merchants and the Roman authorities bribed and threatened the priests with death if they did not convict Jesus. Even so, the priests were reluctant to convict Jesus. When the High Priest saw he wasn't getting anywhere, no matter how many false witnesses he produced, he finally asked Jesus directly if he was the Messiah. Jesus said he was not the Messiah. But he did tell them he was God's messenger, and then he prophesied that the Kingdom of Heaven was about to come and that all the hypocrites and sinners would be left to die. At that point the High Priest charged Jesus with blasphemy, and the Council of Priests found him guilty."

Mary would have none of this. "This Emet fantasy directly contradicts the gospels and sounds very much like it was made up by someone who wanted to rewrite history. They will have to find more than one phony manuscript in a cave if they want us to throw out what we've believed for over 2,000 years."

"Well, Mary, the problem with your theory is that it's possible the gospels contain Christian rewrites of history," Winston said. "For example, I have always been puzzled about how the High Priest could have asked Jesus if he was the 'Christ' or the 'Son of God' because those terms were not used in those days. Jesus may or may not have believed he was the Messiah, but no one in those days thought in terms of 'Son of God'. It was only after he was resurrected that he claimed that title for himself."

No one had anything else to add, so Mary went on to the next topic.

Jesus Before Pilate

"After being condemned by the Jewish court, Jesus was brought before Pontius Pilate, who asked him if the charges against him were true. Jesus refused to answer. So Pilate asked the crowd watching the proceedings what they wanted to do with Jesus, and they told Pilate, 'Crucify him!' Pilate thought he was executing an innocent man, but the crowd was insistent. So Pilate said he was washing his hands of this miscarriage of justice and then did what the crowd demanded. All of this had to happen so that Christ would be crucified on the cross as the Savior of the whole world. He came to shed his blood out of his great love for us so we would be cleansed of our sins and granted eternal life."

Mary had tears in her eyes, as she once again felt the love of Jesus surge through her, and warm her, and give her renewed courage and strength.

Joshua was feeling a surge in his own strength. He was feeling very in tune with God, and that was always when he was at his best and most confident.

"In the Book of Emet, Pontius Pilate was himself part of the conspiracy to kill Jesus, along with the wealthy Roman merchants,"

Joshua said. "The merchants wanted Jesus dead because he was a threat to their business interests. Pilate wanted Jesus dead because he presented a threat to Roman control. Some of the Jews believed Jesus to be of royal blood from the House of David and they hoped he would lead a revolt to throw the hated Romans out. Contrary to what the gospels said about the Jews wanting him dead, the last thing most Jews wanted was for the Romans to kill their hoped-for champion.

"Emet tells us that the crowd watching the proceedings at Pilate's court was stacked with Roman hirelings. It was the Romans, not the Jews, who were demanding that Jesus be crucified, and Pilate was in on the charade."

"The primary duty of any Roman governor was to collect taxes and keep the peace throughout his jurisdiction," added Winston. "The last thing his office needed was a rebellion. He could have lost his job, or even his life, for failing to handle the situation before it got out of control. Furthermore, Pilate would not have been the least bit concerned if Jesus posed a threat to the established Jewish religious authorities. I am quite sure he knew the theory of divide and conquer. Pilate would have been delighted for the religious authorities to have less power and control over the populace.

"No, the threat he was concerned about would have been the threat Jesus posed to the *Pax Romana*, the Roman peace, and the claim of Jesus' followers that he was King of the Jews. The placement of the words 'King of the Jews' on Jesus' cross was to show that Rome was more powerful than any supposed king the Jews could have had."

"There is another point that is being overlooked," said Joshua jumping back in, encouraged by what Winston had just said. "If the mob that called for Jesus' crucifixion was in fact dominated by hirelings of the Roman merchants, an onlooker might think it was really the Jews calling for Jesus' execution, because that is how it was made to look. Don't forget, none of the gospel writers was there. They had all fled Jerusalem fearing for their lives.

"If the Jews thought Jesus was their King, the rightful descendant of King David, who would free them from the yoke of the hated Romans, why on earth would they call for his death? It makes no sense at all. It was obviously a put-up job, and by making it look like the priestly class was at fault, Pilate cleverly turned Jesus' followers against the religious authorities."

"Yes, yes," Winston said, warming to the argument. "Divide and conquer! Pilate's strategy worked very well indeed, because the followers of Jesus ended up by hating the Jews and allying themselves eventually with the ruling powers in Rome.

"Another thing that needs to be pointed out is that Pilate was a bloodthirsty blackguard. His behavior of murdering people was so bad that even the brutal Emperor Tiberius eventually fired him. You know that Pilate must have been very very bad for the Romans to fire him for killing too much! The Romans were not known for their humanity in dealing with occupied peoples. I find it highly doubtful that Pilate cared much whether Jesus was innocent or not, and he had every reason for wanting Jesus dead when he heard Jesus was being called King of the Jews."

Mary was beginning to see the merits of what Winston and Joshua were saying. "Many Christians have said we were mistaken in blaming the Jews for the death of Jesus, especially the Jews living today who had nothing to do with it. I've always agreed with them. Also, I personally have a problem with the grossly anti-Jewish writings of the Gospel of John and do wonder whether those particular words came from God."

Someone in the back of the Chapel shouted, "Kill the bitch! This whole thing is a Jewish conspiracy and she is part of it too." The guards were unable to find the man who had uttered those words.

George again asked the audience to be respectful.

The Crucifixion

"Getting back to the story," Mary said defiantly, "Jesus was immediately taken away to be crucified after Pontius Pilate made his decision. But first the Roman soldiers flogged him and mocked him. Then, in a severely beaten condition, he was nailed to the cross and left to die. He suffered horribly." Mary had tears in her eyes as she recalled the feelings of empathy she always had when thinking about the death of Jesus.

"Yes, he suffered horribly," Joshua said softly and with sympathy, "as did all those who were crucified by the Romans. He was made fun of because he was able to save and heal others he had met, but was unable to save himself." Joshua looked tenderly at Mary and his affection for her grew all the more for her soft heart.

Mary tried to answer, but she had trouble getting the words out. Finally, she was able to say in a broken voice, "Of course he would not save himself! He had to die, so that his followers could live eternally with him, after the resurrection."

Winston jumped in to give Mary a breather. "In the final verse of this section, Jesus addressed the robber who stuck up for him, saying, 'Today you will surely be with me in paradise'. This is a key verse in the discussion of what happens to Christians after they die. Some say one goes immediately to heaven, as this verse would suggest. Others say that one awaits the resurrection of the dead, which is said to occur at the return of the Messiah. That would surely be a sight to behold!"

"Mainstream Judaism teaches that all Jews, and the righteous of all peoples, will be resurrected when the Messiah comes," said Joshua. "That is why they are so diligent in Israel about finding all the body parts and identifying them after a terrorist bomb explodes. They believe the body parts will all be needed to resurrect the whole person when the Messiah comes.

"But I personally agree with the Kabbalah when it says we are reincarnated many times till we get it right. In that, I believe the Buddhists and the Jewish mystics are on the right track. I don't believe we stay dead until the Messiah comes. I think we have a lot of progress to make if we want to help God perfect His creation. As we progress through several reincarnations, we become progressively better people, and the world becomes a progressively better place."

"Those are very noble thoughts Joshua," Winston whistled admiringly. "I hope the world is becoming a better place, but many of us are not so sure about that."

The Death of Jesus

"The world is a better place because God gave us Jesus," Mary said gratefully. "His death was horrible. He was tormented and mocked and thankfully he died within a few hours after he was crucified. His last words were 'Forgive them Father for they know not what they do.' Even in death and pain and agony, he loved us. When he died the sky stormed, the wind blew and the earth shook. All of God's creations mourned Jesus' passing."

"In Emet, Jesus cries to God wondering why he has been forsaken," Joshua said. "And God answers him and comforts him by saying: 'Be comforted my son, for it is partly through you and your followers that my covenant with Abraham will be fulfilled.' By that, God was telling Jesus that His covenant with Abraham would be filled by Christians as well as Jews, and by Muslims too I believe. We are all followers of the God of Abraham. And Jesus' last words were the prayer I mentioned earlier, the *Shema*, that recites one's belief in the One God."

"That is a very nice thought," said Winston enthusiastically. "I wonder why we cannot all get along."

"I wonder that too," said George sadly.

"Bye the bye, the suffering thing is problematic," Winston said as if he were teaching students in his class. "In Matthew and Mark, yes Jesus suffered. But in Luke, he did not. He was in total control of the situation. This is one of those contradictions in the Bible that Joshua was talking about yesterday. There are many, many more."

The Resurrection

Mary resumed telling the story. "After his death, Jesus was taken down from the cross and buried in a cave and a huge stone was put in front of the mouth of the cave. Then two guards were placed by the cave to make sure no one came to steal the body. Mary Magdalene and a couple of other women who had been with Jesus at the end of his life went back to the cave after the Sabbath was over and discovered that the large stone had been rolled away from the mouth of the cave. They went inside and were met by an angel who told them that Jesus had arisen and that he would meet them later.

"Shortly thereafter Jesus appeared to the disciples and others in several places and at several times and told them to spread the Good News that he had arisen and that those who believe in him would experience God's love and grace and be given eternal life. Completely inspired by seeing the resurrected Christ, Jesus' followers spread the word far and wide. Christianity has been by far the most successfully spread religion by peaceful means in the history of the world."

"Emet said that Jesus was indeed risen," Joshua agreed, "but not as the Messiah or the Son of God. Rather Jesus was risen because he was a great prophet and teacher, and he was chosen to accompany Elijah and Moses and Abraham at God's side up in heaven. According to Emet, it was partly because of Jesus that God's covenant with Abraham has been fulfilled. That is just part of what Jesus accomplished in his short life and ministry, and that is why, in my opinion, he should be considered one of the greatest Jews of all time."

"You know what," Mary said, to Joshua's surprise, "now that I think about it, I like the idea that Jesus helped fulfill God's covenant with Abraham."

"I like it too," added Winston. "It is very romantic, but has a ring of truth to it."

George agreed. "Certainly my congregation believes we are all children of Abraham, and I know the Muslims believe that too."

Discussion

"The Bible says Jesus is the Christ, our Lord and Savior, and the Son of God," Mary said, starting the discussion phase of the final chapter of the Book of Emet. "Only this so-called Book of Emet says it differently. The God-given Bible is clearly the better source.

"Furthermore, just as Jesus instructed them, the apostles went throughout the known world preaching the Good News of God's love in Jesus the Christ. Spreading the word of the One God, as Emet put it, has never been part of the gospel message. It has always been about Jesus Christ as Lord and Savior. And that God showed his love for us by giving us His only begotten son to die for our sins, so we may have life eternal.

"The arrival of the Christ was foretold in Isaiah and other prophesies in the Old Testament. So when those prophesies were fulfilled, how can someone who considers himself a good Jew not believe?"

"Isaiah said a lot of things," Joshua countered. "To take one thing out of context, as the Christians have done, does not persuade a reader of Isaiah that he was talking about someone like Jesus, and even less so someone who is called the Messiah or the Son of God. The passage from Isaiah that the Christians rely on never says the suffering individual he talks about is the Messiah. In fact, it sounds more like he was talking about Job than Jesus. Lots of people throughout history have suffered, many of them more than Jesus. One of our greatest sages, Rabbi Akiba, was flayed alive by the Romans for the crime of teaching the Torah." Joshua shuddered at the visual image this always evoked for him.

"Furthermore, in so many other places Isaiah talks about sins being forgiven through prayer and repentance. Nowhere does he say that sins can only be forgiven through the Messiah or any other way. *To say that salvation can only be achieved through believing in Jesus as the Son of God is something the Christians made up. It's that simple.*"

That was it!

All hell broke loose!

Paul Lindenbaugh up in the balcony sent a signal to the five shepherds outside, and they brought the mob running to the chapel.

Outside the Chapel

Judith and Bryce were still sitting on the lawn wrapped in a blanket Judith had brought along.

"Thank God it's almost over," she said. "I want my father out of there safely. That mob has been getting more and more scary."

Bryce put his arm around her comfortingly and kissed her cheek. Meanwhile he was keeping an eye on the mob. He too was scared of them. Terrified, in fact. They reminded him of his ancestral heritage — fearing large groups of angry white men. He had visions of the Ku Klux Klan, church burnings and tree hangings. He shivered against the cold.

Judith had her own ancestral fears. She had visions of pogroms in Eastern Europe that killed thousands of Jews at a time. She had visions of Nazi Germany, and of the occupied populations of Poland and Ukraine eagerly helping the Nazis find Jews to murder them.

The mob had been drinking beer and chanting slogans all evening and had booed and denounced parts of the debate they did not agree with. They were an ugly sight and were getting uglier by the minute. They were continually being whipped up by the five shepherds dressed all in white.

Suddenly, the lead shepherd fired a gun in the air and on cue the mob began to storm the chapel. Although they lacked pitchforks and other primitive tools, the mob was no less frightening than the mob that stormed the Bastille to mark the start of the French revolution. Some in the mob had guns, some had clubs and knives, and some just threw their bodies into the fray.

The policemen guarding the front door of the chapel saw the mob coming and got out of its way. There was nothing to stop the mob from crashing the chapel and doing whatever it wanted inside. Their cries were, "Get the Jew! Get the Jew! Get the Jew!" The doors were quickly breached and the mob stormed inside.

"O my God," Judith exclaimed; "they're going to kill everyone inside!"

Back Inside

When the people inside the chapel heard the shouts and the noise and saw the mob pouring in from every door, they ran around chaotically, as if they were in a building on fire. They did not know where to go or what to do, but that did not stop them from running helter skelter in every direction. Some of them fell down or were knocked down and trampled in the melee. Many were badly injured and five were trampled to death.

While this was going on Paul Lindenbaugh sent another text message to Joshua. "Prepare to meet your maker and be sent straight to hell" it said.

Joshua read the message and stopped dead in his tracks like a deer in the headlights. He could not move. This was exactly what Paul Lindenbaugh was hoping for. He quickly pulled out a handgun, put the sights on Joshua's forehead, and fired!

Simultaneously, George Turner courageously rushed to the front of the stage and tried to quiet the crowd and the mob.

A shot rang out, and…it was *George Turner* who dropped to the floor with a bullet in his forehead. He had inadvertently put himself in the line of fire between Joshua and Paul Lindenbaugh!

Everyone was stunned, including Paul Lindenbaugh. People looked around to see who fired the shot, but Paul Lindenbaugh got low so no one on the main floor or stage could see him. He did not have time to take a second shot at Joshua, lest he be seen. Instead, he quickly discarded the fake beard and the black coat he was wearing, donned his customary white coat and ran down to the main floor to take charge of the mob. Pointing at Joshua, he screamed:

"It's his fault! He has caused all this. Get the Jew!"

The mob responded to its leader's instructions and they rushed the stage.

Joshua was still frozen, all the more so because George Turner had just been shot. Now that they were clamoring for his head, he had no idea what to do.

Suddenly he felt someone tug at his arm and pull him toward the back room. It was Mary. He yielded to her pull and followed her, and then they broke into a run. She took him through the corridor going past the bathrooms that led to a seldom-used double-door service entrance on the backside of the building. They opened the door and saw people running this way and that. No sign of the mob. They ran to the parking lot at the southern edge of the campus, where Mary's rental car had been sitting since the first evening of the Great Debate. She nervously searched in her purse for the keys. After what seemed like minutes, she found them and quickly unlocked the car doors. She had always been a cool customer in a crisis. She started the car, pulled out of the campus parking lot, and headed to their hotel.

"No one is following us," Mary finally said with relief. Joshua was breathing heavily and shaking. Mary worried he might be having a heart attack.

"Are you okay honey?"

Joshua did not answer.

"Are you okay?" Mary asked again, with an almost panicky concern in her voice.

"Yes, yes, I think so. I can't seem to stop shaking, but I think I'll be alright eventually," Joshua said, managing a weak smile.

Mary smiled back and began to rub his neck and back with her right hand while steering with the other.

Joshua began to calm down and soon the shaking subsided.

"Thanks," he said with a better smile, "I needed that."

Mary smiled back with a look that melted Joshua where he sat. Being with her made him feel surprisingly safe.

Twenty minutes later, they arrived at their hotel.

"Get your things before they figure out where we are," Mary told Joshua, taking command. "I'm going to get my things too. We'll meet me in my room."

They quickly gathered their belongings from their respective hotel rooms, jamming them into their suitcases. Joshua ran down the hall to Mary's room. She left her door ajar so he could easily enter.

Mary had put the television on while she was refreshing her makeup, and they watched the news together with open mouths and a feeling of impending doom. The television reporter on the scene reported on the massive injuries, and the five deaths of the people who had been trampled in the melee, as well as Reverend George Turner's shooting death.

A young distraught Washington University student was being interviewed out on the grass. Her name was Judith Isaacson, and she said she was the daughter of Reverend Turner, and that he was unaware he had fathered her. She was sobbing uncontrollably.

Then the reporter interviewed the St. Louis County Sheriff who announced that the police were looking for one Joshua David Hertzel, who the Sheriff said had provoked the riot, and was being blamed for George Turner's death. He was also being blamed for the five who had been trampled to death. Mary and Joshua exchanged disbelieving glances.

Then Paul Lindenbaugh was interviewed, and he squarely put the blame on Joshua for provoking the riot and causing Reverend Turner's death. While admittedly no one seemed to know who the shooter was, Paul Lindenbaugh said it did not matter. It was all Joshua's fault for spreading the 'devil's lies'. "This man is the worst evil-doer since Judas," Lindenbaugh was quoted as saying.

"We better get the hell out of Dodge," said Joshua, who then looked apologetically at Mary for getting her into this mess. Mary squeezed his arm as if to say, "I wouldn't want it any other way."

They hurriedly went down to Mary's rental car, put their bags in the trunk, and jumped in, slamming the car doors shut. Mary quickly pulled the car away from the hotel and headed toward the highway that would get them out of town.

"Where are we going?" Joshua asked.

"Home!"

The Conversation

I applied my heart to seek and to explore by wisdom concerning all things that are done under heaven. It is a heavy burden that God has given to men to do! [Ecclesiastes 1:13.]

"Home" was Colorado Springs, Colorado, a ride of over 800 miles in mostly empty, flat, prairie country. As is often the case on long car trips, conversation came easily and the two new friends soon came to learn a lot about each other.

After escaping the St. Louis metropolitan area, the events of the evening began to sink in and Mary began to cry uncontrollably. She had to pull the car over, being unable to drive any further.

"I can't believe they shot George! Whatever for? He was a good man, wouldn't hurt a fly," Mary sobbed.

Joshua had tears in his eyes too and was still shaken up from his own near escape from the mob. There is nothing like having a mob after you to scare you to the depths of your soul. For Joshua, it was pure terror.

Joshua reached over to hug Mary and she turned and grasped him like a tree in a hurricane. He was surprised at her strength and the energy with which she held onto him. He in turn clung to her the same way and the two of them, sitting in a car on the shoulder of the dark nighttime interstate highway, held each other and cried the cry of the miraculously saved.

After several minutes of clinging to each other, they began to calm down, and fell away from each other back to their respective seats in the car, but kept contact by holding hands. Mary leaned back in her seat and Joshua leaned back against the passenger side door. They looked at each other, in total exhaustion, relief and affection. Nothing is more bonding than having lived through a harrowing event together and surviving it.

After a while, Mary spoke. "How can they possibly blame you for George's death?"

"I have no idea. It's unbelievable. It's totally bizarre. I'll bet Paul Lindenbaugh has something to do with it."

"How could he? He's such a good man!" Mary did not feel as convinced as she sounded. She added, "At least, I used to think he was a good man."

"You know what; I'd better call my best friend Barry and see if they've done anything to my sister." Joshua picked up his cell phone and called Barry.

"Hi Barry, what's going on?" Joshua asked tremulously.

"Really? Are you sure? Okay, talk to you later. And thank you!"

Mary heard relief in his voice. "What happened?" she asked anxiously.

"Esther is okay! Nothing has happened. Barry is going to stay with her for a while and they are putting an extra police guard around her for the next couple of days. He heard that I am wanted for George's murder and said he would help me if he could. He knows I'm not guilty. Everyone seems to know that back in Chicago."

"Maybe so, but I don't think you should turn yourself in," Mary said presciently. "Something is not right there, and that mob scares me."

"I think you're right," Joshua said with fear in his voice. "That mob would have killed me, and I don't know how they got the cops to blame me for George's death. He was killed by a bullet from someone in the audience, and I was clearly not in the audience."

"I don't even see how they could blame you for the ones who got trampled. What a horrible way to die!" Mary shuddered.

"As I understand it, they are saying I caused the mob to come in, and therefore I am responsible for the death of those who were trampled. That's crazy too, but it's not as crazy as blaming me for George's shooting."

"Let's drive to Columbia," Mary said. "It's only an hour and a half away and it's a college town with lots of hotels. We can stay there tonight, and then get to my place by tomorrow night."

"Okay," said Joshua without conviction or resistance. "Whatever you think is best."

They drove to Columbia, Missouri, which is halfway between St. Louis and Kansas City, and found a nice-looking hotel. Mary went alone into the hotel and registered for a room with two queen beds while Joshua stayed in the car. After all, they reasoned, no one was looking for Mary.

While in the lobby of the hotel, Mary's cell phone rang. It was her best friend, Lizzy calling for the umpteenth time. This time Mary answered the phone.

"Thank God you answered Mare," Lizzy exclaimed with relief in her voice. "I've been so worried about you. Are you okay? Where are you? What's going on?"

"I'm sorry Liz," Mary said warmly. "I'm with Joshua. I'm taking him home till we can decide what to do. I didn't mean to scare you, but we've been rather busy." Mary laughed at the understatement and Lizzy joined in.

"It's good to hear you laugh," Lizzy said. "What are you going to do? Why are you getting yourself involved with this?"

"I don't know what we're going to do; I just feel like I need to help Joshua," Mary answered without hesitation.

Lizzy thought for a few seconds. "Have you thought about what this will do to your marriage and career?"

"No, not really. I haven't thought it through very much, but I know that this is what I need to do right now."

Lizzy had always encouraged Mary to leave her husband and try to find some happiness in her life. Lizzy had been in a physically abusive marriage and herself had incurred the opprobrium of their evangelical friends when she divorced herself from that dangerous situation. "You know what I think Mare, if you have feelings for this rabbi, you should go for it. Wayne is a soulless dead end for you."

"Yes I know," Mary said with a laugh. "But having feelings for someone isn't enough to throw away my whole life. There is a lot more to making a relationship work than being in love."

"Oh dear," Mary thought to herself, shocked that she used the "L" word. "Am I in love with Joshua?"

"Leave it to you to fall in love with a jailbird," joked Lizzy. Mary laughed hysterically at the thought of it, fueled in part by her worries of what might happen to Joshua in the end.

"Oh Liz, you know he did not do anything. I don't know why they're chasing him. It makes no sense. I'm so scared for him. Well, I better go, he is waiting in the car. We shouldn't talk for awhile because they might trace my phone."

"Goodbye Mare," Lizzy said with deep concern in her voice. "God bless!"

"I love you Liz."

"I love you Mare."

Mary went out to Joshua and told him she got a room. They took a few things up to their room on the third floor and Joshua collapsed on one of the beds. Mary sat on the other bed and put the TV on to see what news there was.

The news was the same. The police were combing the city looking for Joshua. They had not thought yet to spread the search beyond the St. Louis metropolitan area. They had checked his hotel room in St. Louis and found that he had left. That was all the news had to say.

Mary turned the TV off and found a soothing classical music station on the radio in their hotel room. Mary joined Joshua on his bed and he put his arm under her head. They both felt comforted by the closeness they were experiencing, though both were lost in their own thoughts.

"Let's go to sleep," Mary finally said. "I'm exhausted."

"Me too," said Joshua, already half asleep.

They took turns putting on some night clothes in the bathroom. Mary came out in a light blue nightgown and Joshua had blue and white print pajamas.

"Which bed do you want?" Mary asked.

"The one with you in it," Joshua said half teasingly and half hopefully.

Mary's face softened as she laughed. "Now now *Mister Rabbi*," she said, "I'm a married woman you know."

"I know, I know. You don't have to keep reminding me," Joshua joked back. He got into the bed he had collapsed onto earlier. Mary turned the lights out and got into the other bed. It was a long restless night for both of them, with frightening nightmares alternating with romantic dream interludes.

Bad Things Happening to Good People

The next morning, Mary and Joshua put on jeans and casual tops. They went down for a free breakfast at the hotel dining room and got off to an early start.

"I'm worried about you Josh," Mary said after they had been driving for a few minutes. "What if they convict you for murder?"

"I guess it could happen. I don't really trust our judicial system. A friend of mine got totally screwed in his divorce. And everyone knows innocent people have been executed and guilty people have been acquitted. It's easy to be sanguine about it in the abstract, but when you are the one in their crosshairs, it's positively frightening."

"God won't let anything bad happen to you," Mary said with conviction. "He knows you're innocent."

"God might help or He might not," said Joshua a little angrily. "He certainly didn't do much to help us during the Holocaust."

"I always thought that happened because you all didn't accept Jesus."

"Yeah, that's one interpretation, and some Orthodox Jews say it happened because we quit following the rules in the Torah. I don't believe any of it."

"Well what do you believe honey?"

"You won't like what I believe. Certainly the Jewish establishment doesn't."

"Now you have me really curious. Will you tell me?"

"Okay. Let's start with the question of why is there evil in the world if God is all good, all powerful, and all merciful?"

"We believe there is a heaven and hell," answered Mary, "and that you won't go to heaven if you don't accept Jesus as your savior. The world is not a good place, but our reward for believing in Jesus and following him faithfully is to go to heaven afterwards."

"Well, Jews have various explanations. One, of course, is that God acts in inscrutable ways and that we don't know the divine plan behind what happens."

"Yes, we believe that too."

"Another is, as I said, that God punishes Jews for misbehaving and not observing the covenant we have with Him. They say we were being punished because a lot of Jews became assimilated and quit following most of the rules. Then I ask why most of the six million killed were Orthodox Jews. Did God punish the majority because of what the minority did, or failed to do?

"Then some say that man is responsible for what man does. And others say that God does not act in the world anymore. And some say that God does not interfere with the laws of nature or that He doesn't interfere with the natural consequences of things.

"Everyone has an explanation that somehow gets God off the hook," Joshua concluded.

There was silence for a while.

"So are you saying God should be on some kind of a hook?" asked Mary hesitantly.

"No," Joshua laughed, "I get Him off the hook too."

"Okay, so what do you believe?"

"To those who say God doesn't act in the world anymore, or who say that man's actions are man's responsibilities, I say then, what good is God if He doesn't help you? Why do we pray to Him if He doesn't act in the world or can't or won't help us? Or, to those who say He is a punishing God, I say then that He is either not all good or not all merciful. Today, even parents know that punishing is not a good way to raise their children. Teachers are not allowed to punish their students. They used to day, 'spare the rod, spoil the child'. You never hear that said anymore. Do we really think God is less advanced than we are on this subject? Do we really think that an all powerful God would also be such a horribly punishing God and still be thought of as good and loving?

"So to me, it comes down to whether God is all good or God is all powerful. I don't see how you can have it both ways. If God is all good, then He wouldn't let so many bad things happen in the world *if* He could prevent them. If He could prevent them, but chooses not to, then He could not be viewed as all-good, all-loving, and all-merciful.

"My conclusion is that you have to choose in your mind whether you believe God is all good or God is all powerful. You can't believe both at the same time. I choose to believe that God is not all powerful. I prefer to think He is all good. If He isn't all good, then He is not the kind of God I want to believe in."

"What about believing that God is all-loving but we mortals cannot understand His ways?" Mary asked. "That is certainly what we Christians believe. We start from knowing that Jesus loves us and that the Father loves us."

"Well sure, you can *believe* whatever you want, which is fine for you, but Jews believe there is a cause and effect between our behavior and how God treats us. We are supposed to be the 'chosen people', who God chose to carry His message to the rest of the world. Why do so many bad things happen to us? They say it's because we've misbehaved and God punishes us for it. Looking at our history and what kind of 'misbehaving' they say we must have done, I think that explanation is crazy.

"It goes even further in my opinion. If God is capable of punishing us that much, without most of us being at fault, it calls into question whether we still have a covenant with Him. I would say that if He is all-powerful, then in the Holocaust He broke His end of the covenant, which is to help and protect us, and so we are not obligated any more to uphold our end either. I think a lot of Jews today believe some variation of that, whether consciously or subconsciously. That is one reason why so few Jews today are Orthodox."

Mary decided to try another approach about the nature of God. "How can you have a God who is not all powerful and still believe in monotheism?" Mary asked.

"That is an excellent question, and one that has bothered me quite a bit. I believe in monotheism because I think God is the only god, but I think He is not all powerful because I believe there is an evil power out there that is just as strong or probably stronger than He is."

"You mean the devil, Satan?"

"I don't know about that. It may be the devil or a Satan-like character, but I personally don't think so. I think it may just be an evil or non-caring energy, sort of like gravity or a black hole. Or it just may be Chaos with a capital 'C.' I just call it the Dark Side, for lack of a better term. But in any case, God often can't defeat it, much as He would like to. I think He suffered with all of us in the Holocaust, but He couldn't stop it. If He could have, He would have."

Pain and Suffering

"Are you saying that God suffers? That's kind of crazy." Mary looked very skeptical.

"That's what the sages used to say—that God suffers with us. I don't think they meant God suffers in a physical way. They said He would be like a parent seeing His child in pain. How do Christians think God felt when Jesus was on the cross suffering? You do call him the Father."

"I believe God, our Father, felt His Son's suffering when the soldiers flogged him, when people taunted and spat on him, and when he was dying on the cross. If not, He wouldn't be a loving God," Mary said. "So do you believe pain and suffering come from the Dark Side and God feels bad about it, but doesn't do anything to help?"

"I think God helps when He can, and when He can't He feels bad because He loves us and wants only good things for us. I also think our pain and suffering help change the world for the better in some small way. Like when you throw a stone into a pond, creating outward-flowing concentric circles, our suffering goes out into the universe and changes it in some kind of way. It's another way we help God change the universe for the better."

"Are you talking about Jewish suffering, or everybody?"

"I'm talking about everybody."

"But," Mary protested, "we believe that when we suffer, it is God punishing us for our sins or testing our faith. The Old Testament is full of passages talking about a punishing God."

"Like I said in the debate," Joshua said slowly, "I don't think everything in the Bible is correct. Do you remember the debate Abraham had with God about whether to destroy Sodom and Gomorrah?"

"Yes, of course."

"God told Abraham that he would not destroy the evil cities of Sodom and Gomorrah if there were even ten righteous men there. So if He felt that way then, how can people think that God punishes the innocent along with the guilty *en masse* now? They say God punishes the Jewish people for their sins and transgressions. I don't believe that. Some extremist Christians say God has made catastrophes happen to America because we allow gay rights, for example. I don't believe that either. Based on what God told Abraham, I don't believe He punishes anyone the way other parts of the Bible say He does."

"So you would say the fire and brimstone preachers are totally wrong?"

"Absolutely!" Joshua answered with conviction.

Mary smiled at the decisiveness of his answer. She had never liked fire and brimstone preachers either. They always blamed the victims for the bad things that happened to them. But when bad things happened to those they approved of, they said God was just testing them. That was not Jesus' take on things. In Luke 13:4, Jesus said that when a tower fell over and killed some people but not others, the ones killed were not any more blameworthy than the ones not killed.

"So if God can't help us, what is the point of praying to Him, in your view?" Mary asked dubiously.

"Sometimes God can help us, and sometimes He can't. I think praying helps focus His attention and maybe gives Him extra energy to help us. It isn't a sure thing though."

"I'm hungry, and have to go use the rest room," Mary said. "Let's stop for lunch and we can talk more about this later."

"Okay," said Joshua. "I have to go too. Let's get off the highway at the next place they have a decent restaurant and take a break."

Life After Death

Back in the car after lunch, with Joshua driving now, Mary wanted to resume their conversation.

"Honey, if you believe in a good side and an evil side, isn't that a kind of dualism that Jews rejected in ancient times?"

"Hmmmm, it is similar, except if the evil is just a force like gravity or a black hole, it wouldn't do anyone any good to pray to it. I believe there is God and there is an evil force. God will try to help you if He can, but the Dark Side will not spare you even if you pray to it because it has no consciousness or purpose."

"So are you saying God created evil when He created the universe? That doesn't sound like an all-good God either. Where did the evil come from, if not from God?"

"I think God created the universe out of a chaotic void, but He couldn't overcome all the chaos. The chaos comes to us as evil, or what I call the Dark Side."

After a pause, he continued. "I believe that every religion has a piece of the truth. I think there is a yin yang element in the universe, half good and half evil, although I'm guessing that the Dark Side is stronger. In fact, I think the reason God created people was not because He was lonely, but because He needed help to fight and overcome the chaotic Dark Side."

Mary paused for awhile to think about that, and then asked "But you said people have evil in them too. So how can they help God defeat evil?"

"People are perfectible, which is not to say we can ever become perfect. We are the only one of God's creations who can raise our consciousness and improve our nature over time. That is one of the functions of religion, to teach us how to better ourselves and bring us closer to God. If we as a species can succeed in improving ourselves over time, we will tilt the balance of power toward God and help God overcome the built-in chaos in the universe."

"That is very cool," Mary whistled with growing admiration. "But as I said before, we are taught that life is a veil of tears, and that we will get our rewards in heaven. However, I believe that we as Christians can always experience grace and joy in life. Joy is knowing that Jesus loves us no matter what, and he proved his love by dying on the cross for our sins so that we can have eternal life. When our sins are forgiven, through Jesus, we are given God's grace so that even our life on earth is rewarded. What do you believe about heaven and grace and joy, Josh?"

Joshua thought for a few seconds before answering Mary's question.

"Judaism is mostly focused on this life," Joshua said, "not the hereafter. We have traditionally focused on following God's laws and commandments. We figure if we do that, the future will take care of itself.

"Mainstream Jewish philosophy about the afterlife is very unclear. It says there is a heaven that we all go to somewhere along the line. It's not clear who goes or when. The rabbis of Jesus' time talked about the 'world to come' — *olam haba* in Hebrew — and that is undoubtedly what Jesus was really saying where the gospels quote him as talking about the 'Kingdom of Heaven'.

"When the rabbis talked about the 'world to come', sometimes they meant something like heaven, and sometimes they meant what they called the 'end of days', which meant the Age of the Messiah. Mainstream Judaism says that when the Messiah comes, one of the things that will happen is that the Jewish people will have life breathed back into their bones and they will be physically resurrected.

"But in our own time, Judaism doesn't say much about what happens to us when we die. It only says that when our parents and other loved ones die, they will be kept alive in our memories of them. That is not a very satisfying theology. Then what happens when we're dead? There is no one left to keep their memory alive. So then all we can do is wait for the Messiah to come and be resurrected."

"Well Jesus was resurrected, but as far as I know no one else has been," Mary teased. "It sounds like Christian theology is clearly superior, then," Mary said with pride.

"Yes, absolutely," Joshua agreed. "I think most religions have a better afterlife theology than we do, and New Age ideas are very attractive too. I think that is a huge factor in why so many Jews leave us.

"Like I said before, I believe every religion has a piece of the truth, and none of them has the whole truth. I think the Buddhist idea of reincarnation is very compatible with Judaism, and I think the Buddhist idea of nirvana is similar to our idea of heaven.

"What is really great from my point of view is that, though most Jews do not know about it, the Kabbalah has a belief in reincarnation. It's not quite the same as the Buddhist version, because it says Jews are continually reincarnated until they finish performing all the commandments God gave us.

"My view is more like the Buddhist idea — that we keep getting reincarnated until we get perfected, and then go to nirvana, or heaven. And as we all get more perfected over time, we gradually improve the world as a whole because we have been improving ourselves. And by making the world a better place, we help God overcome the Dark Side."

"Christianity teaches that we are born with Original Sin and that only Jesus dying for our sins allows us to be saved and go to heaven."

Joshua paused thoughtfully. "Well, as I said earlier, I think we are born with inherent perfectibility. Not that we can become perfect in this, or any other lifetime. But I believe God created us to be perfectible so we can help Him perfect the world. I think each of us has a purpose, a God-given purpose, and that He tries to help us discover and fulfill that purpose. Our ultimate purpose is to help God overcome the Dark Side and perfect ourselves and the world around us."

"Christians also believe in making the world better," said Mary. "Jesus taught us to share our possessions with those who have less, seek justice and stand up against injustices, be peacemakers, alleviate suffering, feed the hungry, visit the sick and lonely, help released convicts re-enter society, welcome strangers, and practice hospitality. We can't build the Kingdom of Heaven ourselves—we can only live it, teach it, and invite and welcome others into it."

"Judaism has those same values, which is where Jesus got them. But Christians do it better than we do in many ways, which is something I really admire."

"Equating nirvana with heaven is an interesting concept," said Mary. "What are the chances of mainstream Judaism adopting it?"

"Probably not very good in our lifetime," Joshua laughed wryly. "But mainstream Judaism will have to do something, or its lack of a satisfying afterlife theology will doom it in an open society like we have in America and in other democracies. There is a real issue whether non-Orthodox

Jewry can survive an absence of pervasive anti-Semitism. Anti-Semitism forced us to stay together whether we wanted to or not. Without it, we naturally go in our own personal directions and many of us leave Judaism. Only time will tell whether my ideas will have any effect on this," he added hopefully.

"Are these the beliefs that have you so ostracized from other Jewish leaders," Mary asked.

"Yes. Some of them would like to brand me a heretic or something like that, but we don't really have that anymore. So they just say my ideas are dangerous to maintaining time-honored Jewish traditions. But no one calls for me to be excommunicated or anything like that, so that is how I know that Emet was right about the Jews not being behind the conspiracy to kill Jesus. We just don't do things that way."

"I would like to believe you're right about that," said Mary. "It's possible the gospel writers got that part wrong, but I still think Emet is some kind of forgery or was written by Jewish apologists."

Joshua smiled wryly. "I guess we'll have to agree to disagree about that," he said with a twinkle in his eye.

Mary laughed and squeezed his hand affectionately. Joshua squeezed her hand back. They both felt a warm glow inside that neither had felt since their youth.

After driving in silence for several more miles, another question was on Mary's mind. "Josh, what about those who die young? Like Winston's son?"

Joshua had a ready answer. "What I tell people about that is that we each have our own destiny and our own purpose in life. Each person's life and death serves some kind of purpose for that person that has nothing to do with anybody else. They may die too young for those of us who are still living, but they are on their own personal path, and maybe a step closer to heaven, so we should be glad for them, or at least hopeful. I always say that the ones who passed are okay and that they are doing what they are supposed to be doing."

Mary had tears in her eyes, thinking about her lost baby girl, but she liked that answer and thought it might be a comfort to Winston too. She held Joshua's right arm in both of her hands and rested her head on his shoulder, drying her eyes on his sleeve. She became dreamy and felt at peace.

"I'm getting sleepy Josh," Mary said after a while. "I'm going to put my seat back and take a nap if it's okay."

Joshua nodded his assent and put a hand on her thigh to keep a connection to her. She soon dozed off, with a smile on her face. She was dreaming happy dreams of her and Joshua, and of her baby girl having gone on to a new life. After she dozed off, Joshua put on a soothing classical music station from the car's satellite radio and fell deep into his own thoughts. Most of his thoughts were about Mary and how lucky he was to have met her. He tried not to think too much about her being married and the dangerous forces that were still after him.

Free Will

Mary slept for an hour and a half. When she woke up she stretched, gave a bright-eyed welcoming smile to Joshua that melted his heart, and declared that she was hungry.

"Me too," said Joshua. "We need gas anyway."

They stopped at an obscure gas station on the nearly empty Nebraska highway, filled up the tank, used the facilities, and grabbed some pre-made sandwiches and some snack food, and two large coffees. They did not dare stop to eat at a regular restaurant for fear of being recognized. By this time, Joshua's picture was all over the news and Mary's probably was too. Certainly they were both mentioned on the radio.

Mary was ready to drive again and after eating their dinner, it was Joshua's turn to take a nap. He fell asleep quickly, helped by the soothing strains of the Mendelssohn violin concerto playing on the radio's classical music station.

Joshua slept like a dead man for two hours. Mary occasionally glanced over at him with a motherly smile on her face. She realized she had never really been in love before and the warm feelings she felt were just like she imagined they would be when she was a little girl, dreaming of the man she would love and marry.

Joshua woke up with a start. He had been having a bad dream about wolves chasing him and he was being cornered with no way out when he awoke in a state of panic. When he realized where he was, he felt calmer but he was still shaken up. Mary noticed the look on his face, and he was quick to tell her about the dream. Tears streamed down Mary's cheeks and she told him she would do everything she could to take care of him and keep the wolves away. Joshua was touched by her loving kindness, and he leaned over and kissed the tears away on Mary's right cheek. That made Mary cry even more and she had to pull the car over onto a shoulder of the highway to recollect herself. Joshua reached over and held her and she had a good cry for a few moments. The events of the past day and her unexpected feelings for Joshua had become too much for her and she needed to let it out.

Joshua broke the silence. "I love you Mary," he murmured. "I've never felt like this in my life."

"Me either Josh. I feel like I've known you my whole life."

They kissed and hugged some more, and both wished they could feel the way they were feeling now forever.

"We better get going," Mary finally said.

"How close are we?"

"About three hours away."

"Do you want me to drive for awhile?"

"No honey. I'm feeling fine. You just take it easy."

Mary pulled back onto the empty highway, looking forward to being home and having it help her protect Joshua from the wolves.

"I have another question about your philosophy," Mary said after a period of thoughtful silence. "It would appear that we would have to have free will if we're going to make ourselves better over time and help God."

"That's right," said Joshua. "If God isn't all powerful then He doesn't control everything that happens to us. God also isn't all knowing. He doesn't know everything that is going to happen in the future. Some people believe everything happens for a reason, but I don't think that's true. I think *some* things happen for a reason though. The big things. The more important things."

Mary laughed. "How do you know what things happen for a reason and what things don't?"

"I don't," Joshua confessed. "I think that we each have a purpose in the world that has been given to us; that some things that happen to us, or that don't happen to us, are to help us fulfill that purpose. But I think a lot of things are irrelevant and even random. And some things are from the Dark Side and are bad for us."

"How do we know what our purpose is and whether things that happen to us are leading us in the right direction?"

"I don't know the answer to that either," Joshua confessed again. "I think there is something within us that steers us in a certain direction, and sometimes there are things outside us that steer us in a certain direction. I like to think those things that steer us are from God. But sometimes, and for some people, it is the Dark Side steering them. All we can do is the best we can. And if we realize God needs our help and we know what kind of world a good and loving God would want, then hopefully we will know what to do."

"That really does put a premium on free will," Mary said. "Not only do we have the ability to make decisions, but it puts on us the responsibility for making the right decisions. I'm not so sure as a group we can handle that, nor that we merit so much trust."

"God apparently thinks we do," said Joshua. "I hope He's right," he laughed. "Otherwise we're not going to be much use to Him." Mary laughed too.

"The Kabbalah says something about this too," Joshua continued after a pause. "It says when you do something good, it not only changes the universe for the better, but it also comes back to help you personally. And the opposite is true when you do something bad. It is a lot like the Hindu concept of 'karma.' So you see that it wouldn't be so hard for Judaism to accept some 'truths' from other religions if it would only open itself to them. That is one of the things I'm trying to teach and that is what I consider part of my purpose in life. To expand Judaism and make it receptive to the 'truths' of other religions. More than any other religion, I think Judaism can do this without losing its organic essence.

Whither Thither

They rode in silence again, each lost in his and her own thoughts. After a while, Mary broke the silence.

"You know, I've been thinking about this Emet thing. I can see why it would appeal to you. It's really very nice." Then she added in a teasing voice, "It's wrong, but still very nice."

"Well, who knows what really happened way back then. Hey, maybe one day you'll come over to our side," he laughed teasingly and half hopefully.

"Oh honey, I have a personal relationship with my Lord Jesus Christ. He is with me day and night and is my guide and my inspiration. I feel his love and I know I am saved through him. I could never turn my back on him."

"What if Emet is right and Jesus wasn't resurrected and was not the Messiah or the Son of God? What if the whole idea of a Messiah is just wishful thinking by Jews in times of trouble? Have you considered those possibilities?"

"I can consider them intellectually, but my heart and my soul tell me that Jesus is my friend. I feel him in every fiber of my being."

"I see," said Joshua with a disappointment he could not hide.

Mary noticed Joshua's disappointment and feared this unresolvable problem would keep them apart. Her heart was beating heavily, and she felt like she might have to pull off the road.

"Mary...." Joshua said softly.

"Yes honey..." Mary answered with fear in her heart.

"My congregation and my followers and those who I hope to make followers someday will think I'm insincere and a hypocrite if I were to make a life with you. And those who have been my detractors will have a field day." Mary's heart sank, but she told herself to be brave, as she knew this was true. "But right now I can't see living my life without you," he added to her surprise and delight. "And I hope I don't have to," he said bravely in an almost questioning voice, not knowing what she would say in response.

Mary was deeply touched. "I have my problems too. I am married. Getting divorced would probably ruin my career." Now it was Joshua's turn to feel his heart sink. His brave question had been answered. He turned away from her and felt like he wanted to jump out the window. Mary made him feel more alive than any woman he had ever been with, and the thought of losing that was crushing. "But I am in love with you and can't see living my life without you either!" she said. Joshua was beside himself with delight and hugged Mary so hard she nearly lost control of the car.

"I have a secret to tell you," Mary said softly. "No one knows this except Lizzy. One time when we were students, we went to a psychic. I didn't believe in them but Lizzy did and she wanted me to go with her. So I went, and after Lizzy got her reading, she insisted that I have one too."

Joshua nodded that he understood, but inasmuch as he had mixed feelings about the professionalism of most psychics, he wasn't paying too much attention to what Mary was about to say.

"I was completely amazed by what the psychic told me. I didn't tell her anything about myself and Lizzy didn't tell her anything about me either. She knew my parents' names, how they met, and how they came over to America after my father won the Irish Sweepstakes. She knew the name of my sister and that she had behavioral problems. She told me that I would have a bad first marriage and that I would meet the love of my life afterwards. And here is the part you will find very interesting. She told me that I was Jewish in several of my past lives and that I have a Jewish soul."

Joshua was stunned. He believed in past lives but didn't have any knowledge about any of his past lives. To hear that Mary had been Jewish before resonated with him. Now he knew why he felt so surprisingly comfortable with her — he instinctively felt that she had a "Jewish soul" also.

"Of course I didn't pay much attention to what she told me because I didn't want to believe that I would have a bad first marriage," Mary continued, "but the Jewish soul thing has always stayed with me. I thought of Christianity as an advance on Judaism, so I didn't see a conflict there."

"I think I feel your Jewish soul myself," Joshua said softly.

Mary smiled brightly.

"In fact, I feel surprisingly comfortable with you considering you are a *goy*," Joshua teased. "You know that there is a legend that all Jewish souls were standing at Mt. Sinai when the Ten Commandments and the Torah were given. Who knows, we might have been standing there next to each other."

Mary loved that idea. She already felt like she had known Joshua all her life. The idea that they could have been close in past lives, especially at that very special time stirred her soul. She took Joshua's hand and held it tight.

And so they drove on into the night, holding hands in silence, each thinking their own thoughts and feeling their own feelings. They felt the heaviness and joys of love at the same time. They were happy, and they were in awe. They each thanked their own God in their own way, yet felt very together in doing it. A Christian would say they were in a state of grace.

On The Lam

And the king of Jericho sent a message to Rahab, saying: "Bring out the men who came to you and are inside your house, because they have come to spy out all the land." But the woman had taken the two men and hidden them and she had taken them up to the roof and hid them under the stalks of flax, which she had spread out upon the roof. [Joshua 2:3-6.]

Mary and Joshua arrived at her home in Colorado Springs very late that evening. Mary's house was a sprawling tri-level raised ranch home, featuring a combination of brown brick and pale yellow siding. It was in an upscale neighborhood with tree-lined streets.

Wayne had gone to Denver for his cousin's pre-wedding festivities, and Mary's mother and Christa were fast asleep. Now Mary had to decide what to do with Joshua. She showed him around the house, including the three bedrooms on the second floor. One was the master bedroom, one was Christa's room where Christa and Mary's mother were sharing a bed, and the third one was being used as Mary's study and doubled as a guest room when necessary. It was filled with wall-to-wall books and photos of Mary with famous people. Joshua was quite impressed and said so. Mary beamed with pride.

"I'll put you in here," she told Joshua graciously. "The sofa there is a sofa-sleeper. I'll make the bed and give you some towels. This room has its own bathroom."

"That will be great," Joshua said. He was hoping he could sleep with Mary, but he was not surprised she did not invite him.

"Maybe you could join me in here on the sofa-sleeper...." Joshua suggested slyly.

Mary's face brightened. "What a wonderful idea," she teased back. "I hadn't thought of that."

"It would be a wonderful idea!" Joshua said more seriously.

"Please honey," Mary said, getting emotional now, "I can't sleep with you in my husband's house. It's just too much of a betrayal."

"But you told me he's had women over when you've been gone."

"Yes, but I can't do the same thing. It just doesn't feel right."

"I understand," Joshua said with sincerity. "That is what I thought you'd say."

Mary smiled, and began making up the sofa sleeper and getting Joshua some towels.

"I don't feel ready to sleep just yet," Mary said when she was done. "I'm too wound up. Let's go down to the kitchen and have some tea."

"Do you have any wine? I think in these circumstances I'd rather have wine."

Mary laughed easily. "Sure, I'll have some with you."

They went down to Mary's modern kitchen, where she poured two glasses of white merlot and put them on a silver serving tray. She led Joshua to her large formal living room and put the tray on the glass coffee table in front of her flowery white and turquoise sofa. They sat down and began to discuss their predicament between sips of wine.

"Wayne won't be home till the day after tomorrow. I want to leave before he gets here. Besides, at some point the police will be looking for you here. So I suggest we leave sometime tomorrow."

"I agree. It's probably not safe to stay here for very long." Joshua was looking pale again.

Mary decided to change the subject. They chatted about other things for awhile until suddenly they realized how really tired they were. Mary suggested it was time for bed and, leaving the wine cups and the tray on the coffee table, led Joshua to the stairs.

Then suddenly, and without warning, Joshua literally swept Mary off her feet, eliciting a shriek of delight. He carried her upstairs and into the master bedroom, where he slowly laid her on the perfectly-made king bed. Mary's head felt like it was swirling; she was dizzy, but relishing every spin of the room. Joshua gave her a big hug and kiss and walked sexily out of the room. Mary laughed while the butterflies of love in her stomach matched what was going on in her head.

Joshua had trouble falling asleep at first, full of loving and sexual thoughts about Mary, but luckily for him, the wine took effect and he eventually fell asleep with a big smile on his face. His dreams alternated between happy thoughts of Mary with scary thoughts about being chased by wolves again.

"Would you like some coffee, honey?" Joshua heard Mary ask from beside his bed the next morning.

"I'd love some," he said sleepily. Noticing that she was wearing a robe, he reached out toward her, hoping to bring her to him, but she giggled and artfully dodged his grasp.

"In bed or downstairs?" she asked.

"Oh, in bed for sure," he said hopefully with a big smile on his face.

"Downstairs will be fine," she laughed. "I'll be waiting for you," she added coquettishly and sashayed out of the room, completely capturing Joshua's attention. He jumped out of bed, brushed his teeth, got dressed and glided downstairs.

Meanwhile, Mary had gone downstairs to prepare the coffee, after first looking in on Christa and her mother, who were still asleep. She started the coffee and then decided to cook up some breakfast. She was hungry and she knew Josh would be too, so she fried up some eggs and sausage and made some toast.

Joshua smiled with delight when he saw her busy in the kitchen, looking quite adorable even without any makeup on.

"Oh dear," she exclaimed when she saw him, "I forgot. Do you eat pork?"

"Oh it's okay, Mary," Joshua said softly. "I don't keep all of the kosher rules, but I don't eat pork or shellfish. I'll be happy with the eggs and toast."

"But you're a rabbi. Can you pick and choose like that?"

"My connection to God and Judaism isn't through the rules. In the Reform movement, we believe in informed individual choice. I believe that the kosher rules are a time-honored Jewish tradition, but I don't believe they are mandated by God. After I became a rabbi, I decided to follow the dietary rules that are directly mentioned in the Torah, but I didn't follow them before that."

"But the Old Testament comes from God," Mary said getting upset. "You really don't believe it is God's Word?"

Joshua answered slowly. "I believe the Torah was written by man and inspired by God, but I don't believe the ritual rules there are mandatory.

Those rules were important then, and have certainly kept the Jewish people alive through the centuries. We were attacked and thrown in and out of countless places in our history, and those rules were the main reason we still exist today. But in this country, following the ritual rules only serves to drive Jews away, because they won't follow them. Most Jews in this country either don't believe in them or just don't do them. I think that Judaism has to embrace non-observant Jews and offer them spiritual sustenance in other ways or we will lose them forever. Let those who believe in the rules keep them, and God bless them for it. But most of us need a different connection to Judaism."

"That is very interesting," Mary said, still feeling a bit offended. "If you don't believe Scripture comes from God, that changes everything. That is why this Emet thing is so upsetting for everyone. It implies that Scripture is wrong. I have a lot of trouble accepting that."

"Here is what I believe," shared Joshua. "The historians say the Old Testament was written by different people at different times, and their arguments are very convincing, so that is why I believe our Bible was written by man and inspired by God. I don't believe every word in it is God's word.

"And they say the New Testament was written by four different men who did not even know Jesus, and they don't agree with each other. There are other gospels out there besides Emet that don't agree either. The Church decided which ones were 'from God' and which ones weren't. And the gospels you have were significantly altered over time because earlier versions of the gospels don't agree with the later ones. So I don't believe they are the word of God either."

"And I like to believe that however they ended up was how the Lord wanted them to be," Mary countered. "And I believe the same about the Old Testament too."

Joshua smiled weakly. There was nothing more he could say. He could not argue against her kind of faith. He knew some of his own beliefs also would not stand up to logic. He had debated agnostics and atheists before, and they felt the same way about his belief in God that Joshua was now feeling about Mary's faith. He knew that they would never agree on some of these issues, but he loved her anyway. And he could see by the look in her eyes that she loved him anyway too.

After they finished their breakfast, Mary went upstairs to check on Christa and her mother. Mary's mother was up and dressed, while Christa was just waking up. They were surprised and delighted to see Mary. They had been watching television when the debate had ended so dramatically and of course they had watched the follow-up news reports. Their calls to Mary had gone unanswered. Mary had decided to turn off her cell phone to prevent the police from tracking her calls. Joshua of course had done the same.

"Are you okay honey?" Mary's mother wanted to know with great concern in her voice.

"I am fine," Mary answered giving her mother a warm hug. "The rabbi from the debate is here. He is being falsely accused of murdering George Turner and those other people."

"You better call the police," Mary's mother said absent-mindedly, not totally understanding the situation.

"I will Mama," Mary lied to her so she would not worry. "Would you like some breakfast?"

"No," Mary's mother answered. "Now that you're here, I want to go home."

"Okay, drive carefully," Mary said worriedly.

"I will. Call me later."

"Bye Mama!"

Meeting Christa

Mary now turned her attention to Christa, who was sleepily sitting up in bed and only vaguely listening to the preceding conversation.

"Are you hungry sweetheart?" Mary asked. "That rabbi from the debate is here. We already ate, but we'll have some more coffee while you eat. Would you like that?"

Christa sleepily nodded her head yes. She was excited to meet the rabbi from the television debate, but she wanted to wake up a little more first. She went into the bathroom and brushed her teeth, combed her hair and washed her face.

"Is it okay to wear my pajamas Aunt Mary?" she called down to Mary who was making her breakfast.

"Yes," Mary shouted back, "just make sure you are all buttoned up." Sometimes Christa forgot to check her pajama buttons after getting out of bed in the morning.

A few minutes later Christa came bounding down the stairs into the kitchen. Joshua was already sitting at the table sipping another cup of coffee, and Mary was just putting Christa's fried eggs and sausage onto a plate.

"Orange juice or milk?" Mary asked her.

"Hmmmm," Christa thought for a few seconds, then enthusiastically cried out "Orange juice!"

"Orange juice it is!" Mary laughed.

"Christa, I'd like you to meet Joshua, the rabbi from the debate."

"Pleased to meet you sir," Christa said with her best manners.

"And I'm pleased to meet you too Christa. I've heard so much about you. You are even prettier than Aunt Mary said."

Christa beamed at the compliment. It was something she rarely heard from men.

Joshua asked her about school and her friends and other things of interest to a young pre-teen girl. Christa was glowing from all the attention she was getting, and Mary just listened in with a huge smile on her face, glad for Christa that she was getting so much male attention. Christa's father did not pay much attention to her, and when he did, it was usually to find fault with her. Her Uncle Wayne resented having Christa in the house at all, and also resented the attention Mary gave to her. He was cold to Christa and basically wanted nothing to do with her. Whatever attention he had to give her was given grudgingly, and he made little effort to hide it.

Following breakfast, Joshua and Christa helped Mary clean up the kitchen. Mary excused herself so she could take a shower. Christa invited Joshua to join her in the den.

"I have learning disabilities," Christa confided to Joshua.

"I know. How do you feel about that?" Joshua asked kindly.

"I believe everything happens for a reason," Christa answered slowly, "but it makes me feel like I am a mistake in the world and I wonder why God put me here."

Christa had obviously given this subject a lot of thought, and Joshua decided to tell her what he thought about this.

"I don't think everything happens for a reason," Joshua answered carefully, "but I think important things do. I think everyone has their own destiny and you have one too. It is one of your purposes in life to find out what it is. I don't think you are a mistake at all."

Christa's face brightened, and she grinned broadly. "Do you really think so?" she asked.

"I absolutely do," said Joshua with conviction. "You are a wonderful young lady and I think you have important things to do in this world. That is why God made you and that is why God made you the way you are. Just look for it and you will find it."

Then he told Christa his own story, how he had planned to be a professional tennis player, but had found his real calling in being a rabbi.

"Things don't always happen when you want them to, and the first thing you choose might not be the thing you want to choose later on. One of the true things you can say about life is that things don't always stay the same. If things aren't going well for you right now, just hang in there and eventually things will change."

Christa was totally rapt at the things Joshua was teaching her. No male adult had ever taken the time to talk to her like a real person.

"He's right," Mary said, having come in on the tail end of the conversation. "God will tell you what to do. Jesus loves you and will help you. Don't ever forget that Christa."

"I know Aunt Mary," Christa said. Mary talked to her often about God and Jesus.

Joshua excused himself to go get cleaned up too.

Something was obviously on Christa's mind and Mary asked what it was.

"Oh Aunt Mary," Christa said with urgency in her voice, "the church is having a father-daughter dance the weekend after Easter. I asked Uncle Wayne if he would go with me and of course he said he would be too busy." Christa was pouting now. "Do you think it would be okay to ask Rabbi Joshua?"

Mary was stunned. Christa had always been wary of the male friends and colleagues Mary brought to the house for meetings or dinner parties. Some of them had been polite and feigned interest in Christa, but none of them seemed sincere and Christa did not respond to them with anything except the manners she had been taught.

Mary's face softened at the thought that Christa felt comfortable enough with Joshua to entertain asking him for a favor. She gave Christa a big smile and said "Why don't you ask him." She was fervently praying that Joshua would not hurt Christa's feelings.

When Joshua came down, refreshed from his shower, Christa ran up to him and excitedly asked him if he would go with her to the church father-daughter dance. He paused at first, trying to untangle the words that had rapidly tumbled out of Christa's mouth. Mary's heart sank.

"He has a lot of things to do, Christa," she said. "And he doesn't even live here."

"I would love to go Christa," Joshua smiled sincerely. "When is it?"

"The weekend after Easter! Will you really go with me?"

"I promise, cross my heart and hope to die" said Joshua, crossing his heart and hoping not to die. "I wouldn't miss it for the world."

Christa ran up to him and gave him a hug and held on as Joshua hugged her back. The happiness on Christa's face melted Mary's heart, and her love for Joshua took on an even greater dimension. Mary ran up to Joshua and Christa and joined in the hug.

Wayne's Intervention

They were still hugging when Mary's land phone rang. Reluctantly, she went over to answer it. It was her husband Wayne on the other end. He had heard about the events in St. Louis and wanted to know what was going on with her and if the rumors were true that she was with that rabbi who was wanted for murder.

"Yes, he's here with me now," she said evenly. She was not one to tell a lie even if it would benefit her to do so.

"I'll be right over there," Wayne shouted angrily. "You better still be there." And he slammed the phone down.

The drive from Denver to the Roberts house was about an hour. Mary told Joshua what was about to happen, and they discussed whether to stay there or not. Mary said she wanted to wait for Wayne and have it out with him. She did not want to sneak off like a criminal. They were concerned that Wayne would call the police on his way there, but Mary was of the opinion that he would not. She was right about that.

She rehearsed everything she wanted to say to Wayne, but wondered how long she would be able to follow her "script." She also suggested to Joshua that he go for a long walk so Wayne would not see him, but Joshua insisted he would never leave her alone…just in case. Mary knew her husband had a violent temper, and she was concerned for Joshua's safety. After all, Joshua had nothing to do with her and Wayne's relationship.

But truth be told, she felt much safer with Joshua there and gratefully thanked him for wanting to stay.

Mary had decided she was leaving Wayne and she knew why. He had cheated on her for years and obviously did not love her. Having felt a taste of love from Joshua awakened something in her that had long been dormant. Whether or not things worked out with Joshua, she knew that she could never live with Wayne again. Her eyes had been opened to the possibility of a loving relationship, and she knew she deserved better than what she had with Wayne.

The idea of getting divorced was monumental for Mary. This was more than a personal failure. The teachings of Jesus were part of her DNA, and her brain kept replaying the greatest commandment: "Love God with your entire being and love others as you love yourself." Mary firmly embraced the sanctity of marriage—a forever bond created by God that man may not "put asunder"—and she taught and believed that divorce was a sin. She did not want to be a sinner, but she desperately knew she had to leave Wayne. She hoped God would understand.

Mary's adrenaline was pumping now. She was fretting over the confrontation she was about to have with Wayne, but foremost on her mind was Josh's safety. They had to find somewhere they could lie low for a while, at least until reason could prevail and everyone would see that Joshua was innocent of the crazy charges against him.

At 11:05, Mary heard the automatic garage door open.

"Here goes," she said to Joshua, "you'd better wait in the living room. I'll greet him in the kitchen." Wayne stormed into the kitchen from the garage, his usually pale face as red as a beet. He was a tall slender man with blonde hair and blue eyes. He normally had a benign smile pasted on his face, which is what originally attracted Mary to him, but he had a dark side.

"What the hell is going on here?" he shouted. "You're in big trouble lady!"

Mary had decided to confront him immediately. "There's something we need to talk about, Wayne. I've put up with your affairs and your lies as long as I'm going to. You left our marriage years ago and now I will also. My bags are in the car. After I talk to a lawyer, I'll be filing for divorce."

"What?" Wayne was stunned. This was not the conversation he was expecting to have. He quickly realized that he did not care if Mary divorced him, knowing that the opprobrium would be on her head, not his. Then he realized all that Mary would be giving up and he concluded she was just spouting off, probably because of the rabbi. He guessed when she calmed down, she would change her tune.

"You're bluffing," he declared. "You won't do that because if you do your career will be over."

"I'll have to find something else to do, yes, but in the meantime, I'll be happier without you."

"Does this rabbi murderer you're with have something to do with this? Have you been sleeping with him? I'll bet that's it, you whore!"

"How dare you talk to me like that! If you want to know the truth, yes, I have feelings for him. But I have not violated our marriage vows, yet."

"You bitch! I'm going to ruin you! You'll never get another Christian job in this country again!"

"Ruin me? You've been ruining yourself, me, and this marriage since the beginning."

Wayne advanced menacingly toward Mary with his fist clenched and arm raised, the way he always looked like when he was about to strike her.

Joshua, having heard the shouting, came quickly into the kitchen, ready for whatever might come. Mary viewed him with relief mixed with apprehension. Wayne glowered at him but lowered his arm and unclenched his fist.

"This is Joshua Hertzel, the rabbi from the debate," Mary said, not knowing what else to do. "Josh, this is my husband Wayne."

"He's the one that murdered all those people in that church…and you brought him to our house! Are you crazy?"

"That's what the police say, but it's not true. I was there. I saw it all! The shot came from the balcony. Josh had nothing to do with it. It was awful in there. These crazies came running into the chapel and were coming after Josh. It was so scary, but he and I were able to get out somehow. We got in the car I rented and drove here. He would probably be dead by now if I hadn't helped him escape."

"You've been brainwashed. The police say he is the murderer, and they wouldn't lie about something like that. You're going to get into as much trouble as he is in and I'm not going to lift a finger to help you if that's what you want to do with your life."

"I don't need your help, Wayne. I've been wanting to get away from you for a long time and just didn't have the courage to do it. I don't know what the future will hold, but I'll take my chances with him."

"You're leaving me for a Jewish rabbi? You know all the Jews are going to hell, and you will deservedly be going there with him."

Mary looked shaken. That remark hit home. She did believe that all the Jews are going to hell. Anyone who does not accept Christ as their savior is going to hell. Yet, her love for Josh was unassailable.

"Well maybe I am going to hell, but the Lord has graced our love. I have felt it. Whatever happens will be the right thing. Anyway, as sinful as you've been, you have no room to talk about who is and who isn't going to hell. Come on Josh, let's go."

"Well, you won't get far," Wayne replied, as he walked to the telephone in the kitchen and pressed 9-1-1, the emergency police line. "Hello, I want to report...."

Mary gasped as Joshua sprang forward and leveled Wayne with one punch, knocking him out cold. Then he unplugged the phone, and Mary, taking his cue, unplugged all the other phones in the house and threw them down the basement steps. Then she took Wayne's cell phone out of his pocket and put it in her own pocket. Meanwhile, Joshua finished loading up the car.

"Let's get out of here," Mary urged as she ran to get Christa.

On The Road Again

Christa had been in the den watching television. Mary urged her to quickly get her stuff together because Mary and Joshua had to leave, and they would be taking her to Grandma's. Christa quickly gathered up the things she would need and, together with Mary and Joshua ran outside to the rental car.

Mary drove to her mother's house to drop off Christa, explaining that she would be gone for a few days. Then she drove to her Ministry's headquarters, located in a suburban business park. Only four of her employees were at work and their cars were parked in front of the building. Mary drove the rental car to the rear parking area, where two large company cars were parked by themselves in a detached garage. Quickly Joshua and Mary transferred their belongings into the large trunk of the dark blue Lincoln Town Car. Mary knew that no one would notice it missing for quite some time.

They drove both cars to the airport. When they arrived, Joshua circled the airport in the Lincoln while Mary ditched the rental in the long term parking lot, and caught the little shuttle to the Departures level. The day was cold and sunny for early April in Colorado Springs. Mary did not think anyone would recognize her wearing a ski jacket over an Air Force Academy hoodie that framed her face, a long scarf covering her mouth and nose, and big sunglasses. Within two minutes, Joshua drove up and they were on the road again, returning to the Midwest, but this time to Joshua's home town, Chicago.

Joshua stayed behind the wheel and drove the first leg on I-80 East out of Denver. By his estimation, the 1,000 or so miles would take about 16 hours, which included time for stops for food and fuel. They hoped to use older gas stations with the restrooms accessible only from the outside, so fewer people would see either of their faces. For food, they would stop at fast food places with drive-thrus.

With such a long drive ahead of them, it was natural that the two runaways would have additional serious conversations.

The Importance Of Being Jewish

"Josh, you told me you are committed to trying to bring "lost" Jews back into the fold, right?"

"Yes I am, that's right."

"Tell me why it's so important to you to do that."

"I think it's important to the world to always have a significant Jewish point of view in it. Although Jews, Christians and Muslims worship the same God, we do it from different points of view. Christians focus primarily on Jesus and Muslims focus on Mohammed and the Koran. Jews focus primarily on Abraham and his family, the Torah and the God of the Torah.

"In my view, Jews have had a more historical relationship with God than any other religion. God was in dialogue with our forefathers— Abraham, Isaac and Jacob, and of course very extensively with Moses. The Jews also had an up-close and personal relationship with God when He freed them from Egypt and while they were wandering in the wilderness for 40 years. God also gave them the Ten Commandments at Mt. Sinai and punished them for the golden calf. No other group has had that kind of a relationship with God."

"That sounds right," Mary said thoughtfully, "but what is the significance of that? We've had an up-close and personal relationship with God in human form. I think that is infinitely preferable to talking to an invisible God somewhere up there in heaven."

"The primary significance is that all these experiences color how Jews think about things. There is a definite Jewish point of view about all kinds of things that you don't find elsewhere. I'm not saying it is better or worse than other points of view, but I am saying it's an important point of view that the world would be much poorer without."

"Okay," Mary said unconvinced. "Can you give me an example?"

"Sure Mary. One of my favorite examples is the way Tevye talked with God, almost like a personal friend, in *Fiddler on the Roof.* There is a unique Jewish comfort with God that I don't believe exists elsewhere. Also Jews believe that God has given us a special mission to teach others about Him, and as we keep learning more about Him over time, we can pass on what we've learned."

"I like the way Tevye bantered with God in that movie," said Mary. "But you can't beat the relationship we have with Jesus. 'What a friend you have in Jesus'" she sang. "We are constantly taught that Jesus loves us and that he is very approachable, more approachable than even Tevye's God."

"Yes, I think that is true," Joshua conceded. "The genius of Christianity is that you have a human to talk to, who does seem more approachable than the Jewish God will ever be. I don't see anything wrong with that, except the belief that he is God's son, or even God himself.

"My mother used to talk to her mother to help her sometimes, and now I do the same with my mother. It is very comforting and also more approachable, but we never thought they had a direct line to God. I imagine its the same with ancestor worship in China. We hope they can help us, but we know that maybe they can't."

"Yes," agreed Mary, "sometimes I talk to my father up in heaven to help me with things, but mostly I talk to Jesus."

"I think a key factor for Jews is that God is our family God. I believe Abraham "discovered" Him, and they established a special relationship with each other. That relationship has been passed on from Abraham through Isaac and Jacob, to the twelve tribes, and so on till today. Sometimes we pray to Him as the God of Abraham, the God of Isaac, and the God of Jacob, and ask Him to remember His relationship with them in asking for something today. We have been through good times and bad times together."

"Ah, but there's a big flaw in your thinking," countered Mary. "With all the intermarriages, conquests, and rapes your people have been through over the centuries, it is very doubtful there are any pure blooded descendants of Abraham among you."

"That's true," Joshua answered quietly. "Most Jews prefer not to think about those things so we imagine ourselves direct descendants of Abraham. But what most of us don't realize is that, as a family, there are the normal additions and subtractions that occur in any family over a long period of time. If someone intermarries, the non-Jewish spouse and the children are still included in the family, if they want to be and are allowed to be. If there is a rape, the child is still included in the family. If someone converts and joins us that way, they become a part of the family. We don't have to be pure-breds to be in the same family. I personally think that mixing with other groups from time to time is a good and healthy thing for us."

Mary was quiet for a while. "So if you were to marry someone who was not Jewish, she would become part of the family?"

"Yes, just as she would become part of my personal family, she would also become part of the Jewish family. That would be true whether she converts or not, but of course it would be better if she would convert because that is the only way the Orthodox would consider the children Jewish. But I don't care what they think, and eventually it won't matter anyway."

"Are you planning on having more children Josh?" Mary asked apprehensively.

"No," Joshua chuckled, "not me. I was talking in hypotheticals."

Satisfied, Mary was quiet for awhile as they drove across the Nebraska border into Iowa. It was getting dark out.

The Core of Judaism

Mary dozed off for almost two hours, and when she awoke, she wanted to drive to give Joshua a break. It wasn't long before she had another question.

"Josh honey, you say you want to change Judaism to be more appealing to secular Jews today, and we've talked about some of those changes. But if you make all those changes, will Judaism still be Judaism, or will it be almost like a different religion altogether?"

With Mary driving, Joshua was starting to doze off, but the question woke him up. Mary had touched on the question that most worried him about his philosophy.

"I think we need to get back to our roots, and touch people that way. Most of the rules and rituals that we've developed over the centuries were fine in their time, but most of them are not meaningful for secular Jews today.

"The essence of Judaism has a lot to recommend it, and most Jews instinctively know that. Abraham had a relationship with God where they each tested each other. It was not just a one-way street. Abraham tested God's character with the debate over Sodom and Gomorrah, and Abraham and God tested each other with the sacrifice of Isaac. There is a feeling of being partners with God. Some of our sages tell us we are partners in God's creation. But if God comes up short in our eyes, some of us lose interest in Him and our religion."

"That sounds rather presumptuous to my ears," Mary interrupted. "You think you are partners in creation with God? What about the rest of us? Are we chopped liver?"

"Well we might be a little arrogant about ourselves," Joshua conceded. "Not everything is to be taken literally. But there's no doubt that we have always believed that we have a special relationship with God. It comes from our history."

"It also sounds presumptuous to talk about God coming up short. Who are you to decide that?"

"Well we supposedly have a covenant with God, where we do what He wants and He takes care of us. The holocaust caused many Jews to lose faith in God taking care of us, and that is a major reason Jews feel less attached to Judaism today. I think if they accept my view that God is not all-powerful, and He needs *our* help, they would feel better about Him.

"Also, Judaism has championed a lot of human rights views because of our belief in a moral God. We've always been told to take care of the widow and the orphan. We were advised to respect animals and other people. We were not allowed to eat the meat or drink the blood of a live animal, something that was common in those days. On the Sabbath, not only were we commanded to rest, but we also had to give a day of rest to animals and slaves. That also was very unusual in those days. We were told to pay a man his wages every day, so that he not be sent home unable to feed his family. Judaism at its best is a very ethical religion and we have centuries of discussion about all kinds of things to refine what is right and what is wrong in almost every life situation."

Joshua paused to drink some bottled water they had with them. All this talking had made him thirsty.

"We've also been charged with giving charity," Joshua continued, "trying to make the world a better place, and testifying that there is a moral God in the universe. We've been taught to look inside ourselves and see how we measure up to God's standards. If we fall short, and we always do fall short, we're asked to repent and try to do better in the future. There is more to being Jewish than being in the same family and following all the rules and rituals. I think getting back to our root values will bring a lot of Jews back. A lot of secular Jews are proud of being Jewish even if they don't like Judaism the way it is practiced today."

"You might be right," Mary said. "But we're losing people too, and it's not because of the holocaust. I think people today put more faith in science and the reality they can see than in an invisible God. But they are missing something in their lives, and they know it, so they keep looking elsewhere for it. It is right in front of them, but they don't want to believe."

"I totally agree," said Joshua. "But I don't think it's that they don't *want* to believe. I think it's because what we've been teaching them doesn't sound true to them. That's why I think my idea of saying God isn't all-powerful is important. I think my ideas would help Christians as well as Jews."

A few minutes of silence followed, with both religious leaders lost in their own thoughts.

"Getting back to your original question," Joshua finally said, "about whether the Judaism I'm advocating will be recognizable. What I'm proposing might not be recognizable to observant Jews who follow all the rules, but it would be authentic Judaism. I would hope there would be favorable recognition of each other on the part of all sides. We don't all have to be Jewish in the same way to be doing God's work.

"Getting back to our roots might make all the difference in whether Judaism survives in any meaningful way in this country. I know most Israelis look at us and think we're doomed. I'm going to do whatever I can to make sure that doesn't happen."

Mary looked at Joshua adoringly, warming him all over. Having unburdened his heart to her, he felt entitled to get a little sleep, and that is what he did, with his left hand on her thigh to keep the special connection with her that he was feeling.

When they started getting close to Chicago, Mary woke him up because she didn't know where they were going in the vast sprawling city that lay before them.

In Chicago

Be merciful to me, O God, for men hotly pursue me; all day long they press their attack. They twist my words; they are always plotting to harm me. They conspire, they lurk, they watch my steps, eager to take my life. [Psalms 56:1, 5-6.]

Just before dawn, Joshua drove the car into the parking lot of his synagogue. He unlocked the building and turned off the alarm system. "We'll do the tour later. Let's get our bags upstairs before the neighbors wake up. Oh, the ladies' room is down that hall, the first door on the right." Mary thanked him and disappeared for three minutes. Joshua was waiting for her with both of their suitcases in hand. Mary followed him upstairs to the room once reserved for the custodian.

A bed, dresser, and two old stuffed chairs composed the entire furnishings. It was like a very tiny motel room. Assuring Mary that no one would enter the building until just before 9:00, Joshua left her there to organize their room while he drove to a gas station that he knew still had a payphone. Joshua guessed that the synagogue telephone might be tapped, and the FBI would be tracking his cell phone calls. Nevertheless, he decided to turn his cell phone back on just in case.

First, he used the payphone to call the president of the congregation, who was also a good friend; then his secretary Stephanie, before she left home. He explained everything to each one, including Mary's presence. On her way to the synagogue office, Stephanie purchased five pre-paid phones, one each for herself, the synagogue president, Joshua, Mary, and Joshua's best friend Barry, the friend who had looked in on his sister. Soon, they would be able to communicate freely.

That night was going to be the first night of Passover. Barry invited

Mary and Joshua and some of Joshua's most loyal congregants to join him and his wife and kids at their home to celebrate the holiday.

Mary was exhausted and fell asleep in the custodian's room while Joshua was making all the arrangements with everyone. When he returned to the custodian's room, he got himself comfortable in one of the old stuffed chairs and soon fell asleep himself.

After a couple of hours, Mary woke up, and taking pity on how uncomfortable Joshua looked in the chair, roused him and beckoned him to join her in the bed. He gratefully accepted, and putting his arm under her head, quickly fell asleep again, as did she.

And that is how they woke up in the late afternoon when Joshua's personal cell phone rang. He looked at the incoming phone number on it and decided to take a chance and answer the call. Accustomed to seeing Joshua receive bad news on his cell phone, Mary immediately became fully awake and watched his face intently, while straining to hear whatever she could. She saw Joshua's face turn to horror, unlike anything she had seen before. He hung up the phone without saying a word and his body began shaking uncontrollably. Mary instinctively put her arms around him and hugged him hard. Joshua put his arms around her and began sobbing.

Mary waited a while until his sobbing and shaking body began to ease. "What is it honey?" she asked, fearing the worst, whatever that would be.

It seemed like ages until Joshua was able to answer. "It's my son," he said. "He's missing in action!"

The Stakeout

Even though there were reports that Joshua and Mary had been at her house in Colorado, Judith and Bryce decided to drive to Chicago on the theory that at some point Rabbi Hertzel would show up at his synagogue, Temple Menorah, located in the far northside Chicago neighborhood of West Rogers Park. It was an unobtrusive two-story building made of red bricks that looked like the Georgian-style houses around it. Its claim to fame architecturally was a huge stained glass window depicting a giant Menorah, the venerated ancient Jewish candelabra. What most people did not know about the building was that it had begun life as an Army

surplus chapel at Ft. Benjamin Harrison in Indiana. It was brought to
Chicago after World War II by truck and, at one point, when the truck
turned a corner too sharply, the steeple fell off and broke apart. The rest
of the building, now a block long, was built around that little chapel,
which came to form the Community Hall portion of the building.

It was late afternoon when Judith and Bryce arrived after a five-hour
drive from St. Louis to Chicago in Bryce's car, a sporty red Ford Mustang
convertible. Upon arriving at the Temple, they observed that nothing
appeared to be going on, even though it was about to be the first night of
Passover, so they got some carry-out food and drinks and settled in for a
possible all-night stakeout.

"I shouldn't be eating this," Judith said with some guilt in her voice.
"It's the first night of Passover and we're supposed to eat 'kosher for
pesach' things. But catching my father's killer is more important right
now."

"I'm sure God will forgive you," Bryce said gently. He was not sure
he believed in God, but he knew Judith did. Judith gave him a knowing
look.

As they ate and waited, Judith began to tell Bryce about her father,
Reverend George Turner.

"My mother was in love with George Turner when they were back in
high school. Their relationship was that of best friends, with no romantic
or sexual involvement. Mom said George was the nicest, classiest man
she had ever met and, even though he was not Jewish, she fell head over
heels in love with him. But she could see that he didn't feel the same way
about her, so she never let on.

"Even when they went off to separate colleges, they talked to each
other almost every day. George was totally oblivious to how my mother
felt about him, and of course she later found out the reason — that he
was gay. She pretty much guessed that, but she always lived in hope that
somehow he would 'see the light.'

"One time he came to visit her at college for the weekend. My
mother's roommate in the sorority house was out of town that weekend,
so she was able to put George up in her own room. On Saturday night,
there was a party in the sorority house, with a lot of frat guys coming
over, and the booze was really flowing. Although George didn't drink
very often, somehow the frat guys teased him enough that he got totally
drunk. My mother got drunk too.

"My mother helped George up the stairs to her room on the second floor. She could hardly walk herself. They fell into bed together and they started giggling. My mother started helping George get out of his clothes, which were soaked with beer. Before she could finish, George passed out.

"In her drunken state, my mother couldn't resist making out with George, something she had fantasized about for years. She was totally surprised when George got an erection, and it didn't go away. Quit laughing Bryce, I'm trying to finish the story," Judith giggled.

"So she took her clothes off, put Ravel's Bolero on her stereo (Bryce really laughed at this), and was able to wake George up. Anyway, one thing led to another and that's how I got started."

"That's an amazing story," Bryce stopped laughing long enough to say, tears streaming down his face, and his hands on his belly, which was sore from laughing so hard. His laughter was infectious and soon Judith also had tears streaming down her face and was holding her belly. Every time one of them managed to stop laughing, the other one's laughter got him or her laughing again. Finally, their bellies hurt so much they were able to stop laughing. They rested for several minutes until Judith was able to continue the story.

"George never knew that he fathered me, and my mother never told him because she found out that he was gay shortly after that. My mother met my stepfather a few days later, before she started showing, and they fell in love, and he agreed to say I was his child and that is what Mom told George. And everybody else."

"So how did you find out George was your real father?" Bryce asked.

"Shortly after my Bat Mitzvah, my mother decided I was old enough to know."

"That must have been a real shock to you!"

"Yes, it was," Judith said with a trace of hurt in her voice. "It really set me back. We went to counseling, my mother and stepfather and me, and we were able to work it all out. My stepfather really loved me, and I knew it, and that helped me a lot."

"So if you were cool with your stepfather and never had a relationship with George, why are you so broken up that he's dead?"

"I did come to have a relationship with George in my mid-teens. I decided to sit in on some of his classes on Bible study. My mother asked him if it was okay, being that I was Jewish and not a member of his church, and he did it as a favor to her, not suspecting my real motivation.

I became one of his favorite students — he liked me anyway because of his affection for my mother, and we ended up having many conversations and even eating out together occasionally. When I had personal problems, with girlfriends, boyfriends, or my parents, he was very kind to me and gave me a lot of good advice and empathy in a fatherly way. I came to love him as a person, not just as my biological father."

"I'm so sorry," Bryce said tenderly, putting his arm around her and giving her a big hug. She cried a little on his shoulder and then straightened up and told him that is the reason she wanted to make sure her father's killer is brought to justice.

"I wrote you a little poem to help you feel better," Bryce said gently.

"Really, that is so sweet. Will you read it to me?"

In the fading light, Bryce read:

Death leaves a heartache
That no one can heal
But love leaves a memory
That no one can steal

Judith started sobbing. "That is so beautiful," she said. She gave him a prolonged hug, shedding tears on his neck. He held her and patted her back. "You don't have to burp me," she was finally able to say laughing. Bryce started laughing too, but then he stopped abruptly, because he saw some figures coming out of the Temple. Judith turned to where Bryce was looking.

"That's them!" she said, suddenly becoming very businesslike.

Bryce started the car and, with the headlights off, followed Joshua and Mary to the dark blue Lincoln and then followed them further to Barry's house, which was just three blocks away. They waited a while to make sure the fugitives weren't going somewhere else, and then Judith called the police.

The Two Sons

The two sons Joshua had sired with Patricia were now in their 20s. The oldest one, Ross, who was named after Joshua's deceased mother Rose, was inspired by Joshua's career calling and followed him into the rabbinate. He was currently studying in the Reform movement's seminary in Cincinnati, the same one Joshua attended decades earlier.

His second son, Kalman, was named after Joshua's uncle on his mother's side who had died heroically as a pilot in World War II. Kal was a bit of a rebel, something he also got from his father Joshua, but he chose to follow in his namesake's footsteps and joined the United States Air Force. He was a very patriotic American and believed that the United States was the best country ever conceived by man. Unlike his older brother Ross, who was serious and studious, Kal was a bit on the wild side and had lots of friends, both male and female. He enjoyed partying but was as true as the day is long. He was liked, admired and trusted. Like his father, he was an athlete, but his chosen sport was football. He was a running back and also a punter and field goal kicker. He went to the University of Iowa on a full football scholarship and studied International Relations. He also joined the Reserve Officer Training Corps (ROTC) in college and on joining the US Air Force after graduation, became an officer and a helicopter pilot.

Kal volunteered for two shifts in America's war in Iraq and then volunteered to join the war in Afghanistan. He was supporting a secret commando mission in Afghanistan when his helicopter was shot down.

The Air Force representative who had just called Joshua with the bad news said they did not know if Kal was dead or alive, and if he was alive, they were not sure where he was. It was possible he could have been captured by the enemy, in which case anything could happen. Other U.S. military personnel who had been captured were often tortured and then killed. Some of them were even beheaded.

Joshua related all this to Mary between sobs of anguish, his body still shaking uncontrollably. Mary held him tight, alternately holding his hand, stroking his head, cradling him in her arms, whatever seemed to elicit a comforted response from Joshua.

And Joshua *was* comforted. Slowly, his sobbing eased and his body stopped shaking, although there were intermittent paroxysms of both before he calmed down. He hugged Mary back and kissed her gratefully many times. Soon their embraces became passionate, and Mary knew she would not be able to resist Joshua if he wanted more from her. She was lulled into a feeling of floating on air where everything around her felt safe and magical.

Suddenly, breathing quite heavily, Joshua broke their embrace.

"Not this way Mary," he said affectionately. "There is nothing in this world I want more right now than to make love with you, but not this way. I want to have you when things are right and good between us and we are doing it for the right reasons."

Mary was breathing heavily too, and at first she was almost angry at Joshua for interrupting her dream-like state. But soon she was feeling grateful that Joshua had saved her from doing something she knew she would regret later. She gave him a big smile and a hug of gratitude and they lingered there, embracing each other and talking softly.

Before long, it was time to get ready for the Seder at Barry's house.

The Last Seder

The Seder recounts the story of the Israelites' departure from Egypt, highlighted by the ten plagues and the crossing of the Red Sea. As Joshua and Mary sat at the Seder table, one of the congregants suggested they should pray that their rabbi and his friend would elude Pharaoh's soldiers and arrive in freedom to the Promised Land. Everyone heartily agreed, moving Joshua and Mary to tears. They both were warmed by the affection of the group.

"He's a good man," Mary said, looking at Joshua adoringly. The conviction with which she said that immediately made her part of the group.

"We're so glad to have you with us," Barry told her, with nods of assent all around.

"I also need you to pray for my son Kal," Joshua informed them. "I got a call today that his helicopter has been shot down in Afghanistan and they don't know if he is dead or alive or where he is."

Of course everyone was upset at this piece of unexpected news. They all knew Joshua's sons and Kal was popular with them in his own right. Both of Joshua's sons routinely attended the Seder in Barry's house when they were in town. Ross was not there this year either. He was on spring break from the seminary, and he and some of his friends went to Israel to celebrate the Passover holiday. They were camping in the desert to emulate the experience of the Israelites many centuries earlier and were therefore unreachable by phone. Ross had no way of knowing the predicament his father was in or of his brother's helicopter crash.

This Seder was unlike any Joshua—or Mary—had ever attended for other reasons as well. Mary was reminded of the Last Supper of Jesus and for the first time, through Joshua, she personally felt the impending doom Jesus must have felt. The presentation of the matzoh (the "bread of affliction") and the wine (for the celebration of freedom) reminded her of the flesh of Jesus and the blood of Jesus. The Israelites' escape from Egypt reminded Joshua of his own escape from the police so far and of Kal's hoped for escape from the helicopter crash. He hoped that God would save them both and give them back their lives as free men.

Both Mary and Joshua had similar thoughts about the Passover lamb. Mary thought of Jesus and the words of John's gospel, "Behold the lamb of God that takes away the sin of the world!" Joshua wondered if Paul Lindenbaugh and the others saw him as a sacrificial lamb, who they might want imprisoned as a way of discrediting the Book of Emet.

They went through the normal order of the Seder service. When the time came to drink the first of four cups of wine, they all did so, even most of the children (although some had grape juice instead). When it came time to eat the matzoh, Joshua took the middle piece and broke off a piece for himself and one for Mary, and then passed it around so everyone could do likewise. Then it came time to dip the parsley into salt water, which was to remind everyone of the tears the Israelites shed as brutalized slaves in Egypt. Then the horseradish was passed around and eaten with the matzoh to remind everyone how bitter was the life of a slave.

Finally, it was almost time to serve the Passover meal and the women went into the kitchen to make things ready and bring out the traditional matzoh ball soup as the first course. Mary went with them to help, earning her immediate popularity with all the women. But before they could serve the soup, everyone was startled by the ring of the front doorbell. "Who could *that* be?" asked Barry. "It's too soon for Elijah to come," he joked. Every Seder table throughout the world put out an extra wine cup for Elijah, the legend being that he might come and partake of it. "Sort of like the Jewish version of Santa Claus," Joshua had whispered to Mary with a wink.

Barry's wife, Sylvia, came out from the kitchen and said, "I'll get it dear, you continue." She opened the door, and was shocked to see two uniformed police officers, plus several others in the front yard.

"Good evening, ma'am. We have a warrant for the arrest of Joshua D. Hertzel, and have reason to believe he is on your premises. May we come in?"

"Honey, you'd better come here," Sylvia called out, "there are police officers looking for Joshua."

Immediately, Joshua jumped up from the table. "Joshua, go through the kitchen and out the side door," Barry whispered. "It's very dark and no one will see you!" Joshua grabbed Mary on his way out of the kitchen and quietly slipped out the kitchen door.

Then Barry went to the door to meet the police.

"What is this about, officers? We are Jews celebrating the Passover. Why would you disturb us on this sacred occasion?"

"I understand, sir, but your rabbi, Joshua Hertzel, is wanted for murder. We had a tip that he might be with you this evening. May we search your home?"

"That seems highly irregular. I don't like this one bit."

The search lasted all of ten seconds until Mary and Joshua were led into the house by the officers who had nabbed them outside. Before Mary's horrified eyes, Joshua was hand-cuffed and was given his Miranda rights. Two of the police officers put Joshua into a squad car, while the arresting officers interviewed everyone in the house, including a sobbing Mary. The police then took Joshua to the police station, where he was incarcerated. The next day, he would be driven to St. Louis to stand trial for George's murder.

After The Arrest

You are my rock and my fortress, therefore for Your name's sake lead me and guide me. Free me from the trap they have set for me, for You are my refuge. Into Your hands I commit my spirit. [Psalms 31:4-6.]

After a sleepness night in Chicago's infamous jail at 26th and California, two St. Louis County police officers arrived in the mid-afternoon to take custody of Joshua. Wearing shackles on his hands and feet, Joshua was led by the heavily armed officers into a white and red twelve-passenger police van. A third officer drove the first leg of the 320 miles, playing a couple of CDs by two anti-Semitic white supremacist rock bands. This was completely against department policy, and the other officers put up with it grudgingly.

Joshua began to feel overcome by his fears. They rose within him and he thought he was going to be sick. He tried to ignore the music by meditating on one of the Bible's Psalms, the one praying for deliverance from personal enemies, the first part of Psalm 109.

O God, whom I praise, do not remain silent,
for wicked and deceitful men have opened their mouths against me;
they have spoken against me with lying tongues.
With words of hatred they surround me;
they attack me without cause.
In return for my friendship they accuse me,
but I am a man of prayer.

Joshua was rudely roused from his prayer by the lyrics of a song blaring from the van's speakers. "Oh my God!" he thought, "they're using another part of that psalm against me!" Indeed, they were. The words were hate-filled paraphrases of several lines of that same prayer of David. The song was not about Joshua, of course; it was aimed at all Jews. This is what Joshua heard, made all the more frightening because the driver was singing along:

Send righteous men to accuse;
Lord of Hosts will prosecute.
When he's judged his guilt will show
and when he prays, just say No!

Give him short life and long pain,
His kids see him marked with sin.
Dress his wife in widow's weeds;
Chop down those Jewish family trees!

Joshua had never heard songs like this. He knew these rock bands existed, but had always assumed their songs were just angry, adolescent rants. He now realized the source of what he was hearing: evil, pure evil. He began to shudder. He already feared for his freedom. Now it occurred to him that he was in the middle of something much bigger. What if he was caught in the middle of a great spiritual battle between Good and Evil, God and the Dark Side, Yin and Yang? Like a modern day Job.

Noting Joshua's condition, the officer sitting closest to him asked, "Are you okay, Rabbi? You look like you've seen a ghost."

"Heard one, is more like it," replied Joshua wryly.

"Don't worry about him or that garbage. It's our job to deliver you safely to the jail in St. Louis, and we will. It wouldn't look very good for us to transport you straight to the Barnes Hospital ER. Can I get you anything? I have an extra bottle of water."

"Thanks, water would be good."

The officer opened it and handed it to Joshua. It was cool, and quite refreshing. Joshua felt a bit better, especially knowing that at least one of the officers in the van was a decent person.

Before too long the van pulled into a rest area. They changed drivers and continued on their way. The new music was by Lady Antebellum. As a rule, Joshua did not listen to country music, but after hearing a few songs, he considered becoming a fan of the innocent pop and rock-influenced band. The songs helped Joshua escape his fears momentarily. The next time he looked up, he read a sign listing the exits into the twin towns of Bloomington and Normal, Illinois. He recalled another van ride to that area when he was in college. His men's tennis team had played in an invitational tournament hosted by Illinois State University. As they drove south on I-55 he reviewed his matches from that weekend long ago. He seemed to remember every serve, volley, and point scored. For a moment, he longed for the simplicity and happiness of those days.

Then his thoughts turned to Mary. He wondered where she was now and how she was feeling. He knew she would have been distraught and hoped she was okay. He thought about her inner strength and deep faith. Joshua liked to think he was a strong person too, but he longed to have her beside him now. He missed her so much! He let himself sink into a reverie about her, imagining her warmth and affection. He felt that if she were there next to him, everything would be all right.

As they drove past the Illinois state capital of Springfield, the sun began to set. Springfield was the home of Abraham Lincoln, where one will find many historical and commemorative sites, plus the state-of-the-art Lincoln Presidential Library and Museum. Nearby is the reconstructed town of New Salem, which is where Lincoln lived as a young adult. All the buildings in New Salem are log cabins, and there are actors and tour guides dressed in the clothing of Lincoln's time.

The Yellow Butterfly

They stopped in Springfield for a bathroom break, and then after taking Joshua back to the van, they left him alone to get some hamburgers. Joshua was feeling miserable and very alone, and again prayed to God without any real conviction his prayers would be answered. Deep in thought, he looked out the side window of the van where he saw some trees standing and was comforted by them. Then he happened to see a large yellow butterfly dart by. The butterfly fluttered back and forth among the trees and Joshua became mesmerized by it.

His thoughts wandered aimlessly and then he was struck by a thought that had never occurred to him before. Like most secular people who believed in God, he agreed there was no scientific proof for God's existence. But upon thinking of the life cycle of the butterfly, he felt that he had found that proof.

If you didn't believe in God as the Creator, then you had to assume that life started spontaneously in some primordial soup that existed at one time on the Earth. The first life was a tiny cell, which divided itself and created more tiny cells. Eventually these tiny cells combined in amazing ways to create all the plants and animals that exist today. According to Darwin, the mechanism that made this happen was evolution—natural selection and survival of the fittest. Some religious leaders did not accept evolution and said the way one cell got to the amazing diversity in life that we have today came from "intelligent design," in other words from God the Creator. Joshua believed that evolution and intelligent design somehow worked together.

He started thinking about the life cycle of the butterfly, where it starts out as a caterpillar, and then spins a cocoon around itself, and exits the cocoon as a butterfly. He could not imagine any set of circumstances, *based only on natural selection and survival of the fittest,* that would come up with such a strange life cycle. He felt the only way a caterpillar could become a butterfly was through intelligent design. It defies reason to imagine it happening any other way. There, he thought, is the proof that God exists!

"What a great time to have these thoughts!" he thought to himself. Then, perhaps grasping at straws, he wondered if God sent him the big yellow butterfly as an answer to his prayers, as if to say "Don't worry Joshua, I will help you." It was a comforting thought, but Joshua also knew it could just be a coincidence. Some things happen for a reason, he believed, but not everything, probably not even most things.

On to Prison

He continued watching the big yellow butterfly and thinking these thoughts until the officers returned to the van with the hamburgers. They gave a hamburger and some fries to Joshua, and without missing a beat, the third officer took over the driving. This driver was a U2 fan, which was fine with Joshua. He had long admired their strong stances on social justice, especially on AIDS eradication in Africa and debt forgiveness for third world nations.

A smile formed on his lips. Earlier in his career, before he had developed his unique new age theology, he had spoken one Friday evening about the Israelites' forty-year journey through the Sinai desert. To help his congregants imagine with him the spiritual desert-like experiences the Israelites had during those years, he played the U2 song, "I Still Haven't Found What I'm Looking For." It was one of several great songs from a CD he especially enjoyed—*The Joshua Tree*. Unfortunately, several of the older members of the congregation were a bit disconcerted to hear non-Jewish music (and rock music in particular) used in worship. Slowly, Joshua would win them over with his charisma and his personal attention to their needs and concerns. He was a truly gifted spiritual leader.

The van crossed the Mississippi River at about 8:30 p.m., entering the state of Missouri and the city of St. Louis. The tall St. Louis Arch was well lit at night, a usually welcoming sight. It symbolized St. Louis as the gateway to the West, but to Joshua it was the gateway to an uncertain future. They followed the Daniel Boone Expressway through the middle of St. Louis until they reached the exit for Clayton, the upscale suburb adjacent to the western border of St. Louis. Joshua was being taken to the new St. Louis Justice Center, which housed the County Jail, in downtown Clayton.

Then, he caught sight of his destination, a tall attractive reddish building with green glass façades. As they pulled onto the property, Joshua noticed there were a lot of people milling about outside the building. The van pulled into the docking station and stopped. Joshua was let out and led straight into a secure elevator heading upstairs. He wondered what awaited him and where Mary might be.

Meanwhile, Mary had followed Joshua and the officers the entire distance to Missouri. When they stopped in Springfield for a bathroom and hamburger break, she stopped in Springfield for a bathroom break. But she did not dare let the van out of her sight for more than a couple of minutes, so she got a fast-food fish sandwich and fries from the carry-out window across the street. She yearned to see Josh and comfort him, but she was afraid to show herself to the police. So, like a good detective trailing a suspect, she kept a respectful distance behind the van so she would not be spotted.

She followed them to downtown Clayton, and when the van pulled into an area of the Justice Center that she was prohibited from entering, she spotted a parking lot across the street. She planned to go in and see Josh if she could. There were dozens of people milling about in front of the Justice Center, some carrying signs and shouting slogans. They were not as numerous or frightening as the mob had been at Graham Chapel, but there were enough similarities to reawaken those bad memories. She pulled into a parking spot but did not turn the engine off. She sat frozen in her car, not knowing whether to drive away to safety or take a chance by getting out of the car.

Finally, her desire to see and protect Joshua overcame the terror she was feeling. She got out of the car, made sure her clothes were in order, and determinedly marched across the street towards the front door of the Justice Center as if nothing was wrong.

The crowd was not organized, so she was able to wend her way through it, occasionally bumping into someone or being bumped by someone in return. In a few seconds, she arrived at the front entrance and went into the small vestibule of the Justice Center that preceded the security area. It was much like going through security at the airport, except she did not have to remove her shoes. Nevertheless, security was extra tight this day because they knew that Joshua was coming there. He was the highest profile "guest" they'd ever had there.

"Who you going to see ma'am," asked a heavy-set female African-American guard with long straight hair.

"A friend of mine was arrested and I believe he was brought here," Mary stated with her voice quivering.

"Who that be, this friend of yours?"

"Josh Hertzel…um, Rabbi Joshua Hertzel, from Chicago."

"He here all right," she said, "but you can't see him. Visiting hours are over. You all have to come back in the morning. We open to the public at 10:00 a.m."

"That's it? Can't I find out how he is, or where they are holding him, or if he has been able to contact an attorney?" Mary was panicking.

"You that preacher lady on television, aren't you?" asked a tall heavy African-American male guard who had been listening in. Mary nodded her head yes. "I be there at the dock when Mr. Hertzel brought in. He seem okay; like anybody who be riding in a van all day. They be processing him in right about now. No place to visit him anyway right now. You can try to visit him tomorrow."

Mary was crushed. "Do you know what will be happening tomorrow? When would be a good time to see him?"

"I don't rightly know, ma'am," said the male guard. "He probably be arraigned tomorrow morning, maybe early, maybe late. No way to tell right now."

"Arraigned…I'm sorry, I forget what that is."

"It's when they tell the judge what he be accused of and he say he guilty or innocent."

"Will he need a lawyer for that?"

"Yes ma'am," answered the female guard. "If he don't have one, they give him a public defender."

"Then what happens?"

"The judge set a trial date and determine the bail. That be about it."

"Thank you both," Mary smiled gratefully. "He's not guilty, you know. I was there and I saw it all."

"We all did," the female guard said sympathetically. "They play that scene over and over again on the news. But they don't say he killed them folks personally. He be charged with inciting a riot. There surely was a riot there!"

"Can I just get a quick glimpse of him and just let him know I am here?" Mary begged.

"No ma'am," said the female officer. "There be nothing you or anyone else can do about these things tonight. Why don't you go get some rest. You feel better tomorrow."

"You're right; I am really tired. Thank you for being so patient with me."

"That's okay. I know this be upsetting for you," cooed the female guard softly. The male guard nodded sympathetically and smiled at her.

Mary walked back to the car. She called the hotel where she had stayed the previous week, and reserved a room. The man at the front desk who answered the phone told her how to get there, and she pulled out of the Justice Center parking lot having no idea what tomorrow would bring.

Later that evening, Mary called her mother's home to see how she and Christa were doing. Christa answered the phone.

"Hello sweetheart."

"Oh hello Aunt Mary, I'm so glad to hear from you. Rabbi Joshua has been on the news. Is everything going to be alright?"

"I really don't know sweetheart. He will be in court tomorrow."

"I would like to pray for him," Christa said. "Would that be okay, seeing that he is Jewish and all?"

"That would be lovely Christa," Mary answered, touched by Christa's affection for Joshua. "It doesn't matter that he is Jewish. You can pray for anyone you want."

"Then I will pray for him," Christa said with determination.

"I will pray for him too," Mary said softly. "How are you and Grandma doing?"

"We are fine Aunt Mary. Grandma is worried about you. Are you okay?"

"Tell her I am fine. I'm in St. Louis helping to support Rabbi Joshua."

"I will," said Christa. "Good night Aunt Mary."

"Good night sweetheart. I love you."

"I love you too Aunt Mary. Grandma and I will pray for you too."

The Arraignment

The next morning, a Thursday, the accused was taken to a small courtroom where he met a woman from the public defender's office who seemed way too nonchalant for Joshua's situation.

"Hello," the woman said. "I'm Jennie Johnston from the public defender's office. I'll be representing you. What's your name, again?" she asked, glancing down at the legal file folder on the top of her stack. She was a short chunky woman in her mid-thirties with dishwater blonde hair, cut short and wavy. She wore a big cross around her neck and had a fish symbol on her lapel. "Oh, yes, I remember now," she grinned. "You're in big trouble buster."

"And you're a real confidence builder, Ms. Jennie Johnston. Didn't your office have someone with a little more tact they could have sent?"

Jennie Johnston just smiled knowingly back at him. "They sent the best woman for the job," she said slyly.

"Uh huh, I see," replied an angry Joshua. "I'd like to get another attorney if you don't mind. I can pay for my own counsel and don't need a public defender."

She just smiled at him again and didn't say anything.

"All rise!" announced the clerk. "The County of St. Louis…"

Joshua was so startled he missed the judge's name, but loudly and clearly he heard, "The State of Missouri versus Joshua D. Hertzel." The clerk motioned for everyone to sit and the judge called on the prosecutor to speak.

The prosecuting attorney, Bryce's father, did not ordinarily appear at arraignments, but this was a special case because it was receiving worldwide attention. Mr. Patterson began making the State's case against Joshua—to demonstrate that there was probable cause that Joshua was responsible for the shooting death of Reverend George Turner and the five people in the audience who had been trampled to death. He claimed that Joshua had created a dangerous atmosphere with his oratory and had incited the mob to violence. The fact that someone else pulled the trigger on Reverend Turner was a non-factor. He seemed very nervous as he spoke, his words halting, as though he knew he was being scrutinized by more than just those present.

The judge was a balding middle-aged man with spectacles and thick eyebrows and a perpetual sneer on his lips. He looked disapprovingly at Joshua, his eyes burrowing a hole into Joshua's torso. Joshua did not feel encouraged looking at the judge.

Ms. Jennie Johnston then advised the judge that she had not spoken to her client yet, but she would do so later when she had time.

"I find that there is reasonable cause to go ahead with this indictment," the judge ruled. "How do you plead?" he asked Joshua absent-mindedly.

"Not guilty!" Joshua said firmly.

"Okay, when will you be ready for trial Mr. Patterson?"

"I can be ready by tomorrow," Bryce's father said. "All the facts are known and we've already interviewed all the witnesses."

"When can you be ready for trial Ms. Johnston?"

"I can be ready for trial by tomorrow too Judge," Jennie Johnston answered.

Joshua could not believe his ears. How could she be ready in only one day when she had not even spoken to him yet? He felt like he was going to be sick again.

"Wait!" Joshua shouted. "I want another attorney. I can't be ready for trial that soon!"

"Silence!" the judge ordered sternly. "One more outburst like that and you will be gagged. Ms. Johnston, can't you control your client better than that?"

"Sorry, Your Honor. It won't happen again." She gave Joshua a dirty look and told him to shut up.

"I'm scheduling the trial for 10:00 Friday morning. Jury selection will begin at 8:00. The defendant will be held with no bail. Next case...."

"Why didn't you ask for bail?" Joshua angrily asked Jennie Johnston. "I need to get out of here to help work on this case!"

"There is no bail in capital cases buster," Jennie Johnston lied. "Better go make your cell as comfy as you can. You might want to pray too. You will need all the help you can get." The sinister way she spoke those words told Joshua she thought there was no hope.

Two sheriff's deputies approached Joshua to escort him back through the second floor windowed skywalk that connected the courthouse to the jail over the intervening street between them. They re-shackled his ankles and wrists for the ten-minute walk. Joshua felt totally powerless and humiliated. And now his optimism was gone too. He felt utterly defeated, a feeling he had never experienced before. Then, it suddenly hit him. He'd been so used to living in Illinois that he had forgotten that Missouri still had the death penalty. "Oh, my God!" he thought. "If they convict me, they might kill me!" It was a good thing there was an officer on each side of Joshua, because his knees went wobbly and they had to catch him before he fell.

The officers took him up to the eighth floor where there were solitary cells, which were used for the most dangerous prisoners. This was a much more modern jail than the one in Chicago. His room was small but looked like a tiny dormitory room. There was a bed and a sink and a steel toilet with no seat. There were no bars. His room was enclosed by a steel door with a rectangular window in it, which enabled guards to see him without opening the door. The door was locked and could only be opened by an officer who sat at the computer console in an open area beyond the cells.

The officers unshackled Joshua and gave him some magazines to read. They told him he would be allowed out of his cell only one hour per day, and that no one else would be allowed out at the same time he was. He would be brought food by an officer, to be eaten in his cell. And no one would be allowed to visit him.

The Revelation

Meanwhile, flashing back to Tuesday night when Joshua was arrested, after they saw that Joshua was in police custody and taken away from Barry and Sylvia's home, Judith and Bryce decided to go to a nearby restaurant to help calm their nerves. It was called Gulliver's, and was on the street dividing the northern edge of Chicago from the fashionable suburb of Evanston, home of Northwestern University. The restaurant was famous for its many sculptures and stained glass windows displayed by the owner who had spent years collecting them. As they were being seated in a booth toward the back of the restaurant, Judith excused herself to find the ladies' room. Bryce pulled his cell phone from his pocket and called his father to tell him where he and Judith were, and to inform him of Joshua's arrest. His younger brother Richard answered the phone. Their father was not home so Bryce gave Richard the message.

But Richard had a secret he wanted Bryce to know....

"Bryce, I think Dad's getting himself into big trouble."

"What do you mean Richard?"

"Well, you know how I like to listen in on Dad's phone conversations..."

"Yes, I know," Bryce said disapprovingly. He knew Richard liked to do this so he could learn more about the criminal law business, but he disapproved of Richard being so sneaky about it. "What did you hear?"

"It was a four-way conversation with Dad, this preacher called Paul Lindenbaugh, Congressman Fitch from Texas, and a big shot rich dude from Wall Street. They told Dad they wanted this Rabbi dude found guilty of murder and sentenced to death. They said that the judge and the jury would be fixed and that they wanted Dad to rush things through."

"What did Dad say?"

"He didn't want to do it, but they threatened him and us too. They said he would lose his job, and we kids would be blackballed from ever getting a good job. They even threatened that Dad might be killed if he didn't cooperate."

"But why are they threatening him? Isn't the Rabbi guilty anyway?"

"Dad told them no, and they seemed to know that. The charges are trumped up, Dad said. He said anything they did would be overturned on appeal."

"Really?"

"Then they really got scary. They said not to worry about it — that the case would never get that far."

"Why would Paul Lindenbaugh and the other guys care what happens to the Rabbi?" Bryce wanted to know.

"I'm not exactly sure, but it sounds like there are lots of investments involved that could be at risk if the Rabbi isn't discredited. I think they're worried that donations might fall off. Maybe there's lots of other secret stuff going on there too."

"What did Dad decide to do?"

"That's where I'm worried Bro. He said he'd go along with them if they were so sure no one would ever find out. I'm afraid someone will find out and Dad will be in big trouble. And I think they've decided to off the Rabbi one way or another."

"Thanks for the information Richard," Bryce said. "This is terrible. I was wondering how the Rabbi could be blamed for the shooting when he didn't fire the shot. And how he could be blamed for the other deaths when that mob out there was looking for a fight even before the debate began. Now I'm beginning to understand."

"Is there anything you can do to help Dad?" Richard asked.

"I really don't know. And Judith is dead set against the Rabbi because the guy that got shot turns out to be her real father. I don't want to go against Dad and Judith."

"I sure just hope Dad doesn't get caught. Talk to you later Bro."

"Bye Richard."

Bryce's head was still spinning when Judith came back from the rest room. She noticed immediately that Bryce was shook up and asked him what happened. Bryce told her what Richard had said. He was totally surprised at her reaction.

"If the Rabbi isn't guilty then we have to save him!" she said resolutely. "I don't want my father's death to be used to help the people who were really responsible for his death. If the Rabbi isn't guilty then that guy who was connected with the mob must have been."

"You mean Reverend Paul?" Bryce asked incredulously.

"Yes, if he was the guy responsible. It sure looked like he had something to do with it."

"But what can anyone possibly do against the likes of him and all the other big shots?" Bryce asked. "And more particularly, what can *we* do?"

"I don't know. Why don't you call your father and see how much time we have."

So Bryce called Richard back and asked him to have their father call him when he got home.

Bryce and Judith were having beers and a couple of hot appetizers when Mr. Patterson called.

"Hi Dad, do you think you'll be involved in Rabbi Hertzel's murder trial?"

"I am certain I will, Bryce. This case will generate more media coverage than any trial the county's had in ages, and I'm the chief prosecutor. I was told yesterday to start my preparations to convict Mr. Hertzel."

"Wasn't that a bit premature? I mean, to work on a case before the suspect is even arrested?"

"No, not at all. Typically he would be arraigned the morning after he is brought in and processed. The state has to have all its ducks in a row before that hearing happens. One thing I can tell you is this: there is pressure to move this trial through the system quickly. A lot of very powerful people are demanding swift justice."

"Wow, Dad. You said that was one thing you *could* tell me. Is there something else you can't, or aren't supposed to tell me?" There was a pause before Mr. Patterson spoke.

"Yes, there is more."

Neither spoke for a few seconds. Finally, Mr. Patterson broke the silence.

"I need for you to understand that what I am going to tell you is strictly confidential. Can I swear you to secrecy on this?"

"Yes, of course."

"Rabbi Hertzel will be charged with those deaths on the grounds that he created a riot, like falsely shouting 'fire!' in a crowded theater. But that is a theory that will not stand up under appeal."

"Why do you say 'under appeal'?"

"The big shots have already set it up so he will be convicted at the trial level. I don't know what is going to happen after that, but they tell me it will not get to the appeals stage. I'm not sure what they mean by that, but it doesn't sound good."

"Can you alert the defense attorney so this doesn't happen?"

"I wish I could do that, but I'm being told to cooperate by some people you don't want to mess with. These people always get their way."

"Are you talking about the Mafia?"

"No. Even worse. We're talking about some really big shots on Wall Street combined with some of the 'religious right'. They are not going to let this rabbi or anyone else undermine the Christian nature of this country. A lot of important politicians are involved in this too."

"Wow! It sounds hopeless. But Judith doesn't want the wrong man convicted of killing her father. I have to help her!"

"We're in a bad place Bryce. You do what you have to do and I'll do what I have to do. Whatever God wants to happen *will* happen!"

"You know I don't really believe that stuff, but I know you do. Bye Dad, I have to go now."

"I love you, Bryce."

"Love you too, Dad."

To The Rescue

Judith asked what Mr. Patterson said and Bryce told her.

"We have to do something to stop this!" Judith affirmed again. "I was so *sure* Rabbi Hertzel killed my dad...." She started crying. "If he really didn't do it, we can't let them convict him. He's a rabbi, for God's sake!"

"And how are two college students going to fight the courts and a bunch of rich and powerful people who sound like they're crazy?"

"We will need a lot of help," said Judith. "Who do we know that's really smart, would know what to do, and wouldn't be afraid of doing it?"

Bryce thought for awhile, and then his face brightened. "How about that British historian guy? He seems to have it together, and he probably knows the Rabbi isn't guilty."

"Yes, Sir Winston something..." Judith's light bulb went on. "Sir Winston *Hamburley*. He might be perfect for this. He is 'smart as a tack' as my grandmother used to say, very logical and fair-minded, and he was there. He was right there when everything happened."

"He must have seen something that night."

"Yes, and I'll bet he has connections. I read an interview with him before the debate started and he seems to know scholars, political leaders, and CEOs of Fortune 100 companies all over the world."

"Let's look him up," Bryce offered as he reached for his cell phone again. In a matter of minutes, he had retrieved Dr. Hamburley's contact information. He would have called him right then, except that it was 3:30 a.m. in Oxford, England. "If we're still up a couple of hours after midnight we can call him then."

"Why don't we just go wake him up ourselves?" Judith asked.

"OK, I'll call him," Bryce said reluctantly.

"I didn't mean call him," Judith said with a twinkle in her eye. "I've always wanted to see England."

"Are you crazy? I don't have that kind of money."

"But I do," replied Judith, whose mother and step-dad made good salaries in their professions. "Maybe we could have tea and biscuits in the garden tomorrow with Sir Winston and his wife. What are you staring at me for? Find us some tickets!"

An hour later, the two students were checking in at one of the many United Airlines counters at O'Hare International Airport in Chicago. Their parents had promised them a trip to Europe that summer and they already had passports, which they excitedly kept with them at all times.

They were able to get seats on a Boeing 757 headed to Heathrow Airport in London. They would be on their way to a campus they had always wanted to visit, Oxford University.

Early the next day, Judith phoned Sir Winston from the airport. Winston was suspicious at first. He did not know these kids, and after what happened to Rabbi Hertzel, he was reluctant to trust anybody connected with the case. But when he was told the whole thing was a conspiracy and that maybe he could help, he decided to take a chance on them and invited them to his home. He was very moved by the tragic death of George Turner, and would have stayed for the funeral, but he had other commitments back in England that he could not get out of.

The weather was damp and cool when the taxi pulled up in front of the Hamburley residence. Winston and Molly's house was a typical upper class English Tudor cottage, with a rose garden in the front surrounded by a white picket fence. The pathway to the cottage was made of pastel-colored cobblestones and featured a white arched trellis encircled with fragrant yellow roses. Judith and Bryce were greeted warmly at the door by Molly Hamburley, a dignified plump white-haired lady with blue-grey eyes, rosy cheeks and a big friendly smile. Molly led them all to the Victorian-styled dining room and invited the guests to be seated at a large antique oak table with matching chairs where Molly served homemade vegetable soup (everything homegrown) and hot bread. She invited the kids to return in warmer months when she could serve them tea and scones on the patio outside.

Sir Winston, who had already eaten, joined the group presently. After hearing what Bryce had learned about Joshua's predicament, Winston knew what had to be done. He placed a call to the Imam in Israel who had helped the young brothers, Fareydoun and Amir, navigate their way through the cave that led to their heralded discovery. The two men had met a few months after the Book of Emet was discovered, and had come to admire each other. The Imam respected Winston's scholarship and appreciation of Islam and its practitioners. Winston in turn esteemed the wise and generous spirit of this venerated religious leader. By the end of their phone call, they determined that Winston should travel to Israel.

The Muslim holy man had something to give the scholar — something very powerful.

That evening, Sir Winston and the kids arrived in Tel Aviv, Israel, and got a hotel near the beach. Judith and Bryce went for a walk after they got settled in. They had never been to the Holy Land and were so excited to be there. Judith, who knew a little Hebrew from her Bat Mitzvah days, was totally captivated by its use everywhere, with frequent English signs for tourists and others who did not know Hebrew.

At one point in their exploration, they passed an Arab street vendor who was cooking and selling falafel sandwiches from his cart. Judith decided to try one and gave Bryce a taste, whereupon he ordered his own sandwich. They sat at an outdoor café to eat and ordered coffee from the waitress. They enjoyed people-watching from their vantage point. Among the passers-by, Bryce noticed two very dark black men walking by in strange garb, but they did not appear to be tourists. Judith explained that they were probably part of the thousands of Ethiopian Jews who Israel airlifted to safety when they were in danger of extinction due to famine and persecution.

"I didn't know they have black Jewish people," said Bryce with amazement.

"Oh yes, there are Jewish people in Africa and India and even China. There are African-American Jews in the United States. If you're Jewish, it doesn't matter what race you are or what country you're from."

"I have a friend with a white Jewish father and an African-American Christian mother," said Bryce. "He said the Jews told him he is not Jewish because he has to have a Jewish mother, that it doesn't matter what his father is."

Judith frowned. "Yes and no. What they told him is what traditional Jewish law says, but the Reform Movement voted to change that. I think eventually, traditional Jewish law will have to change too. If one parent is enough to make you Jewish, what difference does it make which parent it is. It doesn't make any sense. So your friend would be considered Jewish in my temple, but not in an Orthodox or Conservative synagogue. And not here in Israel either, because they follow Orthodox law here. With all the people we lost in the Holocaust, and our numbers shrinking even now, I think it's crazy to arbitrarily say some Jewish people aren't really Jews. What do they gain by thinking that way? I really don't get it."

"It sounds like some of the arguments in the African-American community. Like my friend, not only what religion he is but what race he is. Whites consider him black and some blacks consider him white."

They both agreed that arguments like this are pretty crazy when there are so many "real problems" in the world.

Later, they walked back to their hotel where they spent the rest of the night. The next morning, Winston hired a cab and they were driven the 100 kilometers to the Imam's home in Nazareth. The Imam's home was a three-story white stucco building with a green door and green shutters. The Imam's study and greeting rooms were on the main floor, while the residence area for him and his extended family were on the upper two floors. The front of the residence was decorated with gorgeous purple, red, pink, and white bougainvillea bushes. A servant greeted Sir Winston at the door and ushered him into the Imam's study, where the two elders exchanged warm hugs and kisses in the Arab style.

While Sir Winston spoke privately with the Imam, Bryce and Judith were introduced to the boys who had found Emet's scroll, Fareydoun and Amir. The boys had been told important visitors would be coming and were waiting excitedly in one of the greeting rooms on the main floor. They were two years older now and had become more sophisticated. The family had been rewarded financially by the Israeli government, which had purchased the scroll from them at a very good price. The Imam had handled the negotiations, with both sides bargaining in the Arab way. The family became celebrities in the Arab world and they were on everyone's VIP guest list. They were also visited by many historians and archaeologists, including of course, Sir Winston Hamburley. They moved to the nicest area of Nazareth, but still kept and worked the olive orchard, which they regarded as a family heirloom. The cave, which was on family land, had already become a lucrative tourist site, but the family donated most of those receipts to their mosque and to the Imam to be used to help the needy. They felt that Allah had given them this treasure, and that the benefit of it must be returned to Allah.

When Winston left the Imam's office, he was carrying a large elongated package. Judith asked him what it was but he said he was sworn to silence and could not tell her. He said they needed to return to the hotel immediately and gather their things, so they could be on the next flight to St. Louis. He hoped they would be in time to help.

The Trial

Their hands are skilled in doing evil; the ruler demands gifts, the judge accepts bribes; the powerful dictate what they desire; they all conspire together. [Micah 7:3.]
Let their lying lips be silenced, for with pride and contempt they speak arrogantly against the righteous. [Psalms 31:19.]

As it turned out, the trial of Joshua David Hertzel was scheduled for Good Friday. That morning, Mary arrived at the courthouse early, hoping to get in so she could support Joshua. There were hundreds of people milling around the outside of the two connected buildings housing the prison and the courthouse, and a couple dozen police, some on foot and others on horseback. The police had the crowds fairly well under control, although there was lots of pushing and shoving. Everyone wanted to get in to see the trial, but the courtroom was not very large and only forty people were being allowed inside. Astonishingly, the press was completely barred from the proceedings.

Mary had to park five blocks away, and she was lucky to find a parking place that close. At first it appeared Mary would not be allowed in the building either, but one of the policewomen knew her from her television show and made sure she got in. As it was still early, Mary was able to get a good seat in the courtroom.

When Joshua was brought into the courtroom in handcuffs, Mary jumped up from her seat and went as close to him as the guards would let her. She put her hands on her heart and mouthed a kiss to him. Joshua was delighted to see her and felt much better. Before the guards shooed her away, Joshua was able to ask her one question, and that was whether there was any word about Kal. Mary, who had been in touch with Joshua's ex-wife Patricia, told him that there was nothing new. Joshua's shoulders slumped.

The trial of Joshua Hertzel for the murder of George Turner was a farce. Any writer describing a kangaroo court could never have invented such a bizarre sequence of events.

The judge, the Honorable Phineas Pilott, was stern and resolute. Mary examined him closely, noticing he had snow white hair encircling a balding head with long white sideburns, and wire frame glasses perched at the end of his nose. As a boy, young Phineas aspired to be a pilot for obvious reasons, but he found that he was not up to the standards required by tough airline requirements. So instead he went to law school, always a little bitter that he had been deprived of what he felt was his true calling. He quickly got in with the "in crowd." And some whispered that he could be had for a price. Judge Pilott was known in St. Louis as "the hanging judge" and he moved the proceedings along more quickly than anyone had ever seen in a murder trial before.

Jury selection had taken almost no time at all. As it turned out, the twelve jurors selected were all out of work, with several of them living in homeless shelters. Each had been well paid to agree with the prosecutor's closing arguments. Jennie Johnston, Joshua's defense attorney, did not object to anyone Mr. Patterson selected. Of course, there was the appearance of a real jury selection, but it was just for show.

None of this made any sense to Joshua. He had never heard of a case coming to trial so quickly. It was apparent that everything was a set up. He wondered who was behind this conspiracy, who had been paid off, and why finding him guilty of a murder he did not commit was so important...and urgent.

At the behest of instructions that had been given him by the conspirators, Bryce's father split the charges against Joshua into two separate trials. First, they would try the hardest, highest profile case, the murder of George Turner. Then, if necessary, they would try Joshua for the trampling deaths of what the press was calling the "Graham Chapel Five."

After the jury selection and the opening statements were concluded, Mr. Patterson called only three witnesses and appeared as nervous and unsure of himself as he had been at the time of the arraignment. The first witness was Paul Lindenbaugh, the second was to be Reverend Paul's chief lieutenant from the outside mob, and the third was to be another Lindenbaugh supporter from the inside audience.

Paul Lindenbaugh, wearing his usual all-white outfit, put his hand on the Bible and swore to tell the truth, the whole truth, and nothing but the truth, "so help me God." When he gave his name and profession, there was a smattering of applause from the guests in the courtroom. The judge did not try to silence them. Reverend Paul then testified that the things Joshua had said against the New Testament were inflammatory to most Americans and that Joshua was responsible for the chaos that had resulted in Reverend George Turner's death. The other two witnesses said the same thing.

Mary was not impressed with Jennie Johnston, the Public Defender, or the young man she had sitting next to her, who Mary guessed correctly was another public defender. The two public defenders whispered to each other incessantly during the proceedings, often ignoring Joshua's questions and comments.

On cross-examination, Jennie Johnston asked Reverend Paul and his associates if they knew who fired the shot that killed Reverend Turner, and they all said they did not. Then she asked them about Joshua's right to Freedom of Speech, and they had no answer, saying they were not Constitutional law experts.

Jennie Johnston called only one witness, Dr. Mary Madelyne Roberts, who did not know until that moment that she would be called. Mary felt a twinge of panic at first, but she quickly regained her composure. She walked with determination to the witness stand and swore on the Bible to tell the truth with great confidence. She was convinced she would be able to help Joshua get acquitted with her testimony.

Jennie Johnston asked Mary if she saw who shot Reverend Turner, and she had to testify that she did not know who did it, but that she thought the shot came from the balcony and that Joshua *certainly* did not pull the trigger. Then Mr. Patterson asked her about the climate of fear in the chapel, and Mary had to testify that there had been earlier incidents that had scared much of the audience away.

"Did Mr. Hertzel stop defaming the New Testament after that?" Mr. Patterson asked. Surprisingly, Jennie Johnston did not object to use of the word "defaming." If she had objected, even this judge would have had to make Mr. Patterson rephrase.

"There were times when he said negative things about the New Testament, yes," Mary testified. "But in the end, he did what he was supposed to do to explain the Book of Emet to the audience."

Mr. Patterson then played a video tape showing the end of the debate, in which Joshua said: "To say that salvation can only be achieved through believing in Jesus as the Son of God is something the Christians made up. It's that simple."

"Did you see the chaos that followed after what he said at the end?"

"Yes, people came in from all over it seemed, and five people were trampled to death and many other people were injured." Mary visibly shuddered at the memory.

"Do you think that chaos would have happened if Mr. Hertzel had not defamed the word of God in the New Testament?"

"He didn't defame anything. He was just explaining the Book of Emet and giving his own take on the life of Jesus from a Jewish perspective."

"Isn't it true that he said Jesus was wrong and that the New Testament had some lies in it?"

"Yes..........." she said slowly.

"You are a preacher and teacher of the Word of God through Jesus Christ, are you not?"

"Yes."

"Do you believe that the negative things that Mr. Hertzel said about Jesus and the New Testament are true?"

Mary looked helplessly at Joshua, tears in her eyes. Joshua nodded to her mouthing, "It's okay Mary."

"No," she finally admitted.

"Are you in love with him? Would you try to exonerate him if you could?"

"Yes," she proclaimed proudly, "but Josh is not responsible for George's death."

"Aren't you a married woman?"

"Yes, I am." She was almost in tears. "But I am going to be getting a divorce."

"Oh, that is very interesting. Haven't you decried divorces on your television show many times?"

Mary was too choked up to answer, but nodded her head affirmatively.

"Well now," Mr. Patterson said to the jury, "we do not have an objective witness here. She has already sacrificed her morality for the defendant. We can't believe anything she says here now. I have no more questions of *this* witness," he concluded scornfully.

Mary stepped down from the witness stand badly shaken. She looked at Joshua imploringly, as if to say "I'm sorry Josh!" Joshua gave her a loving look back, as if to say, "It's okay Mary darling, I love you!" Mary knew she would treasure that look forever.

"The defense rests," Jennie Johnston stated.

"*Wait a minute!*" Joshua said in a voice loud of enough for everyone in the courtroom to hear. "Shouldn't you call more witnesses to say I didn't shoot George?"

"Mr. Hertzel! Close your mouth!" yelled the judge. "You will speak only when spoken to by this court, or you will be gagged! Ms. Johnston, if this outburst happens again I will cite you for contempt of court. Do I make myself clear?" Both Jennie Johnston and Joshua nodded their heads up and down and said, "Yes, your honor." The courtroom was so quiet you could hear Joshua's blood pressure spike. Jennie Johnston also turned a little red and looked at her colleague, rolling her eyes knowingly. They knew something that Joshua was not yet ready to face — the conclusion of this trial had already been decided.

Joshua threw a quick glance back at Mary, who was sitting three rows behind him. He knew Mary was praying for him. He could feel her spiritual strength around him, holding him up. To think how briefly they had known each other, and how in tune with each other they had become. And he was right. Mary had been praying silently for him all morning.

Maybe Mary's prayer helped. Joshua did not know himself, but suddenly he had an inspiration. Jennie Johnston had told him he would not be called to testify in his own behalf because that would only help the prosecutor. He did not understand why that would be so, but he took her word for it. But now he realized he had nothing to lose. He stood up, and risking punishment from the judge, announced that he wanted to testify in his own behalf.

"Your honor, I want to testify. I believe I have that right under the Constitution."

Jennie Johnston's face got even redder, and she quickly jumped up and told the judge she had no intention of calling Joshua as a witness and that she had advised against it.

"Are you sure you want to testify against advice of counsel Mr. Hertzel?" the judge asked.

"Yes, your honor, I do," Joshua said bravely. He had no idea what would happen on the witness stand or even if anyone would offer him a chance to tell his story, but he was determined to insist that he be given that chance.

"The defendant has a right to testify on his own behalf," the judge ruled. "Ms. Johnston, he will be regarded as your witness, so you have the right to question him first."

"I want nothing to do with this," Jennie Johnston replied in a huff. "I'll let my associate, Mr. Cruz, do the questioning of this witness."

Jennie Johnston sat down and the surprised Mr. Cruz stood up, having no idea what he was going to ask Joshua.

"May I have a few minutes your honor?" Mr. Cruz asked.

"Do you have any objections Mr. Patterson?" the judge asked Bryce's father. He indicated that he had no objections.

Mitchell Cruz was of Mexican heritage, but was third generation American. He had been in the Public Defender's office for only a few months and had no experience presiding in a trial of this importance. He wanted to confer with Jennie Johnston before undertaking the questioning of Joshua.

But he was to be disappointed. Jennie Johnston wanted nothing to do with this and told him he was on his own. However, Mitchell Cruz was a cocky young man, 26 years of age, short and swarthy, with a full head of curly black hair. He saw this as an opportunity to make a splash in the Public Defender's office and put his career on the fast track.

He left the courtroom for a few minutes to gather his thoughts and write down some notes and questions he wanted to ask. When he reentered the courtroom, he announced in a confident voice that he was ready to proceed.

Joshua was called up to the witness stand and sworn in. He was nervous but determined to say his piece. After going through the formalities of answering questions to establish who he was and where he lived, the real questioning began.

"Did you shoot Reverend George Turner on the night of the Great Debate?" Mitchell Cruz began.

"No I did not!"

"Did you see who did shoot him?"

"No, I was watching all the people from outside the chapel forcing their way in. I was scared for my life. I heard a shot from somewhere, and Reverend Turner dropped right in front of me, with a bullet hole in his head." Joshua shuddered at the memory of it and tears formed in his eyes. "I don't own a gun and I didn't have a gun with me, so I could not have shot him."

"As I understand the case against you," Cruz said in a clear and confident voice, "the State isn't saying you shot Reverend Turner. They say you inflamed the people outside the chapel and were responsible for their stampeding into the building and creating a situation in which the murder took place."

"Yes," answered Joshua, "that is my understanding too. But it doesn't make any sense. We were debating an issue that has the whole world on edge it seems and all I was doing was giving the Book of Emet's interpretation of who Jesus was. The people outside were carrying signs, drinking beer, and inflaming themselves."

Here was where Mitchell Cruz's inexperience showed itself, because he committed the lawyer's sin of asking a question he did not know the answer to.

"What did you think you could accomplish by defaming Jesus Christ and the New Testament in a worldwide telecast?" Mitchell Cruz asked with a sneer.

Joshua paused for a few seconds before answering, wanting to make sure he would get his answer right. "I had no intention of defaming Jesus or anything else. I don't believe that Jesus was God in human form but I think he was a great man who we all could learn from. And although I believe Christianity is wrong about who he was, I think Christianity is a wonderful religion and I think its adherents are wonderful people who do wonderful things in the world. I hope Christianity lives on forever. I have no reason to defame it."

Joshua paused again, but seeing Mitchell Cruz was about to ask another question, Joshua quickly resumed his testimony.

"You see, I believe every religion has a piece of the truth and no religion has the whole truth. I believe God spoke to different peoples and gave each of them a piece of the truth. I came to this conclusion when I learned that the compilers of the Jewish Old Testament and the Hindu Bhagavad Gita, as well as Plato, Buddha, Confucius, and Lao Tzu the founder of Taoism, all date from roughly the same time, around 400 to 500 BCE. It must have been an era of great religious insight; perhaps an era when God spoke to or inspired them with the great doctrines that are still with us today. After them came Jesus and then Mohammed, who carried some of those great insights to other peoples.

"I believe that rather than fighting each other to see whose religion is right and whose is wrong, we should talk to each other and learn what God taught them that He didn't teach us. Then, together, we can arrive at a higher truth than any of us could reach separately. I believe that is what God wanted us to do and now is a good time for us to do it. Many of our young people are already learning from other religions, and I encourage that. As a rabbi, I believe Judaism can adopt the best principals of the other religions without losing its essence. That is what I think God wants us to do, and He gave us a religion that is flexible enough to incorporate what He taught others. We are taught by Ben Zoma in *Ethics of Our Fathers*: 'Who is wise? He who can learn from every man.' None of us should believe that our religion is the whole and complete truth."

Mitchell Cruz did not know what to do next. He looked helplessly at Jennie Johnston and her face told him it was time to quit. "I have no further questions, your honor. Your witness," he said to the prosecuting attorney.

Mr. Patterson quickly got back to his talking points. Did Joshua know about the mob outside? Did earlier events indicate that people were disturbed by the arguments Joshua was making? Did Joshua say the words that preceded the mob rushing into the chapel? Joshua could only answer "yes" to each question. By the time Bryce's father was done with the questioning, the atmosphere in the courtroom had once again turned decidedly against Joshua.

The entire trial did not last more than two hours. After Joshua's testimony, the judge told the attorneys to make their closing statements. Each was disturbingly brief. The judge then gave his instructions to the jury. He told them that Freedom of Speech considerations did not apply to this case. He told them to find Joshua guilty if he defamed the Word of God as encoded in the New Testament and if he caused the chaos that ensued. The judge told the jury that the fact that Joshua did not personally fire the shot that killed Reverend Turner was irrelevant, because he was responsible for the conditions that resulted in George's death.

Jennie Johnston did not object to the judge's instructions, although they were clearly not a correct statement of the law. Mitchell Cruz pulled Joshua aside and told him not to worry, that the instructions would be overturned on appeal. Something in the way he said that made Joshua feel like that day would never come.

By 12:00 noon, the court was recessed for lunch and the twelve jurors were sequestered in the jury room for lunch and deliberation. To the surprise of none of the "actors", the deliberations were finished before the sandwiches were. They had reached a verdict on the first vote. At 2:00 p.m., everyone was called back to the courtroom to hear the verdict.

Mary was frantic. She tried and tried to visit Joshua, but was not allowed to. One officer even told her that the visitation room was closed for the day, when she could clearly see people coming and going. Meanwhile, Joshua's best friend, Barry, had flown down that morning. He was not allowed into the courtroom, but after consulting with Mary, he contacted several local lawyers to see if anyone could intervene on Joshua's behalf. They all told him that because Joshua already had legal representation, there was nothing they could do to help him at this time. Barry and Mary had lunch together to commiserate and strategize. Each was feeling that further efforts were futile, but would not admit that out loud. They were two tenacious people with a shared love for Joshua; surely they would think of something to save him.

At 2:00 p.m., the court was reconvened. The judge entered the courtroom from his chamber, sat down, and asked the foreman if the jury had reached a verdict. The foreman stood and replied, "Yes we have, your honor. We find the defendant guilty as charged." Many people gasped at the news, especially Mary, Barry, and Joshua. Several people began to cry, while many more applauded and cheered.

"Quiet down, everyone," the judge said as he pounded his gavel on the large wooden desk. "I will not allow a circus in my courtroom. Will the defendant and his counsel please rise." Joshua and the two public defenders did as they were told.

"Joshua David Hertzel," the judge intoned, "a jury of your peers has found you guilty in the murder of Reverend George Turner. As this is a capital crime, the Prosecutor has requested the death penalty, with which I concur. Joshua David Hertzel, I sentence you to be executed by the State of Missouri at midnight on July 4th of this year, to be hung by the neck until dead. You will no doubt observe that July 4th is our Independence Day, and that is the day we will bid good-riddance to you and those heretical documents of yours."

Joshua's knees gave way, plunging him against the front edge of his wooden chair, and then bouncing him to the floor. A pain shot up his back so fast he thought his sciatic nerves were on fire. Two sheriff's deputies pulled him back into a standing position. Joshua gazed up at the judge with eyes that could not focus and a dizzy feeling in his head. "Surely this is all just a nightmare and can't really be happening," he thought.

His wishful thinking was interrupted by the fall of the judge's gavel. "I hereby declare the case of the State of Missouri versus Joshua David Hertzel closed."

The Hanging Party

*Then Moses said, "This is how you will know that the Lord has sent
me to do all these things and that they did not come from me:
If these men die a natural death then the Lord has not sent me.
But if the Lord brings about something totally new, and the earth
opens its mouth and swallows them, with everything that belongs to
them, and they go down alive into the pit, then you will know that
these men have treated the Lord with contempt."
And it came to pass, as soon as he finished speaking these words, the
ground under them split apart and the earth opened its mouth and
swallowed them, with their households and all their possessions.
So they went down alive into the pit, with everything they owned;
and the earth closed over them, and they perished and were gone
from the community. [Numbers 16:28-33.]*

Immediately after the verdict was announced, the two sheriff's deputies
who were holding Joshua up hauled him quickly out of the courtroom.
He had just enough time to turn toward the sound of Mary calling out,
"Josh, I love you! We will get you out of this!" Barry then telephoned
several of the lawyers he had contacted earlier to file a motion to appeal
the verdict. Most of the attorneys Barry called were too intimidated by
the power of the religious right to risk the loss of business, and possibly
the protests, that they felt would ensue if they took the case. Only
one attorney was willing to touch the case, and he said he would file
an emergency motion after the weekend. However, he wanted a huge
amount of money upfront before he would do anything.

Meanwhile Mary followed the deputies who were escorting Joshua,
hoping to get a chance to talk to him or give him a hug. She saw them

get on an elevator and Mary got on another elevator. She punched 2 for the second floor. On the second floor was the skywalk connecting the court building to the jail building. She did not see Joshua in the second floor lobby when she got out of the elevator, so she ran to the entrance of the skywalk, expecting to see him and the deputies there a few yards ahead. But he was nowhere to be seen. "Where could they have taken him?" she wondered.

She looked out the concourse windows and she gasped at what she saw. There was what appeared to be a well-organized mob outside, led by Paul Lindenbaugh and the St. Louis County Sheriff. And what was worse, she saw the deputies and Joshua in front of the court building, just a few yards from the mob. Yes, the deputies had mysteriously decided to escort Joshua to the jail building by taking him from the street entrance of the one building to the street entrance of the other building, bypassing the interior skywalk that they had always used in the past.

"They must have known the mob would be there!" Mary realized. "What are they up to?" She knew the answer as soon as she asked the question. "They aren't going to wait for him to be executed. They want to kill him now. I'd better get down there right away!"

She quickly hopped on the down escalator to the first floor lobby and ran out the double glass doors to join Joshua and the deputies outside. They were still standing under the stone canopy covering the outside entrance to the court building. Facing them on the grassy field north of the court building was an angry mob, almost as large as the one that had rushed Graham Chapel just a few days earlier. Paul Lindenbaugh, using a bullhorn, was demanding that Joshua be turned over to them, to be taken by the mob and hanged from the nearest tree. Standing next to Paul Lindenbaugh was the Sheriff, holding a hanging rope, who was ordering his deputies to do just that. The deputies stood there looking at each other, not sure what to do. They knew it was wrong to turn Joshua over to the mob, but that is what their boss was ordering them to do, and they were trained to follow orders without thinking.

Paul Lindenbaugh was working the crowd, dressed as usual in his white suit and white tie. His associates, also dressed in white, were scattered throughout the crowd, helping to assure that the mob would be whipped into a fever pitch. One of the associates began shouting "Hang him! Hang him!" and the rest of the mob took up the chant. "Hang him! Hang him!" Mary tried to plead with the crowd not to take matters into their own hands, but she was easily shouted down. The deputies began to push Joshua toward the mob, when something unexpected happened.

Three people who were not supposed to be there appeared around the corner of the court building and were walking toward them. Paul Lindenbaugh was startled because he knew one of them and stopped shouting, wondering what they were doing there. The three people were Bryce, Judith and Winston. The latter was carrying two shovels, the same shovels Fareydoun and Amir had used to dig out the cave in which they found the Book of Emet. Bryce quickly approached the mob and wrested the bullhorn away from the shocked Paul Lindenbaugh. Bryce began using the bullhorn to tell the crowd that what they were doing was illegal and that they should disperse so justice could be done in the right way.

Recovering his composure, Paul Lindenbaugh grabbed the bullhorn back while three of his associates assaulted Bryce, knocking him down to the ground, and were encouraging the mob to help them. Judith came quickly to Bryce's rescue and pulled him away from the mob before they could mobilize to join in the fray.

Meanwhile, as he had been previously instructed by the Imam, Winston placed the two shovels on either side of the pillars holding up the stone canopy under which Joshua and the deputies and Mary still stood.

No sooner had he done this than the shovels began to glow. The deputies, who were in the process of handing Joshua over to the mob, were awestruck and did not know what to do. They did not have to wait long for an answer, because Winston told them and the mob not to pass the glowing shovels or they would face the wrath of God. Fervent in the belief that God was on their side, five men from the mob charged past the shovels anyway. When they attempted to get past where the shovels were standing, there was a horrific crackling noise and lightning bolts flashed out from the shovels, striking them and dropping them in their tracks. More of the frenzied crowd, directed by Paul Lindenbaugh and his associates, charged the canopy, with the same result. The smell of burning flesh was in the air.

Paul Lindenbaugh, shouting through the bullhorn, decried the glowing shovels as the devil's handiwork and prayed loudly to Jesus to strike down the evils unleashed by Joshua and his supporters.

"Lord Jesus," he intoned in a hypnotic voice, "strike down these devils who don't believe in you. Show us your power and your glory and wipe out all the evil doers amongst us!"

"Amen! Hallelujah!" the mob chanted over and over again, their crazed chanting growing louder and louder.

And it appeared that their impassioned prayers were working.

The sky darkened, a storm with high winds approached, and a torrential rain began to fall. Before long, lightning bolts were flashing and crackling all around them, giving off an eerie glow. The thunder became deafening and seemed to well up out of the black and roiling clouds above them. The earth began to shake, ever so softly at first, then more frequently, and then more violently. Mary was terrified and did not know what was going to happen next. She ran to Joshua, who threw his shackled arms over her head and around her, holding her tightly against his body. Surprisingly, she felt totally safe in his embrace.

Meanwhile, people in the area were running helter skelter all around them, screaming, tripping, falling all over each other in a complete panic. Even some members of the mob broke ranks and ran off in terror.

Paul Lindenbaugh saw in these events the hand of God doing his bidding and began bobbing and weaving and praying. Again he shouted through his bullhorn, "Lord Jesus, strike down these sinners. Show us your power and your glory and wipe out the ones who hate you!" Again the mob chanted over and over again, "Amen! Hallelujah! Amen! Hallelujah!" They tried to hold onto their fever pitch but the flashing bolts of lightning and the fierce roar of thunder was making it harder for them to focus and be heard.

The meteorological barrage was coming to a climax. The thunder roared louder and louder, the lightning bolts flashed nearer and nearer, the rain poured down faster and faster and the ground shook harder and harder. Paul Lindenbaugh's eyes glowed hypnotically and his lips parted into a sinister smile. He became more and more animated, almost akin to an intoxicated whirling dervish.

Suddenly, the ground on the grassy field where Paul Lindenbaugh and the mob were standing groaned and began to split. Lightning crackled all around them, the shovels glowed even brighter, sending out ever-larger bolts of electricity. The brightness was blinding, like looking at the midday sun. Paul Lindenbaugh's eyes took on a fierce and sinister hue, and his mouth opened wide with glee. He, *Paul Lindenbaugh*, had summoned the vengeful Jehovah he believed in to comply with his demands. He raised his arms heavenward and looked up at the downpouring sky and felt like God's conductor on earth.

But, alas, he misunderstood the score.

For Reverend Paul's expression abruptly changed to surprise and horror. The earth beneath his feet and those of his lieutenants, the Sheriff, and the remaining mob began to collapse and opened up a yawning abyss, too wide, too deep and too fast for them to escape. Suddenly they had no ground to stand on and they screamed in horror and fear as they fell into the depths of the earth and disappeared. And there on the spot where they were going to hang Joshua, they fell into a bottomless abyss and were swallowed up by it. Their screams reverberated back and forth against the sides of the pit, and soon became barely audible echoes as the walls began to close.

Winston, Bryce and Judith joined Joshua and Mary under the stone canopy and huddled together, shaking in fear. The deputies who had been escorting Joshua ran away, as did the remaining members of the mob.

After a few minutes, the sky began to clear, the winds and rain died down, and the tremors of the ground around them began to abate. The glow of the shovels began to fade.

Mary and Joshua looked skyward. Mary thought she saw the face of Jesus in a cloud smiling down at her. "Thank you Lord Jesus," she whispered.

Joshua saw a large white cloud that seemed to be moving toward him and he felt the presence of God in that cloud. "Thank you God," he said to himself silently. "Baruch ha-Shem" (blessed be Your name).

The Imam in Nazareth was watching the whole thing on television, for camera crews from the trial were there capturing everything on film. "Thank you Allah," the Imam said out loud. "Allahu Akbar! God is Great!"

Still looking up at the sky, Joshua and Mary were startled to see three helicopters appear on the horizon. It became evident that the helicopters were coming their way. One of the helicopters circled cautiously, and then gingerly landed a few hundred feet from the court building. The other two helicopters immediately followed suit. Out of each of the helicopters came four heavily armed uniformed men, led by, to Joshua's astonishment and joy, his missing son Kalman.

Kal ran up to Joshua and they hugged each other tightly for several minutes, each relieved the other was alive and safe. The other soldiers quickly took control of the situation. The area of the confrontation was sealed off and the surrounding areas were returned to normalcy. One of the deputies who had been escorting Joshua was found, and he was ordered to give up the key that would release Joshua from his handcuffs.

As order was restored, Kal explained to Joshua that he had survived the helicopter crash in the Afghan mountains and was able to communicate his position by a transmitter he carried with him. Some of his buddies flew in to rescue him, nearly getting shot down themselves. When Kal got back to his base, he learned about what was happening to his father. He succeeded in persuading his superiors to quickly send him back to the States, to declare martial law in the area and save Joshua from his intended fate. He would have arrived sooner except for the severe weather that kept them temporarily at bay.

"Thank goodness we live in a society where the rule of law usually prevails," Sir Winston intoned. Thinking back to an earlier time when another mob was allowed to achieve a different result, he added, "If Jesus had lived in such a society he never would have been crucified."

Bryce's father had been fearfully watching the preceding events from a window in the court building. When he saw Paul Lindenbaugh and the mob being swallowed by the ground, and then the soldiers arrive to take charge of the situation, he knew what he had to do. The building had lost its electricity and the elevators were not working, so he took the stairs to the lobby and came outside to tell Joshua that he was dropping all charges against him and that he was free to go. *Joshua was a free man!*

Bryce gave his father a big hug and both men were smiling ear to ear.

Mary and Joshua thanked Sir Winston profusely and were introduced to Judith and Bryce. Hugs were exchanged all around. It was the most euphoric feeling any of them had ever experienced before.

Back at the Hotel

Having shared in what they all regarded as a miracle, Joshua, Mary and friends did not want to leave each other. Mary invited them all to dinner at her hotel and everyone enthusiastically agreed. All they wanted to talk about was what they had just seen and how they felt about it. They all felt blessed to have witnessed such an event and they wondered what the rest of the world would think about it, the whole thing having been recorded by television cameras.

Bryce could not get over what he had just seen. "I didn't used to believe there was a God," he told his newfound friends. "Certainly not the kind the Bible talked about. I don't see how what we just saw can be looked at any other way."

"I'm afraid this old man has to agree with you Bryce," Sir Winston said. "When I lost my son, I lost interest in God. I didn't care if there was a God or not. Now I'm not sure what to think. What we saw today was quite powerful, I must say."

"It was positively Biblical," Joshua said happily. "Right out of Exodus, when the earth opened up and swallowed those who rebelled against Moses. I guess we know whose side the Lord is on now!"

"I don't know what to think," Mary added uncertainly. "Was that God saying the Book of Emet is right? I saw the face of Jesus in the clouds afterwards. Somehow he was involved in this. That I know for certain."

They could talk about nothing else for the next two hours while they celebrated with food, drinks and ice cream with chocolate cake at the end. It was later learned that there had been extensive fracking underneath where the earthquake had occurred and that the heavy rains had combined with the ground's unsteadiness to create a huge sinkhole. Judith pointed out, however, as she had said earlier, that there are miracles in everyday life if you choose to look at them that way. Joshua added that sometimes the miracle is found not in the event itself, but rather in the timing of the event.

After two hours, Mary smiled at their friends and said that she and Josh had some things they needed to talk about privately. She returned their knowing glances with a wink and a smile. "Come along Josh," she purred. She took his hand and he was only too willing to follow her.

They got into the same elevator they had taken after the first night of the debate. Joshua moved toward Mary, gently pushing her with his body against the elevator wall. Mary's whole body lit up as she felt Joshua's hard body on one side and the elevator wall on the other side. She felt desired and protected at the same time, a totally delicious feeling.

When the elevator door opened, Mary led Josh by the hand to her room and unlocked the door. Joshua started to kneel down on one knee, but in a surprise move, lifted a shrieking Mary into his arms and carried her across the threshold of her hotel room.

"Why sir, whatever does this mean?" Mary said in her best mock Southern accent as she put her arms around his neck.

Quoting lines from two of Mary's favorite movies, he smiled and said "Frankly my dear.....I think this is the beginning of a beautiful friendship."[2]

Mary laughed delightedly and gave Joshua a big hug and kiss as he carried her into the bedroom, kicking the door shut behind them.

---

2   *Gone With the Wind* and *Casablanca*

The Aftermath

In the next few weeks, police and the FBI made many arrests, including Bryce's father and members of the police force who had collaborated with Paul Lindenbaugh and company. In New York City, the three Godfathers were indicted for conspiracy. Because of the extenuating circumstances and his willingness to testify against the three Godfathers, Bryce's father was not indicted, but he did lose his job, and his law license was suspended for an indefinite period of time.

Mary filed for divorce from Wayne and, as predicted, the Christian cable network cancelled her TV show, but while she mourned the loss of what she had worked so hard to build there, she knew that God had other plans for her life and her ministry. "When one door closes, another one opens," she liked to say. After the divorce, she moved to Chicago so she could be closer to Joshua. She became involved in pastoral marriage counseling and was able to help many women in tragic marriages learn how to strike out on their own.

Because of his new-found fame, Joshua's influence was even greater than it had been before. He was in great demand as a speaker all over the country and internationally too. Eventually, he had to leave his congregation so he could better work on his calling to liberalize Judaism from the "shackles of the Middle Ages," as he put it. Gradually his teachings achieved wider acceptance in the mainstream Jewish community, and the incensed attacks of many of his critics subsided.

Bryce decided to convert to Judaism and married Judith. Winston felt his faith restored, and counseled by Joshua, found peace in believing that his son was not really dead. Rather, he came to believe that his son's immortal soul was following its destiny in the cycle of reincarnation in God's service. Kal received several decorations for bravery and got a promotion.

Winston personally returned the two shovels to the Imam in Nazareth, where they are to this very day. Who knows when they might be needed again?

After all the hubbub died down, Mary and Joshua were quietly married in a small family ecumenical ceremony in Jerusalem on the Temple Mount, where the Temple of God had once stood. The ceremony was held outside in the park-like area between the gorgeous gold-domed porcelain-tiled Dome of the Rock and the Al Aqsa Mosque. Winston was Joshua's best man and Christa was the maid of honor. Bryce, Judith, and the Imam were all in attendance.

And yes, Joshua kept his promise and took Christa to her church's father-daughter dance the weekend after Easter!

Postscript

And God said [to Elijah], "Go forth and stand on the mountain in the presence of the Lord." And behold, the Lord passed by, and a great and powerful wind tore the mountains apart and shattered the rocks before the Lord, but the Lord was not in the wind. After the wind there was an earthquake, but the Lord was not in the earthquake.
After the earthquake came a fire, but the Lord was not in the fire. And after the fire came a still small voice.
And the voice said to him, "What are you doing here, Elijah?" He replied, "I have been very zealous for God. But [they] have rejected your covenant, broken down your altars, and slain Your prophets with the sword. I am the only one left, and now they are trying to kill me too." [I Kings 19:11-14.]

Moshe and his twin sister Miriam were done with their work for the day in the olive orchard near the Jewish town of Nazareth. Their father had been killed a few years earlier by the Romans, and now their mother was ill, and there was no one else to take care of the family orchard. They were 14 years old and were strong and energetic.

As they typically did, they took some of the bushels of picked olives into the nearby cave. This time, however, they went even further into the cave to hide them than they usually did because they were afraid the Romans would find them. Deep inside the cave, further in than they had ever been, they came upon two tunnels, one going to the left and the other going to the right. When they saw a light coming from the tunnel on the right, they were frightened. Who was there and was it friend or foe?

The political climate of the time was very bad. The Jews had revolted against the Romans, led at first by the always-rebellious Galileans and later by religious fanatics in Jerusalem. In revenge for the revolt, the Romans had destroyed Jerusalem and the Holy Temple and had driven most of the Jews from there out of the country. After decimating the Jews of Jerusalem, and impoverishing the countryside, the Romans changed the name of the country from Judea to Palestine, the Latin variation of the word Philistines. Yes, the same Philistines who had once been championed by the giant warrior Goliath. The area remained desolate for centuries until the Jews started to come back in the 19th Century.

Cautiously Moshe and Miriam tip-toed further into the cave. The light appeared to be relatively close, no more than 200 cubits away they guessed, and they followed the glow. Breathing heavily, the twins walked slowly and cautiously, not knowing what they would find, and prepared to run at a moment's notice. Miriam gripped Moshe's hand so hard she made it throb. But he barely noticed it.

There was a bend in the tunnel and around the corner they saw an old man with a long beard and ragged clothes sitting against the tunnel wall, accompanied by several candles but with only one of them lit. He also had a piece of parchment and a quill and was laboriously writing on the parchment.

He was old and nearly deaf and blind and did not hear the twins approaching him. Then he noticed some shadows on the wall and he looked up and almost jumped out of his skin. He picked up a nearby rock and cocked his arm, ready to defend himself against the unwelcome intruders.

"Shalom old man," said Moshe fearfully. "Don't hurt us!"

The old man was relieved to hear his native language of Aramaic spoken to him and that told him the intruders were not Roman soldiers or other unfriendlies. He put down the rock and gazed at the twins intently. He was quite relieved when he realized that one of them was a girl.

"Shalom children," the old man said. "You scared me. I thought you were Roman soldiers."

"We're not soldiers," Miriam reassured him. "We live in Nazareth with our mother, and we own the olive orchard out there. We saw your candle and came to see who is here. Are you okay? Do you need anything?"

The old man was touched by Miriam's concern and smiled benignly at the twins. "I haven't seen a friendly face in quite a while. I've been hiding from the Romans. I've been living in this cave for several months and I'm almost out of food and candles."

"Are you a teacher old man?" asked Moshe. He knew that the Romans were especially on the lookout for teachers because they had decided that the Jewish religion was not to be taught anymore. Their intent was to wipe out the Jews as punishment for their revolt. They figured if they could not kill or exile every Jew, they could wipe the Jews out by stopping the transmission of their religion.

"No, I am not a learned man. I was a craftsman who made pottery in my younger days, right here in Nazareth."

"I don't understand, why are the Romans after you then?" Miriam queried.

"They found out I have been writing the story of my friend Jesse – they call him Jesus – and neither the Romans nor the Christians want me to do so."

"You mean the one they call the Christ?"

"Yes. I am almost done with it and I am hoping to finish it before I die or get captured."

"Why is it so important for you to tell Jesus' story," Miriam inquired.

"There are lots of stories about him. Some are true and some are false or exaggerated. Some tell his true motivation and others do not. I saw or heard everything that happened to him and I want to tell the real story. He was a great man and died a horrible death. They say he claimed to be the Christ or the King of the Jews, but that wasn't true. He never thought of himself that way."

"Were you one of his disciples?" asked Moshe in awe. The disciples of Jesus had become famous for spreading "the word" and many of them had been killed by the Romans in horrific fashion.

"No no," the old man said. "I wasn't a follower of Jesus. But when I had time, I went with him on some of his missions. He was glad to have me around. We were best friends as kids and he trusted me more than anyone else around him. And I became friendly with some of the women in his entourage and they told me things that happened that I didn't see myself. After all, I couldn't go with him everywhere. I had to make a living and support my family."

"Our father used to say wonderful things about him," Miriam said with enthusiasm. "He also said some of the things Jesus' disciples said about him weren't true, although he also said that they were telling the truth as they saw it. Our father didn't think the disciples were very bright and they didn't understand a lot of what Jesus said or did. But they were very well meaning and were totally inspired by him."

"Yes, that is true," the old man said sadly. "I think it is important for me to tell the real story."

"Is it true the Jews in Jerusalem had Jesus killed?" asked Moshe with disapproval in his voice.

"No, the Romans killed him. But they made it look like the Jews did it. It fooled the disciples, but I was in the crowd that day, and I know what really happened. It was so sad. Jesus was heartbroken that he didn't live to see the Kingdom of Heaven come, and that he had to die so young. He was the greatest man I've ever known. I miss him terribly and writing his story is something I feel compelled to do."

"Well then," said Moshe bravely, "we'll help you tell the story, won't we Mir?"

Miriam was fairly jumping for joy and her eyes were glowing with excitement. "I was hoping you'd say that Moish. We'll be glad to help you. By the way, what is your name? We can't call you old man forever."

"My name is Emet son of Chaim," said the old man.

The Writing

Emet was sitting next to a large urn that he had made himself. Originally, it had foodstuffs in it that he knew would last for months. The food was almost gone and the urn was empty, so that is where he started storing his scroll. He thought that if he got killed or captured, no one would think to look in the urn and the scroll would survive.

Over the next two months, the twins visited Emet in his cave every day after harvesting the olives. They brought him fresh food and new candles and took several sheets of papyrus for themselves so they could make extra copies of the stories he told them. Miriam made one set of stories and Moshe made another one. Sometimes a whole story would fit on a page and sometimes a story needed two or three pages.

As Emet retold the life of Jesus, sometimes reading from his own scroll to make sure the wording was right, the twins wrote it down, word for word, according to what Emet had said. In those days, people were more used to remembering stories exactly as they happened and stories could be told from generation to generation without significant changes in the wording. Of course, sometimes one storyteller would emphasize something differently than another storyteller, and sometimes a storyteller would embellish something or leave something out, or even change the story to make it more dramatic. Emet's scroll was as precise as possible, and the twins for the most part captured everything Emet told them with the same precision.

As the story unfolded, the twins asked questions about what they were being told.

"So Jesus was like a follower of John the Baptist?" Miriam asked.

"Yes," said Emet. "We went together to be baptized by him, me and Jesus. And Jesus had a profound religious experience during his baptism, much moreso than I did. He thought he saw that the Kingdom of God was about to be upon us, just as John said it would."

"How come you weren't appointed a disciple," asked Moshe, "if you were his best friend?"

"I was more a friend than a follower. And he wanted his disciples to quit everything they were doing and follow him. I had a pottery business and a family to support. I went with him when I could, but I couldn't spend all my time wandering around with him. He understood that and blessed me."

"Did Jesus really raise the dead and heal all those people?" asked Miriam wide-eyed?

"I saw him do some of the healings, but I didn't personally see him do everything I tell about him. But his followers swear they are all true, so I included them in my story."

"Why was Jesus closer to his disciples than to his own family?" Miriam asked.

"His family thought what he was doing was dangerous and would end up getting him killed. They also didn't understand his message and wondered if he was exaggerating his relationship with God. They thought he should keep his preaching and his healing local, and that he should get married and have a family. On the other hand, even though the disciples didn't always understand what he was saying or doing either, they were totally behind him and in awe of him. Naturally, he was much more comfortable with them. Also, they were helping him spread his message and his family did not help him, except sometimes his brother James did."

"Did Jesus really walk on water?" asked Moshe with a thrill in his voice.

"I was not there, but they say he did," Emet answered cautiously. "I have wondered about that story myself, but they swear it happened."

"Were you at the Sermon on the Mount?" both twins wanted to know. That sermon was famous throughout the land.

"I was there," Emet said proudly. "He was magnificent! He was inspired! His face glowed, and I felt I was hearing God talk through him. It was the greatest single experience of my life!"

"Were you there when Pontius Pilate sentenced Jesus to death?"

"Yes, I was there." Emet's body was shaking and his face went white as he remembered those horrific events. He needed to take several minutes before he could continue.

"It was the most unjust thing I've ever seen in my life. All of us there were supporters of Jesus, but the Romans had their paid minions scattered throughout the courtyard where we were standing. They did all the shouting, not us. Those of us who dared to shout something different were beaten or killed by the Roman soldiers who were also there. Jesus knew what was happening and he signaled us to be silent, lest we be harmed too. He knew nothing could save him at that point, and he didn't want us to be killed with him. He was very brave and a great leader. But you know that none of his disciples were there. They had fled to save themselves. They were told later that the crowd called for Jesus to be crucified and they thought the Jews did it. But it was really the Romans."

Epilogue

Inspired by the spirit of Emet, Moshe and Miriam made several copies of Emet's stories. All the copies were on papyrus and they did not survive the test of time. However, some pages survived longer than others. Many of the pages were used by Christian writers, including the authors of the four gospels, to tell the story of Jesus. Some of the pages were changed by the original authors and some of the pages were miscopied or deliberately altered by others over time. Not only did none of the pages written by Moshe and Miriam survive, but none of the pages written by the original four gospel writers survived either. What we have today are copies of copies of copies, plus what we have today are Greek translations of the writings of Moshe and Miriam, which had been written in Aramaic.

After finishing and hiding his scroll in the urn, Emet returned to his family in Nazareth. Just as he feared, the Romans were looking for him, and when he refused to reveal the location of his scroll, he and his family were brutally killed in their home by Roman soldiers.

Moshe and Miriam continued to live in Nazareth until their ill mother passed away. Then they fled Nazareth, which was becoming a predominately pagan town. No one knows where they ended up settling, but rumor had it that they were seen once in Anatolia, which is present day Turkey.

Over time, most of the Jews in the Holy Land were either killed or driven out. Although a few Jews were continuously present in the Holy Land until the present day, the Holy Land suffered from neglect. Without the love of the Jews for their homeland, the Holy Land became progressively poorer, overgrown and sparsely settled. When Mark Twain visited it in the 19th Century, he reported that there were few inhabitants in the Land, that it was in total disrepair, and that abject poverty and disease were widespread.

In the late 19th Century, the Jews of Europe began to return to the Holy Land, in small numbers at first, and in much larger numbers after the Holocaust. In 1948, the State of Israel was born and Jews once again were in possession of the Holy Land after being largely absent for almost 2,000 years. The Jews drained the swamps, "made the desert bloom," and made Israel the most prosperous land in the Middle East.

Today, the Jews and the descendants of the surrounding populations, now called Palestinians, are still fighting over who rightfully belongs in the Holy Land. How this dispute will be resolved is unknown at the present time. It is safe to say that Jesus hopes the Jews will be able to recreate and sustain a Jewish state and that the Kingdom of Heaven will arrive soon and in our own time.

Appendix:
Excerpts from The Book of Emet

Table of Contents

"I am more than ever certain that a great place belongs to [Jesus] in Israel's history of faith." — *Martin Buber, Two Types of Faith (1951)*

Chapter One: In the Beginning

The Birth of Jesus
Mt 1:18

1:1   Joseph and Mary (Miriam) lived in the city of Nazareth in the district of Galilee in the nation of Judea.

1:2   And Mary was without child and prayed to the Lord that she may have a child and promised to dedicate him to the Lord's service.

1:3   And the Lord heard Mary's prayers and opened her womb and gave to Mary and Joseph a child who was named Jesus (Jesse) after the father of Joseph's ancestor, King David.

1:4   And Mary raised Jesus to know that he was promised to the Lord's service.

The Early Years

1:14   It came to pass that Jesus grew up to be a kind and gentle and determined lad who was sensitive to the pain and troubles of others.

1:15   He was interested in the world around him and a strong spiritual nature developed within him.

1:18   His teachers observed the great learning he had for one so young and asked Jesus to help teach the younger children.

1:19   He often taught by story-telling, which helped the children understand better.

1:22   His friends were working people like himself, the sons of fishermen, carpenters, day laborers, farmers, shepherds, even one who was the son of a tax collector.

1:26   He discovered as a youth that he had special healing powers which he said came from God.

1:30   His soul grieved greatly over the cruel and merciless world he saw around him

1:31   and he became convinced that God was about to usher in the Kingdom of Heaven when all things would be set right.

1:32   He hoped and expected that, as a son of David, he would play an important role when that great day arrived.

1:33   He observed that those around him were not ready for the arrival of the Kingdom of Heaven

1:34   and believed he needed to warn them to prepare themselves, lest they miss being included in the Kingdom and having eternal life.

John the Baptist
Lk 3:1-20; Mt 3:1-12

1:35   The word of God came to John the Baptist in the desert.

1:37   He went into all the country around the Jordan River, preaching a baptism of repentance and the forgiveness of sins, saying "Repent, for the Kingdom of Heaven is near.

1:50   And the people who heard him believed John was the Messiah they had been waiting for.

1:51   People went out to him from Jerusalem and all Judea and the whole region of the Jordan.

1:52   Confessing their sins, they were cleansed and had their sins washed away by him in the Jordan River, as John the Baptist proclaimed:

1:53   "I baptize you on behalf of the Lord with the water of atonement for your repentance."

1:54   And the people felt cleansed of their sins and renewed in their spirit.

1:55   And the Romans became concerned about John's following and plotted against him.

1:56   And when John rebuked Herod the tetrarch for marrying Herodias, his brother's wife, and all the other evil things he had done, Herod locked John up in prison.

The Baptism of Jesus
Mt 3:13-17; Mk 1:9-11; Lk 3:21-22; Jn 1:31-34

1:57   When Jesus was 30 years of age, he came from Galilee to the Jordan to learn from John and he was greatly inspired by his teachings.

1:58   And when he felt ready, he asked John to baptize him in the River Jordan, and John did so baptize him.

1:59   As soon as Jesus was baptized, and he went up out of the water, he saw heaven open, and felt the Spirit of God descend like a dove upon him.

1:60   And from that time forth, Jesus knew he was called by the Lord to join in the work of John the Baptist, and to prepare the people for the imminent coming of the Kingdom of Heaven.

The Calling of the First Disciples
Mt 4:18-22; 9:9-13; Mk 1:16-20; 2:14-17; Lk 5:2-11, 37-32; Jn 1:35-42

1:70   Then Jesus said to Peter, "Fear not; from now on you will catch men [instead of fish]."

1:71   When they pulled their boats up to the shore, they forsook all and followed him.

1:72   As Jesus went on from there, he saw a tax collector named Levi, also called Matthew, sitting at the custom house. "Follow me," he told him, and Matthew got up and followed him.

Appointing the Twelve Apostles
Mt 10:1-4; Mk 3:13-19; Lk 6:12-16

1:78   And he chose twelve of them as apostles—that they might be with him and that he might send them out to preach the Kingdom of God

1:79   and gave them authority to drive out evil spirits and to heal every disease and sickness.

Sending Them Out With Instructions
Mt 10:5-42; Mk 6:7 -13; Lk 9:1-6, 9:49-50, 10:4-24

1:82   These twelve Jesus sent out with the following instructions: "Do not go among the Gentiles or enter any city of the Samaritans.

1:83   Go rather to the lost sheep of the house of Israel for they are the ones our Father in heaven sent me to help.

1:84   As you go, preach this message: 'The Kingdom of Heaven is at hand.'

1:85   Heal the sick, raise the dead, cleanse those who have leprosy, and drive out demons. Freely you have received, and freely you shall give."

1:91   When you are persecuted in one place, flee to another. I tell you the truth, you will not finish going through the cities of Israel before the Kingdom of Heaven comes.

1:98   He who receives you receives me, and he who receives me receives the One who sent me.

Chapter Two: The Ministry Begins

Jesus Heals the Sick
Mt 4-23-25; 8:14-16; Mk 1:29-34; Lk 4:38-41

2:1   Jesus went throughout Galilee, teaching in synagogues, preaching that the Kingdom of Heaven is near, and healing diseases and sicknesses among the people.

2:2   And his fame spread throughout the area and people brought to him those who were sick with various diseases and pains, the demon-possessed, and the paralyzed, and he healed them.

2:5   At sunrise, the people brought to Jesus those who had various kinds of sickness, and laying his hands on each one, he healed them.

2:6   When evening came, those who were demon-possessed were brought to him, and he drove out the evil spirits from them.

A Dead Girl and a Sick Woman
Mk 5:21-43; Lk 8:40-56; Mt 9:18-26

2:44   And a woman was there who had a disease causing her to be bleeding for twelve years.

2:45   She had suffered many things with many physicians, and although she had spent all she had, instead of getting better she grew worse.

2:46   When she heard about Jesus, she came up behind him in the crowd and touched his garment, for she thought, "If I just touch his clothes, I will be healed."

2:47   And straightaway the fountain of her blood was dried up and she felt in her body that she was healed of that plague.

2:48   And Jesus immediately realized that power had gone out from him. He turned around in the crowd and asked, "Who touched my clothes?"

2:50   Then the woman, trembling with fear, came and fell down before him and told him the truth.

2:51   He said to her, "Daughter, your faith has healed you. Go in peace and be freed from your plague."

Jesus Goes to the Feast of Tabernacles
Jn 7:2-18

2:95   When the Feast of Tabernacles for Sukkot arrived, Jesus' younger brothers said to him, "You ought to leave here and go to Jerusalem, so that the people there may see the miracles you do.

2:98   About halfway through the Feast Jesus went up to the Temple in Jerusalem and began to teach.

2:99   The people were amazed and asked, "How did this man get such learning without studying at our best schools?"

2:100   Jesus answered, "My teaching is not my own. It comes from He who sent me."

Woe Unto the Hypocrites
Mt 23:1-39; Mk 12:38-39; Lk 13:34-35, 20:45-46

2:103   Then Jesus said to those who came to hear his teachings:

2:104   "The teachers of the law sit in Moses' seat and they tell you what to observe and do.

2:105   But do not do what they do, for they do not practice what they preach.

2:106   They put heavy burdens on men's shoulders, but they themselves are not willing to lift a finger to move them.

2:107   Everything they do is done for men to see: They make their phylacteries wide and the tassels on their garments long;

2:108   They like to have the most important seats in the synagogues and be greeted in the marketplaces, and have men call them 'Lord.'

2:111   Woe to you, teachers of the law, you hypocrites! You shut the Kingdom of Heaven in men's faces. You yourselves can not enter, nor will you let those enter who are trying to go in.

2:118   Woe to you, teachers of the law, you hypocrites! You make others do the work that needs to be done while you live off their alms so you can study. Our Father did not give us the law for such a purpose.

The Widow's Offering
Mk 12:41-44; Lk 21:1-4

2:127   Jesus sat down opposite the place where the offerings were put and watched how the people put their money into the Temple treasury. Many of those who were rich put in large amounts.

2:128   Then a poor widow came and put in two very small coins, worth only a fraction of a shekel.

2:129   Calling his disciples to him, Jesus said, "I tell you the truth, this poor widow has put more into the treasury than all the others.

2:130   They all gave out of their abundance; but she, out of her poverty, put in all she had to live on."

Observation of the Sabbath
Mt 12:1-8; Mk 2:23-28; Lk 6:1-5

2:131   After the conclusion of the Sukkot feasts, Jesus and the disciples who were with him returned to Galilee.

2:132   One day they were walking through the grainfields on the Sabbath. His disciples were hungry and began to pick some heads of grain and eat them.

2:134   When the elders heard about this, they said to him, "Look! Your disciples are doing what is unlawful on the Sabbath."

2:138   [He answered] "The Sabbath was made for man, not man for the Sabbath."

Healing on the Sabbath
Mt 12:9-14; Mk 3:1-6; Lk 6:6-11, 13:10-17

2:139   Later he went into a nearby synagogue and a man with a shriveled hand was there.

2:140   So the elders asked him, "Is it then lawful to heal on the Sabbath?"

2:141   He said to them, "If any of you has a sheep and it falls into a pit on the Sabbath, will you not take hold of it and lift it out?

2:142   How much more valuable is a man than a sheep! Therefore it is lawful to do good deeds on the Sabbath."

Chapter Three: Parables and Miracles

The Parable of the Sower
Mt 13:1-23; Mk 4:1-20; Lk 8:1-15

3:5   A large crowd gathered and Jesus told them many things in parables.

3:6   He told them this parable: "A farmer went out to sow his seed. And when he sowed, some fell by the wayside. Some of it was trampled on, and some was eaten by birds.

3:7   Some fell on stony places, where there was not much earth. Those seeds sprung up quickly, because the soil had no depth.

3:8   But when the sun came up, the plants were scorched because they had no roots and, they withered away.

3:9   And some seeds fell among thorns, and the thorns sprung up and choked them.

3:10   But other seeds fell on good soil and brought forth plentiful and delectable fruit."

3:13   This is the meaning of the parable: The seed is the word of God.

3:14   When anyone hears the message about the Kingdom and does not understand it, the evil one comes and snatches away that which was sown in his heart. This is the seed sown by the wayside.

3:15   Those who receive the seed on stony places are the ones who hear God's word with joy, but they don't have the roots within themselves to sustain it. They believe for a while, but when tribulation and persecution arise, they fall away.

3:16   The seed that fell among thorns stands for those who hear God's word, but they become distracted by life's riches and their souls are choked and do not bear fruit.

3:17   But the seed that falls on good earth stands for those who hear God's word and understand it, and their souls grow and blossom and become the best fruits.

The Parable of the Yeast
Mt 13:33, 44-46; Lk 13:21

3:18   He told them more parables: "The Kingdom of Heaven is like leaven that a woman took and mixed into a large amount of flour until the whole was leavened."

A Prophet Without Honor
Mt 13:54-58; Mk 6:1-6

3:23   Coming to his hometown, [Jesus] began teaching the people in the synagogue on the Sabbath, but they were unimpressed.

3:24   "Where did this man get this wisdom and these miraculous powers?"

3:25   "Isn't this the carpenter's son? Isn't his mother's name Mary, and aren't his brothers James, Joseph, Simon and Judas?

3:26   Aren't all his sisters with us? Where then did this man get all these things?"

3:27   And they were offended by him. But Jesus said to them, "Only in his hometown and in his own house is a prophet without honor."

Jesus' Mother and Brothers
Mt 12:46-50; Mk 3:31-35; Lk 6:16

3:29   While Jesus was still talking to the crowd, his mother and brothers stood outside, wanting to speak to him.

3:30   Some of the people told him, "Your mother and brothers are standing outside wanting to speak to you."

3:31   He replied to him, "Who is my mother, and who are my brothers?"

3:32   And he looked at the crowd around him and said, "You are my mother and my brothers.

3:33   For whoever shall do the will of God, they are my brothers and my sisters and my mother."

The Cost of Being a Disciple
Mt 8:19-22, Lk 14:26-33

3:35   Then a scribe came to Jesus and said, "Teacher, I will follow you wherever you go."

3:36   Jesus replied, "Foxes have holes and birds of the air have nests, but I have no place to lay my head."

3:37   One of his disciples said to him, "Master, I want to go with you, but first let me go and bury my father."

3:38   But Jesus told him, "Follow me, and let the dead bury their dead.

3:39   If anyone comes to me and cannot leave his father and mother, his wife and children, his brothers and sisters—yes, even his own life—he cannot be my disciple.

Mary Magdalene

3:51   One day in their travels, Jesus and the disciples were in the village of Magdala and Jesus was preaching and healing there.

3:52   And one of the healings he did was to expel demons from a woman named Mary (Miriam). After she was cured, she became a devoted follower and helped supply Jesus and his followers with food and places to sleep.

3:53   She was wise and more learned than most of the women in Judea. Jesus quickly came to recognize her wisdom and devoted soul.

3:54   And they had many talks about theology and philosophy and the nature of the world, as well as things in their daily lives.

3:58   The other disciples noticed that Jesus loved her more than all the others,

3:59   but they did not become jealous because Jesus and Mary made sure that their actions were beyond reproach.

John the Baptist Beheaded
Mt 14:1-12; Mk 6:14-29

3:66   Now Herod had arrested John and bound him and put him in prison because of Herodias, his brother Philip's wife, for John said to him: "It is not lawful for you to have her."

3:67   And Herod would have put him to death, but he was afraid of the people, because they considered him a prophet.

3:68   On Herod's birthday, Salome the daughter of Herodias danced for them and pleased Herod. Whereupon he promised with an oath to give her whatever she would ask.

3:69   And she, being instructed by her mother, said, "Give me here on a platter the head of John the Baptist."

3:71   His head was brought in on a platter and given to the girl, and she brought it to her mother.

3:72   John's disciples came and took his body and buried it. Then they went and told Jesus.

Jesus Feeds Five Thousand
Mt 15:13-21; Mk 6:30-44, 8:1-9

3:73   When Jesus heard this, he was very saddened and went by boat to an isolated place in the desert.

3:74   When the people nearby heard where he was, they came on foot to be by him.

3:75   And when Jesus saw them, he was moved by compassion for them, because they were as sheep not having a shepherd; and he began to teach them many things.

3:76   When evening arrived Jesus' disciples came to him and said, "We are in the desert and the time is now past to send the people away to where they can get food for themselves."

3:77   Jesus answered, "They need not depart; give them something to eat."

3:78   His disciples asked him, "Where could we get enough bread in this remote place to feed such a crowd?"

3:79   "How many loaves do you have?" Jesus asked. "Five," they replied, "and two fishes."

3:80   He told the crowd to sit down on the ground. Then he took the five loaves and the two fishes, and he blessed them.

3:81   Then he broke them and gave them to the disciples to set before the people and they did so.

3:82   They all ate and were filled. Afterwards the disciples picked up twelve basketfuls of broken pieces of bread and fish that were left over.

3:83   The number of those who ate were about five thousand men.

Jesus Walks on the Water
Mt 14:22-35; Mk 6:45-56

3:84   After that Jesus told the disciples to get into the boat and go on ahead of him to the other side, while he blessed the crowd and then dismissed them.

3:85   Then he went further up on the mountainside by himself to pray, for his heart was greatly grieved by the death of John the Baptist, who had been his teacher and inspiration.

3:86　When evening came, he was there alone, and the boat was in the midst of the sea. And he saw them, not making progress against the wind.

3:87　During the fourth watch of the night Jesus went out to them, walking on the lake, lost in prayer.

3:88　When the disciples saw him walking on the lake, they thought they were seeing a ghost and cried out in fear.

3:89　But Jesus heard their cries and said to them: "It is okay. It is I! Do not be afraid."

3:90　And he got into the ship with them and the wind ceased.

The Man With Leprosy
Mt 8:1-4; Mk 1:40-45; Lk 5:12-15

3:94　A man with leprosy came and knelt before him and said, "Master, if you are willing, you can make me clean."

3:95　Jesus was moved with compassion and reached out his hand and touched the man. "I am willing," he said. "Be clean!" And immediately his leprosy was cleansed.

Jesus Raises Lazarus From the Dead
Jn 11:1-44

3:97　Now a man named Lazarus was very sick. He was from Bethany, also the village of Mary and her sister Martha, the sisters of Lazarus.

3:98　They sent word to Jesus, "Master, the one you love is sick unto death." Jesus loved Martha and Mary and Lazarus.

3:104　On his arrival, Jesus found that Lazarus had already been put in a tomb.

3:114　Jesus grieved openly and it was obvious to all how much Jesus loved Lazarus.

3:115　"Where have you laid him?" he asked and they showed him. It was a cave with a stone laid across the entrance. "Take away the stone," he said.

3:116　Then they took away the stone. And Jesus called in a loud voice, "Lazarus, come forth!"

3:117　The dead man came out, his hands and feet wrapped with graveclothes, and a cloth around his face.

3:118　Jesus said to them, "Take off the bindings and let him go."

Chapter Four: The Sermon on the Mount

On Prayer
Lk 11:1, 5-13; Mt 7:7-11

4:1   One day Jesus was praying by the Sea of Galilee. When he finished, one of his disciples said to him, "Master, does the Lord answer our prayers?"

4:6   So I say to you: ask and it will be given to you; seek and you will find; knock and the door will be opened to you.

4:7   For everyone who asks receives; he who seeks finds; and to him who knocks, the door will be opened.

4:8   Which of you fathers, if your son asks for bread, will give him a stone; or if he asks for a fish, will give him a snake; or if he asks for an egg, will give him a scorpion?

4:9   If you then, though you are sinful, know how to give good gifts to your children, how much more will your Father in heaven give good things to those who ask Him!"

The Primacy of the Law
Mt 6:17-20

4:23   "Do not think that I have come to destroy the Law or the Prophets. I have not come to destroy them but to renew them.

4:24   I tell you the truth, until heaven and earth pass away, not a letter or a marking will pass from the law.

4:25   Anyone who breaks one of the least of these commandments, and teaches others to do so, will be called least in the Kingdom of Heaven. But whoever shall do them and teach them shall be called great in the Kingdom of Heaven.

4:26   And I tell you this, the oral law and rules of the rabbis do not carry the same weight and are not as binding for you."

Murder, Anger and the Judicial System
Mt 5:21-26; Lk 12:58-59

4:27   "You have heard that it was said to the people long ago, 'Thou shalt not kill, and anyone who kills will be in danger of God's judgment.'

4:28   But I tell you that anyone who is angry with his brother without just cause will be in danger of the judgment.

4:30   Agree with your adversary quickly, while you are still with him on the way;

because if he takes you to court, the judge may hand you over to the officer, and you may be cast into prison.

4:31   I tell you the truth, you will not get out until you have paid the last penny.

4:32   For the laws almost always favor the rich and powerful, and you by yourself can not defeat them."

Adultery
Mt 5:27-30

4:33   "You have heard that it was said, 'Thou shalt not commit adultery.'

4:34   But I tell you that anyone who looks at a woman lustfully has already committed adultery with her in his heart.

4:35   If your right eye causes you to sin, pluck it out and cast it away. It is better for you to lose one part of your body than for your whole body to be thrown into Gehenna.

4:36   And if your right hand causes you to sin, cut it off and cast it away. It is better for you to lose one part of your body than for your whole body to go into Gehenna."

On Women

4:37   "Eve was given to Adam to keep him company for he was lonely without her.

4:38   Do not think of women as secondary, for they support you and all that is best in you.

4:39   God gave them smaller bodies but greater love. Hearken unto them and do what they say, for the word of God is within them."

Homosexuality

4:40   "You have heard that it was said, 'Do not lie with a man as one lies with a woman; for that is an abomination to the Lord.'

4:41   But I tell you this law was meant to apply only to those who are given to procreate.

4:42   For the Lord made men who lie with men as well as men who lie with women and He loves them both."

Turn the Other Cheek
Mt 5:38-42, 7:12

4:46   "You have heard that it was said, 'An eye for an eye, and a tooth for a tooth.'

4:47   But I say to you, do not resist an evil person. If someone strikes you on the right cheek, turn to him the other also.

4:48   And if any man will sue you at the law and take your coat, let him have your cloak as well.

4:49   If someone forces you to go one mile, go with him two miles."

Love Your Enemies
Mt 5:43-48; Lk 6:27-38

4:50   "You have heard that it was said, 'Love your neighbor and hate your enemies.

4:51   But I say to you, love your enemies, bless those who curse you, do good to those who hate you, and pray for those who hurt and mistreat you.

4:52   Give to he who asks you, and do not turn away he who would borrow from you.

4:53   So in everything, do unto others as you would have them do unto you, for this sums up the Law and the Prophets.

Giving to the Needy
Mt 6:1-4

4:61   "We are commanded to give to the needy, for the poor will always be with us.

4:62   Take heed not to do give your charity in public, to be seen by others. If you do, you will have no reward from your Father in heaven.

How to Pray
Mt 6:6-15; Lk 11:2-4

4:69   This, then, is how you should pray:

4:70   'Our Father Who art in heaven, hallowed be Thy name,

4:71   Thy Kingdom come, Thy will be done on earth as it is in heaven.

4:72   Give us this day our daily bread. Forgive us our trespasses, as we also forgive those who trespass against us.

4:73   And lead us not into temptation, but deliver us from evil.

4:74   For thine is the Kingdom, and the power, and the glory, forever. Amen.'

Treasures in Heaven
Mt 6:19- 21

4:80 "Do not store up for yourselves treasures on earth, where moths and rust destroy, and where thieves break in and steal.

4:81 But store up for yourselves treasures in heaven, where moths and rust do not destroy, and where thieves do not break in and steal.

4:82 For where your treasure is, there your heart will be also."

Judging Others
Mt 7:1-2; Lk 6:37-40

4:106 "Judge not, and you will not be judged.

4:107 For in the same way you judge others, you will be judged, and with the measure you use, it will be measured to you.

4:108 Condemn not, and you will not be condemned. Forgive, and you will be forgiven. Give, and it will be given to you.

4:109 Do unto others as you would have them do unto you."

We Are All Children of God
4:125 "You have heard it said that I have a special relationship with the Father.

4:126 I tell you the truth, I have been called to a special mission. But we all have missions given to us.

4:127 We all of us have God-given souls and that makes us all children of God. We all have God within us.

4:128 Follow the murmurings of your soul and you will be following the Father and He will love you as much as you need.

The Little Children
Mt 19:13-15, 11:25-30; Mk 10:13-16; Lk 10:21, 18:15-17

4:129 Then little children were brought to Jesus for him to place his hands on them and pray for them. And the disciples rebuked those who brought them.

4:130 But Jesus said, "Suffer the little children come to me, and do not hinder them, for the Kingdom of Heaven belongs to such as these.

4:131 I tell you the truth, whoever will not receive the Kingdom of God like a little child will never enter it."

4:132 And he took the children in his arms, put his hands on them and blessed them.

4:133   At that time Jesus said, "I praise you, Father, Lord of heaven and earth, because You have hidden these things from the wise and learned, and have revealed them to little children.

4:134   Come to me, all you who are weary and burdened, and I will give you rest.

Chapter Five: Teachings

Divorce and Adultery
Mt 19:1-9; Mk 10:1-12

5:2   A rabbi asked, "Is it lawful for a man to divorce his wife?"

5:3   "Haven't you read," he replied, "that at the beginning God 'made them male and female.'

5:4   And He said, 'For this reason a man will leave his father and mother and cleave to his wife, and the two shall be one flesh.'

5:5   So they are no longer two, but one. Therefore what God has joined together, let not man put asunder."

5:8   I tell you that anyone who divorces, except for marital unfaithfulness, and marries another commits adultery.

5:10   And then he said: "Woe to those who profit from divorce and the unlucky ills of others, for they will surely go to the lowest reaches of hell."

The Adulteress
Jn 8:3-11

5:11   The elders of the community then brought in a divorced woman caught in adultery. They made her stand before the group and said to Jesus,

5:12   "Master, this woman was caught in the very act of adultery. The Torah commands us to stone such a woman. But what do you say?"

5:15   "He that is without sin among you, let him be the first to cast a stone at her."

5:17   And when the elders heard this, they left one by one till all were gone, and Jesus was left alone, with the woman still standing there.

5:18   He asked her, "Woman, where are your accusers? Has no one condemned you?"

5:19   "No one, sir," she said. "Then neither do I condemn you," Jesus declared. "Go now and sin no more."

5:20   And he said to his disciples, "Just because there is a law, it does not follow that she who breaks it should be punished by it.

The Rich Young Man
Mt 19:16-24; Mk 10:17-25; Lk 18:18-25

5:13   Now a man came up to Jesus and asked, "Good teacher, what good things must I do to have eternal life?"

5:14   "If you want eternal life, obey the commandments." "Which ones?" the man inquired.

5:15   Jesus replied, "'Do not murder, do not commit adultery, do not steal, do not give false testimony, honor your father and mother, and love your neighbor as yourself."

5:16   "All these I have kept since I was a boy," the young man said. "What do I still lack?"

5:17   Jesus answered, "If you want to be perfect, go and sell all your possessions and give to the poor, and you will have treasure in heaven. Then come follow me."

5:18   When the young man heard this, he went away sad, because he had great wealth.

5:19   Then Jesus said to his disciples, "I tell you the truth, it is hard for a rich man to enter the Kingdom of Heaven.

7:20   It is easier for a camel to go through the eye of a needle than for a rich man to enter into the Kingdom of God."

Who Will Be Saved
Mt 19:25-29; Mk 10:26-30; Lk 18:26-30

5:21   When the disciples heard this, they were taken aback and asked, "Who then can be saved?"

5:22   Jesus looked at them and said, "With man this is impossible, but with God all things are possible.

5:26   Jesus said to them, "I tell you the truth, at the renewal of all things, when God's messenger sits on his glorious throne, you who have followed me will be rewarded for doing God's work.

5:28   Then Mary Magdalene asked him, "And what will become of you when the Kingdom of Heaven comes?"

5:29   Jesus said to her, "I have a special relationship with our Father because He has called me to His service and I believe we will continue that relationship in the world to come.

The Parable of the Good Samaritan
Lk 10:25-37; Mt 22:34-40; Mk 12:28-31

5:33   On another occasion an expert in the law stood up to test Jesus. "Teacher," he asked, "which is the greatest commandment in the Torah?"

5:34   He answered: "'You shall love the Lord your God with all your heart and with all your soul and with all your mind.'

5:35   And the second is 'You shall love your neighbor as yourself.'

5:36   On these two commandments hang all the law and the prophets."

5:37   Then the man asked, "And who is my neighbor?"

5:38   And Jesus said: "A man went down from Jerusalem to Jericho, and fell into the hands of thieves. They stripped him of his clothes, and stabbed him and then went away, leaving him half dead.

5:39   A priest happened to be going down the same road, and when he saw the man, he passed by on the other side.

5:40   So too, a Levite, when he came to the place and saw him, passed by on the other side.

5:41   But a gentile Samaritan, as he traveled, came where the man was; and when he saw him, he had compassion for him.

5:42   And the Samaritan went to him and bandaged his wounds, pouring on oil and wine. Then he put the man on his own donkey, took him to an inn and took care of him.

5:44   Which of these three do you think was a neighbor to the man who fell into the hands of thieves?"

5:45   The man of law replied, "The one who had mercy on him." Jesus told him, "Go and do likewise."

The Parable of the Unmerciful Servant
Mt 18:21-35

5:51   The Kingdom of Heaven is like a king who wanted to settle accounts with his servants.

5:52   As he began to do the accounting, a servant was brought to him who owed him ten thousand talents.

5:53   Since he was not able to pay, the master ordered that he and his wife and his children and all that he had be sold to repay the debt.

5:54   The servant fell on his knees before him. 'Lord, have patience with me and I will pay back everything.'

5:55   The king was moved to compassion and forgave the debt.

5:56   But when that servant went out, he found one of his fellow servants who owed him a hundred denarii.

5:57   He grabbed him by the throat, saying 'Pay back what you owe me!

5:58   His fellow servant fell to his knees and begged him, 'Have patience with me, and I will pay back everything.'

5:59   But he refused. Instead, he went off and had the man thrown into prison until he should pay the debt.

5:60   When the other servants saw what had happened, they went and told the king everything that had happened.

5:61   Then the king called the servant in and said to him, 'You wicked servant, I forgave all that debt of yours because you begged me to.

5:62   Shouldn't you have had compassion on your fellow servant just as I had on you?'

5:63   And the king was angered against the wicked servant and had him put in jail until he should pay back all he owed.

5:64   So likewise, our heavenly Father will do to you unless you forgive your brother's sins from your heart.

Jesus Anointed by a Sinful Woman
Lk 7:36-50; Mt 26:6-13; Mk 14:3-9; Jn 12:1-8

5:73   Now one of the scribes called Simon invited Jesus to have dinner with him, so he went to Simon's house and sat down to a bounteous table.

5:74   When a woman in that city who had lived a sinful life learned that Jesus was eating at Simon's house, she brought an alabaster jar of perfume,

5:75   and as she stood behind him at his feet weeping, she began to wash his feet with her tears. Then she wiped them with her hair, kissed them and poured perfume on them.

5:76   When Simon saw this, he said to himself, "If this man were a prophet, he would know who is touching him and what kind of woman she is, that she is a sinner."

5:82   Then he turned toward the woman and said to Simon, "Do you see this woman? I came into your house. You gave me no water for my feet, but she has washed my feet with her tears and wiped them with her hair.

5:83   You gave me no kiss, but this woman, from the time I came in, has not stopped kissing my feet.

5:84   You did not anoint my head with oil, but she has anointed my feet with perfume.

5:85   Therefore, I tell you, her sins, which are many, are forgiven, for she loved much. But he who loves little will be forgiven little."

Chapter Six: Toward the Kingdom of God

The Day and Hour Unknown
Mt 24:36-42; Mk 13:32-37; Lk 12:35-40

6:1   The disciples came to Jesus and asked him how they would know when the Kingdom of Heaven is coming.

6:8   No one knows about that day or hour, not even the angels in heaven. Only God knows.

6:9   As it was in the days of Noah, so it will be at the coming of the Messiah.

6:10 For in the days before the flood, people were eating and drinking, marrying and giving in marriage, up to the day Noah entered the ark;

6:11 and they knew nothing about what would happen until the flood came and took them all away.

6:12 That is how it will be at the coming of the End of Days

A Seat at the Table
Lk 14:8-24; Mt 22:1-14

6:91 One Sabbath, Jesus went to eat in the house of a prominent teacher of the law.

6:92 When he noticed how the guests picked the places of honor at the table, he told them this parable:

6:93 "When you are invited you to a wedding feast, do not take a place of honor, for a person more distinguished than you may have been invited.

6:94 If so, the host who invited both of you will come and say to you, 'Give this man your seat.' Then, humiliated, you will have to take the least important place.

6:95 But when you are invited, take the lowest place, so that when your host comes, he will say to you, 'Friend, move up to a better place.' Then you will be honored in the presence of all your fellow guests.

6:96 For everyone who exalts himself will be humbled, and he who humbles himself will be exalted."

6:97 Then Jesus said to his host, "When you give a luncheon or dinner, do not invite your friends, your brothers or relatives, or your rich neighbors; if you do, they may invite you back and so you will be repaid.

6:98 But when you give a banquet, invite the poor, the crippled, the lame, and the blind, and you will be blessed.

6:99   Although they cannot repay you, you will be repaid at the resurrection of the righteous."

6:101   Jesus [continued]: "A certain man was preparing a great banquet and invited many guests.

6:102   And sent his servant to tell those who had been invited, 'Come, for everything is now ready.'

6:103   But they all began to make excuses [and said they could not come].

6:106   The servant came back and reported this to his master. Then the master became angry and said to his servant, 'Go out into the streets and alleys of the city and bring in the poor, the crippled, the lame and the blind.'

6:107   Then the servant said, 'Lord, it is done as you commanded, but there is still room.'

6:108   Then the master told his servant, 'Go out into the highways and country roads and urge them to come in, so that my house may be filled.

6:109   I tell you, not one of those men who were invited will get a taste of my banquet.'

Preparing for the Kingdom of God
Lk 17:20-32; Mt 24:37-39

6:111   Once, having been asked by an elder when the Kingdom of God would come, Jesus replied, "The Kingdom of God does not come with outward observation,

6:112   nor will people say, 'Here it is,' or There it is,'

6:113   because the Kingdom of God is also within you."

Chapter Seven: To Jerusalem for Passover

The Arrival
Mt 21:1-11; Mk 11:1-10; Lk 19:29-38; Jn 12:12-13

7:1   And Jesus and his followers left Jericho and made their pilgrimage to the Holy City of Jerusalem for the Passover Feasts. As was the custom, they arrived a week before the Feasts so they could be ritually purified.

7:2   A large crowd formed of his followers and others who had heard of Jesus and his teachings and healings and miracles.

7:3   Some went ahead of him shouting, "Hosanna to the Son of David!"

7:4   When the residents of Jerusalem saw the crowds and heard the shouting they asked, "Who is this?"

7:5   They answered, "This is Jesus, the healer from Nazareth in Galilee."

7:6   But those who were followers of Jesus answered, "Blessed is the King who comes in the name of the Lord!"

7:7   "Blessed is the coming Kingdom by the son of David! He will restore our nation and drive out the pagans!"

7:8   Now Herod the tetrarch heard about all that was going on.

7:11   And he sent a messenger to Pontius Pilate and told him to beware of this man Jesus who some of the people were calling King.

Jesus at the Temple
Mt 21:12-17; Mk 11:15-17; Lk 19:45-46; Jn 2:12-16

7:12   Jesus entered the outskirts of the Temple area, where cattle, sheep, and doves for sacrifice were sold

7:13   and Roman moneychangers converted the various currencies into the Roman coins accepted by the vendors.

7:14   And he saw that the people were being cheated by the moneychangers and the vendors and his anger was kindled.

7:15   So he made a whip out of cords, and drove the sheep and the cattle from the Temple area and he scattered the coins of the moneychangers and overturned their tables and the benches [where they] were selling doves.

7:16   The astonished onlookers asked him, "Where do you get your authority to do all this?"

7:17   "It is written," he said to them, "'My house will be called a house of prayer,' but they are making it a den of thieves."

7:18   Then he invited the blind and the lame among the onlookers to come to him at the Temple, and he healed them.

7:19   But when the powerful and wealthy Roman merchants who hired the cheating moneychangers and vendors saw the wonderful things he did, and the people shouting his praises in the Temple area, they became angry and afraid.

7:20   "This man will turn the people against us and destroy our businesses," they said.

7:21   And they decided he must be stopped and they conspired against him.

The Fig Tree Withers
Mt 21:18-22; Mk 11:12-14

7:23   In the morning, as he was on his way back to the city, he was hungry.

7:24   Seeing a fig tree by the road, he went up to it but found nothing on it except leaves, for the fruiting season had not yet begun.

7:25   And his anger was kindled and he said to it, "May you never bear fruit again!" Immediately the tree withered.

Paying Taxes to Caesar
Mt 22:15-22; Mk 12:13-17; Lk 20:20-26

7:30   Then some of the priests went out and posed a question to Jesus that had been troubling them.

7:31   "Teacher," they said, "we know you are a man of integrity and that you teach the way of God in truth.

7:33   Tell us then, what is your opinion? Is it right to pay taxes to Caesar or not?"

7:34   And Jesus said, "Show me the coin used for paying the taxes." And they brought him a Roman coin.

7:35   And he asked them, "Whose portrait is this? And whose inscription?"

7:36   "Caesar's," they replied. Then he said to them, "Render unto Caesar what is Caesar's, and to God what is God's."

7:37   When they heard this, they were very impressed and had no more questions. So they left him and went away.

The Greatest Commandment
Mk 12:28-34; Mt 22:34-40

7:48   One of the teachers of the law came and heard them debating. Noticing that Jesus had given them a good answer, he asked him,

7:49   "Teacher, which is the greatest commandment in the Torah?"

7:50   "The most important one," answered Jesus, "is this:

7:51   'Hear, O Israel, the Lord is our God, the Lord is One.

7:52   You shall love the Lord your God with all your heart and with all your soul and with all your might.'

7:53   The second is this: 'You shall love your neighbor as yourself.' There are no commandments greater than these.

7:54   On these two commandments hang all the Law and the Prophets."

Signs of the End of the Age
Mt 24:1-34; Mk 13:1-30; Lk 21:5-38

7:58   As he went out of the Temple one of his disciples said to him, "Master, see what beautiful stones and buildings are here."

7:59   And Jesus answered, "Do you see these great buildings? There will not be left one stone on another; every one will be thrown down."

7:60   [S]ome of the apostles came to him asked, "Tell us, when will this happen, and what will be the sign of the coming of the Messiah and of the end of the age?"

7:61   Jesus answered: "Watch out that no one deceives you.

7:62   For many will come in the Lord's name claiming, 'I am the Messiah,' and they will perform great signs and miracles and will deceive many. Do not follow them.

7:63   For as lightning that comes from the east is visible even in the west, so will be the coming of the Messiah.

7:64   You will hear of wars and rumors of wars, but do not be troubled. Those things must happen, but that will still not be the end.

7:65   Nation will rise against nation, and kingdom against kingdom. There will be famines and earthquakes and pestilences in many places, but these are only the beginnings of the sorrows.

7:69   At that time many will turn away from the faith and will betray and hate each other, and many false prophets will appear and deceive many people.

7:70   Because of the increase of wickedness, the love of most will grow cold, but he who stands firm to the end will be saved.

7:83   I tell you the truth, this generation will certainly not pass away until all these things have happened."

The Authority of Jesus Questioned
Mt 21:23-27; Mk 11:27-33; Lk 20:1-8

7:86   The next day, some priests from the Temple came to him, and said,

7:87   "By what authority do you do these things? And who gave you this authority?"

7:88   Jesus replied, "I will also ask you one question. If you answer me, I will tell you by what authority I do these things.

7:89   John's authority to do baptisms—where did it come from? Was it from heaven or from men?"

7:90   They discussed it among themselves and said, "If we say, 'From heaven,' he will ask, 'Then why didn't you believe him?'

7:91   But if we say, 'From men'—we fear the people, for they all hold that John was a great prophet."

7:92   So they answered Jesus and said, "We cannot tell."

7:93   Then he said, "Neither will I tell you by what authority I do these things."

The Parable of the Prodigal Son
Lk 15:11-32

7:109   Jesus continued: "There was a man who had two sons.

7:110   The younger one said to his father, 'Father, give me my share of the estate.' So he divided his property between them.

7:111   Not long after that, the younger son got together all he had, set off for a distant country and there squandered his wealth in wild living.

7:112   And when he had spent everything, there was a severe famine in that land, and he began to be in need.

7:115   Then he came to the realization, 'How many of my father's hired servants have bread enough to spare, and I perish from hunger!

7:116   I will go back to my father and say to him: Father, I have sinned against heaven and against you, and am no longer worthy to be called your son; make me as of your hired servants.'

7:117   So he got up and went to his father. But when he was yet a long way off, his father saw him and had compassion for him; he ran to his son, threw his arms around him and kissed him.

7:119   [T]he father said to his servants, 'Bring the best robe and put it on him. Put a ring on his finger and sandals on his feet.

7:120   Bring the fatted calf and kill it, and let us eat and be merry.

7:121   For this son of mine was dead and is alive again; he was lost and is found.' And they did as they were told and began to be merry.

7:122   Meanwhile, the older son was in the field. As he got close to the house, he heard music and dancing.

7:125   The older brother became angry and would not go in. So his father came out and pleaded with him.

7:126   But he answered his father, 'Look! All these years I have served you and never disobeyed your orders. Yet you never gave me even a young goat so I could make merry with my friends.

7:127   But as soon as this son comes back, who has devoured what you gave him with harlots, you kill the fatted calf for him!'

7:128   And the father said, 'Son, you are always with me, and everything I have is yours.

7:129   But it is proper that we should make merry and be glad, for this brother of
        yours was dead and is alive again; he was lost and is found.'"

Chapter Eight: The Final Events

Judas Agrees to Betray Jesus
Mt 26:14-16; Mk 14:10, 11; Lk 22:3-6

8:1   Then the chief priests met with the cabal of powerful and wealthy Roman
        merchants in the palace of Caiaphas the Sadducee high priest.

8:2   And they plotted to have Jesus arrested on some charge, for the merchants
        wanted him dead.

8:3   So they sent out two guards with instructions to bring one of Jesus' followers
        to them.

8:4   They found one of the Twelve alone—the one called Judas Iscariot—and
        threatened to kill him unless he helped them capture Jesus.

8:5   Judas did not believe they could hurt Jesus, so he asked "What are you
        willing to give me if I hand him over to you?" They decided to give him
        thirty silver coins to do their bidding.

8:6   From then on Judas watched for an opportunity to hand him over.

The Last Supper
Mt 26:17-30; Mk 14:12-26; Lk 22:7-34

8:7   On the first day of the Passover holiday, when it was customary to eat
        unleavened bread and sacrifice the Paschal lamb, the disciples came to Jesus
        and asked, "Where do you want us to go to make preparations for us to
        celebrate the Passover?"

8:8   So he sent two of his disciples, telling them, "Go into the city, and a man
        carrying a jar of water will meet you. Follow him.

8:10   He will show you a large upper room, furnished and prepared. There make it
        ready for us."

8:11   So the disciples did as Jesus had directed them and prepared the Passover Seder.

8:12   When evening came, Jesus was reclining at the table with the Twelve and he
        interrupted the Seder to say:

8:13   "I tell you the truth, one of you will betray me this very night."

8:14   They were very disturbed and protested to him one after the other, "Surely
        not I, Master?"

8:15   When Judas, the one who would betray him, said in turn, "Surely not I, Master?" Jesus looked at him sadly and answered, "Yes, I know it is you."

8:16   With everyone looking at him with fury, Judas hastily left the table and the house.

8:17   Then Jesus told them, "This very night you will all leave me, for when the shepherd is struck, the sheep of the flock will be scattered."

8:18   Peter replied, "Even if all fall away on account of you, I never will. I am ready to go with you to prison and death."

8:19   "I tell you the truth," Jesus answered, "this very night, before the rooster crows, you will deny me three times."

8:20   But Peter declared, "Even if I have to die with you, I will never disown you." And all the other disciples said the same.

8:21   Continuing the Seder, Jesus took the unleavened bread, gave thanks and broke it, and gave a piece to each of his disciples, saying,

8:22   "Take and eat; for this is the symbol of the day that the Lord took us out of Egypt to give us our freedom. May we see freedom again in our own day."

8:23   Then they took the first cup of wine, and Jesus raised his cup and said,

8:24   "This is the wine of freedom, that you shall know our freedom shall always be sweet." And all drank from their cups.

8:25   When they had finished the Passover Seder, with food and wine and prayers and songs, they went out to the Mount of Olives.

Jesus Arrested
Mt 26:36-56, 69-75; Mk 14:32-50, 66-72; Lk 22:40-62;
Jn 18:1-11, 15-18, 25-27

8:26   Then Jesus went with his disciples to Gethsemane on the Mount of Olives, and he said to them, "Sit here while I go over there and pray."

8:27   He took with him Peter and the two sons of Zebedee, and he began to feel sorrowful and heavy.

8:28   Then he said to them, "My soul is exceedingly sorrowful to the point of death. Stay here and keep watch with me."

8:29   And they did so, because they had seen him sad many times before, nearly overcome by the weight of his mission.

8:30   And he went a little farther, and he fell with his face to the ground and prayed, "My Father, I am greatly afraid for what awaits me.

8:31   If it be possible, let this cup pass from me, for I want to live to see the coming of the Kingdom of Heaven. Yet, not as I will, but as You will."

8:37   When he came back, he found them sleeping, because their eyes were heavy with food and wine.

8:40   [He said] "For now the hour is at hand, and I see I am already betrayed into the hands of the evil ones. Here comes my betrayer!"

8:41   While he was still speaking, Judas Iscariot returned.

8:42   With him were two officers from the Temple guard accompanied by a large mob armed with swords and clubs, hired by the Roman merchants who had plotted against him.

8:43   Now Judas Iscariot had arranged a signal with them: "The one I kiss is the man you are looking for. Then you can arrest him."

8:44   Going at once to Jesus, Judas said, "Forgive me, Master!" and kissed him.

8:45   Jesus replied, "Friends, do what you came for." Then the two officers stepped forward, seized Jesus and arrested him.

8:46   With that, Peter reached for his sword, drew it out and struck one of the officers and cut off his ear.

8:47   "Put your sword back in its place," Jesus said to him, "for all who take the sword will die by the sword. This man is just doing what he has been commanded to do."

8:48   And he touched the man's ear and healed him.

8:50   But the mob became loud and menacing, and all the disciples saw this and deserted him and fled, lest they also be condemned.

8:51   The two officers took Jesus to Caiaphas, the Sadducee high priest, and several other Temple priests who were called to assembly.

Before the Council of Priests
Mt 26:57-66, 27:3-8; Mk 14:53-65; Lk 22:66-71; Jn 18:12-14, 19-24

8:61   Now the Temple priests and Caiaphas, the high priest who had been appointed by Pontius Pilate, were bribed and threatened with death by the wealthy and powerful Roman merchants,

8:62   and they were looking for false evidence against Jesus so they could persuade the Council of Priests to turn him over to the Roman authorities.

8:63   First, the high priest Caiaphas questioned Jesus about his disciples and his teachings.

8:64   Jesus answered him, "I spoke openly to the world. I always taught in synagogues or at the Temple, where all the Jews come together. I have not said anything in secret.

8:65   Why question me? Ask those who heard me what I said to them. They know what I said."

8:68   Many false witnesses came forward and testified against him and others accused him of blasphemy and heresy. But the witnesses contradicted each other and the Council seemed unpersuaded.

8:69   Then the high priest said to Jesus, "Are you not going to answer? Don't you hear this testimony that these men are bringing against you?"

8:70   But Jesus was silent. The high priest said to him, "I charge you under oath by the living God: Tell us if you are the Messiah as your supporters say you are."

8:71   "I am not him," Jesus replied. "But I say to all of you, I am God's messenger and servant. In the very near future the Kingdom of Heaven shall be upon you and you hypocrites and sinners will be sent to Gehenna for your crimes."

8:72   Then the high priest tore his clothes and said, "He has spoken heresy and blasphemy! Why do we need any more witnesses?

8:73   What do you think? Is he not worthy of condemnation?" Caiaphas asked them.

8:74   Some of the members of the Council nodded their heads for they knew Caiaphas spoke for the Roman authorities and they were afraid.

8:75   Early the next morning, the Council came to a majority decision to recommend that Jesus be turned over to the Romans.

8:76   He was then bound and handed him over to Pontius Pilate, the evil and murderous Roman governor of Judea, who had the sole power of life or death in Judea.

Jesus Before Pilate
Mt 27:11-31; Mk 15:2-20; Lk 23:1-25; Jn 18:29-40

8:84   Meanwhile, Jesus was brought before the murderous Roman governor Pontius Pilate.

8:85   Pilate had financial and social associations with the wealthy and powerful Roman merchants who wanted Jesus dead and had already been bribed by them to order Jesus killed.

8:86   And he remembered the warning Herod had given him about Jesus being called King of the Jews, by virtue of being a descendant from the House of David. And he worried that the people would make a revolt in his name.

8:87   "Are you the King of the Jews as they say?" he asked. "It is you who says it," Jesus replied.

8:88   Then Pilate asked him, "Aren't you going to answer? Don't you hear the testimony they are bringing against you?"

8:89   But Jesus made no reply, not even to a single charge.

8:90   Now it was the governor's custom at the time of Jewish Feasts to release a prisoner chosen by the crowd.

8:91   A man called Barabbas was in prison as one of the Jewish insurrectionists who had killed Roman soldiers during an unsuccessful uprising.

8:92   So when the crowd had gathered in the courtyard, Pilate asked them,

8:93   "Which one do you want me to release to you: Barabbas the killer, or Jesus who they say calls himself King of the Jews?"

8:94   The Roman merchants had packed the courtyard with the same hired mob that had helped arrest Jesus. They were instructed to ask for Barabbas instead of Jesus.

8:95   The people who were there to support Jesus saw dozens of armed Roman soldiers surrounding them and they were afraid to try to outshout the mob. Those who did try were quickly beaten and silenced.

8:96   "Which of the two do you want me to release to you?" asked the governor.

8:97   The mob shouted "We want Barabbas."

8:98   "What shall I do, then, with Jesus who is called King of the Jews?" Pilate asked with great pomposity.

8:99   The mob shouted, "Crucify him!"

8:100   "Why? What crime has he committed?" asked Pilate, continuing the charade.

8:101   And the mob kept shouting "Crucify him! Crucify him!"

8:102   Pilate played along with the mob. He dipped his hands in a cistern of water and washed his hands in front of the crowd.

8:103   "I am innocent of this man's blood," he said. "It is your responsibility!" And the mob cheered wildly.

8:104   Then he released Barabbas to the priests (later to be rearrested after the Feast days were over and quietly executed).

8:105   And he had Jesus flogged publicly, and handed him over to the Roman soldiers to be crucified.

The Crucifixion
Mt 27:32-44; Mk 15:21-32; Lk 23:26-43; Jn 19:17-24

8:112   As they were going out, they found a man from Cyrene, named Simon, and they compelled him to carry the cross.

8:113   A large number of people followed him, including his women followers who mourned and wailed for him.

8:118   They came to a place called Golgotha (called Calvary in Latin). And it was there that the soldiers attached him to the cross.

8:119   Above his head they placed the written accusation against him: THIS IS JESUS, THE KING OF THE JEWS.

8:120   Two thieves were crucified with him, one on his right and one on his left.

8:121   The leaders of the mob passed by and hurled insults at him,

8:122   "Save yourself! If you are the Messiah, come down from the cross!

8:123   "He saved others, but he can't save himself! He's the King of Israel? Let him come down now from the cross, and we will believe him.

8:124   He says he trusts in an invisible God. Let this God rescue him now if He wants him, for his followers say 'He is the Messiah.'"

The Death of Jesus
Mt 27:45-66; Mk 15:33-47; Lk 23:44-56; Jn 19:28-42

8:130   From the sixth hour until the ninth hour darkness came over all the land.

8:131   At the ninth hour Jesus cried out in agony in a loud voice, *"Eloi, Eloi, lama sabachthani?"*—which means, "My God, my God, why have you forsaken me?"

8:132   When some of those standing there heard this, they said, "He must be calling the prophet Elijah."

8:133   And the leaders of the mob laughed and said, "Let's see if Elijah comes to save him."

8:134   And then Jesus cried out again in a loud voice, and this time God answered him.

8:135   And God said "Be comforted my son, for it is partly through you and your followers that my covenant with Abraham will be fulfilled, that his seed shall be as plentiful as the sands of the seashore and the stars in the sky."

8:136   And Jesus was comforted, and as he felt his life slipping away, he sanctified the name of God (*Kiddush HaShem*) like the Jewish martyrs of old, by reciting the *Shema*.

8:137   *"Shema Yisrael Adonai Eloheinu Adonai Echad,* Hear O Israel, the Lord is our God, the Lord is One."

8:138   Then he fell into a deep sleep and he drew his last breath.

8:139   At that moment the sky grew dark, there was a great storm, and the earth shook.

8:140   When the centurions and those with him who were guarding Jesus saw the storm and the earthquake, they were terrified, and exclaimed, "Surely this man was favored by the gods!"

8:141   When all the people who had gathered to witness this sight saw what took place, they beat their breasts and went away.

8:142   But all those who knew him, including the women who had followed him from Galilee, stood at a distance, watching these things. Among them were Mary Magdalene and the mother of Zebedee's two sons.

8:143   As Sabbath Eve approached, there came a rich man from Arimathea, named Joseph, who was also a follower of Jesus.

8:144   And he went to Pilate and he asked for Jesus' body, and Pilate ordered that it be given to him.

8:145   Joseph took the body, wrapped it in linen, and placed it in a sepulcher that had been hewn out of a rock.

8:146   He rolled a big stone in front of the entrance to the sepulcher and went away.

8:147   Mary Magdalene and the other women mourned in front of the sepulcher.

8:148   The next day, the Roman merchants went to Pilate.

8:149   "Your Excellency," they said, "we are concerned that his disciples may come and steal the body and bury him in a secret place

8:150   and tell the people that here lays the martyr Jesus, the King of the Jews.

8:151   And they will use him to make rebellion against you and us."

8:152   "Take two guards," Pilate answered. "Go, make the tomb as secure as you know how."

8:153   So they went and made the tomb secure by putting a seal on the stone and posting the guards.

The Resurrection
Mt 28:1-20; Mk 16:1-20; Lk 24:1-53; Jn 20:1-31

8:154   On Sunday morning, after the Sabbath day, Mary Magdalene and some of the other women went back to mourn at the tomb.

8:155   But when they arrived there, they saw that the stone, which was very large, had been rolled away.

8:156   As they entered the tomb, they saw an angel dressed in a white robe sitting on the right side of the sepulcher, and they were alarmed.

8:157   His face was like lightning, and his clothes were white as snow. The guards were so afraid of him that they shook and became like dead men.

8:158   The angel said to the women, "Do not be afraid, for I know that you are looking for Jesus of Nazareth, who was crucified.

8:159   He is not here; for the prophet Elijah has come for him and has taken him up on a cloud

8:160   to join with Abraham and Moses and Elijah and sit at the foot of the Lord our God who is in heaven."

8:161   When the disciples were told this by the women, they were encouraged, and they went out among the people

8:162   declaring that Jesus was the Messiah all had been waiting for, and that he would soon come again and save the world.

8:163   And although it did not happen in their lifetimes, as they expected, the disciples of Jesus and their progeny fulfilled God's promise to Abraham,

8:164   and they spread the word of the one God throughout the Western world.

8:165   And many years later, we are told, another messenger will rise in the East to also spread the word of the One God.

8:166   And God smiled, for He knew that one day all His children would be reconciled and worship the One God in harmony and peace.

8:167   My name is Emet son of Chaim, and I was Jesus' best friend from the age of three until his death, and I saw or was told about all the things I have written herein.

Made in the USA
Lexington, KY
08 February 2015